THE FIRST THIRTY-THREE

Stories in the Make 100 Challenge

DEAN WESLEY SMITH

The First Thirty-Three: Stories in the Make 100 Challenge
Copyright © 2020 by Dean Wesley Smith
Published by WMG Publishing
Cover and layout copyright © 2020 by WMG Publishing
Cover art copyright © by grandfailure/Depositphotos

ISBN:13 - 978-1-56146-199-8
ISBN: 10 - 1-56146-199-7

CONTENTS

THE FIRST THIRTY-THREE

INTRODUCTION

A Fun Idea

From the start of the indie publishing movement, I have wanted to get my short stories into paper books of their own. Stand-alone books, short story paperbacks in other words. It has sort of been a passion, to be honest.

And for about eighty of my short stories in 2010, I did that as a challenge. But that was a decade ago now. Wow, time does fly. I just never had the reason to spend the time and energy to do the covers and get the remaining two hundred to three hundred stories into paper form.

Or for that matter, redo the covers of the eighty I did ten years before, rebrand them.

This passion to do short stories in stand-alone paper form comes from my days with Pulphouse Publishing. Way back in 1990 we started a line of books called "Short Story Paperbacks" that had one author's story in a stand-alone paperback. Regular paperback size.

I loved them.

And we even took it another step and did fifty copies of the same short story in stand-alone, hand-bound in leather hardback, signed by the author and numbered 1-50. (Go ahead, try to buy a copy of the George R.R. Martin's limited hardback of his story in that series. If one is for sale, it is amazingly expensive now.)

The series was very successful and we did over sixty science fiction and fantasy authors and ten mystery authors. Wonderful fun, so when the indie movement started up, I came back to the idea for my own stories.

But now, after a decade, I really wanted to do more and along came Kickstarter with their Make 100 Promotion. It dawned on me that with a lot of help, a bunch of learning curves for me, and some time, I could do one hundred paperbacks of my short stories.

The Kickstarter got more support than I had hoped it would, which was wonderful. But it turned out the learning curves I had to go through slowed down the process. I wanted to redesign a website to get the new branding on, and completely rebrand collections and redo covers from my *Smith's Monthly Magazine*.

And to do all that I not only had to learn better website design, but I had to completely relearn both InDesign and Photoshop. Not small tasks.

But now, after a year, I am working away at redoing *Smith's Monthly* covers, and am about halfway through the 100 covers and gaining speed. As the first part of 2020 goes along, the paperbacks will be appearing and now I feel I can put together the three anthologies of the one hundred stories that I promised in the Kickstarter.

In this volume are the first 33 stories of the Make 100 Challenge. They cover many of my series and many are stand-alone stories.

The introductions ahead of each story will be basically the sales copy, with a few changes, on Amazon and other sales sites.

I hope you enjoy these short stories. I can say that not only was it fun to write them over the years, but even more fun to get them up stand-alone, paperback, and in this volume.

Dean Wesley Smith
Las Vegas, Nevada.
December, 2019

THE BIG TICK OF TIME

USA Today *bestselling writer, Dean Wesley Smith twists you into a* Twilight Zone *type of story and then beyond.*

A long ways beyond.

Clarice Williams dreams of a fantasy lover, her standards set so high she seems destined to live out her lifetime in Boise alone. Then her dream lover tells her his name.

Real or a dream, she must find out.

One

CLARICE WILLIAMS listened intently to the faint hum of her alarm clock.

Outside the pulled shade of her bedroom window, she could tell the sun wasn't even thinking of coming up. And yet she knew, without a doubt, that any moment now that alarm would go off, the annoying sound of a shrill buzz able to wake even the dead across the street in the cemetery.

Yes, she had bought a house directly across the street from the Morris Hill Cemetery, oldest cemetery in Boise. And she liked it that way. Better looking across the grass and through the old trees than at

1

the garage door and scattered kid's toys of another house in some subdivision somewhere.

And she had a high wooden fence around three sides of her large property, so it felt like she actually had no neighbors.

As a senior attorney for one of the largest and most powerful law firms in the state, she could have bought anywhere in town, or up on the foothills above the city. But she liked this old neighborhood and the peacefulness of the cemetery.

She had always liked it, for as long as she had been in this town.

Those people across the street seldom demanded her time and energy or asked stupid questions.

She had sat the alarm for buzz, because she really, really needed to get out of bed every morning and into the office before seven. But no sane person should ever be forced to get up on a cold winter morning at 5 A.M. and at some point she would cut back the schedule, slow down, take more vacations.

She had been promising herself that now for three years. Soon, it would have to happen. This pace was wearing on her.

She burrowed down into the soft cotton sheet and the two quilts and pretended the alarm wasn't about to go off.

Instead she let herself imagine her dream man, the one she knew deep down that in this life she never would meet. She was just too picky when it came to men.

The past had spoiled her, of that there was no doubt.

As one of her friends had once said, no man could live up to her standards.

Her friend had been right. But Clarice did have a dream man who was just perfect. He was six-two, with dark hair slightly long in the back. She imagined him wearing jeans, a dress shirt open at the neck, a duster-like leather jacket, and a dark cowboy hat.

He would smile at her, tip his hat, and then ask her to dance.

And from there, she imagined they made passionate love.

With the help of a wonderful device she had been given as a gag gift one Christmas party, she often felt satisfied for days after those long adventures with her dream man.

Clarice knew that she didn't have time this morning to fire up her special gift before the alarm went off. So instead she just lay there, waiting for the buzzing that would start yet another day that would be like most every other day.

She had never made up a name for her perfect dream man. She closed her eyes and let her mind roam trying to imagine what he would be named if he actually existed.

In her mind she was now dressed in a wonderful, blue evening gown, tight around her chest, but flowing to the floor in sweeping lines. Her brown hair was pulled up on her head and done perfectly.

Her dream man stood in front of her and she could feel herself tingle just staring at him.

"James Tick Edwards," he said, his voice deep and almost rumbling as fit his look and frame. He tipped his hat. "My friends just call me Tick."

"Tick it is, then," she said, smiling at him.

And her alarm went off.

She sighed, rolled over, turned the alarm off, then slipped out from under the quilt and put on her slippers to protect her feet from the cold tile of the bathroom floor.

Another day had begun.

Two

AS THE DAY WORE ON, Clarice just couldn't shake the strangeness and the exactness of her dream man's name. Had someone else she had met had that name and she just wasn't remembering and now associating it with her dream man?

James Tick Edwards seemed far too exact for her imagination to come up with, especially so early in the morning.

By eleven in the morning she decided she needed to find out.

With her fifth cup of coffee for the day in her hand, she headed two floors down to the firm's research department. She had done a computer search on her own and found nothing, so she needed better help.

The firm occupied a four-story office building tucked back in the trees near the Boise River and only about four blocks from the university campus. The area was packed with restaurants catering to both the university crowd and the varied office buildings nearby.

Her office was on the top floor with a wonderful view out through the old trees and over the slowly flowing river. Right now the river wasn't much more than a trickle and the leaves were all gone from the trees. A little snow still clung to the shaded areas from the last snow a few days before.

She loved the view, but as a senior attorney in the firm, she seldom had time to turn away from her desk to enjoy it.

The head of research was a young guy named Stanton, not more than twenty-five, who had long blonde hair, solid shoulders, and a tan that couldn't be beat. His passions were skiing and he managed to spend most late afternoons and all evenings in the winter up at nearby Bogus Basic Ski Area.

And in the summer he spent his weekends and spare time on rivers, rafting some of the most extreme water the area had to offer. Every woman who had met him found him fantastically attractive, but sadly for all women, he found men more to his liking and had been with the same partner now for six years. His partner worked at the university.

Stanton was the best person she had ever known with computers, and if something needed to be found or tracked down, he could do it.

When he saw her coming his smile lit up his face. "Clarice, what can I do for you?"

She smiled back, pushing away the wish that she could just jump him once. Totally inappropriate thinking for a senior attorney in the firm.

"I need to see if you can find someone for me?"

"Sure," he said. "Which case do I bill the time to?"

"No case yet," she said. "This is background, so put it to my office."

"Got it," he said, nodding and making a note on his ledger as he was supposed to do. "Who are you looking for?"

"James Tick Edwards," she said. "I have no other information but the name.

He shrugged. "I'll see what I can do."

"Thanks," she said. "I appreciate it.

And with that, she headed back upstairs to her office, feeling silly that she was wasting the firm's time on her fantasy. But she worked enough extra hours for the firm. It could afford a little payback.

Three

THREE HOURS LATER her secretary said that Stanton was here to see her.

He came in, smiling, a brown research folder in his hand. "Only one James Tick Edwards that I could find in all of history."

"Really?" she asked, her heart suddenly beating harder. More than likely the guy was a five-two bank manager instead of her dream guy, but she had to know.

"You two are neighbors, actually," Stanton said, handing her the file. "He's buried in the old section of the Morris Hill Cemetery right across from your house."

She looked up at Stanton, who was still smiling and clearly not noticing the shock and surprise she was feeling.

"Buried?" she asked.

Stanton nodded.

"He was an amazing man in his day," Stanton said, pointing to the file that she could see also contained printouts of old newspapers. "That was some fun reading."

With that Stanton turned and left the office, leaving the file open on her desk in front of her.

And there, staring out of an old newspaper photo was her dream lover.

"Well, that figures," she said, shaking her head. "So just where did the name come from?"

She stared at his picture. He was the man she had had numbers of wonderful dreams about. He was tall, seeming to tower over other men in the picture. He wore a duster and a dark cowboy hat. He seemed to be looking out of the image at her.

"So, if this was a Twilight Zone episode, he will appear right about now."

She looked up from her desk, but no dream-lover ghost standing there. Her office was empty.

She glanced out the window at the river walk below her office. No one there either.

She felt both relieved and disappointed.

She couldn't believe he was dead.

And buried.

For the guy in that picture, that didn't seem possible. Her dream lover was too powerful, too much to be killed.

The intercom on her desk buzzed telling her it was time for her next meeting, so she carefully closed the file and tucked it in her case to take home.

Maybe she'd read it later tonight, in the bathtub, with a bottle of wine and her favorite Christmas gift.

Four

CLARICE DECIDED there was no point in waiting to read the file, so after her meeting she told her secretary that she wasn't to be disturbed for a half hour, then went back and opened up the file, spreading it out on her desk.

Stanton had been right, James Tick Edwards had been an amazing man. An early pioneer to the area, he had owned a large mansion outside of town above the river and had helped in the construction of the capitol building. He had remained single, but was seen regularly with the appropriate ladies of the time, as the articles said.

He supported numbers of good causes, was free with his money and time, but yet remained a private man. No one was sure where his money came from, or where he was from, although there was speculation he was from New York. He left a large part of his fortune on his death to a number of charities and the rest to a young nephew in London.

She stared at that nephew sentence for a moment, then went on reading.

James Tick Edwards died in 1927 at the age of forty-two in a massive house fire. What was left of his body was buried across the street from her in a ceremony attended by the governor and the mayor and many others.

"Wow," Clarice said after finishing the file. "At least I have great taste in fantasy lovers."

Then she stared at the closed brown file in front of her. How in the world had she gotten his name? She must have read something about him somewhere.

Otherwise she really was in a *Twilight Zone* episode.

She clicked her intercom and had her secretary ask Stanton if he could come back to her office when he had a moment. She needed to find the nephew.

She knew without a doubt that until she figured out where she had seen a picture of that man, and gotten his name, she wasn't having any more fantasy dates.

And with her workload, she needed those dates.

Five

THE NEXT MORNING Clarice made it in before seven like normal. The sun was barely lighting the winter sky and it would be dark by the time she left the office. Damn she hated winters. At least in the summer she could take a break and stroll on the river walk. Right now it was too cold out there to do any strolling, at least in comfort.

Usually she was the first person in, even ahead of her secretary, because she liked the quiet, but this morning Stanton was waiting for her when she arrived, drinking some sports drink and pacing in front of her secretaries' desk. He had a large file in his hands and an excited look on his face.

"You're never going to believe what I found," Stanton said, holding up the file before she could even say good morning. "I stayed up all night researching this after I got back from skiing. Not sure what case you are working, but this is really something."

She motioned for the excited young man to come in and then she closed the door behind him. She took her coat off and hung it on the coat tree behind her door.

"Okay," she said, "go slowly. Start from the beginning."

He nodded, took a drink from the sports bottle, then placed it on her desk with the folder and started pacing. She left the folder closed even though she wanted very much to open it. But first she wanted to find out what had Stanton so excited about the research on her mystery man. And why he had stayed up all night doing the work.

She moved around behind her desk but did not sit. Instead she leaned against the desk sipping her own Mocha she had gotten on the way in, just as she did every morning. At some point she would have breakfast brought in and eat it at her desk.

"I started with the nephew who inherited all the money in 1927," Stanton said. "He was twenty-two and his name was James Edwards as well. James T. Edwards, actually. I could not find out what the middle initial stood for."

Clarice nodded, but sat her coffee down.

"That James T. Edwards died in a fire in 1947 at the exact age of forty-two and was buried in London. He was never married and gave

7

all his money to a James Edwards from New York. A twenty-two-year-old nephew."

Now Clarice had to pace.

"That's a very strange coincidence," she said, her hands clasped behind her back because she didn't want to let Stanton see them shaking.

"That's what I thought," Stanton said, "which was why I came back after skiing last night. But it gets even stranger."

She nodded and motioned for Stanton to go on.

The file on her desk beckoned her to open it, but she kept her hands off it.

"The nephew died at 42 in 1967, in a house fire. Unmarried."

"And he gave all his money to?" Clarice asked.

Stanton stopped and smiled. "A twenty-two-year-old nephew named James T. Edwards who lived in Australia. He died exactly twenty years later in 1987, in a house fire, unmarried, and he gave his fortune to his nephew, James Edwards from Phoenix."

"And let me guess," Clarice said, her stomach twisting like the morning after a long night of drinking. She couldn't believe this was even possible. "That James Edwards died in 2007 in a house fire, never married, and gave his fortune to James Edwards, his twenty-two-year-old nephew."

"Exactly," Stanton said. "James Edwards of Boise, Idaho. No middle name or initial listed."

That froze Clarice in her tracks and she managed to get to her chair and drop into it before her knees gave out.

He was here?

Now?

After all this time, could he really be here?

Stanton stopped his excited pacing and opened the file and turned it for Clarice to see. On top was a driver's license picture of James Edwards. And he was the same exact man of her dreams, staring into the DMV camera with a slight grin on his face.

"That's either some very powerful genetics or something very, very strange is going on here," she said. But she said that for Stanton. She knew exactly what was happening if she could let herself believe it.

He was here. That thought just kept echoing in her mind over and over.

"Exactly," Stanton said. "I went back and tried to find birth records for any of these men. Nothing. I could find no record of any of them being born. Not unusual for most of them, but odd for the last two."

"But there were bodies in those burned out houses?" she asked.

"Always," Stanton said, nodding.

"Looks like I need to talk to this guy," she said, feeling some excitement about finally meeting the man of her dreams. "Do you have his address and where he works?"

"Careful," Stanton said, suddenly worried. "Are you sure?"

She smiled. "I'm sure there's a perfectly logical explanation for all this. I need to talk with this man about a legal matter, which is why I wanted you to find him, and I'll ask him about his relatives when I see him."

Stanton nodded, clearly not happy. "He works about three blocks from here as a financial investor, even though he doesn't need to work."

That close! Amazing.

She had no idea how that was possible. Why hadn't she seen him, run into him in a restaurant?

She wasn't even sure how she had gotten his name in the first place. She needed answers and she needed them now.

And she needed to see him.

That more than anything.

"Thanks," she said, smiling at Stanton and raising. She moved the file to the top drawer of her desk. "I'll let you know what I discover. And I really, really appreciate the extra work on this. Take the rest of the day off and put your hours last night in as overtime and I'll approve it."

"Thanks," he said, smiling. "You sure you don't want me to go with you to meet him."

She laughed. "No thanks. Let me read up on him first before I go." She pointed to the file. "He has strange ancestors. That doesn't make him a killer."

"Yeah, good point," Stanton said, nodding and smiling. "It's just all so weird."

"That it is," she said. "And I'm going to find out why. I'll let you know tomorrow."

"Thanks," he said and left.

On the way down the elevator a half hour later, her hands were shaking so much, she could barely get her coat buttoned before she walked out into the cold air to meet her fantasy lover.

The very man she could not believe was alive and so close.

Six

IT WAS BARELY EIGHT in the morning when she reached the offices of Daniels and Associates, financial investors. But the place looked like it had been going for hours. More than likely there were people here before the stock market opened on the east coast.

She had decided to walk the few blocks up Boise Ave to the two-story office complex tucked back in the trees. The walk allowed her to clear her mind and figure out what she was going to say.

The investment office radiated money and power from the outside, which was what it needed to do if customers were to trust them. She went in through the large wooden front door and then through another inner door.

A large trading floor was to her right behind glass, and a wide staircase led up behind the reception area. There were very plush and expensive couches along one wall with plants. No one was sitting in them.

Clarice walked up to the middle-aged secretary with dark brown hair at the front desk who greeted her with a large smile, more than likely sizing up Clarice's clothing and measuring her for money. Clarice dressed the part of a powerful attorney. That was enough for the woman.

"I'd like to see James Edwards, please," Clarice said.

She managed to sound in control, somehow. Was this going to be even possible?

"Do you have an appointment?" the woman asked, going through the routine she was trained to do.

"I do not," Clarice said, smiling. "But please tell him that Clarice Williams is here to see him. I am a fan of his great, great, great uncle."

Then she slipped the lady her card, which had the name of her firm on it.

The receptionist glanced at it, nodded and stood, moving to the wide staircase that led up to what must be the executive offices above.

Clarice forced herself to take a deep breath and relax. She needed to know how this happened and what it meant and that meant she had to stay as calm as possible.

A moment later the secretary came down the stairs followed by James Edwards.

If he had on a long duster, jeans, and a cowboy hat, he would have been the replica of the man of her dreams.

This James Edwards wore a silk suit like it was the most comfortable thing he had, and he had loosened his tie some around his neck.

He saw her about halfway down the stairs and actually jerked, catching himself on the railing. He paused for a moment just staring at her, clearly not believing what he was seeing any more than she believed he was standing there.

Clarice felt relieved that he was as shocked as she felt.

Finally he regained his composure. As he reached the bottom of the stairs, he extended his hand and smiled that wonderful smile of his. "James Edwards."

She took his hand and felt the electricity between them. His skin was firm, his hand slightly calloused like he actually did physical work at times.

"Clarice Williams," she said, smiling back, not letting go of his hand.

She stared into those wonderful brown eyes and he stared back, clearly not wanting to let go of her hand either.

Finally both of them came to their senses and he said, "Let's go to my office." He indicated they should go back up the stairs and she shook her head.

"If you wouldn't mind," she said, smiling, "I could use some breakfast and a large cup of coffee."

"I'd love that," he said. "Café right around the corner is wonderful."

"I know," she said, smiling, "I eat there regularly."

"You do? How have we missed each other?"

"I honestly don't know," she said. Then she whispered so that the secretary couldn't hear. "And I understand you own it."

He leaned back and looked at her, then smiled. "How much do you know about me?"

"More than you can ever imagine," she said as they went out the door and back into the cold morning air.

"Oh, I can imagine a great deal," he said. "Don't you remember?"

She smiled. "It's only been four hundred and twelve years since our last few lifetimes together. How could I forget?"

"I was afraid you were dead," he said as they reached the cold air and started through the parking lot. "I've really missed you, but had no real idea how to track you. You cover your tracks well."

"Better than you do," she said, laughing.

He reached over and took her hand.

"I worried about you as well," she said. "And dreamed about you all the time."

"Starting in the last few years?" he asked, smiling that impish smile she loved so much.

"More so, yes," she said, staring up into the smiling face of the man she had loved for centuries, ever since they had first met in an Egyptian Court over three thousand years before.

"Remember Jimmy David?" he asked.

She nodded. "I've run into him off and on for centuries since we met him."

"He's a computer nerd now, one of the best," James said. "He's figured out a way to get in contact with more of our kind, maybe bring a number of us together, help us cover our tracks a little better in this new information world."

"He put your name in my head?"

James nodded. "Among other things. He's been working on this special linked communication thing for three years now, trying to pull us all together. I'm funding him. He even guessed you might be in this area six years ago if you were still alive, which is why I came back here."

Then her fantasy lover smiled and looked into her eyes. "Was it good for you, having me in your mind?"

She laughed and squeezed the man of her dreams hand. "Better than you can ever imagine."

"Show me after breakfast?" he asked, laughing.

"With pleasure," she said, smiling at her no-longer-fantasy lover. "With pleasure."

THE CASE OF THE DOG-BIT ARM

A Pilgrim Hugh Incident

USA Today *bestselling writer, Dean Wesley Smith asks you to once again climb into Pilgrim Hugh's famous limousine, this time with a new assistant in training.*
The case? Possibly a murder.
A human arm found by a dog their only clue.
And the real test? The new assistant.

One

PILGRIM HUGH seemed to thrive on strange phone calls. He got a lot of them from all over the Portland area, asking for his help with one thing or another. Almost always the calls came from police departments stuck on an odd problem of some fashion or another.

The call that came in on this fine, warm September morning was no different. Just flat strange, plain and simple. And yet interesting enough that he took the call.

The day was one of those perfect days that often happened in Oregon in the fall. Cool morning, warm afternoon, no real humidity. In September the kids were back in school and the world to Pilgrim just seemed to be at peace with itself as people went about their lives and jobs.

Except that Pilgrim was in a very foul mood. Carrie, his best friend and assistant, was leaving him next week to go back to school and the very idea of that just depressed the hell out of him, even on a perfect day.

He had on his normal jeans and a blue t-shirt that said simply, "Don't Ask."

So far no one had. And that suited him just fine.

He was peddling slowly on a stationary bike while looking out over the city. He felt at thirty-two that he needed to start doing something to keep in shape. His doctor said he was in great shape and at the perfect weight, but Pilgrim still felt like he needed to do something. He called it his "Portland Rich Guilt."

Pilgrim was so rich, he really didn't need to work at any job. His grandmother on his mother's side had left him more money than he knew what to do with just two months after his one and only divorce. At that point he had been out of law school for three years and pretty much hated working corporate law. His stint in corporate law lasted almost exactly the same amount of time as his marriage. Two years.

He had been good at corporate law and really bad at marriage. And had hated them both.

Somehow, after the money had arrived and he drank and traveled for a year, he had managed to start a law firm and hire great lawyers who liked working in law a lot more than he did. And then he had gone back to school and gotten his private investigator's license because it sounded like fun.

After a short time he sort of combined the law firm and the private investigation firm into what was now one of the largest and most powerful law firms in the state.

Hugh and Associates now occupied five floors of a downtown high-rise that Pilgrim also owned. His office and the entire private investigation section filled the top floor. The four floors below were the legal part of the firm. He had started out rich from his grandmother's money and now was even richer by hiring the right people and taking the right cases and buying the right buildings.

Carrie, Pilgrim's assistant, limo driver, and best friend since grade school, would be heading off to law school this fall for her third and final year before joining the legal side of his firm. He secretly hoped she would come back and remain on the investigation side of the business. They were a great team and he was going to miss her while she was down south in Eugene at school.

But he knew she was never coming back to be his assistant. Unlike him, she discovered she had a passion for the law and loved it.

And that thought of her not returning to be his assistant had him depressed. They would stay friends, sure. But he had loved all the time she had worked with him.

When the morning's strange call came in from the Tigard police chief, Pilgrim listened to the story while working at a Diet Coke and exercising on his stationary bike and looking out over the city and the Willamette River, trying to let the beautiful fall day brighten his darkening mood.

Everyone in this city rode bikes. Riding a stationary bike sort of made him feel a little more like the rest of the population. Carrie thought he was just fooling himself and had warned him a few times that to get any benefit from being on the bike, he actually had to peddle it faster and sweat a little.

He saw little point in that. Especially today.

From what the Chief of Police of Tigard told him in the call, it seemed they had a body.

A dead body.

Sort of.

Actually, they only had a male arm and a right hand that a dog had brought back to the dog's home in a neighborhood of Tigard. The Chief wanted Pilgrim to come and see if he could make any sense of it and try to help them figure out where the rest of the body was located.

It seemed the dog was being of little help.

Pilgrim told the chief they would be there in thirty minutes, then climbed off the bike, took a damp towel to his face even though he hadn't been sweating at all, and headed out of his office door.

Carrie was as tall as his six feet and today wore tight white short-shorts and a green t-shirt from the University of Oregon. As normal with Carrie, her outfit left little to the imagination.

She could walk down a sidewalk and cause car wrecks from both men and women staring at her.

Beside her stood Donna Marks, the assistant Carrie was training to take her spot this year. And, as Carrie reminded him, to take her spot permanently since after graduation Carrie was coming back and working with Ben two floors down in the corporate legal department of the firm.

Donna was shorter than Carrie, maybe five-six, and today she wore jeans and a blue blouse tucked-in. She had short brown hair and wide brown eyes that made her seem far more innocent than Pilgrim figured she was. She was thirty and divorced and had a smile that could light up a room when she used it.

Carrie loved her and said he would as well given time.

He would see about that. At the moment he didn't want anyone but Carrie.

"Did you get all that?" he asked as the three of them headed for the door to the office suite. He had always told Carrie to listen in to all his phone calls on cases. The practice just saved him time in explaining things to her and she often heard things he missed.

"We did, boss," she said. "The Case of the Dog-Bite Arm sounds like it's going to be interesting.

Pilgrim just moaned and shook his head.

Carrie always named all their cases like they were old detective books. Pilgrim liked that habit, he had to admit, even though he always made snide comments about it.

He glanced around at Donna as they reached the elevator. "So what's your take on this?"

Donna had a small notebook in her hand on top of a small tablet. She also had a pen stuck behind her ear being held there by her hair.

"I think this is a case of one hand not knowing what the other is doing."

She actually said that directly to Pilgrim without looking away and without breaking into a smile.

Pilgrim laughed and shook his head, then looked at Carrie who was smiling. "You found one like you?"

"She's better," Carrie said as they got into the elevator.

"I am," Donna said, smiling at Pilgrim. "I'm faster on computers, been trained in high-speed driving and car chases, and I am an expert marksman on ten different categories of guns."

"Are you going to decide to go to law school on me?" Pilgrim asked as the elevator doors closed. He had known all that about Donna before Carrie decided to bring her on board. But it was nice to see her stand up like that for herself with humor. On some of the things they did, she was going to need it.

Just putting up with him every day she was going to need a really good sense of humor and patience.

"Already been to law school," she said, smiling. "Dropped out before the last finals of my third year because I hated the idea of being a lawyer."

Now that hadn't been on her resume, so he turned and faced her. "So now you decide to come to work for a law firm?"

"I want to work as a private investigator and you're the best in the business."

He turned and smiled at Carrie. "I'm starting to like her."

"Good thing, Boss," Carrie said. "Because I'm not coming back. Remember?"

"Something I'm trying not to think about," he said, his mood suddenly foul again.

Two

DONNA WAS DRIVING and pulled the limo up to the curb in front of a brown house in a quite neighborhood in Tigard, Oregon, a suburb of Portland about five miles to the south of the downtown area. The area was built on rolling hills covered in large pine trees.

Three Tigard police cars blocked the street in both directions and one had had to move to let them through.

Carrie sat in the back with him, but they hadn't talked much on the way out, thanks to his mood.

The stretch limo served as their office and had more high-tech computer gear and surveillance equipment than Pilgrim could remember. A bunch of it Carrie had had installed over the years. And she knew how to run it all. He was good on computers, but not as good as she was. He hoped Donna was as good as she said, otherwise, this beast of a vehicle was just going to be a very expensive limo and nothing more.

The Tigard Chief of Police came down the sidewalk from a 1960s style ranch house to greet them. The house looked well-kept and had a fence around the backyard, more than likely to keep the dog in.

Chief Danny, as Pilgrim liked to call him, had red hair, far too many freckles on his face, and brown eyes that seemed to see everything. He was at least fifty, but looked younger unless you actually got close.

He extended his hand to Pilgrim and shook the firm, calloused hand. "Thanks for coming."

The Chief nodded to Carrie, who then introduced Donna as Pilgrim's new assistant and he nodded to her as well before turning back to the house to explain the situation.

Around them the wonderful day was starting to warm up just slightly, but in the shade of the large trees it felt perfect to Pilgrim. The neighborhood was an older one, the trees all grown, the sidewalks cracked with tree roots. The Portland area was full of perfect family neighborhoods just like this one. Sometimes he wondered why he didn't live out like this instead of in a penthouse condo in the Pearl District downtown.

"Dog came from that direction," the Chief said, pointing up the street. The dog dropped the arm on the back porch. You want to see it?"

"Pictures would be enough," Pilgrim said.

The Chief nodded to Carrie and said, "I'll have someone send them along in a moment."

"Thanks," Carrie said.

"So you have men searching the park at the top of the hill?" Pilgrim asked.

"We've already been all over it and up and down every alley around here. Nothing."

"Fingerprints?"

"Nothing on file local," the chief said. "We're searching larger data bases now."

"Send those fingerprints along as well, would you?" Pilgrim asked and the Chief nodded.

"Any identifying marks on the hand or arm?" Carrie asked.

"Besides a dog's teeth marks, nothing," the chief said. "No ring or ring mark, no tattoos, no scars, nothing."

"How was the arm removed from the body?" Pilgrim was starting to get an idea of what they were dealing with here, but he still needed more information.

"The bone and skin looked like it was cut cleanly right below the shoulder with a very sharp blade."

"Before or after death," Carrie asked a fraction of a second before

Pilgrim could.

Donna just stood taking notes.

"The guy was dead when the arm was cut off," the Chief said. "And at one point the hand and arm had been cleaned and put on ice."

Pilgrim nodded. He knew exactly where the arm had come from and why. He was surprised no one on the force had clued to it as well.

"Give us five minutes. But do send those pictures and fingerprints as soon as possible."

Carrie handed him a card with the e-mail address on it as Pilgrim turned back to the limo and crawled in. This was going to be an interesting case for Donna to start on.

A great test.

He took a can of Diet Coke from the fridge and then sat in his normal chair near the back of the limo's large passenger area. He flipped a switch hidden under his seat. Two computer screens appeared out of the side and a desk with a keyboard swung up out of the floor and clicked into place in front of him.

Carrie crawled in behind Pilgrim, grabbed a bottle of water, and took her normal spot up behind the driver's seat. She punched a hidden button and a computer console and two large screens wrapped out around her, making her look like she was suddenly in more of a command chair than a limo seat near a wet bar.

Her fingers instantly went to work on the keyboard.

Pilgrim looked at his screens and didn't bother. Carrie or Donna would find the information far faster than he would. So he just left the computer screens in front of him sit idle.

"You going to miss this?" he asked Carrie as Donna climbed in and pulled the door closed.

Donna sat facing the wet bar in the middle of the limo and in a moment was also surrounded by keyboards and screens as well.

"A little," Carrie said. "Not so much the private investigation cases, but I'll miss being around you all the time."

"A very nice thing to say."

Three

CARRIE TURNED TO DONNA who was typing faster than Pilgrim

had ever seen anyone type before. "So, you know where the arm came from?"

Pilgrim knew generally where the arm had come from, but not how the dog got it. He liked how Carrie was using this to test Donna as well.

"Oh, sure," Donna said as her fingers flew over the keyboard. "Just trying to get the address now."

A moment later Donna hit one last key, studied the screen for a moment, then smiled. "Three houses up the street on the same side of the street as the dog's home."

Carrie actually seemed slightly surprised. "And how did you get that information?"

Donna shrugged and looked at Pilgrim. He was doing his best to keep a straight face.

"Easy," Donna said. "The arm was clearly from a medical school here in the area. More than likely a student took it home for study, so I did a search cross-referencing this neighborhood with all the medical students at all the universities in the entire Willamette Valley and southern Washington and included the teaching hospitals in the area."

Donna twisted a screen around so that both Carrie and Pilgrim could see the picture of a young woman with black hair smiling for her student id.

"Peta Edwards," Donna said. "Part Native American, part German. Perfect grades. She lives here with her parents to save money."

"Shall we go tell the poor girl about her missing homework?" Pilgrim asked, punching the button that retracted all the computer equipment around him.

Donna and Carrie both did the same and then Donna went out into the wonderful, fall afternoon air first.

Pilgrim followed carrying his Diet Coke can and motioned for Chief Danny to follow them up the sidewalk as Carrie got out and locked the limo.

As they walked, Donna explained to the chief where the arm had come from.

"And you figured all that out in two minutes in that limo of yours?" the Chief asked, clearly surprised and happy he didn't have a murder on his hands.

"Actually," Pilgrim said, "Donna got the address of the student. And I'll bet you'll find an empty medical school cooler on the back porch. More than likely the poor student doesn't even know the arm is gone yet."

The Chief laughed as the four of them turned up the sidewalk toward the front of another 1960's ranch-style home nestled in among the trees. This one had no fence around the backyard.

"Chief," Donna said, "I kind of feel bad for this poor girl. You're more than likely going to have to write her instructor an official note."

Pilgrim moaned softly and looked at Carrie, who was smiling from ear-to-ear.

But Chief Danny didn't see the next thing coming at all and Donna was keeping a perfectly straight and serious face. Pilgrim was going to have to remember his new assistant could do that, or he would walk into a few of these traps as well.

"Why's that?" the Chief asked, stumbling and falling into Donna's punch line.

"Because no one's going to believe her when she says the dog ate her homework."

Chief Danny just shook his head as he looked at Donna who was still holding a perfect poker face.

Then he turned back to Pilgrim. "Where did you find this one?"

Pilgrim pointed to Carrie, trying to look innocent. "She found her."

And then as the chief turned away to knock on the door, trying to contain his laughter, Pilgrim mouthed to Carrie.

"Thank you."

THE ROAD BACK

A Doc Hill story

USA Today *bestselling writer Dean Wesley Smith returns to the world of his acclaimed thriller* Dead Money *with a new problem for professional poker player, Doc Hill.*

Doc agrees to help find a missing college student, the son of the Las Vegas Chief of Police. But little did Doc know that such a simple case would turn out to be so large and ugly and dangerous.

"The Road Back" gives readers a perfect introduction to the world of Doc Hill and professional poker.

When you are short-stacked in poker, and in life, the road back to being in contention often has a very sudden end.

One

"DO WE HAVE any idea where he might be?" I asked Annie over my shoulder.

She had crouched down behind my chair at the no-limit ring game I had joined a few hours before at the Bellagio. I was almost a thousand up and had been enjoying the game as a warm-up for a series of poker tournaments coming later in the week to the Bellagio.

I seldom played regular ring games anymore, only tournaments. But at times it felt right to just sit and play for a time. This hot September afternoon was one of those times to relax in the air-conditioned poker room and drink iced tea and win a little money in the process.

"Not a clue," she said. "Dad's got all the information."

Annie had her long brown hair pulled back and the white blouse and dark slacks she wore accented her perfect body. She was the best-looking *former* Las Vegas detective I had ever met, with brown eyes that could stare through to your soul. Actually, she was one of the best-looking women I had ever met, and also one of most deadly poker players in the modern game.

In the year we had been together, she had taken down a dozen tournaments and won two World Series of Poker bracelets for two different events.

Now she wanted my help to find some guy her dad thought was missing. Actually, her dad, Detective Bayard Lott, also a former Las Vegas police detective, wanted her help and she was asking if I would help out as well.

"You want me to deal you in, Doc?" the dealer asked.

"No, thanks, Al," I said, pushing back from the table as Annie stood and stepped back. I flipped him a twenty-five dollar chip and he tapped it and nodded thanks before slipping it into his tip slot.

I turned and nodded to Ben, the brush in charge of the room at the moment who was headed my way from the poker room desk.

"Cash you out?" he asked.

I flipped him a twenty-five dollar chip as well and said, "Thanks. Just add it to the account."

I had had a running account at the Bellagio for almost ten years now. Made it easier than hauling racks of chips to the cage all the time. And after the two tips, I had five hundred in starting money in my stack and another eight hundred and fifty in winnings.

My chip vanished into Ben's pocket and he worked to rack the rest as I turned and headed with Annie out of the poker room and into the noise and bells of customers filling the slots.

"Dinner?" I asked, realizing I was starting to get hungry as we turned toward the front of the casino.

"Dad's meeting us in the Café Bellagio," she said.

I laughed, taking her hand. "You were pretty sure I was going to help you, huh?"

"Not really," she said, smiling at me as we wound our way through the people toward the restaurant. "I would have gotten the information from Dad and told you later if you were really interested in staying in the game."

"It was enough warm-up," I said. "More than enough, actually."

"Lucky for those guys at the table," she said, laughing. "You warm-up much more and they would have been broke."

"That's the point, isn't it?" I asked.

She agreed and then waved at her father sitting at a semi-private four-person table off to one side of the café where it looked out over the pool. The smell of hamburgers and steaks drifted from the direction of the kitchen and my stomach rumbled. I really was hungrier than I had realized.

I liked her dad a great deal. He looked pretty sharp for his sixty-three years with short-cut white hair, broad shoulders, and only a hint of a gut around his stomach. He had a wicked sense of humor and his laugh could start an entire room laughing with him.

He and a bunch of his retired detective friends played poker every week in the basement of his house and worked to solve cold cases for the Las Vegas Police Department on the side. They called themselves the Cold Poker Gang. Annie and I helped them when we could.

But from what Annie said, this didn't sound like a cold case. More like a missing person problem. And in Vegas, there were always a lot of those.

For all sorts of reasons.

Two

I WAS INTO my rib steak and onion rings, Annie was picking at her hamburger, and her dad was about halfway done with his French Dip before Annie finally broached the subject.

"So who is missing and why are you involved, Dad?"

"Steve Benson Junior," he said between bites.

Both Annie and I glanced at him.

Finally Annie asked exactly what I was thinking. "The son of Chief of Police Steven Benson?"

"One and the same," her dad said. "Chief Benson called me, asked if I would look into it for him."

"He thinks his son is in trouble?" I asked.

Annie's dad shook his head. "Not that kind of trouble. He's a good kid, graduate student at UNLV focusing on Nevada history. But his dad this morning went to meet him for breakfast and Steve didn't show up. Steve's best friend hasn't seen him either."

"And his dad's worried?" Annie asked.

"I would be too," her father said, smiling at her. "Steve is like you in that he calls when he has to cancel something."

"He have a car?" I asked.

"Red Jeep SUV," he said. "About a year old. It's missing as well."

"So he went somewhere and hasn't returned yet," Annie said. "More than likely he's fine."

Her dad nodded. "That's what the Chief thinks as well, but he's still worried. Steve's cell isn't picking up. I think that's really why the Chief called me. He doesn't want this out yet, so he's just calling in personal favors at the moment."

I sat back munching on a crisp onion ring, thinking. My little voice was telling me that something was wrong with this kid. I didn't know him and I didn't know his father, but this felt wrong for some reason I couldn't put my finger on.

However, when at a poker table, I had learned to trust that little voice when it told me something was wrong with a play another player made. And in life I had also learned to trust that voice. And right now the very same voice was telling me we needed to move on this and fast.

I finished the onion ring and leaned forward toward Annie's dad. "Could you call the chief and ask him if Steve is back yet? And if not, could we go look at his apartment?"

Detective Lott slid the key across the table at me, smiling. "Steve wasn't back five minutes before you two showed up, and I got this key from the Chief before coming over here."

I just shook my head and grinned as Annie patted her father's arm, smiling. It was no wonder the guy had been such a great detective in his day. He was a half step ahead of everything.

Three

STEVE'S APARTMENT near the university seemed far neater than I would have expected a grad student's apartment to be. And it was clear with only a quick look that there was nothing at all out of place.

Nothing.

The apartment had one bedroom with a living room with only a couch and chair and a large desk in it. A small, clean dining room table with four chairs sat near the open kitchen. There was a bathroom off the bedroom.

There was no sign at all of any woman's touch in here. Everything was standard apartment except the large computer on an L-shaped desk on the left side of the living room and large wall of books on the right side, mostly textbooks that at a glance I was glad I never would have to read. My college days were a long ways behind me now.

However, one full shelf was full of books on various aspects of Nevada history that looked very interesting, from the gold rush towns to railroad history to the founding of Las Vegas.

All of them in perfect order by author.

Annie was looking through Steve's desk. There were a couple of books open on the desk on Nevada place names and another on lost mines of Nevada.

"Can you access that computer?" I asked Annie. "See what he was researching before he left?"

"If it's not password protected," she said, sitting down in the chair and moving the wireless keyboard closer toward her.

Her father came out of the bathroom shaking his head. "This kid is the cleanest kid I have ever seen. Nothing out of place, no sign that anyone else but him even visited here. Not even a hair on his comb."

"He folds his socks and underwear," I said. "His bed is made, even though he slept in it recently. And he washed his breakfast dishes before he left, more than likely yesterday morning, since the dishes are completely dry as is the dish towel."

Annie brought the computer up and then shook her head. "Protected."

"He's going to have a password book," I said. "Upper drawer on the left."

She opened the drawer and pulled out a small notebook, shaking her head. "How did you know that?"

"Someone like Steve is completely predictable. Every move, every detail. It's how his mind works. He has no choice."

"Easy pickings on a poker table," Annie said.

"He'd never sit down at one," I said. "He wouldn't be able to handle the uncertainty that comes naturally with the game."

"Obsessive-compulsive?" Annie's dad asked.

"Borderline," Annie said, nodding. "It goes toward hoarding or being neat freaks."

"We know which way Steve goes," I said.

As Annie worked on the computer and bringing up the history, I went back into the small apartment bedroom. Steve had his shoes lined up perfectly along the bottom of his closet, from dress shoes through tennis shoes to boots. There was an empty spot between a pair of tennis shoes and a heavy pair of boots. That's where he would put his hiking boots.

His shirts were lined up hanging in his closet and there was a clear opening where a light casual shirt had clearly hung. More than likely brown from the patterns of the colors.

I went into the bathroom and opened the medicine chest. There was an empty spot where a tube of suntan lotion would have sat right between a small jar of Vaseline and a tube of blister cream.

I closed the cabinet and went back into the living room with the desk and books. "He's gone into the desert. More than likely yesterday morning. My guess is he was planning on returning before dark last night and something happened."

Annie's dad looked around at the apartment. "I can see why the Chief was worried, now."

"Got it," Annie said, moving back through the history of what Steve had last looked at on his computer.

The very last thing was a map of an area of the Nevada desert to the north and west of Las Vegas along Highway 95.

"Skeleton Mountains," Annie said, hitting a button to print up the map just as I was sure Steve had done.

One of the books open on the desk referred to the area as well, and I picked it up as Annie kept going back through the history on the computer.

Seems the Skeleton Mountains were a group of rocky peaks sticking up out of the desert about ten miles to the west of the highway. The article said that no one knew exactly how it got its name. From what I could tell in the book, the rocky peaks had just always been named that.

And they weren't that big, with the largest being not more than six or seven hundred feet off the desert. Compared to the mountains I spent the summer in every year in central Idaho, guiding rafts on the River of No Return, these Skeleton Mountains were nothing more than large piles of rocks.

"He was researching some old patented mining claims in those mountains," Annie said, again hitting the print button. "All of them are long dormant and never produced anything of real value."

"So we know where he went," Annie's father said, nodding.

"Get a search team set up from the Chief," I said to him as Annie printed a second copy of the map of the small group of mountains.

"Where are you going?" Annie's dad asked, as he pulled out his phone.

"Fleet's in town and he loves testing out his new helicopter," I said, and Annie laughed. "He'll get us up there and we'll see what we can see from the air, see if we can spot his car before you and the Chief get there."

I was on the phone to my best friend and business partner, Fleet, and Annie's father was talking with the Chief of Police as we headed out into the hot early evening air and Annie pulled the door to the apartment closed behind us.

Four

FLEET LIVED IN BOISE with his family. Annie and I had a house there as well, but unlike Fleet, we were seldom in Boise. Fleet had a wonderful wife and two kids there, but at the moment they were all here, letting the kids have one last vacation before school started up again.

Fleet had decided that our company needed a helicopter to go along with our own private jet. It seemed that over the years, his investments of my poker winnings had made us, as he said, stupidly rich. We gave millions away to charity every year and spent what we wanted and somehow just managed to get richer.

Fleet was that good with business and investments.

My father's death a year ago had just added more millions than I wanted to think about into the picture.

When Fleet bought the jet helicopter for the company, he had decided he wanted to fly it, much to his wife's horror. And in the last year he had become a very good pilot.

On the phone I told him what was going on and he almost beat us to the airport, even though we had a shorter distance to go. Any excuse to take out the helicopter was a great idea as far as he was concerned.

Within forty minutes after leaving Steve's apartment, we were airborne and headed for the Skeleton Mountains, the loud drone of the chopper a constant noise around us.

"So what do you think we're going to find?" Fleet asked through the communications links we all wore.

Annie was in the co-pilot chair because she had taken a few lessons with the chopper last year. I was behind them, strapped in tight. I wasn't afraid of flying, but I had to admit having my friend from childhood doing the flying didn't instill great confidence, even though he had a lot of hours in the air already.

"Besides rocks and snakes?" Annie asked.

She moved slightly so I could see the wink she gave me.

I smiled. Fleet was deathly afraid of snakes. Any kind and size of snake, actually. And everyone knew it.

"Not funny," he said.

"If we have to land, you can stay in the chopper," I said. "There will be snakes."

Fleet shook his head. "You two sure know how to kill a good flight."

Less than fifteen minutes after leaving the Las Vegas airport, the mountains sort of rose from the rolling desert floor in front of us. They were sure nothing to look at. Mostly rocks and scattered open areas covered in scrub brush. I hadn't been kidding Fleet. Those rocks would be infested with snakes, since it was clear the area got little or no attention by humans at all.

"Come in from Highway 95," I said to Fleet. "See if you can spot a road into those mountains."

Fleet nodded and slowed until Annie pointed ahead.

A bare excuse of a dirt road left the highway and wound toward the mountains.

Fleet banked over it and followed the road, moving slowly as we all studied the area.

There was no place to hide below us at all. Just open desert and scrub.

Up ahead the road started to wind up a small canyon and then seemed to break out into an open flat area before going back into another canyon and deeper into the piles of rocks laughingly called mountains.

Nothing but huge rocks and scrub brush.

"On the right," Annie said, pointing.

It took me a moment, but finally I saw what she was pointing at. A glint of the sun reflected off some metal. At closer look I could see hints of a red car hidden beside a rock and covered with scrub brush. Someone had spent a lot of time in the task of hiding the car and had the car off the road so it couldn't be seen by anyone driving in.

"Someone really wanted that hidden," Fleet said, shaking his head.

My stomach was twisting like my rib steak was suddenly not agreeing with me.

"Same speed," I said to Fleet. "Just keep going straight and off into the desert on the other side of the mountains."

"Like we're on Fleet's tour of the desert," he said and did as he was told.

Annie had her cell phone to her ear as all of us watched the ground below. To the right of our flight path I could see a trail going up to what looked to be an old mine entrance. There was no sign of anyone there, but that meant nothing.

Then, near where the dirt road came out the other side of another rock canyon and started across the desert, I spotted an old pickup truck parked under a rock outcropping. It was brown and clearly dusty and blended in perfectly with the rocks.

"Truck on the right," I said as we went past and out into the desert just as if we were a sightseeing chopper doing nothing unusual.

"Get us away from these rocks and turn back toward Vegas until we are completely out of sight," I said to Fleet.

"Looks like the kid found some real problems he didn't expect in there," Fleet said.

"Dad," Annie said into her cell. "We found Steve's car, but looks like he's in trouble with someone living in an old mine in the Skeleton Mountains."

She waited for a second. "They hid his car," she said. "Spent a lot of time doing so, actually."

Again a pause as her father said something on the other side of the conversation that I couldn't hear.

"There is," Annie said. "A brown pickup, dirty, also hidden. We've moved away from the mountains to not spook anyone in there."

Then she gave a description of the truck to her father.

This one-sided conversation was driving me crazy. I had a hunch that the longer we delayed, the less chance Steve was going to make it. He had clearly walked into something ugly. You don't go to that much trouble to hide a person's car if you ever plan on letting them leave.

She nodded for a long minute, then she glanced at me, her brown eyes big. Then she said, simply, "Shit."

Then she hung up.

Fleet had the chopper flying low over the desert and had turned back for Vegas. We were out of both hearing and sight of the mountains.

"Dad and the Chief and a bunch of Vegas police and the State Police are all coming hard and silent from all directions. They are going to button up all ways in and out of that group of mountains."

"What did he say?" Fleet asked just before I could.

"A brown truck matching the description of the one back there has been connected to a string of disappearances. Maybe up to a dozen women going back years."

Now the steak in my stomach was really twisting around. Steve really had stumbled into something far, far bigger than he could handle.

"Take us back up to where the road into the mountains hits Highway 95," I said to Fleet. "Drop us off there and then make a wide circle out and around the rocks to the other side and out of sight and watch the road on that side. We don't want this guy getting away before the police get here."

Fleet nodded and two minutes later had us on the ground next to the highway. Then he lifted off and swung back to Vegas, climbing and moving fast.

I had tossed in an older twenty-two Remington saddle rifle from my car in case we needed to take out a couple of snakes and Annie had brought along her revolver. We had both grabbed bottles of water.

The air around us was hot, and there were very few cars passing by on the highway. The sun was low on the horizon, but not low enough to cut off the heat. It would be dark in less than two hours.

As Fleet vanished and the sound of the chopper faded off, Annie pulled out her phone to call her dad.

She told him what we had done and then asked how far out they were. As she listened to the answer, she shook her head.

"They are still a good fifteen minutes out," she told me. "And it will be thirty minutes or longer before they can have the entire place locked down from all sides.

I glanced at the half mile of road between us and the first edge of the rocks they called Skeleton Mountains. I wasn't sure that Steve had that long. If the guy had a police scanner, he would know the police were on the way.

I glanced at Annie and she could read my mind. She nodded and then said to her dad. "We're going in on foot. Warn everyone we're in there. And don't put that on the scanner."

Then before her father could object, she clicked off the phone and tucked it in her pants pocket.

"Up for a jog?" I asked.

"Why not?" she said, smiling as she made sure the clip in her gun was in place and ready. "Seems like a perfect evening for some exercise."

I knew there was a reason I loved this woman.

Five

IT TOOK US less than five minutes to run the length of the dirt road to the edge of the first rock canyon. It was a tough and hot run since we both had to keep looking ahead and also down at our feet to watch ruts and rocks that could twist an ankle.

We slowed as we entered the shadows of the canyon and walked, both of us drinking from our water bottles.

The rocks towered a good hundred feet over the road that ran up a wash. Annie watched the left side, I watched the right.

And I had been right about snakes. A couple nasty Speckled Rattlesnakes lay on rocks. As we approached, they slipped down into the brush. Both of them were large, far larger than I had seen in some time, actually.

In Idaho, as a guide on the summer rafting trips on the River of No Return, I warned people away from climbing the rocks near the river.

The rattlers there were much smaller, but could still ruin a good rafting trip if you cornered them or got too close.

The road came out of the rocks and opened up through an open area a quarter mile across before ducking back into the rocks on the other side. Steve's Jeep was hidden to the right about a hundred yards into that canyon ahead.

We stopped, still in the shadows and both took another long drink. Then we left the bottles beside the road. I had a hunch we were going to need our hands free from here on out.

I glanced at my watch. Eight minutes had passed since we left the highway.

"You ready?" I asked?

She nodded.

Running low, bent over, we headed out into the sun and across the open area. I kept expecting to hear a shot or something, but we made it quickly to the shade of the other canyon, both of us panting.

From there we slowed to a walk, Annie again watching the right walls of rock while I watched the left.

As we got even with where Steve's Jeep was hidden, Annie pointed it out. No one would have ever seen it simply driving this dirt path up this narrow canyon between all the rocks.

We kept moving up the road and within a minute we were at the place where the path left the road through some scrub and up a narrow cut in the rocks toward what looked to be an open mine.

"Got any ideas?" Annie asked as we stopped in the shadows and studied the path.

"Nothing," I said. "Trying to climb these snake-infested rocks to get up there another way would be suicidal."

"Going up that trail won't be very healthy, either," Annie said, studying the trail up to the mine opening a hundred feet above us. "It would be like shooting ducks in a pond for anyone above."

We both stood there, with not an idea in the world between us. The heat of the day had really baked the rocks around us and even though we were in the shade, everything was just radiating heat. I would have bet the temperature was a good hundred and twenty and there wasn't a breath of wind. Sweat dried so fast it left my skin feeling coated in dust and salt.

Annie took out her cell phone, then shook her head and put it back.

Then an idea hit me. "Car alarm."

Annie glanced at me, puzzled and listening. There was no sound at all out here in the desert in these rocks.

"Steve's car," I said. "I'm going to go back and see if I can set off that car alarm. If the guy up there doesn't know anyone is on the way to look for him, he's going to come out thinking a snake set it off or something."

"Good idea," she said.

"Don't let him get back in that cave or Steve is dead."

She nodded and glanced around for a place to hide. I started back down the road and behind me she whispered, "Watch out for snakes."

"You too," I whispered back.

Actually, snakes were my biggest concern with this entire plan. With brush all over that Jeep, there could be a dozen rattlers in there already, both in the car, in the engine, and under it. The car formed a perfect snake cave and I wasn't looking forward at all to wading in there.

I spotted a long piece of brush in the ditch beside the road and grabbed it. It was a good six feet long and sturdy. A rattler needed to get within four feet to strike, maybe more if they were big ones like we had seen coming in.

I glanced at my watch as I neared the Jeep's hiding place beside the road. Annie's dad and the State Police would be almost into position. If this guy ran, and Annie couldn't stop him, they would.

I just hoped Steve would still be alive if the guy did run.

I took a deep breath of the warm afternoon air and started off the road toward the red Jeep buried in the brush. Then, before I had taken two steps, I heard Annie's clear voice ring out through the rocks.

"Stop! Police. Let him go and put your hands up!"

Then two shots filled the air.

Running low and silently, I headed back up the road, not allowing myself to think about Annie getting hurt.

As I neared a corner in the road that would allow me to see the road ahead and the area where the trail left the road to the mine, I slowed.

Annie somehow had gone up the trail a dozen steps and then climbed into some rocks. Somehow she had managed to stay hidden as the guy holding Steve had come down the trail to the road. He must have had a scanner and finally clued to the fact that they were coming for him.

She now had him basically pinned on the road using Steve as a shield.

Steve looked tired and scared out of his wits in his tan slacks, hiking boots, and tan shirt. The guy holding him was short, about five-four, and wore jeans and a light green T-shirt that was stained by sweat. His face looked like it had a five-day growth of beard and his dark hair looked like it hadn't seen a comb in days.

He had a large pistol pressed against Steve's temple and was holding it as if he knew what to do with it.

Annie saw me and nodded.

"Police!" I shouted. "You are surrounded!"

The guy spun in my direction, trying to drag Steve with him, but Steve tripped. The guy's gun left the side of Steve's head as he fought to get his hostage back into position. In doing so he gave Annie a clear shot.

And she took it.

The guy spun from the impact and smacked back into the rocks and brush in the shallow ditch beside the dirt road. His gun flew away from him to the left.

Steve spun the other way, tumbling to the ground in the middle of the road.

I came in fast and Annie was almost faster down the trail, both of us watching for any movement in the guy. Annie had gotten him in the right shoulder. He had been holding his gun in his right hand. It didn't look like the wound would be fatal. There was blood, but not enough to cause him any danger.

A huge rattlesnake came out of the brush under him and struck at the guy's left arm. Clearly the snake wasn't happy about some guy landing on him.

The kidnapper moaned and jerked away.

All I could do was laugh.

"That's going to make his recovery a little longer," Annie said, laughing and shaking her head as she turned to help Steve to his feet.

"You all right?" she asked the son of the Las Vegas Chief of Police.

Steve nodded and didn't say anything. He was clearly in shock.

"You dad will be here shortly," Annie said, patting Steve's shoulder. "Is there anyone else up there in that mine?"

Steve shook his head. "No one alive."

Then he dropped to the road and buried his head in his hands and just sobbed. The guy in the ditch moaned and the large rattler slithered off down the ditch, clearly not happy, as I glanced at Annie.

She looked up at the mine entrance and shook her head.

I had a slight desire to see what was in there, but my better judgment quickly got control.

Some things were better just left unseen.

Six

I HAD MANAGED to go up the dirt road a short distance and get a clear enough phone signal to get word out that it was clear.

Then I called Fleet and told him it was clear and to meet us back at the intersection on Highway 95. But I told him that it might be awhile. He might have to transport Steve to the hospital with his dad before he could take us. We had some paperwork to fill out and a story to tell before we would be released, of that I had no doubt.

By the time I got back to Annie, I could hear two Las Vegas Police cars powering up the road.

They slid to a stop just short of us in a cloud of dust and Annie's dad and Steven's dad both piled out.

"You two all right?" Annie's dad asked.

"Had to put a bullet in his shoulder," she said, pointing to the guy in the ditch.

"And then a snake helped keep him down as well," I added, smiling.

Annie's father just shook his head and studied the moaning man for a moment before turning back to us.

The Chief helped his son to his feet and eased him back toward the patrol car as a number of State Police officers arrived on the scene sending up even more clouds of dust into the hot evening air.

As we watched, two Nevada State Police officers carefully worked to extract the guy from the ditch and made sure he didn't have any other guns on him. Then they flipped him over on his face in the dirt and handcuffed him in the middle of the road, not seeming to care at all that he had been shot and snake bitten.

I moved over to the tall State Police officer who seemed to be in charge and pointed up the trail. "From what the Chief's son said, that cave up there isn't pretty. More than likely a major crime scene."

The guy nodded. "Which one of you put the bullet in this guy?"

"I did," Annie said, coming up and handing him her gun. "Retired Detective Annie Lott."

"Thank you, Detective," the officer said, handing the gun to one officer to put away. He didn't seem to care at all about the rifle in my hand.

Then he motioned for two other officers to follow him up the hill.

Annie's dad, Annie, and I moved into a deep area of shade and stood watching as the three State Police officers went into the cave while another stood near the prisoner in the road.

A short minute later one came out, moved to the edge of the mine entrance, and threw up.

"That can't be good," I said.

Both Annie and her father just shook their heads. In their days I was sure they had seen things I flat didn't want to know about.

A few minutes later the other two came out and came back down the trail, a haunted look in all of their eyes.

The Chief climbed out of the patrol car where he had been sitting with his son.

"Your son is going to need counseling help after what he saw up there," the officer said. "He's going to have a long road back to normal."

"That bad?" the Chief asked.

"Worse," the officer said. "This is going to solve a lot of missing persons' cases. More than either of us care to think about."

I had never seen a police officer look so haunted in his eyes. He also was going to have some trouble dealing with whatever horrors were in that old mine.

Then the State Police officer walked over to the guy lying hand-cuffed face-down in the dirt and kicked him square in the side of the stomach.

After that, the officer turned and walked away down the road past the patrol cars, leaving the desert silence and heat closing in around all of us.

At that moment I was so glad I had resisted the slight temptation to go up to the mine opening.

The Chief glanced over at us, a look of relief in his eyes. Then he said simply, "Thanks."

"You are more than welcome," Annie said as her father put his arm around her.

"Just take care of Steve," I said.

The Chief nodded and went back to the car to sit with his son.

As the door to the patrol car closed, I turned to Annie's father. "Think all the good feelings will cut down some on the paperwork for us?"

Both Annie and her father laughed, as did the state cop standing near the prisoner on the ground.

"Not a chance," Annie's father said between laughs.

Annie stepped over and kissed me. "You always were a dreamer."

THE SECRETS OF YESTERDAY

A Poker Boy story

Former professional poker player and USA Today *bestselling writer, Dean Wesley Smith returns to the world of Poker Boy.*

When Poker Boy senses someone watching him as he stands in his invisible office high over Las Vegas, he knows only trouble lurks. With his boss, Stan, the God of Poker at his side, they go to investigate and what they find gives Poker Boy a glimpse into Stan's past.

A glimpse he did not want to see.

One

FROM MY OFFICE floating a thousand feet over the MGM Grand Casino and Hotel in Las Vegas, the city and surrounding area seemed painted in light brown. I could almost see the heat shimmering off the concrete and streets below as the record temperatures continued for a third day.

For a change I was alone in this office that I had designed to look like a booth in a fifties retro diner. All four walls were clear and the red vinyl booth sat in the middle of the room, two fake trees behind it to give it a feel of containment.

I had put in a wooden railing in front of the glass walls all the way around because it felt like I could fall off the edge of my office floor.

Before I put those railings in I couldn't even walk near the edge. Just too creepy.

The place was invisible to anyone from below and there were only three ways to get here. You either had to teleport, which I knew how to do, or go through the door from my girlfriend and sidekick Patty Ledgerwood's apartment. But most of the team entered through the secret door from The Diner off Freemont Street in downtown Vegas.

This office looked exactly like a booth in The Diner, actually. We used to meet there when dealing with a problem, so when I built this office, it just felt right to make it look like the old booth in The Diner.

Most everyone on my team except Stan used The Diner entrance. Patty tended to either come with me, or use the door from her apartment.

At the moment I was waiting for Patty and we were going to head to dinner, but she didn't get off work at the MGM Grand Hotel front desk for another twenty minutes.

It felt kind of odd being here alone. Normally at least three or four of the team were with me, talking about one thing or another.

And Madge, from The Diner, was always coming in and out serving us milkshakes and burgers.

At times the room had held up to fifteen people, but Madge had had to bring chairs from The Diner for that. The booth only held eight when we crowded in, and three chairs could be pulled up at the head of the table.

Right now I sat in a chair, my feet up on the wood railing around the room, facing downtown Las Vegas.

What a view. It just didn't get any better.

I felt about as relaxed as I ever could feel as a superhero always chasing down one bad person or another. Usually I only felt this relaxed while playing poker.

Suddenly one of my faint alarms in the back of my head went off.

As a poker player, before I had become a superhero, I had learned to trust those alarms. They warned me when I was up against another player who had better cards or who might be cheating or who was getting angry.

I called the feelings my "super powers" back then. Little did I know that many of them actually were superpowers. All I had done was learn to trust them.

This time my little voice was telling me someone was watching me.

But at the same time I knew that wasn't possible. I was in an invisible office floating a thousand feet over the Las Vegas Strip. No one could see this place.

As Stan, my boss and the God of Poker, told me one day, the office was slightly out of phase with the real world. A plane trying to land at the nearby McClaren airport could fly through the office and no one would notice.

I expect that if I saw a plane coming directly at this place I would notice.

So who could be watching me now?

And why was my little voice considering that a threat?

A God of something or other might be able to see the office.

Or maybe another powerful superhero like me.

But not many others.

In fact, no one else that I could think of.

I stood and stared in the direction of downtown Vegas. The new Rush Tower of the Golden Nugget stood above most of the buildings there, but I still had to look down on it from my height.

My little voice was telling me that tower was where the problem was coming from.

And I didn't like this at all. Not one little bit.

Two

"STAN?" I shouted upward as I always did when calling my boss.

Stan appeared almost instantly beside me, also looking out toward the downtown area.

He had on his normal gray slacks, gray shirt and sweater and had his brown hair combed perfectly. He was the most nondescript man I had ever known. You could walk right past him in a hallway and never notice him, which was one thing that made him so deadly on a poker table.

I had yet to sit across from him at a poker table, and honestly had no desire to do so any time in the near future.

"You feeling it as well?" I asked as he stared at the downtown area.

"Someone's watching," he said. "And they are not blocking the fact that they are watching."

"That's why I could sense it?" I asked.

He nodded.

"Can you get a spot on the location?"

"A suite on the 25th Floor of the Golden Nugget. Corner suite. The person is staring at us?"

"Suggestions?"

"I'm going to jump us there and take us out of time," Stan said.

I nodded and a moment later we were standing in a large suite on the top floor of the Golden Nugget. The place was decorated in brown tones, with a large brown couch and chairs in an area under a large screen television.

A made king-sized bed filled another part of the huge room, with a brown comforter and white pillows. A large vanity with a marble surface faced the bed with a desk and another large flat-screened television.

Someone was in the bathroom to my right, pocket-doors slid closed.

And standing in front of the window facing in the direction of my floating office over the strip was a teenager, not more than sixteen at the most.

He was frozen, his hand holding open the drape, as was the news-caster on the television screen, since Stan had taken us out of time.

Actually, I knew how to do that as well. It was more that he had slipped us between two instants of time, but it had the affect of seeming to stop time for anyone taken out of time.

The kid was dressed like most normal teenagers with jeans and a blue tee-shirt not tucked in. His hair was cut short and he looked like he played sports because his shoulders were broad and he didn't have an ounce of fat on him.

"He's powerful," Stan said, nodding at the kid. "I can feel it."

Actually, I could as well. "Is this unusual for someone his age?"

"Very," Stan said, his voice serious.

"Can he sense us here?" I asked.

"He might be able to."

"I can hear you as well," the kid said, turning to look at us.

His face was angular and his eyes a deep black. And as he turned just about every alarm I had as a superhero went off in my head.

More than anything I just wanted to jump and run. But Stan stayed put beside me and so I did the same, my best poker face firmly in place.

"You were looking for us?" Stan asked, his voice as neutral as it always seemed.

"I was," the kid said, nodding and moving away from the window. He moved past us and sat on the couch. "Actually, I was looking for more people of my kind. Guess I found a few, huh? That your place out there floating over the Strip?"

I nodded and said nothing more. At this point, I was glad, more than glad, to let Stan handle this.

"So who are you?" Stan asked.

"Jason King," the kid said. "My mom, Bonnie, is in the bathroom. She doesn't have any of these powers I have, or at least doesn't seem to."

"Oh, I do, dear," a voice said as the pocket doors to the bathroom slid back. "I just never let you know about them."

I glanced around.

Stan still held us in a time bubble. The newscaster on the television was still stuck in mid sentence and outside the window I could see a jetliner headed for McClarin just hanging there in mid-air. And there were no sounds coming from the city around us at all.

Yet two people had broken into the time bubble Stan had set as if it were nothing unusual. I couldn't do that and I was supposedly one of the most powerful superheroes out there.

Or maybe no one had taught me how to do that yet.

"Hi, Stan," the woman said as she came around the corner in the suite from the bathroom area.

She was attractive and thin and looked to be about the same age as all the Gods and superheroes, mid-thirties. It seems we all pretty much stopped aging at that point for some reason or another.

She had long brown hair pulled back off her face and dark brown eyes. She wore a red summer dress and was barefoot. And she was smiling, but I wasn't sure the smile was reaching her eyes or not.

"Bonnie?" Stan asked, actually sounding shocked.

I glanced at my boss. He was the God of Poker. Even when something shocked him, he never showed it. He was the master of poker faces. But right now he was showing surprise just as any normal human would.

This time the smile actually did reach her eyes. And there was more there. A love, a fondness.

"It's great to see you again," she said, moving over and taking his hands and then reaching up and kissing him on the cheek.

"But I thought... I thought..." Stan couldn't seem to finish his sentence.

"That we were dead," she asked, still smiling. "We were."

"And it wasn't a lot of fun, either," Jason said, dropping onto the couch and putting his feet up on the coffee table.

Stan stared first at Bonnie, then looked at Jason. Then back at Bonnie with a questioning look.

I was reading Stan's face. In the years I had worked for him, that had never happened. Not once.

"Is he...?" Stan asked.

Bonnie nodded. "Jason," she said, turning to her son slouched on the couch. "I would like you to meet your biological father, Stan, the God of Poker."

"So," Jason said, nodding, but not acting surprised or shocked. "He's the guy who killed us."

Three

THE SILENCE in the room couldn't have been cut with a chainsaw.

I moved silently over and dropped onto a chair near the vanity, doing my best to just pretend I wasn't here. I had no idea what was happening, what had happened between Bonnie and Stan, and not a clue why Jason scared me to death.

This all seemed way, way out of my league at the moment. I really, really, really needed someone to spend some time filling me in on the history of all this, including the history of the people I worked with. I had only been a superhero now for a short ten years. I was an open book, but it sure seemed that everyone around me had a lot of history and secrets.

"I didn't..." Stan said, shaking his head, clearly upset and clearly surprised at meeting his son.

"Oh, we know you didn't," Bonnie said, smiling at Stan. "Don't we, Jason?"

"Yeah, whatever," he said, shrugging like any teenager.

Bonnie smiled again, but this time the smile once again didn't reach her eyes.

Every alarm in my body went off again.

I focused all my powers and without saying a word out loud, I shouted the thought, *Laverne!*

Watching. Her voice came back strong in my head. *And no need to shout.*

Laverne was Lady Luck herself, one of the most powerful Gods there was. I felt a lot better with her watching this. Whatever this was.

Stan shook his head and then regained his calm poker face. "If you didn't die, then where have you been for the last sixteen years?"

"Oh, we did die," Bonnie said.

"Buried," Jason said.

I almost shuddered at the very idea, but managed to stay still, tucked off on the side in my chair.

"Buried?" Stan asked. "How can that be? I saw the cabin burn to the ground with you in it. I couldn't get to you and couldn't stop the flames."

"Did you find a body?" Bonnie asked.

Stan shook his head. "The magic in those flames took everything down to fine ashes. I killed Crystal for what she did to you."

Holy smokes. Stan killed someone?

Bonnie nodded, clearly sad. "I know you did. And I know what that cost you."

Don't ask, Laverne's voice said softly in my head before I could even form a thought about asking Stan what had happened later. *Don't ever ask him. Ever.*

Understood.

"I had crawled under the floorboards of the cabin," Bonnie said, her voice soft. "I dug down into the mud and soft dirt, but I still died. And our unborn child, Jason, died with me."

"But how?" Stan asked. Then clearly, as I watched his face, he seemed to understand something. "Osiris?"

Bonnie nodded.

Laverne put in my mind an image of a tall, thin, green-skinned man wearing a white long beard and carrying a black stick. He wore robes that seemed to shimmer in the image. *One of the great old ones. The major God of Death and of Life.*

I didn't know there were great old ones.

Laverne thankfully said nothing to that stray thought by me.

Bonnie went on. "Osiris took my remains while the flames were still

45

hot and put me in an ancient wooden coffin in an old cemetery in Boise, Idaho. The previous resident had gone mostly to dust. In there, in that darkness, Osiris slowly let life come back into my body."

"I was born in that coffin," Jason said, clearly disgusted. "We were in that old coffin until I was five living on worms and grubs and dripping water from above."

Now I actually did shudder. There were many things about the Gods and superheroes I had come to dislike, but whatever had happened to these two topped anything I had learned so far.

Stan's face looked white and he turned away. I had no idea how he was even holding it together. His son had been born six feet underground in a coffin. And had to stay there for five years.

"It took that long before we regenerated completely," Bonnie said softly. "But we are now alive. Osiris accepted us into his world and we live in comfort there. Osiris is training Jason."

I wanted to ask what he was training him for, but then Laverne thought *To replace him as the God of Death.*

Oh.

Stan looked at his son and then bowed slightly to him. "I did try to save you. I had no idea you survived. I owe Osiris a great debt."

Jason just sat on the couch under the window and shrugged like any bored teenage kid would do.

A moment later a very tall, very green man with a long white beard appeared beside Bonnie. He wore a silk robe that shimmered and radiated power like I had never felt before.

Suddenly the suite smelled of a beach fire and rose petals.

Laverne appeared beside him and bowed to him.

Stan bowed to him and I scrambled to my feet and did the same, stunned that Laverne would bow to anyone. Wow did I have a lot to learn about the Gods and this world I played a very small part in.

I so wanted to just jump away from this, but instead I backed up as much as I could and tried to make myself as unnoticed as possible.

Jason just sat on the couch looking bored.

Osiris faced Stan. "I am sorry I could not tell you about your wife and son. I did not know if I could save them or if they would come through the process sane."

"I am very glad you did save them," Stan said.

"We cannot return to you," Bonnie said to Stan, a sadness now in her brown eyes.

46

Stan nodded. "I understand."

Osiris reached over and took Bonnie's hand and it was clear they were now a couple of some sort.

Stan nodded and smiled and after a moment Bonnie also smiled.

Then something happened that I am sure would give me nightmares for years. Osiris, the God of Death and one of the ancient ones that even Laverne bowed to, turned and faced me directly.

His eyes were a swirling pool of silver and black and he seemed to have a sly grin hidden in that white beard.

"Poker Boy," he said and I swore his voice seemed to echo into all parts of my head. "I have watched you and your team save this world and the gods in it many times. I now ask for your help."

I nodded and somehow said with a slight bow, "Anything you desire, sir."

"In a few years Jason will require training in the arts of discipline and control of his emotions if he is to someday rule in my place."

On the couch Jason just snorted. I did not look away from Osiris.

"When the time comes, I would like you to teach him those arts through the game you call poker. You are the best poker player in the world. Jason will require the best."

I don't think I was breathing, but I did manage to say, "I would be honored, sir."

"Very good," Osiris said, smiling and showing me a mouthful of rotted and yellowed teeth.

He turned to Laverne. "It is always an honor."

"The honor is mine, Great One," Laverne said, bowing slightly.

Osiris then turned to Stan. "I am deeply sorry for your loss."

Stan nodded and then glanced at Bonnie with a smile. "It seems that from the ashes has come some good."

Bonnie smiled back and the smile reached her eyes. And the relief that Stan understood.

Stan was letting her go.

Osiris nodded and bowed slightly to Stan. "You are as great a young god as Bonnie led me to believe."

Then Osiris, Bonnie, and Jason were gone.

My legs gave out and I dropped down onto the chair.

Laverne stepped over to Stan and put her hand on his shoulder like a parent comforting a small child.

Then without a word they were both gone and the sounds of the city outside the suite came crashing back in as they let go of the time bubble we had all been inside.

I was now alone in a plush hotel suite trying to catch my breath. I took two deep, shuddering breaths, working to slow my heart that seemed to want to pound right out of the front of my chest.

I worked to just clear my mind and relax as I had learned to do at a poker table in times of stress.

In a moment I felt better.

I stood, went to the window, and looked out the window at my office floating there in the sky over the MGM Grand. There were still almost thirty minutes before Patty got off work. She'd never believe what had just happened. Or maybe she would.

And then I realized that I had just agreed to give the adopted son of the God of Death poker lessons.

Once again I had to sit down and try to catch my breath.

And that wasn't easy to do.

A NIGHT WITH A FORGOTTEN GOD

A Poker Boy Story

USA Today *bestselling writer Dean Wesley Smith returns to his most popular series that features the superhero Poker Boy and all his sidekicks.*

Poker Boy once again finds himself facing the task of saving someone. But this person seems to be a ghost.

Can a simple poker player give a ghost a reason to live? If anyone can do it, Poker Boy can, all between hands of cards on a great Saturday night.

One

YOU WOULD THINK that with all my varied superpowers, I would have one that would warn me when a really good night was about to turn into something else. Just a tingling, maybe a little buzz behind one ear, something.

But nope.

This Saturday night started off as normal as a Saturday night gets for a superhero working for the gods of gambling.

I was playing in a great no-limit game in the poker room at Spirit Winds casino. Since I was Poker Boy, and playing poker was what I also did for a living between rescuing people and saving the world, finding a good game with decent players on a Saturday night was about as good as it came.

The noise from the nearby casino was a steady background sound of people excited at the craps table and bells and alarms of slot machines.

A faint smoke smell drifted in from the casino floor where smoking was still allowed. At times I figured it was almost demanded that a person had to smoke to play a slot machine. Smoking in poker rooms had been banned a decade ago, and for that I will be forever grateful.

I had just had a snack at the free buffet that they set up in the poker room. The entire five-foot buffet was basically some crackers and cheeses and curled up vegetables of one sort or another. I stuck with the crackers and some cheese and a bottle of water. I figured that would get me to a late dinner.

The Spirit Winds poker room had fourteen tables and right now there were seven games going, with another table about to start up. The game I was in was the major game in the room, and we were tucked to one side of the big room so that people could stand and watch from the edges of the room.

Right now we had about ten people watching the play.

I loved this casino and considered it my home casino even though I spent most of my time in Las Vegas and had an invisible office floating a thousand feet over the MGM Grand Hotel and Casino. This little casino tucked off in the Oregon mountains felt like home.

I had played here before I met Stan, the God of Poker and my boss, and before I found out I was a superhero. So my roots were here.

And no one in this casino really knew anything about my alter identity as Poker Boy. They just all called me "Hat" because of the black fedora-like hat I always wore and the black leather coat. No one in Oregon knew that hat and coat was my superhero uniform that helped strengthen my superpowers.

I loved the area of the Oregon Coast Mountains so much, I was building a huge home about a mile away from here on some land I owned. Actually, Patty Ledgerwood, aka Front Desk Girl, and I were building the home, paying a guy I had helped rescue a year or so ago.

We weren't married, but we had been an item now for years and I had a hunch the marriage thing would come at some point. We had talked about it, but since we were both superheroes, we figured taking our time wouldn't hurt. Especially since we were both basically immortal now. I still looked like I was thirty, as did all gods and super-heroes. I was going on fifty in real years.

Patty wouldn't tell me her real age, but I had a hunch from some of the things she had said, she was well past one hundred years old. Thankfully, she just looked thirty as well.

The home we were building was tucked back in the trees on forty acres. When done, it would have a huge indoor pool and game room. It was being built partially out of local logs. It was costing me over two million to build and wouldn't be done for almost another year, but Patty and I loved to visit it every week or so and see the progress and just sit and stare out over the valley. The view from the new house could take your breath away at sunset and at sunrise.

Patty had been surprised I had so much money that I could afford a two-million-dollar home, and honestly I was surprised as well. I had just never really counted it up. Since I learned how to teleport, I no longer had to fly anywhere, so about all I spent my winnings on was food.

And other investments, which, it seemed, often turned out to pretty good investments.

Patty helped me figure it all out once before we started construction and the total had shocked both of us. Two million for the home wasn't going to dent how much money I had.

I had bought into the no-limit game for two hundred and in over two hours I had built that up to over a thousand. And had fun doing it, and it seemed the players around me were enjoying the game as well, which made it even better, even though they were losing.

It was still just a little before eleven in the evening. Patty worked the front desk at the MGM Grand Hotel in Vegas and I didn't have to meet her until two in the morning. So I had three more hours of play left before I had to cash out, teleport to Vegas, and go out for a late dinner with the woman of my dreams.

The noise from the nearby casino floor for a moment seemed to suddenly fade, then came back again strong.

I glanced around, but no else had noticed and I could see or feel no reason for anything like that to happen.

And none of my warning senses were going off at all.

Weird, just weird.

Then, out of the corner of my eye I caught a glimpse of a guy standing to one side of the room, just watching the game.

But he wasn't really there. More like a ghost.

I could see the wall right through him without a problem.

My wonderful Saturday night had just taken a turn onto a new road. Which road would depend on what the ghost wanted.

Two

NOW, I HAD come to believe in a lot of things since becoming a superhero, such as aliens, old races of Titans, and powerful gods of math. But I still hadn't heard a word that ghosts were real, and I kind of still doubted they were.

With one eye on the ghost, I took myself out of time.

Around me the noise of the casino shut off, leaving the entire place instantly silent. And everyone froze in the instant.

People's faces do not belong frozen in an instant. It twists them all up into something not natural or attractive.

Jumping into an instant of time felt like I was actually stopping time, but all I was doing was moving into an instant.

Time was still going on just fine and I hadn't stopped anything. I just existed outside of the flow of time.

I stood and headed toward the ghost.

He was frozen as well, his attention focused on the table I had been playing at. He wore an old-fashioned dark cloth shirt, dark cloth pants, and a wide rope belt. Over that he had what looked like an 1800s dress jacket. He had short dark hair and no beard at all.

He stood not more than five foot tall and he looked around thirty or so.

I studied him for a moment, not having a clue what to do next.

I could see right through him, of that there was no doubt. And from the looks of a woman's face standing about five feet away, she had noticed him as well just as I froze time.

So it wasn't just my powers that saw him.

I had no idea what to do, so when that happened, I did the most logical thing.

"Stan!" I shouted at the ceiling.

I have no idea why I always shouted his name and why it was at the ceiling. Just an old habit from my first days as a superhero when I was calling for him all the time it seemed.

He appeared between me and the ghost looking like the God of Poker always looked. He had on tan slacks, a tan shirt, a slightly darker sweater without an identifying mark on any of it. His hair was cut perfectly and his face always neutral. He stood exactly five-ten, not too short and not too tall. And he seldom smiled, although over the years I had seen him shocked a few times and smile a few other times.

In other words, he was the kind of guy who could walk by you in a hallway and most people would never remember anyone walked past them.

"Winning?" he asked.

"Of course," I said.

"So what's the problem?"

I pointed to the short ghost standing behind him.

Stan turned and then just shook his head.

"What is it?" I asked.

"Not what, who. That's Ben."

"So he's not a ghost?"

Stan shook his head and I felt relieved.

"Nope, he's a god."

Three

OF ALL THE THINGS Stan could have told me about the nearly invisible guy wearing rumpled old-style clothing, the fact that he was a god stunned me.

And as a god, he had let me get out of time and approach him. All the gods I had met, and that was no small number, were able to sense when someone slipped out of time around them.

"So what's he the god of?" I asked.

"Lamplighters," Stan said, his voice sad.

"Lamplighters? What's that?"

"And thus the reason for his condition," Stan said. "His entire area is being forgotten. Lamplighters used to be a huge number of men, and a few women, who went around city or town streets all over the world and lit the lamps. They reached the height of their profession in the gas-lamp era."

"There was a god for that?" I asked.

Stan gave me a dirty look. "I'm the God of Poker. There's a god for everything."

I looked at Ben the god ghost and finally caught a clue. When a god's area went away, eventually the god did as well.

"How come he couldn't shift to another area?" I asked.

"Some are able to," Stan said. "Some would rather just fade away as their area of expertise does with time."

"So what's he doing here?" I asked.

Stan shrugged. "Let's ask him."

A moment later Ben realized he had been taken out of time and that Stan and I stood there staring at him.

"Stan," Ben said, his voice not much more than a distant whisper even though he seemed to be talking normally. If we hadn't been out of time and the casino completely silent, I never would have been able to hear him.

"Ben, great seeing you again," Stan said. "Haven't found a new area that interests you yet, I am gathering?"

Ben held up his nearly see-through arms and laughed. "Yeah, pretty obvious. You know there are less than one hundred professional lamplighters left in the world?"

I almost said I was surprised there were that many, but I managed to keep my mouth shut and let Stan do the talking to someone he clearly knew out of the past.

"So what are you doing here?" Stan asked.

Ben sort of half-pointed at me. "Since I have a lot of time on my hands, I've been following Poker Boy and his team and all the good work all of you are doing. And how many times the team has saved all of us."

I nodded my thanks and again kept my mouth shut.

Stan did the same thing, so Ben went on in his whisper-sounding voice.

"So I wanted to come and see if I could get a chance to ask Poker Boy what area of expertise his team was missing and I would move in that direction with the hope that in a few hundred years or so I might have enough of my powers back to be able to help out in a crisis or two."

Areas we lacked?

I honestly hadn't given that any thought. Not one.

The team consisted of Patty, aka Front Desk Girl who had the ability to calm anyone into a smile, including me in the most stressful of times.

Screamer was an original member. He could link people's minds together and read thoughts.

We had Smoke, part wolf, part human, who could walk through walls and sense and smell things from great distances.

Madge, a superhero in the area of food service, added in her keen eye and ability to cut right to the point of something. Plus she made the best milkshakes ever made on the planet.

And then there was Stan, my boss, a god who seemed to know almost everyone, kept us all balanced, and knew were to go for help when we needed it.

We had a few others who had helped on certain missions, but that was the core. What were we missing?

A very good question.

And clearly a question that just might save Ben's life. But, one thing I didn't know about Ben. Did the powers-that-be want him saved? I had met my share of gods and not all of them were liked.

Maybe Ben's demise was something no one wanted to stop.

"That's very flattering," I said to Ben. "And let me think for a minute. And I'm going to need to talk with Stan, if you don't mind, since he's my boss in all this."

Ben smiled and meekly waved. "Oh, sure, no problem. Thanks for even considering my crazy question."

With that Stan put Ben back frozen, and we turned and walked away, weaving between the people stuck in real time in varied poses.

The silence was intense and I wanted to make sure Ben couldn't hear my next question to Stan.

Finally Stan stopped near the tiny buffet of crackers and cheese and browning lettuce, frowned at it in clear disgust, and then turned to me.

"What's he like and can he hear us?" I asked.

"He barely has enough power to maintain his essence in the world," Stan said. "He can't hear us. And he's a very, very nice man, from everything I heard and know about him."

"So people would welcome him being saved?"

Stan nodded. "I don't think he has an enemy anywhere, and that's saying something with gods."

I agreed with that. I had seen more bickering and feuding among the gods than I would have seen watching kids play on a playground during recess. With great power and years of age comes great pettiness, it seemed.

"Why didn't he just move around into other areas of city government?" I asked Stan, glancing back at the ghost that was Ben.

"He doesn't interact well with people," Stan said. "He's very shy and not strong enough for management, not physically able to handle something like garbage, and besides, there just aren't a lot of slots sometimes for a god to move to."

"So he just stayed where he was and the world went past," I said.

"Exactly," Stan said.

"I wonder what he's been doing with his time for the last hundred years?"

Stan just shrugged.

My little voice, which was part of my superpowers, kind of dinged me. The answer to Ben's problem had something to do with what he had been doing since electricity started lighting city streets.

"Let's go ask him," I said.

Stan looked puzzled, but just shrugged why not.

I turned back and weaved my way in and around the frozen people.

As we got close, Stan brought Ben out of time and into the silence of our little bubble.

Before Ben could say anything, I asked him point blank. "What have you been doing to fill your time over the last one hundred years?"

He looked down at the floor, clearly embarrassed. Then he said even softer than normal, "I read."

"Read?" I asked. "Read what?"

"Everything," he said, clearly a glow filling him slightly. "I love books, all sorts of books. I love bookstores, libraries, everything about any form of books. I even love the new electronic books."

He reached into a pocket of his loose old jacket and pulled out an electronic reader.

I glanced at Stan who seemed as shocked as I felt, but it was hard to get a read on the emotions of the God of Poker.

"How much do you remember about what you read?" I asked.

"Everything," he said. "My memory is photographic, even slipping away like this. I know which book I read what in and when and who the author was and everything. I own a large castle outside of London and it's completely full of books. I guess you would say I'm a hoarder."

I flat didn't want to think about an entire castle full of ancient books. I could easily see his passion was everything books and reading. Everything.

"When did you start this reading?"

"Gutenberg invented the press and it wasn't long after that. But I also have collected and read a lot of old scrolls and have spent many a wonderful day in the Library of Alexandria."

"That still exists?" I asked, stunned.

Beside me Stan said, "Oh, sure."

Ben nodded.

Damn I had a lot to learn about history and the gods and everything else. I really hated always being the young and stupid one in a conversation among old gods and superheroes.

Then it dawned on me what I had just thought.

Knowledge. If my team had the knowledge of history stored in Ben's head, we would be a ton stronger.

A million times stronger, actually.

I turned to Stan. "Is there a god of books, a god of libraries, a god of bookstores?"

"Yes, yes, and yes," Stan said.

"Can a god go back to being a superhero if there are no spots open?"

"Sure," Stan said, nodding and thinking.

"Good," I said. "We need to find a spot somewhere in the book world for Ben, because we need him now on the team."

Ben looked stunned and Stan just smiled.

I looked at Ben feeling how lucky we all were that all the knowledge that Ben had gathered had not just faded away with him.

"I'll be right back," Stan said.

He vanished and I smiled at Ben, who was looking stunned and very shy. I could see why he hadn't been able to stay in the city government world of gods.

"I don't understand," he said, looking up at me.

"Do you trust me?" I asked.

He nodded.

"Do you love books and reading?"

"More than anything in the world."

"And you can remember everything you've read?"

"Everything."

I nodded. "Then the team needs you now, not a hundred years from now. So we just got to get you out of this fading-away state."

Ben was about to say something when Stan reappeared with a striking woman in a white blouse, long black skirt, and black glasses. Her shiny black hair was pulled back and tied in a bun to the back of her head. She was short, maybe five-two at the most, but she radiated power.

A lot of power, actually.

She saw Ben and instantly put a hand over her mouth in shock. "Oh, my, Ben, what's happened? You didn't move from the lamplighter position, did you?"

He just shook his head and looked down at the ground, ashamed.

"Baalat, I'd like you to meet Poker Boy," Stan said. "Poker Boy, this is Baalat, the god of all reading and books."

She turned to me and smiled. I managed to bow slightly and she extended her hand and I shook it. Her skin felt smooth and firm and her grip firm as well.

"I have heard so much about your team," she said. "We all owe you so much."

"Thank you," I said. Then somehow I managed to focus my attention away from one of the most powerful and stunning gods I had yet to meet and back to the problem at hand.

"Ben has a photographic memory for everything he has ever read since books were invented."

"You do?" Baalat asked Ben directly, looking at the ghost of a man.

Ben nodded and said nothing, still staring at the ground at his feet.

So I kept going, pitching his case. "And Ben has been reading scrolls as well from before books. And he loves electronic books. He tells me he loves all books, no matter what type or shape. He loves reading. Period."

"Is this true?" Baalat asked, looking away from me and back at Ben.

Ben this time looked up and nodded, staring into her eyes. "Completely. It's all I ever do is read. I haven't had much work to do for a very long time."

I went on. "The knowledge he holds of history and facts and lost arts in that photographic mind would be invaluable to my team and some of the major problems we face. But he needs to have a position somewhere that will allow him to regain strength. Stan and I are hoping you might have that spot available, and let him have the time to work with my team as well."

Baalat smiled at me and I darned near melted. "Poker Boy, you are as amazing as everyone says."

Then thankfully, before my knees gave out under the high-wattage smile, she turned to Ben.

"Would you like to work for me as one of the Gods of Reading and Books?"

I thought Ben was going to turn into a ghost child right in front of us, his smile was so big. "I would so much enjoy that?"

"So we need to get you transferred, but I don't think your old boss will much care, do you?"

"He's been pushing me for fifty years to find something," Ben said.

"Good," Baalat said.

Then she turned to me. "As soon as I get Ben squared away and trained in some of his new duties, I'll have him contact you."

"Thank you," I said. "But please not too long. If something big comes up, we're going to need him."

Baalat smiled. "When you need him, he will be there."

She nodded to Stan and then she and Ben vanished.

"Looks like we have a new team member," I said, smiling at Stan.

He just shook his head and patted me on the shoulder, smiling. "Now I understand why you also save stray dogs."

And with that he was gone.

I headed back over to the table, sat back down and released myself back into the flow of time.

The sounds of the casino smashed in around me.

And the wonderful Saturday night went on.

Then, to one side of the table, I caught something out of the corner of my eye.

It was ghost Ben standing there, smiling at me.

And then I saw his lips move as he clearly said, "Thank you."

And then he vanished.

And the very next hand the dealer dealt me pocket aces, so I knew Lady Luck was smiling as well.

A PITY ABOUT THE DELUSION

A Bryant Street story

USA Today *bestselling writer Dean Wesley Smith returns to his acclaimed world of the novel* Dust and Kisses *with a side adventure.*

Mandi Meyers wants to find her parents' bodies. So she takes a trip to their home outside of Portland, Oregon, only to find impossible, yet familiar things.

Sometimes we all must learn that nothing with parents ever changes.

One

MANDI MEYERS TURNED the big, white Ford Explorer SUV onto Bryant Street and drove slowly past all the suburban homes that were damn hard to tell apart. Luckily, most of them had big numbers attached to the wall beside the standard two-car garage door.

She was looking for 1622, which would be on her right side.

All the lawns had once been beautiful, but now were patches of weeds, brown and dead now that it was summer and hot. All the cars left on the street were parked in the driveways or along the curbs. There clearly hadn't been that many people in this neighborhood home when the world ended. She figured that most everyone here had jobs in downtown Portland and had died there, their cars more than likely parked in a transit-station parking lot.

The few that had died here on Bryant Street in that mid-morning were either self-employed or the parent that stayed home with the kids. But school in this town had already started in late August when the world ended, so she doubted there would be many kids' bodies here either, even though this neighborhood was clearly one for young families.

She was used to mummified bodies in cars and along sidewalks, still in the same positions where they had fallen three years before. It felt strange to not see any bodies at all.

And if not for the weeds and brown lawns from the summer heat, she wouldn't have been able to tell anything at all was wrong with this subdivision.

When the world ended, she had been working for the United States Air Force after finishing college. She had been twenty-three that day three years ago and had survived because she was working about thirty feet underground when the electromagnetic pulse hit the Earth and killed everyone who wasn't inside protection.

No one knew the pulse was coming from space. One minute the world had billions of people, the next there were only millions left, most scattered across the planet wondering what had happened.

Many of the survivors killed themselves shortly after the first wave of deaths or went insane, unable to come to grips with everyone they loved being dead. But Mandi had been single and young. When the wave hit, her parents, her only family, had just moved to a small town in the Portland, Oregon metropolitan area.

She actually hadn't seen them for a number of years, so she really didn't miss them that much.

She had stayed with the other survivors in her unit and slowly, over time, a form of national organization started to come back together.

It seemed a lot of people in the military had survived, and a lot of people in subways and in tunnels and so on. And everyone wanted to rebuild before too much was lost.

Now, there was a national plan to restart five cities in the country and Portland had been picked as one of those cities because of its nearness to clean water, its long growing season, and mild winters. She had volunteered to come here and live and work.

Mostly she had picked Portland because she knew she would find the time to finally deal with her parents.

She had arrived last week in the first wave and had been too busy setting up everything for the thousands more that would follow to try to get here, to her parents' home, before now.

So finally, after three years of wondering, it was time for her to face the loss of her family. She had always known they would be dead, but seeing them was another matter. She needed to do that, then at some point get help coming here to bury them.

Her best friend, Donna, had offered to come along to her parents' new home on this first trip, but Mandi had declined, saying she needed to do this herself. She didn't even know if they had been home that morning of the electromagnetic wave.

If not, her parents were somewhere in the city and were going to be tough to find among all the bodies. But since the new government was working to give every body a decent burial and record what information was with the body, she might find them eventually.

Donna had been really, really worried about her coming alone. She said what little Mandi had said about her parents had not been complimentary. But Mandi had insisted she would be fine.

It had taken her almost an hour from downtown Portland to work her way out here into the suburb city called Lake Oswego. Part of the way the big freeway had been cleared by her people.

And part of the way she had been forced to use the police bumper attached to the big SUV front to gently nudge a car or two out of the way.

But now this suburban street was clear.

The winding street turned to her right and then wound back to the left.

She was getting close. Then, as she came around a gentle bend in the street she could see her parents' home.

The lawn was green.

Flowers were growing in the flowerbed along the sidewalk.

That wasn't possible.

Two

MANDI STOPPED THE CAR and closed her eyes, then opened them again.

The lawn was still green among rows of brown lawns and the flowers were clearly being watered.

From military satellites, she knew that only two people had been living in downtown Portland itself, and there were scattered survivors living out in the suburbs, but she hadn't really paid any attention to see if any of those survivors lived close to her parents' address.

Let alone their very address.

She shook her head to try to clear it, but the green grass and flowers remained.

She pulled the big SUV over near the front of the house and sat there, shaking.

Then she took a couple of deep breaths.

She had to think and be clear or this could turn out very ugly.

She had no idea who was in that house or how sane they might be. She leaned over and took out the loaded service pistol she had put in the glove box of the big car.

Donna had insisted on that just in case.

With the pistol in one hand, she slowly climbed out of the big SUV and into the heat of the later afternoon sun. She tucked the pistol in the back of her jeans and ran her hands through her short, brown hair.

She had kept it short for the last three years since it was just easier to keep clean and take care of.

The green lawn was still there in front of her parents' house, as impossible as it was.

She moved slowly up the walk towards the front door, some of her basic training coming back in.

She moved slowly, one hand on the gun, as she scanned the neighborhood, looking for anyone watching her.

Nothing moving at all in the heat.

Except for this one house, the neighborhood was dead.

She reached the front porch and rang the bell, feeling so numb she couldn't believe any of this was possible.

Was she having a hallucination?

Had she gotten sick on the way out here, or was she having some sort of reaction to actually finally seeing her parents dead?

She had no idea who was going to answer that door or what kind of reception she was going to get. For all she knew, one of her parents had survived and had gone completely crazy in three years and wouldn't even recognize her.

After a moment the door handle turned and the door swung open.

Her father stood there, trim and fit and looking younger than she remembered him.

And he was as naked as the day he was born, with a drink in one hand.

She forced herself to look only into his eyes.

Music drifted from the inside of the house and Mandi could smell the wonderful odor of baking cookies.

"Hey, Mandi," her father said, smiling at her. "Glad you could make it. Come on in."

She started to open her mouth, but she knew she could say nothing.

That was not the response she had expected at all.

"Don't let all the cold air out," he said, standing back from the door. "It's hot enough in here as it is."

He laughed at that for some reason.

It was a saying he always had said when she was growing up with them in Southern California.

She nodded to him and stepped through the door.

He shut the door behind her.

The cool, air-conditioned air felt wonderful after the heat outside.

And all the lights were on.

Somehow her father must have set up a generator to run the lights and the air-conditioning.

The home looked standard, right out of the 1990s, just as their home had been when she was growing up. Couches were nice brown cloth and the carpeting tan. A large-screen television sat in a large entertainment center on one wall, and two recliners faced that area.

There was a large dining area off the living room with an oak table with ten matching wooden chairs. A wide, carpeted hallway disappeared off to the right. It must go off to bathrooms and bedrooms.

This was a nice, spacious suburban home, nicely furnished and kept clean.

Then from the kitchen area off the dining room, Mandi's mother shouted, "Who is it, dear?"

"Come see," her father said, smiling at her. "Mandi has decided to join the party."

Mandi recognized that phrase, but darned if she could place it.

Her mother came out of the kitchen, also totally nude and thinner than Mandi remembered.

Her mom smiled at her. "Glad you could make it, dear. Jim, get her a drink before the other guests get out of the pool."

Mandi again just opened her mouth, then closed it.

What the hell could she even say?

It had been three years since the world had ended. Yet her parents seemed to think everything was normal and there were other guests in the pool.

And why were they standing around naked.

And why weren't they excited to see her?

It felt more like she had just stepped back in time, into her own past. There was so much of that past she had pushed away and forgotten. This felt like part of it.

But that wasn't possible.

She could feel the room spinning some, so she moved over to a chair at the kitchen table and dropped into it.

Her mother smiled at her and went back into the kitchen while her father went to the bar in one corner of the family room and started working on a drink for her.

Neither of them made any movement to cover up their nakedness in front of her.

At that moment, the sliding back door to the kitchen area opened and four other naked people walked in, all of them in their late twenties, all of them laughing and dripping wet.

Somewhere, in her distant memory, she recognized them.

All of them.

"This can't be happening," she said to herself, shaking her head.

She closed her eyes, but the laughing and the voices continued.

"Not feeling well, dear?" her father asked. "It's okay if you just go back to your room."

"Sure is," her mom said, coming in and putting a plate of chocolate chip cookies on the kitchen table.

The four other nude people gathered around, each grabbing a cookie.

"You better get a couple of those before they're gone," her father said, winking at her.

Then all of the naked people went into the living room and sat down, laughing and talking while Mandi sat at the kitchen table, stunned.

She put her head down on the hard wood, jammed her eyes closed as she used to do when she was a young girl and didn't want to see or know something her parents were doing, and just let the voices and the scene of six naked people sitting around fade away.

Three

THE NEXT THING MANDI KNEW, a hand was gently touching her shoulder.

"Mandi? Mandi?" the voice whispered. "Are you all right?"

She pushed back from the table, stunned, almost tipping her chair over in the process.

The house was dark and hot and smelled like a tomb. She had dust on her hands and, she was sure, on her face where she had put her head on the dusty tabletop.

Donna stood there with Henry Stevens, one of the main contractors working on getting the airport back up and running. Both of them had flashlights tied to their heads and another in one hand.

"I got worried when you didn't come back," Donna said, "so Henry and I came to see if you were all right."

"How long have I been gone?" Mandi asked, trying to brush herself off.

"Seven hours," Donna said.

Mandi nodded and stood.

Donna handed her a flashlight and Mandi went out into the living room.

Six bodies were there, on the couch and chairs, none of them wearing clothes.

They had basically become mummies in the heat of the house.

Donna recognized her father in a big recliner and her mother sitting next to another man on the couch.

"My mother, my father," Mandi said, shining a light on the two grinning skeletons as a way of introducing them to Donna and Henry.

Mandi just shook her head, staring at the scene. It had been just after eight in the morning on a weekday when the electromagnetic wave hit and killed most everyone. And yet her parents, even here in Portland, even at the age of forty, were still up to their old games.

"Do you know these other four?" Henry asked.

"More than likely neighbors," Mandi said. "Over for a morning of sex and mate-swapping, more than likely, considering none of them are dressed."

Donna glanced at her, a very worried look in her eyes.

"Don't worry," Mandi said, smiling at her friend. "I dealt with my parents' behavior a long time ago, when I was very young. I had forgotten it until now."

"Wow," Henry said, shaking his head. "Way beyond my comfort level."

Both Donna and Mandi nodded.

It had always been beyond Mandi's comfort level. She had grown up with naked adults coming and going at all hours and the sounds of sex coming from strange places in the house. It was no wonder she wasn't interested in sex or getting married.

She was really going to need some help getting past that childhood, if she ever could.

Maybe seeing them like this would help.

Maybe.

With one last look at her parents, she said, "Let's get out of here. Let them have their party. For them, it was the perfect way to leave the planet."

She went toward the front door and waited until Henry and Donna were outside ahead of her. Then with one last look at the six naked mummified bodies in the suburban house, she said what she had always said to her parents when they told her they were "getting together with friends."

"Have fun."

As she pulled the door closed, she thought she caught the sound of laughter and ice in a glass making a clicking sound as someone drank for courage.

Or maybe that was just her memory.

LONG SHADOW

USA Today *bestselling writer Dean Wesley Smith once again returns to the world of his acclaimed novel* Dust and Kisses *with a story set a few years ahead of the novel.*

Buster and Ben, two time travelers from a hundred years in the future harvest what they call "Shadows," people destined to be killed when most of the population of the planet gets wiped out. The future needs those people to help society rebuild.

But an alien human might have other ideas.

One

"YOU KNOW there's no such phrase as "Long Shadow Best Eaten?""

The time was ticking at five and people were already starting to pour out of the tall buildings around us on Forty-First Street. New York was always tough around quitting time because of all the office workers. The sidewalks got packed, everyone had something to carry, and the entire city seemed to be in a hurry to be somewhere else.

I leaned against the stone side of the Grant Building, letting the firmness of it hold me up and keep me out of the way of the passing crowd. The key with living in this city was to just step off to one side of the flow. No one saw you when you did that. New Yorkers were trained to not look at any person who wasn't moving.

Not moving made me feel invisible, and I liked to feel invisible. Invisible was good in my line of work.

My best friend, Ben Longknife Jump, leaned against the building beside me, also standing still. His long black hair was pulled back tight and a floppy cloth hat with decorations on it covered his head. Most of the decorations were parts of old jewelry and buttons he had found in the gutters.

Both of us had on Army jackets with about six billion pockets and old jeans. The evening was a little too warm for the big Army jackets, but neither of us ever took our coats off. The coats were sort of our walking homes. Especially when we were out on a job like we were now.

I had on a tan baseball cap without any baseball team logo on it. Both of us wore tennis shoes, dirty and scuffed-up so that they didn't look out of place.

We both wore our standard issue sunglasses that were not so standard, but they served us fine.

"Sorry, Bub old buddy," Jump said, not even much moving his lips as he talked. "The saying has magic to it."

Jump called me Bub most of the time since my real name, Buster, just made him laugh. I had always gotten that reaction while growing up as well, so Bub suited me just fine.

None of the regular folk streaming past us noticed us in our lack of movement. Not one woman in a business suit or a man in a tie and jacket even glanced our way.

We were nothing more than decoration along the sidewalk to pay no attention to.

Invisible.

Invisible was a ton better than being laughed at or punched aside.

"What kind of magic does it have?"

"The good-eaten kind," he said.

I had to admit I was hungry and had no doubt Jump was as well. We'd been out on the street for too long this time. But I couldn't make the connection between a shadow and food. All I knew was that pretty soon we were going to need to get something to eat.

Pretty darned soon, actually. My stomach was starting to make sounds I could hear over the traffic.

Before I could ask him to explain a little more, he said, "Target. Ten o'clock."

Without moving or turning my head I looked in that direction.

The display on the inside of my glasses gave me all of the target's vitals. Judith Benz, thirty-one, single and in no relationship. She lived alone in a small rent-controlled apartment up near Columbia. She stood five-two, with short red hair and golden-brown eyes.

I had been attracted to her in her picture, but now, seeing her, I was instantly in love. I thought I was hot in my big jacket before, now I was sweating.

She was amazing.

Completely amazing.

In all my life I had never been attracted to a woman like that so instantly.

She actually was trying to hide her incredible looks. Today she had on a black business suit that seemed a size too large. She wore white tennis shoes, with her working shoes sticking partially out of her black purse over her shoulder.

She walked with an intense stride that told me that she was in charge and didn't like to be messed with.

The information about her kept scrolling past my left eye as I watched her walk in our direction. She was brilliant, far, far too smart for her senior editing job at some publisher. She had two degrees in higher mathematics and had moved to New York to follow some friends on an impulse and just stayed.

Her genetics were pure and she was free of disease.

Targets didn't come any better.

Or any better looking.

No one was going to miss her, and we really, really needed her.

And I really, really wanted to get to know her better. I hoped to if she ever forgave me for what was about to happen.

We were actually saving her, since she would die anyway in just over two-and-a-half years.

Jump moved over about a half a pace in a way that no one noticed. Now there was a Judith-sized hole between us.

I clicked the link between Jump and me as she got closer and the air between us sort of shimmered. That was the gate to the holding cell in our ship in orbit. From there we would jump her back home and if I were lucky, I'd get a chance to show her around her new home and explain what happened.

Jump and I both stood completely still as she got close to us. With targets we just set out a shield that slid the target into the field between us without so much as them missing a step.

They didn't feel anything at all and still thought they were moving forward. They never knew what hit them until they were on the other side.

We never moved and no one around ever noticed that a person had just vanished into a hard wall.

But Judith surprised us both.

One step short of the screen as it extended out in front of her, she just stopped and looked at both of us.

"How stupid do you two think I am? I have a few questions for both of you idiots."

She touched a watch on her wrist and I could suddenly feel myself being transported.

And I had no way of knowing where.

But even with that, I didn't like being called an idiot by a woman I was lusting after.

Two

"OKAY," SHE SAID, sitting and facing us across the table. "Where are you two from?"

We were in what looked like the control room of a huge ship. Out the window or view screen that was an entire wall of the room, I could see the Earth floating below us. From the looks of it, this ship was in high orbit.

There was no one else in the control room and Jump and I were both sitting in chairs in front of what looked like a conference table to one side of the control room. There were three plates and silverware on the table, but no food.

Judith sat across from us, still dressed in her black business suit like a normal New Yorker, which she clearly wasn't. She looked a little angry and her golden-flecked brown eyes were pretty intense.

And I still found her amazingly attractive.

I was still half-angry with her for calling me an idiot. But that anger was vanishing quickly considering where I found myself.

The entire place smelled of roast beef and some sort of potatoes and I realized once again how hungry I was. My stomach actually rumbled loud enough to hear.

I glanced at Jump and he just shrugged, saying basically at this point we had no other options but to tell her the truth.

I turned and looked her in the eyes and almost couldn't get a word out. For a second I felt like a teenager facing my first date.

"We're from one hundred years in the future," I finally said. "We're trying to take some likely people to help us jumpstart the energy back into our rebuilding. And in the process we're trying to save their lives, basically."

She frowned, clearly surprised at my answer. "Assuming I believe you can travel in time, what exactly are you saving them from?"

It suddenly dawned on me she wasn't a time traveler. We were actually in an alien spaceship. And more than likely miss red-haired Judith that I was lusting over was an alien as well.

Jump looked at me, just as surprised. He clearly had come to the exact same conclusion.

"Answer for answer," I said, leaning forward toward her. Alien or not, I still wanted to get to know her a ton better. "Where are you from?"

"Originally, two galaxies over from here, but I've been working with the Seeders now for longer than you want to think about. This spiral arm of this galaxy is my sector to watch over all the planets and to help each civilization along in its growth."

"You human?" Jump asked.

"As much as you two," she said.

I liked the sound of that. And if I hadn't been sitting in a monstrous control room on a big space ship in orbit over Earth a hundred years in my own past, I would have thought her a lunatic. But she had said all that with a completely straight face, like she was reporting it.

"So, my turn," she said, "what are you saving these people from by kidnapping them into your future? Again, not saying you can travel in time, but that ship of yours in orbit below us is certainly for some sort of travel and I sure wouldn't trust it out of orbit."

"You can see our ship through our shields?" Jump asked, sitting forward as well. He had been the one to design those shields and he was very, very proud of them.

"Not really shields by my standards," she said, smiling at him. "But you didn't answer my question."

"In two years and six months and eight days," I said, "a seemingly harmless electromagnetic cloud will sweep over Earth for exactly five seconds."

Her pale skin seemed to be turning even paler. So I went on.

"The wave will short-circuit the human brain and only those inside something metal or a distance underground will be spared."

"About two million out of the billions down there live through it," Jump said, his voice low and clear. "And by the time the survivors start to reorganize three years later, there are only about that many left."

I went on, continuing the story of my planet. "The number drops even farther in the following fifty years before finally stabilizing. We need help from more humans to really start growing again as a culture. We are technologically advanced in some areas and far, far behind in others."

"And most of the planet of our time is a wasteland," Jump said. "So we are back here in our own history pulling out the shadows of the dead to come forward in time and help us."

"That's what we call the people walking down there," I said. "Shadows."

Jump nodded. "Because to us, in the future, they are all ghosts and shadows is a better term."

Miss Red-Hair and Golden-Eyes sat there, staring at both of us.

I felt like her eyes were boring into my soul and I honestly didn't mind. She could stare at me like that for as long as she wanted.

After a moment of silence, she said, "Shit, you two are telling the truth."

I was stunned that aliens swore in American slang.

She stood. "Dinner is on the way. I'll be right back."

Then talking into the air she said, "Benson, we have a major problem. I'm coming to you."

And then she just flat vanished.

Again the silence filled the big command area like a thick weight on everything.

I just sat there smiling at where she had been. "She's really something, isn't she?"

"Oh, no," Jump said, shaking his head at me.

"I'm still fairly young and have emotions," I said. "So sue me."

He just kept shaking his head.

A moment later some of the best smelling pot roast and potatoes and brown gravy appeared on the table in front of us. There was also corn, slices of wheat bread, and glasses of water.

I glanced at Jump who was smiling at the food.

"Long shadow, good eaten," he said as he reached for the bowl of potatoes. "I told you."

"I'm fairly certain this isn't what you meant," I said as I went after the pot roast.

"Magic is magic," he said.

Three

WE FINISHED EATING and then both of us went over and stood in front of the image of Earth floating below. It sure looked like some big window, but I had no idea how that could be possible, so I figured it was an image on a screen.

Judith appeared beside us, staring down at the planet below.

"You are correct, we can see the electromagnetic pulse wave. The planet's speed and the speed of the pulse will bring them together at exactly the moment you stated."

"Can you stop it?" Jump asked.

"No," she said. "And we can't protect the planet. This event has been known for some time. I was just not informed. I can tell you that in a more advanced sector of this galaxy we are now frantically mounting a rescue mission to build enough ships to take as many people off planet as possible."

"Rescue mission?" I asked, turning to face her.

She nodded. "We have no way to stop the first wave or rescue enough people from that first wave, but we will rescue about two million people from being killed in a second pulse wave following the first. You are proof of that."

"Because we are still standing here," Jump said.

I realized at once what he meant. If the aliens had been able to stop the first wave or block Earth from it, we would no longer be standing here, since we would have had no reason to come back in time.

And we were still standing here because we instigated the rescue of the survivors.

"Exactly," she said to Jump, nodding, clearly very sad. "I wish we could do more."

I looked over at her with another thought that sent chills through me. "When we get back to our normal time a hundred years in the future, you are going to disable our time-travel capabilities, aren't you?"

"We will," she said, nodding. "It's far, far too dangerous for a young culture like yours to have."

"So our mission concludes?" Jump asked.

"No," she said.

I was surprised at that. Very surprised, actually.

"I will monitor you and your other operatives to make sure you take no one that survives the first wave," she said. "You have done fine so far from what we can tell from your ship's records."

Now I was flat stunned.

She smiled, but the smile was sad.

"We rescued almost two million from being killed by the second wave," she said. "If you and your teams pick up the pace, you could rescue thousands and thousands more into the safety of your future."

"Would you help us?" Jump asked.

She sadly shook her head, staring at the Earth below.

"And we won't remember any of this, will we?" I asked, knowing full well the answer.

"I'm afraid not soon," she said. "But maybe, in a hundred years or so, we'll meet again and I can refresh your memory."

"I'd like that," I said, smiling at her, not wanting to think about how old she would be or how she could live that long. I just didn't care.

She looked at me and smiled as well. "So would I."

I damn near melted right there.

"Long shadow," Jump said, nodding.

Four

I STOOD WITH MY BACK against the stone wall of the Grant Building, not moving, letting the crowds of New Yorkers flow past.

Only it seemed the sidewalk wasn't as busy as it had been a moment before.

"Looks like our target isn't showing," I said to Jump. "Let's move to our next target."

I was really, really disappointed. I really hoped we could somehow get Judith. Everything about her attracted me, and I had spent an hour last night just staring at her picture.

"How did we lose the last hour?" Jump asked as we pushed away from the building and headed toward Broadway.

I glanced at the time in the upper corner of my glasses. It had been just before five, now it was almost six.

That wasn't possible.

"Did we both just fall asleep?"

"If we did, we ate while we were sleeping," he said.

I suddenly realized that I was no longer hungry as well.

"Okay, maybe both of us need a day off, some rest back on the ship," I said. "When we forget we ate, we need rest. I can't even remember what we had for dinner."

"Pot roast," he said. "And it was really good, but damned if I can remember where."

I took one more look at the image of Judith on my screen, then with a sigh flicked her off and brought up the next target. A white kid around twenty living alone four blocks from here. He had an IQ that couldn't be measured.

Maybe tomorrow we could try to rescue Judith again. I would hate to see her turn into just a shadow, a fleeting memory in my life.

She felt special for some reason.

MATCHBOX AGENDA

Ben Trager sucks as a person, a father, a husband. And he knows it. Everyone around him knows it as well.

Lost, he stumbles into a Denny's Restaurant and gets a special box of matches. Very, very special matches.

Matches, that if used correctly, will save his life.

USA Today bestselling writer Dean Wesley Smith opens the door to a simple Denny's Restaurant and gives us all a tiny peek into Rod Serlings' Twilight Zone world just one more time.

THE SOUNDS of the crowded Denny's Restaurant faded around him as Ben Trager stared at the little red box with the black stripes on both sides. The cardboard box held his entire life.

One match his luck, another his loves, another his actions. Everything his future held, all bundled up in the dark in nice neat rows. Each match facing the same direction, each match having the same potential, each match promising the same opportunities.

This morning he had felt like one of the matches: Wooden, explosive, and ready to burn up at any moment. But unlike his real life before now, the matchbox was full, giving his life a newness, a freshness he could have only dreamed of a few minutes before.

This morning, when leaving his four-bedroom home in Stevens Heights, his life had basically been over. His future was clouded and meaningless. He had nowhere to go, no place to be, nothing he wanted to do.

He and his wife had argued again, he had hit her again. His two teen-aged children hated him for good reason, he hated his job, and he hated himself for hitting his wife and messing up his life so completely.

He had driven around, lost, directionless, until he saw a Denny's Restaurant. He had pulled in and got out of his van, standing there staring at the newspapers in their dispensers trying to decide if he should go in and eat or not. It didn't seem to matter either way.

How could he, a man with a good college degree and wonderful potential fifteen years before, end up like this? Where had he gone wrong, what had he missed, how could he have been so stupid?

Then, as he stood there, staring at nothing but a blank future, a man coming out of the restaurant asked if Ben needed some matches.

Ben had only shrugged. He wasn't even thinking clear enough to tell the man he didn't smoke.

The guy tossed him the box of matches hitting Ben in the chest. "Decided to give up smoking while having breakfast," the guy said, shaking his head. "No smoking, no matches."

With that the man walked off leaving Ben standing there holding the box of unused matches from a man who had made a decent choice about life.

It wasn't until Ben sat down inside that he understood that his future had been given to him. He had been tossed the secret to putting his life in order.

He turned the box over and over in his hands, not even daring to set it down on the Formica-topped table. The sounds of the wooden matches inside were reminders of all the possibilities ahead. He could either start something fresh and growing, or sputter out useless and spent. It would be up to him.

The damn box held his life.

What was he going to do with it?

"You going to play with those things all mornin'?" the waitress asked, putting a large glass of water in front of him. "Or you want some breakfast?"

Ben placed the matchbox carefully down on the table and glanced up at her. She was early forties, about his age, with a wonderful, welcoming smile. She had on a blue uniform, a blue hat that sat slightly tipped on her blonde hair, and rings on every finger but the important one. The empty skin of that finger glared at him as she held her order pad and waited for him to move.

He smiled back at her and managed to not glance down at her chest any farther than her name badge. "Jenny," he said. "Nice name."

Her smile got even larger. "Thanks."

Today, with a new life in front of him laid out in the box, he knew that everything was possible again. Even good sex.

Of course, he had his future in the box, she had her life stretched out ahead in order tickets hung on a swirling ring that took her life into the kitchen and then sent it back, burnt and overcooked.

But who knew what might happen with a carefully chosen match.

"Bacon and eggs, eggs over easy, bacon crisp, wheat toast light."

"Drink?"

"Small orange juice," he said.

She raised an eyebrow as she wrote that, then gave him a large smile and turned away.

The orange juice had been the perfect touch. Had he given her the hint that her ringless finger needed? He doubted his marriage could be saved, not with his past actions, so it sure wouldn't hurt him to start thinking of other chances.

Wow, what a difference a box of matches and a future could make, and he hadn't even used up a match yet.

He took off his overcoat and adjusted his tie. If he was going to keep his job with the county auditors much longer he was going to have to shape up there as well. No doubt that would take a match or two.

Wait. Was that worth it? Or should he use a few of the matches to find a new job, one that he would like to do. Suddenly the possibilities were endless, and he loved that feeling. It felt young, healthy, vibrant.

He picked up the box and rattled it carefully, not wanting to damage any of his future chances. The morning felt brighter, some of the weight was lifting off his shoulders.

He took a deep breath and kept staring at the matches as the waitress placed his orange juice on the table, smiled at him again, and left.

Good contact, no wasted match.

He slowly opened the box and looked at the neat row of sticks there with their bulging ends. One match seemed to stand out more than any other, and he touched it with one finger, then picked it out of the box.

He slid the box closed and put it on the table, staring at the one match. Such a simple little thing to have such possibilities.

It could light a cigarette for a man who would die of cancer.

It could start a camp fire to keep a family warm on a camping trip.

It could light a gas stove to feed hungry children.

It could start a raging forest fire.

For him it could do so much more. This box held his plans for the future.

He held the match between his thumb and index finger of his left hand. The first thing he needed to do was settle the situation left over at home.

One match in one hand.

One problem to fix.

He pulled out his cell phone with his right hand and punched in the number for home.

The phone rang until the machine picked it up. He didn't blame Gloria for not answering, if she was even still there. More than likely she had already left, going who knew where.

When the message machine came on he said calmly, "I know you understand I am sorry for what happened this morning, but sorry is no longer enough. This afternoon I will find a counselor who will take me on an emergency basis, and I will check myself into a hotel until I can be sure I will never strike another woman again. If I have to check myself into a hospital, I will solve this problem. I know this will take time. I don't expect you to forgive me or even help me. I'll call you tonight to let you know where I am."

He clicked off the cell phone, surprised at the words that had come out of his mouth. He had always been adverse to counseling.

The last flame of the match burnt his finger slightly and went out.

He stared at it the burnt remains, shocked at those as well. He didn't remember lighting that match. Yet the burnt smell of sulfur mixed with the smell of coffee and bacon as a faint wisp of smoke vanished into the air.

"Hey, no smoking in here," the waitress said, sliding his plate of food in front of him, then almost dropping the smaller plate covered in toast.

"Not smoking," he said, smiling at her. "Sorry about that. Didn't mean to light it." He pushed the last of the burnt match away.

She smiled and winked. "No more accidents, honey," she said, putting her hand on his shoulder. She turned away, letting her hand linger a fraction of a second longer than it should.

He watched her walk, her ass moving in a very fine fashion under the tight uniform. There, in that blue uniform, was a future that might be fun exploring.

He stared at the matchbox. He had used a match, a possibility in his new future, and it felt good to be on the right road. No matter what happened at home, or with this waitress, or any other woman, he would never allow his temper to run loose again. He would find a way to control it. The match had made sure of that.

He dug into the eggs, hash browns, and crisp, perfectly cooked, bacon, staring at the box of matches in front of his plate while he ate. To have a future again felt so wonderful he wanted to just shout to the world.

About halfway through the eggs he opened the box so that he could stare at the pile of matches, and all the possibilities laid out there in neat rows.

His hopes.

His dreams.

A saved marriage, a better job, a new house, more money, respect for himself. All of those things were there, one match after another.

For the first time in years he felt less angry about everything.

He finished his eggs, crunched on the wonderful taste of the last piece of bacon, then washed it all down with the orange juice. Perfect breakfast for a day of major life changes.

"Done?" the waitress asked, appearing at his shoulder and reaching for his plate.

"Just beginning," he said, smiling up her. If she could only see all his dreams and hopes and roads to travel, she would screw his eyes out tonight.

She was smiling at him, not looking at the table, when he said "Just beginning."

She stopped suddenly, the plate halfway off the table, then went to put it back down, clearly thinking he meant that he wasn't done with breakfast.

But she wasn't looking at the plate, but instead into his eyes.

The edge of the plate hit the large glass of water and tipped it over, pouring the water into the open box of matches, washing away every-thing in a pool of ruin.

"Shit, shit, shit!" she said, tossing a dirty towel she had with her into the puddle of water. "Sorry, I'll get some more towels."

She turned to the counter as he just sat there, the water dripping coldly onto his suit pants and down into his crotch.

He didn't even shout, he didn't cry, he didn't even move.

He just sat there starting at his water-soaked, scattered future, ruined on the table.

The room grew dark as his anger flooded back.

Clumsy bitch had ruined everything.

The waitress grabbed a few towels behind the counter and headed back his way.

He wanted to hit her, break her damn neck.

He didn't dare let his anger come out at her. Not here, not now.

He stood, took out his wallet, and put twenty bucks into the puddle. Then he turned, leaving his future on the table, and walked out the door.

By the time he reached the sidewalk outside, he could barely move his feet. He felt as if he were walking in quicksand, the anger gone as quickly as it had come.

Nothing mattered anymore.

He had hit his wife.

His children hated him.

He was about to lose his job.

He hated himself.

There had been enough matches in that box to help him, but he had let those chances be wasted as well by flirting with a woman instead of paying attention to what mattered.

His entire life was a waste.

He climbed inside his van, put the keys in the ignition, but didn't start the car.

He couldn't think of any reason to start the car. He had nowhere to go.

So instead he just sat there, staring blankly ahead, a man with no future.

No hope.

No matches.

A STORM FROM THE RELIC

A Poker Boy story

USA Today *bestselling writer Dean Wesley Smith writes about many regular characters, the most popular being Poker Boy.*

In this adventure, Poker Boy starts off spending a quiet evening in his favorite casino, playing poker and wining a little money as he waits for his girlfriend, Patty Ledgerwood, to get off work.

Then a man walks in and sits at the table with a lucky charm that would turn out to not be so lucky for all of humanity. Can Poker Boy and his team act quickly enough to stop an ancient war from erupting once again?

GOOD POKER PLAYERS never really believe in luck. Good players know that luck levels out over time and that skill always wins in the long run.

But as Poker Boy, I knew luck very much existed, and I had met her many times over the years. I even saved her life once. Lady Luck, known as Laverne, was a very real and a very powerful god.

But most players, especially newer players, had never had the chance to meet Lady Luck, so they often used something lucky to try to get her attention in some way or another.

That was silly, of course. Laverne had far, far more pressing matters to deal with than rewarding some idiot for bad play because he had a polished rock on his bad cards.

But players of all types used talismans of one sort or another to put on their cards when in a hand.

There was a practical reason for it, of course. It was called "protecting your cards" in case a careless dealer tried to take them before the hand was over, or some careless person tossed their cards and hit yours. If your cards were protected with a chip or something on top of them, they were fine.

Over the years of sitting at poker tables, I had seen players use polished rocks, polished bones, chess pieces, Risk pieces, lucky tokens, and so much more.

It was almost two in the morning on a late Saturday night. Outside it was a beautiful fall evening in the Oregon Mountains. The sounds of bells ringing and excited people at the craps table drifted in from the main part of the casino along with the faint smell of smoke. It was legal to smoke on the casino floor, but not in the poker room, a rule which I was very thankful was in place.

I had only thirty minutes to keep playing in my favorite small poker room at Spirit Winds Casino before I had to teleport to Las Vegas to meet my girlfriend, Patty, aka Front Desk Girl. I had managed to get a couple thousand up for the evening. Considering how small the room was, and how few tourists were in the casino at this time of the year, I felt as if the night had been a success.

Then a man wearing a large winter coat and black stocking cap came toward the table carrying a rack of red chips worth five hundred dollars, the maximum buy-in to the table.

Normally seeing someone like that coming would get me excited and force me to stay a few more hands to see if I could nab some of those chips.

But suddenly every danger alarm I had went off at once, almost rocking me back in my chair. I had never gone from completely calm and with no alerts to completely on alert in such short notice before.

The guy put the rack of chips on the table and took off his coat. He wore regular jeans and a plaid shirt under the big winter coat. He seemed trim and in shape.

He nodded to one of the other men at the table, took off his stocking cap and stuffed it in his coat, then hung his coat on a nearby coat tree against one wall.

I couldn't figure out what about the guy was causing the danger signals. He just seemed like a regular guy, clearly from outside the area. I had never seen him in this casino before. And considering he was about to sit down in a no-limit game with five hundred dollars, the guy clearly wasn't that worried about money.

There was nothing at all about him that seemed dangerous in the slightest.

The guy turned from his coat, then seemed to remember something and dug something small out of one of the coat pockets.

And when that item came into the light, I almost had to put my hands over my ears to try to cut down the screaming alarms of all my warning superpowers going off at once.

Everything inside me just shouted "Run!"

That was not a feeling I was used to having.

I pushed back from the table. "Got to go pick up my girlfriend," I said to the dealer.

The dealer, a nice guy named Carl, motioned for James, the room's brush, to come over and rack up my chips.

I stood and stepped a few feet away from the table to try to catch my breath and think.

The guy set a golden-looking piece of metal on the table and sat down and started to stack his chips.

Whatever that thing was on the table, it was frighteningly dangerous.

The guy wasn't dangerous.

The talisman was.

How the heck was that even possible?

I froze time around myself, but it did nothing to calm my alarms. Basically what I did was just step between two moments in time, but it felt like I had frozen time since all the noise from the casino stopped and everyone looked frozen in mid-step. Besides teleportation, stepping between instants of time was my favorite superpower.

I wanted to get a better look at that talisman, but as I stepped toward it, every warning alarm I had as a superhero went off even louder than before.

And that was a lot of alarms.

I felt as if a thousand little voices were all shouting at me at once. All inside my head.

All of them shouting for me to turn and just run.

Nothing like that had ever happened before.

I staggered back like a drunk coming out of a bar at closing time. I almost bumped into James frozen on his way toward the table with empty racks to get my chips.

"Stan!" I shouted toward the ceiling, even though I didn't need to shout upward to get his boss, the God of Poker to come running.

Stan appeared beside me and before I could get a word out he staggered slightly and spun around, staring at the table.

"What is that thing?" I asked.

Stan shook his head and pulled me a dozen more steps back away from the table.

With each step away from the talisman, the warnings faded slightly. It was no wonder the guy could get so close to the table with that thing in his pocket before I felt it. Whatever it was, it had a limited range.

"So you don't honestly know what that thing is?" I asked Stan.

Stan just shook his head. "Never felt anything like that before. But it feels very, very old."

I realized Stan was right, it did feel old. And powerful. And evil, all rolled into one tiny little shiny piece of metal.

"Can you get Ben?" I asked. "He might know what it is."

Stan nodded and vanished.

I stepped even farther away from the frozen table. Ben was an old god who loved to read. He looked like an old man you would see shuffling down the street in baggy pants and an old ill-fitting jacket. His hair was gray and very thin. He had been the god of lamplighters for centuries until that profession faded and he faded with it. I had managed to get him in with the gods of books, since he loved to read and remembered everything he had ever read since the beginning of printing and even before.

He was a gentle man and very nice and very shy. He was the newest member of my team, but so far we hadn't had a mission that we needed him on yet.

And at some point I was going to get him to show me the Library of Alexandria.

Stan and Ben appeared beside me. Ben smiled at me and I could tell he was recovering quickly from his ghost state. He looked almost solid now and much healthier, although still very thin.

He started to say something to me and then froze.

He turned in the direction of the table, staring.

"Do you know what would cause that?" I asked. "It's coming from that gold talisman on the table."

"The Relic," Ben said, his voice so soft that if I didn't have time frozen and all the noise from the casino gone, I never would have heard him.

"Oh, shit," Stan said and vanished again, leaving me standing there with Ben.

"What is the Relic?" I asked.

Ben indicated we should move even farther away from the table and I was glad to do so. We moved back so that we were almost out of the poker room and onto the casino main floor.

My danger alarms were still going off strong, but more distance from that thing eased them even more. Clearly Ben and Stan had the same kind of thing.

"The Relic was a spaceship," Ben said. "The legends have it that the ship crashed here in the early days of humans on this planet. It was filled with the vilest of evil aliens. The Titans, the Giants, and the early days of the Gods all banded together to fight the creatures of extreme power who came off that ship."

I looked at him and all I could say was, "Oh."

Ben said nothing more and I went back to staring at the table, wondering just where Stan had gone to.

Finally, my mind cleared enough so that I had another couple of questions for Ben. "How did that guy get a piece of the ship? And why is it still dangerous?"

"In the final great battle, the evil aliens were pushed back into their ship," Ben said. "With that kind of pressure, the ship exploded, scattering the ship and the aliens into millions of pieces. Every piece of the ship contained an essence of an alien. The evil creatures still inhabit the remaining pieces."

"And that's why it feels dangerous?" I asked.

"No, it doesn't just feel dangerous, it is dangerous," Ben said, his voice firm and clear. "The man who has it clearly has no magical powers, but he is being controlled by the entity in the metal. If a magical person touches that piece, the evil will escape from it and inhabit that person."

"That's happened in the past?"

Ben nodded. "Hitler."

"I thought he was a troll," I said, completely shocked.

"He was," Ben said. "Inhabited by the evil from that ancient battle."

Now I finally understood something. "That's why Hitler was always searching for more magic and religious items?"

Ben nodded. "He was looking for more of his kind to bring them back. He found a few of them before he was stopped and they were all killed."

I just stood there staring at the frozen poker table. It was common for a player to show other players their "lucky" talisman, especially if it had a cool look to it. So a poker table was a perfect place for the alien in that piece of metal to find someone even slightly magical.

"I wonder how he found it," I said out loud.

"That's the most important thing we need to learn," Ben said. "We must get that man away from that piece of the Relic to find out."

Stan and Lady Luck appeared.

She was wearing her standard business suit and had her hair pulled back tight. She turned to the table. "Oh, my," was all she said.

I had never seen Lady Luck look worried before, but right now she was clearly upset and very worried.

I looked at the table and at James frozen in place as he headed toward where I had been with empty racks for my chips.

"I assume none of you dare go in there," I said to the three gods standing beside me.

Laverne and Stan and Ben all nodded.

I had a hunch that was going to be the case. The more power, the more that evil would push them away. I was barely able to just be near the table.

I turned to Stan. "I need Patty and Screamer."

Stan nodded and vanished.

"So we need to get that man away from that piece of the Relic, right?" I asked Ben. "To find out where he found it and if there are more pieces."

Ben nodded. "Critical."

"Will the evil be able to go through him to get to anyone here?" I asked.

This time both Laverne and Ben said no.

"And if we get him away from the Relic piece," I asked, "what can we do with it then?"

"Without the man close to it," Laverne said, "we can send it into the sun as we have done with all the other pieces. But we first must disconnect anyone attached to the piece, otherwise the evil flows back instead of being destroyed."

"And you can do that?" I asked.

Laverne nodded. "Given enough distance between the two, I can break the bond the piece has over the man."

"And it won't transfer to anyone else?"

"Not unless another person touches it," Ben said, and Laverne nodded.

A moment later Stan appeared with Patty and Screamer.

Patty had on her uniform from the front desk of the MGM Grand Hotel and her long brown hair pulled up and back. She looked as beautiful as ever.

Beside her Screamer looked as Screamer always did in his jeans, long-sleeved shirt and short brown hair. Both of them were looking worried. I was sure Stan had told them nothing.

"Oh, oh," Patty said as she appeared, turning toward the table.

She could clearly feel it as well.

"What the hell is that?" Screamer asked, also turning toward the table across the poker room.

"Part of the Relic," I said.

Screamer looked puzzled, but Patty softly just shook her head. "I had hoped to go my entire life and never have to deal with another piece of that evil."

"All right," I said to my team. "It's going to take all three of us if we're going to go drag that guy away from that table and out here. Without breaking the time bubble."

Patty nodded and Screamer looked like he had about a thousand questions, but kept them to himself.

"Stan, Laverne, can you hold the bubble?"

"Got it," Stan said, nodding.

"The evil in that piece will not want you doing what you are going to attempt to do," Laverne said. "It will fight you."

"How?" I asked.

Laverne shook her head. "I do not know."

"You will need a magic-based shield," Ben said.

Now all of us turned to look at him. Both Stan and Laverne were looking as puzzled as I felt.

Ben nodded. "A magic-based shield is an old and almost lost art, but Poker Boy, I think you could do it, with help from Patty."

Ben turned to the table. "Feel the evil coming from that piece like waves of energy?"

I nodded. Once I had my warning powers cut down, I actually could sense the energy waves coming from the piece.

"Hold Patty's hand now," Ben said, "and focus about a foot in front of you both all the good energy you can muster. Hold it there like a wall. Imagine it a wall. Patty, focus as much good and calming energy as you can into Poker Boy."

I could feel Patty's energy coming into me and I did as Ben had told me to do, building an imaginary wall with good energy in front of me, between all of us and that table.

Suddenly I could barely sense the evil. And I could almost see the shield shimmering in front of me.

"Stan," Laverne said, "you and I funnel him more energy."

Suddenly I could no longer feel the evil at all as energy poured through me from Stan and Laverne and Patty.

"Screamer, behind me," I said. "Let's go get that guy out of there."

I kept hold of Patty's hand and kept the image of the shimmering screen between me and that piece of metal sitting on the table.

The closer we got, the more I focused on the shield.

I could feel the evil in that piece pushing back, fighting to keep us away.

It felt like I was pushing a wide board against a river current, working it upstream.

We came in behind the guy frozen at the table. I did not let go of Patty's hand, but with my free hand I took one side of the guy's chair and tipped it back while Screamer took the other side.

The energy coming from Laverne and Stan and Ben now increased as the energy from the evil fought us.

I felt like I was caught between two intense currents and that imaginary shield in front of me was all that was keeping us in place.

The evil in that piece of energy was very, very powerful.

We pulled, moving the guy back from the table, dragging the chair along the carpeted floor.

I wasn't sure how much longer I could hold up that imaginary shield, but I somehow did as we got the guy back away from the table and Ben and Stan came ducking in to help as we beat a full retreat, the frozen guy not even having a clue that he was being pulled away from the table in an instant of time.

We pulled the guy clear out onto the casino main floor.

I could almost not feel the energy from the evil, so I dropped the screen, panting.

"Ben," I said, looking at our newest team member, "will it be safe for us to go into the guy's mind and find where he found the piece?"

"At this distance it should be if we don't release the time bubble. But it wouldn't hurt to have the screen back up as well."

"Got the time bubble solid," Stan said, indicating the time bubble that kept us out of the normal flow of time.

I took a deep breath and could feel the energy coming back into me from Patty's grasp as I again imagined the screen between us and that piece of metal on the table.

Then Screamer touched me and I could feel all of us linked inside Screamer's head. It was such a familiar thing now, it didn't even bother me.

Keep that screen up, Screamer thought at me.

Then he touched the poor guy we had hauled away from the table.

I was right. He wasn't from around here. He was from a mountain town in Northern California, just south of the Oregon border. And he wasn't a poker player either. And he didn't have the five hundred to lose. He had been forced to sit at that table to find someone with magic. Clearly the evil entity in the piece had felt me sitting there and thought I would be an easy mark.

Screamer dug down into the guy's mind as I held the screen between all of us and the evil Relic piece.

I could see where the evil had taken over, the darkness in the guy, the unexplained actions, everything. Normally, he was a good man, but he had been controlled to go in search of magic.

Then the image became clear and I damn near let go of everything I was so shocked.

Patty thought clearly, *Oh, oh. Hold on.*

The guy had found the piece in an old mine in Northern California, just south of the Oregon border. He had dug down and ran into a cavern. And there in that underground cavern were many, many more pieces of the Relic. A vast number as far as I could see from the guy's mind.

Thousands at least.

If just one piece had caused Hitler, I could only imagine what all those pieces could do if let lose with magic in the world.

Screamer got the exact location of the cavern, then backed us out of the guy's head, then let go of me so the contact between the three of us was broken.

"Bad?" Laverne asked, looking worried.

"Really bad," I said, holding up the screen. "An entire cavern of pieces of the Relic."

"But he's the only one who knows about it," Patty said.

"I have the exact location," Screamer said.

"Stan, Ben, stay here," Laverne said. "Poker Boy, hold that screen up for as long as you can."

I nodded and Patty gripped my hand even tighter as Laverne, Screamer, and the poor miner from Northern California vanished, chair and all.

We all stood there like that for at least a minute. I was doing my best to hold that wall of good energy up between all of us and that piece of metal on the table.

Then suddenly there was a white light, very bright, that formed on the surface of the poker table and then vanished.

I could feel now that the screen I was holding up was no longer getting attacked from the other side.

A moment later Laverne appeared again with the guy in the chair.

"We broke the connection and that piece has been tossed into the sun, she said."

I sighed and dropped the shield I had just learned how to do, feeling the relief of the lack of energy drain.

And I realized I was suddenly very, very hungry.

"I got him," Stan said.

He touched the back of the chair and teleported the guy to his position at the table.

"What is happening with the cavern?" Patty asked a moment before I could.

"We're going to teleport them all into the sun," Laverne said. "After I broke the connection with the Relic, Screamer and I got the information from the man's head as well. They will all be gone within the next few minutes."

"That place was flat scary."

"We came very close to another major war with the Relic," Lady Luck said, nodding. "Great job once again, to all of you."

And then she turned to Ben. "It sure seems Poker Boy was correct. You are greatly needed on his team."

Ben smiled and I could see him gain energy. "It feels good to be needed."

He turned to me and said simply, "Thank you."

Then he vanished.

Lady Luck smiled at me once again. "Yes, thank you."

And she vanished.

I turned to Patty. "See you in about twenty minutes when you get off work?"

"Dinner is on me," Stan said. "Steaks. We'll meet in the lobby at the MGM in thirty minutes."

Then my boss looked at me.

"You got it?"

"I got it," I said and took back over the time bubble as he and Patty and Screamer vanished.

I moved back over to the table and tried to remember where I was standing when I took myself out of the time stream.

Then I let the time bubble go.

The sounds of the casino crashed in on me again. Amazing how loud a casino can be and how I only really notice it when the sounds are gone.

The guy who had the Relic suddenly looked around, clearly very puzzled.

I turned to James as he approached. "Rack that guy's chips back up first. He doesn't belong at this table."

James looked puzzled, but went around and did as I suggested as the guy stood, clearly very, very puzzled and with only a fuzzy memory of how he had gotten seated in a poker game four hundred miles from his home.

"Better call your wife," I said to him, smiling and sending him a calming influence. "She's going to be worried."

James handed him his chips.

"Help him cash those out," I said to James. "I'll rack my own."

Then I handed James a twenty-five dollar chip and he nodded, leading the guy from the table.

"What just happened?" Carl the dealer asked, glancing back at the guy walking away as I started racking up my winnings for the night.

"Besides stopping an alien invasion and saving the world from being taken over by great evil, not much."

Carl laughed, shaking his head as I took my chips. I tossed Carl a twenty-five dollar chip as a tip and went to the coat tree and got the guy's coat and took it across the room to him.

Sometimes telling the truth seemed funny.

Even when it wasn't.

I KILLED ADAM CHASER

USA Today *bestselling writer Dean Wesley Smith writes not only science fiction, but many thrillers and mystery stories.*

In "I Killed Adam Chaser" he introduces us for the first time to a very special secret agent. An agent who kills. An agent who prides himself in taking out the garbage of humanity.

The agent likes his job until the day comes along that he meets one of the wives of the garbage he needs to send to the curb. And everything changes, but only in a way Dean Wesley Smith can imagine.

THERE ARE A LOT of people like me, and not enough people like me.

I kill people. It's what I do. It's my job, although I do not need the money and seldom accept it.

Unless I make a mistake, which I never do, no one knows that I have killed a person. Or that anyone has been killed, for that matter.

I am a hired contractor for Clean Sweep, a simple company with a simple slogan: We Take Out the Garbage.

Human garbage.

So let me tell you the story about one sack of human garbage named Adam Chaser. It's a heartwarming story of a simple garbage man (me) doing my simple job, and meeting the love of my life in the process.

At least she could have been.

One

THE SNOW FELL in lazy flakes, blowing on a light Portland wind on the day I met Adam and Lori Chaser. The temperature was hovering at freezing, but it didn't feel cold out. The snow wasn't sticking. Twenty days before Christmas and the people of Portland were celebrating the snow in the air as a sign the season was really upon them. They could do that because Portland seldom got snow that actually became a problem.

The meeting was casual, in the elevator on our way up to our respective condos. We nodded, I refrained from looking at Lori.

I had been given my assignment to dispose of Adam five days before while living in a rented condo in Phoenix. I always rented under an assumed name while on a job and never stayed long in any one place.

That name was now gone.

I have no permanent home and my real name and history have long since vanished from any database. I always became the person I needed to be in the city I live in for the job at hand.

In Portland, I became Dan Garton.

I wore my now dark-brown hair short and stylish to match a look of extreme money. I usually wore expensive sweatshirts and expensive jeans, with five hundred dollar loafers around the building, but I also had a closet of silk suits and everything needed to pull that look off as well. Nothing about me said "fake money." I made sure of that.

The condo I rented was located in an upscale fourteen-story building in a Portland district called The Pearl District. The building had high ceilings, a doorman, and stone and wood and art everywhere. It was first class all the way and comfortable in brown and gold tones that only can be found in the Northwest part of the United States.

The neighborhood had lots of coffee shops, high-end decorator stores, and bookstores. It was a district where most everyone walked or took the electric streetcars that crisscrossed the area. I had hired a limo service to take me anywhere I needed to go at any time of the day or night. A limo and driver remained on duty within one minute of my building's front door.

I seldom used them.

Adam and Lori had a condo in the same building three stories below mine. Adam worked in his family business of investing, and he forced Lori to remain at home at his beck and call.

I had many cameras in every area of their condo so that I could watch their every move.

He forced her to do all the cleaning and demanded that the huge three-bedroom condo be spotless at all times. He forced her to cook a major meal for him every evening, but seldom came home to eat it. Instead he spent many evenings with high-end hookers in a bondage club.

As far as in business, Adam had been the force and money behind two major projects that had caused two hundred families to suddenly become homeless in three major cities. His company had also bought up and closed down five family businesses in the last five months, forcing almost six hundred people to lose their jobs.

He loved causing that kind of pain while making more money than he needed.

I could track his business dealings easily by hacking his company's computer network. They seemed to think no one would be interested in them, thus had taken few precautions. I read every e-mail he sent from work and listened in on every meeting through someone's computer in the room.

I was a master at all things electronic and digital.

I stood exactly six-foot tall and worked out every day. Adam was one inch shorter and weighed one hundred pounds more than I did. In the ten years since he had graduated college, he had become a fat slob who thought himself untouchable and enjoyed inflicting pain on others, including his wife.

Somehow, even with all the abuse from her husband, Lori had maintained her looks and weight since she had married him. She managed to exercise two hours a day. She said on her driver's license that she was five seven, but I would say it was closer to five-five. She had a tiny and perfectly-proportioned body and long black hair that when released reached her butt.

She also spent almost two hours per day on her computer, but I could not follow most of what she did on that computer and could not seem to find the connection into it. It seemed she was not online at all. More than likely Adam didn't let her, so she only played games.

But that was what made me understand her and finally figure out who she really was. What gave her away was my inability to get to her computer.

The exercise and the computer and private time in the bathroom were her only time for herself every day.

She seemed to have some Asian descent in her, while Adam seemed pure white slob.

I had also set up surveillance cameras in the hallways, near the front entrance, in the parking garage, along with every room in their condo. The cameras I used were so tiny that they looked more like the point of a pen than a camera.

Imagine a camera and battery the shape of a small finishing nail with no head. I just had to drill a tiny hole into a wall and insert the camera, usually at a height that no one could touch. And in most cases, the tiny shell of the camera matched the paint color.

And if touched by anyone but me, they generated so much heat from their tiny batteries that they melted and fused into the wall.

They transmitted only to my computer, which only I could access.

For the entire month of December and then most of January, I followed Adam and Lori's routines, their habits, everything about both of them. During that time Adam beat Lori five times, never hitting her in the face.

Clearly she was a strong woman, and she took the beatings almost coldly, which often did nothing more than make Adam even madder. He lived to see the pain on his victims.

After almost two months, it became clear that Adam had no sense that anyone might want him dead, and he took no precautions at all. He was as stupid as he was brutal.

He would be an easy target, which bothered me a great deal. Lori could have cleared him from her life easily with her skills. So before I moved to clear his odor from the human race, I needed to know more about Adam's will and who would take over his company and what Lori would end up with after her husband's sudden demise.

So I dug.

I am an expert on all things electronic and am constantly updating both my knowledge and my equipment.

A garbage man like me has an ability to dig and we don't mind the smell of rot that we often find. And with Adam, I found a great deal of rot.

And I discovered, as I suspected, that Lori would end up with nothing from the company or even the condo if he died.

Not one dime.

It was clear she wanted none of it.

I went in search of why she stayed with him through all the abuse. I discovered that her cover story was that both her parents were dead, but she had a brother who had broken his back in a car accident and his only care was what Adam provided the money for.

Otherwise, she had no assets. Nothing.

Of course, she had assets and it took me some careful digging to find them. She was extremely rich.

And the kid with the broken back wasn't her brother. Her family was as long gone as mine.

She supposedly had stayed with Adam, the monster, because of her brother's care. Not an uncommon story. I had seen similar stories many times in my years working as a disposal artist, so it played.

Over the month of February, without leaving a trace in any record, I fixed all that. By March first, Lori would inherit everything. At least the Lori of her cover story.

That inheritance would anchor her something awful. She would not like that one bit.

And I set up a trust fund that would fund on Adam's death for Lori's pretend brother. It all looked as if Adam had done it over a year's time. And all from his own work computer.

Lori would be so angry when she discovered that. But I knew she never would because she had no idea I knew who she really was.

Or why she was putting up with the false life with Adam.

She was good and I had come to like and admire the small, strong woman.

Emotions were often a bad thing for a garbage collector such as myself. I knew that.

I accepted that risk.

But I had to admit, I was enjoying this just a little.

And I really enjoyed watching her in the shower. Especially since she knew I was watching.

Two

MARCH TENTH, Adam Chaser took a long sip of a cup of mocha his assistant had brought for him. His young female assistant lived in the same fear of Adam as Lori pretended she did.

Exactly fourteen minutes after drinking the coffee, Adam Chaser grabbed his chest while in the middle of a meeting. He fell forward onto a big conference table shouting "Heart! "Heart!"

What I had laced in his coffee was untraceable and forced the heart to shut down just as any normal heart attack.

I returned to my apartment before he collapsed so I could watch the show.

They rushed him to an emergency room at a nearby hospital and called Lori to tell her that her husband was there and more than likely wouldn't make it. She smiled as she slowly gathered up her things and headed for the elevator.

I made sure from my computer that the elevator came up to my floor so I could ride down with her.

"Nice day?" I said.

She smiled at me. "It is now. Thanks."

I assumed she meant to thank me about my comment about the weather since I doubted she would blow her cover just yet. And I was only slightly surprised at her calmness. Usually abused wives are upset when the abuser is taken from them and she needed to be playing that part.

I was wrong.

I held the door for her at the lobby and as she walked past she said, "Would you like to take a drive with me? I have to go play the grieving widow. Or you could call your limo service if you would rather do that."

I stood there holding the door to the elevator open, acting slightly surprised. She was showing herself to me before her job was finished.

That could be a fatal mistake.

She stopped two steps out of the elevator and smiled back at me. "Mr. Dan Garton, or whatever your real name is, you aren't the only smart person on the planet. And you are not the only one who works for Clean Sweep."

In all my life I had never exposed my cover to a target. I knew I was her target. I had known it almost from the beginning. I was the garbage that Clean Sweep needed removed. I knew that day would come some day. More than likely this was her play.

After a moment she laughed. "Close your mouth and call your limo. We have some planning to do."

With that she turned and started across the lobby at a fast walk, nodding to the doorman.

I pretended to pull it together and got the limo out front in less than one minute.

I didn't like this play on her part.

After we got into the back of the limo, she flicked a switch to block all listening devices. I had one on me, but clearly she wasn't trusting me at this moment and I wasn't trusting myself, to be honest, because this play on her part made no sense.

"I want to thank you for setting me up with Adam's business," she said, smiling a smile at me that I had not seen before. "I discovered it yesterday, although like you, I assure you I don't need the money. And the paralyzed kid who's going to get the trust fund really isn't my brother. It just gave me a good cover story."

I said nothing, as she would expect.

"After I get through the grieving widow part and the funeral," she said, "I'll explain everything if you feel like staying around. I hope you do, since Clean Sweep and I went through a lot of trouble to set this up."

We were almost at the hospital.

"Check with them if you don't believe me. They want us to work together on a very special case coming up."

I nodded.

Now I got her cover story. And her actions made sense.

The limo dumped her out at the front of the hospital and then took me back to my condo.

I had known for months that each room had at least three of the tiny black dots that were Clean Sweep cameras.

Adam Chaser died at three-ten of massive heart failure, his grieving widow was at his side.

At four I sent the coded message that the garbage was taken out.

A coded message came back telling me to stay in place.

As I expected.

I wanted to contact them directly, but I stayed with what I had been trained.

I stayed in place and waited and watched Lori.

And she watched me.

And for almost a month we both pretended that we were not being watched.

At times, that was very, very difficult. I did not want to hurt her.

I knew for a fact she was looking for a weakness to kill me. Clean Sweep operatives never retired.

We got retired and taken out to the garbage.

Three

APRIL 12TH she made her first and only move.

I knew she had been watching me in the shower as much as I had watched her in her shower. I tried to vary my morning routine, but I always knew she was there watching me.

And I tried to keep her entertained.

And she did the same for me as well.

This morning, as I started to step into the shower, I could smell the simple poison. It was a slow-acting type that absorbed painlessly through the skin and killed in twelve hours. She had more than likely planted the poison in my showerhead when I had left for lunch yesterday.

I had known she had accessed the apartment. I had put my own cameras in my apartment that she did not know about. I did not have one in the bathroom, however.

I tapped a button under a towel rack.

My special cell phone rang.

She would be able to hear that.

I left the shower running and went to answer the phone I had triggered, wrapping myself in a towel as I went.

I had put a scrambled message to be played to me over my phone in standard Clean Sweep instruction format so she could quickly take the code apart.

The code said I had new garbage to take out in Boston.

I went in and shut off the shower, even though I knew the poison was now long flushed through, I didn't feel safe in there. I dressed quickly in my standard travel clothes.

I quickly packed a suitcase, my computer, and then turned and smiled at one of her cameras.

I slowly mouthed the words "It's been fun."

I went out into the hallway, pressed the elevator button, then stood there waiting.

I knew for a moment she would watch me.

When the elevator dinged only a moment later and opened empty, I knew I had her. Her best bet would have been to get on the elevator first.

I stepped onto the elevator, put my suitcase and briefcase with my computer in the elevator, turned and punched the button for the lobby as if I was about to ride the elevator down. Then as the doors started to close, I triggered a camera loop override showing the door closing to her camera.

I ducked out and into the stairwell.

I silently beat the elevator down the three floors.

She was standing there, gun drawn. She was in her blue nightgown, the one that anyone could see through, facing the elevator as the door opened.

She had her legs spread, gun with sound suppressor aimed at the elevator.

She put four shots into the elevator as the door opened before I put three in her. Two center mass, one in the head.

I doubted anyone heard anything, since both of our suppressors were top rate.

She went down into a pile, showing me clearly that she had no underwear on.

I took my briefcase and suitcase off the elevator.

Then I rolled her onto the elevator and tossed my gun with her. It would never be traceable and I had left no prints on it in any fashion.

I had disabled the cameras on this floor near the elevator and in the stairwell, running them into a loop.

I let the door close and the elevator head for the lobby. Lori was going to expose some of her most private parts to those in the lobby when she reached there. She really should have put on some panties this morning.

I went back up to my apartment and opened my computer back up. Then I sent a virus to her computer that would wipe it clean of everything but standard games.

I also sent a self-destruct to all my cameras, melting them into the walls. And her cameras in my apartment as well. Even if someone dug one out, they would never know what it was.

Then I carefully left tracks on her bank accounts that would let anyone decent with a computer track that she had killed her husband for his money and some of her husband's associates wanted the money back.

I left some videos on her computer of her showing her body to some lover who was not seen behind the camera.

I left threatening e-mails from these made-up associates and love notes from her lover. All dated and untraceable to me.

I unpacked my suitcase and hung up my clothes.

Then I spent one full hour checking every detail of my condo for any traps left by the now very dead Mrs. Adam Chaser.

As with everyone in the building, I was questioned by the police, but I watched their investigation through their computers. They had no leads.

I planted a couple of false ones to help them out a little.

A week later, I gave notice on my condo and paid my last bills and had the limo service drop me at the airport.

Dan Garton stepped into a men's rest room and vanished. The camera in that area of the airport just happened to be having a glitch.

Now I still take out the human garbage.

But now I work for myself.

As I said, there are a lot of people like me. And yet, not enough.

Not by a long ways.

Maybe I'll work on that.

OUT OF COFFEE EXPERIENCE

USA Today *bestselling writer Dean Wesley Smith enjoys playing against the limitations set up by time travel.*

In "Out of Coffee Experience," an artist works in a moment of time to set up a perfect piece of art.

Just hope you are not in his next work of art. But, of course, how would any of us ever know if someone from the future thought of us as nothing more than props?

AS A TIME TRAVELER, I quickly came to hate the smell of burnt coffee far more than I used to as a child. And trust me, I really hated it back then. My parents drank the stuff constantly, day and night, and Mom could never remember to turn off the burner under the coffee pot. I lost count of how many times I would come home from school with the house filled with the burnt smell of coffee.

Not once have I ever been able to even taste coffee because of that.

Now, as an adult with a thousand trips back in time to capture different aspects of life in the year 2004, the very idea of drinking coffee turned my stomach. There's an old expression about great art coming from great emotion. When I realized just how repulsed I was by coffee, I knew it would make great art, if I could just capture my repulsion.

My name is Arrington, and in case you haven't heard of me, which I suppose most have not yet but will at some point, I am a time-artist, one of the new and struggling breed of people who capture moments in the past in artistic fashions. Today I planned to travel to the year 2004 and capture the true nature of coffee in metaphor, using a group of people frozen in time in a diner.

After I entered the small, crowded diner called Henry's Place, the first thing I did was move through the people frozen in their places and around behind the counter. Walking through groups of people stuck in the moment used to make me feel creepy, like being in a forest of mannequins. Now it was part of my art.

I took the three coffee pots off their burners, and waited until the machine making another pot of coffee stopped and then removed it from the burner. Since I was going to be in this diner for at least a few hours my time, the last thing I needed was the smell of burnt coffee in the picture too soon.

I poured the coffee out into a sink and rinsed the sink just to get rid of the smell. Because of the law of conservation of time, matter, and space, the people stopped in time around me would never miss it. The coffee would be back, smelling like coffee, tasting like coffee, the very next instant in time.

But for this instant, for this moment, for this piece of art, I wanted that awful coffee smell out of here.

I stepped away from the sink and took a deep breath, taking in the texture of the air in the diner. Getting rid of the coffee had left the place smelling of bacon, and toast. Perfect.

I next went around into the kitchen and scraped everything the two chefs had cooking off the grill, then turned off every burner. Lastly, I made sure no toast could burn.

It wasn't that doing this was because time traveling had made me sensitive to smells. I just had learned that to keep an environment perfect for my art, I needed to take care to make sure no food burnt. I didn't need that problem today, at least until I was ready for it. This project was going to take long enough as it was.

I stopped in the kitchen door and studied the place, a classic diner for the year 2004, decorated in a throw-back fashion to the 1950s.

Everything was a bright red or polished black or shiny white. The contrasts would make for a great piece.

There were over thirty people in the diner, most sitting in booths, others at the counter, plus two waitresses and two cooks, all posed in what they were doing or saying at this instant in time.

It was a perfect frozen picture of a diner just outside of Seattle, Washington in the year 2004.

Sometimes I was amazed at how time travel had given mankind the ability to understand that old saying of "living in the moment." The frozen people around me were in a moment, passing through, I was in another moment sixty years in the future, passing through it. Time travel had allowed me to live in my moment while visiting other moments.

Who would have thought that right along with the law of conservation of energy, there was a law that governed the conservation of time. So when you traveled back in time, you landed in one instant, and stayed inside that same instant until you went back to your own time frame.

This rule of the conservation of time stopped all paradoxes and made time travel completely safe. Nothing anyone could do in a moment could hurt the time line. If you went back to an instant in time and killed your father, due to the law of conservation of time and energy and matter, he would still be alive in the next instant.

Of course I had heard of really insane people going back thousands and thousands of times to kill a parent, just because their anger was so great. And counselors a few years back in my time line had started using the kill-the-parent technique to help get people past their problems from childhood.

Matter and energy reset every instant of time. So far no one had figured out a way to measure just how small an instant of time was.

I moved over to the spot by the front door that I had figured would be my viewpoint location, the place where the viewers of my art back in my own time would stand and view my work. Everything I did today would focus on this one spot. With any time-art, the most important thing was the viewpoint.

As I stood there, I noticed a few details about how things had moved since I had come in. Mechanical things only. I was sure that the first few time travelers who had had to smell burning coffee were the ones who had come up with the theory of "The Observer Effect on an Instant in Time."

Basically, that effect was that the coffee would not burn on hot burners inside every instant of time in every restaurant unless there was an energy field from a future time moving it forward inside the instant of time.

Humans were energy fields, thus when I entered the restaurant, all inanimate objects continued to move, as if the objects were functioning in my time period. The food on the grill continued to cook, the coffee continued to pour, electricity and lights continued to burn, and so on, as long as I was within observational range.

A waitress had been pouring a cup of coffee for a woman in the second booth from the back. When I became an observer in this instant, the coffee continued to pour out of the pot, overflowing the cup and running down the woman's arm, even though neither the waitress nor the woman moved. I would have to clean that up.

Of course, the woman would never know that during one fraction of a fraction of a fraction of a billionth of a second, the coffee had poured over her arm, then in the next fraction of a fraction of a fraction of a billionth of a second, it hadn't.

Interestingly enough, the observer rule had no effect at all on the thirty plus people around me. Or anything else living. They just stood there in their own instant of time like warm statues.

Besides allowing me to become a time-artist, the good side of all this time travel was control of population. With the advent of cheap and easy time travel, billions of people over the last twenty years had simply moved to different instants of time in the past, setting up a thousand different societies, living off the supplies that existed in that one instant, hurting nothing because time reset everything the next instant.

Just last year a report stated that there were more people alive at that moment who lived in the past than did in their own time frame.

My art was for those who lived in my present. "Henry's Place," named after the diner, would be my best work yet because of my passion for the subject of coffee. It might even get me famous, make my name, allow me to move to a better apartment, sell some of my older work, get me a better agent. Hate often brought out the best in an artist and I hoped my hate of coffee would do so for me this time. I was so broke that anything would help at this point.

I studied the diner for another minute from my viewpoint position, then started with the people sitting at the long counter.

Six men, two women. The two women were together at the far end near the entrance to the rest rooms. The men were scattered along the counter and clearly didn't seem to be together. Both women had their mouths open as if talking at the same point. One looked to be in her mid-thirties, the other might have been her mother.

One thing that always surprised me was how warm human skin frozen in an instant felt. I usually tried not to touch anyone, but for this work, I was going to have to touch everyone in the diner.

I worked quickly, stripping the man closest to me, taking off his suit jacket, his shirt, his pants and shoes, leaving him only in his underwear and socks, the same way I planned on leaving everyone in the diner.

Then I took the man's right hand and used his thumb and index finger to pinch together his nose. In his other hand I put a coffee cup and put him into a position that looked like he was drinking.

I tipped his head back slightly and then pushed the skin around his eyes together a little to make him look like he was squinting, like he really hated the taste of the coffee he was trying to drink.

I stood back and studied him, making sure every detail was right.

It was.

I tossed his clothes in the kitchen out of the way of the image I was building, and went to the next man at the counter. The younger woman at the end of the counter caused me the most problems. She hadn't been wearing any underwear under her business suit, and she was going to be very clear in the final setting.

I didn't want nudity in my work, since so many people had already done that. I wanted everything about this work to be original and focused on the coffee. So I had to go to the woman in the back booth who had her back to where my viewpoint shot would be taken and take her underwear and put it on the woman at the counter. That was a lot more work than I had planned on doing for one person.

By the time I had finished undressing and posing everyone at the counter, I was sweating and needed a break.

And I needed some food. Another good thing about time travel was that the food was free for the taking.

I moved into the kitchen, poured myself a glass of orange juice, and took a couple of doughnuts from a tray in the back. Then I moved to my viewpoint position near the front door and stared at the work so far. It was as good as I had hoped it would be when I came up with the idea.

Excited at the progress I had made, I quickly downed the snack and went back to work, only taking off the clothing of the people in the booths that would be seen from my viewpoint position. And each person I posed in the same fashion, with the same type of coffee cup.

A room full of patrons in their underwear downing a cup of coffee they clearly hated. This was turning out better than I had hoped.

Finally, I moved to the two waitresses, the crowning touch on this image.

One waitress was short and attractive. She stood near a booth where she had been pouring the coffee, and I left her right there.

The other was near the cash register and I moved her a little so that she was in the foreground of the shot more, yet not blocking any other line-of-sight from the viewpoint to another person.

I undressed them both, glad that both had on the standard white underwear and bras of the time. Then instead of putting coffee cups in their hands, I posed both of them drinking right out of an empty coffee pot, only with their other hands on their hips.

They looked like super-coffee-drinkers.

Only in their underwear.

A dozen times I went back to my viewpoint to make sure everything was perfect, every detail in its right place, nothing but underwear and coffee cups and sour expressions showing.

The image I was about to record for all time would have two major parts to it. It would appear life-sized and three dimensional to the observer from the viewpoint, reproduced exactly at this real size in my gallery, an instant in this time caught in symbolism for all to see. The second aspect would be that it would have a sensory impact.

I planned on having the lights dimmed as the observer approached, then bring them up to the brightness of color and intensity of the diner, just like the observer had come in from the dark outside. Of course all of this would depend on selling it to a gallery who could do those sorts of things. But I had no doubt this would be my best, so I would sell it.

As the viewer approached, the smell would also grow stronger. At first it would be the smell of regular coffee, bacon and eggs, then as the observer reached the viewpoint, the smell would turn to one of burnt coffee.

After every detail was right and I had double- and triple-checked everything, I was ready for the final smell touch. That was the critical factor, and to make it right it had to be recorded at the exact moment of capture of sight. It was my attention to those kind of details that I knew would someday make me famous.

I moved around behind the counter and studied the old coffee machines. I had planned on having all four of the coffee makers pouring out coffee onto hot burners with no coffee pots. But I quickly discovered I had a few problems.

First off, I had no idea how to make coffee. I hated the stuff so much, I had no idea how it was made. I know my mother had put some sort of coffee bean in some part of the machine, but I had no idea how or where, especially in the bigger restaurant machines.

The second problem was that I couldn't find any fresh coffee. There was an empty sack beside one coffee maker, but it looked like that the restaurant had run out. I went back and searched the kitchen and the store room, but still couldn't find any.

I ended up standing there by the coffee machine and staring at the scene I had spent hours creating. The smell of burnt coffee, the image of the coffee pouring out of the coffee machines onto hot burners without pots, was the main impact of the image. Without it this work of art would say nothing. It would be just like all the other time-art pieces I had done, and everyone else did.

Yet there was no coffee, and even if there was, I had no idea how to make the big machines make the stuff into liquid form.

What a waste of a day of work.

I couldn't go home and figure out how coffee was made, because time travel would never bring me back to this exact instant again. It would be close, but I would have to do all the work I had already done in the undressing and posing. No exact instant could ever be returned to after going to the present. An instant in time in the past was just too small a unit to hit.

I dropped down onto one of the stools at the café counter and just sat there, staring at all the work I had done, and that was now wasted. I had had other pieces of art go bad before, but never this bad.

There didn't seem to even be much reason to take the image at all. The statement wouldn't be enough without the coffee pouring from the machines and the burnt smell. The piece would have no impact. I was better off just calling it a day, going home, and maybe trying it again at some point later.

But I knew that would never happen. Once I had lost interest and excitement in a project, it never came back. Ever.

I sighed and stood. How could some place like this be out of coffee?

Suddenly that question hit me, and I realized how I could make an even stronger statement about the stuff I hated so much.

I went back to work, my excitement even higher than before, changing each person's pose from one of disgust at the drink, to one of surprise alternating every third person with anger.

I turned the cup in each person's hand over, and moved the position of the cup up above each person's head, as if they were looking up into the empty container.

Then I opened about half of the people's mouths, as if they were trying to catch the last drop from each cup.

I posed two of the customers at the counter licking out their cups.

I posed each waitress with the empty coffee pot upside down, clearly empty, with a look of panic on each of their faces.

Then I stood back at my viewpoint position, checking every detail. It took me another fifteen minutes to get a few expressions right, a few arm angles in the right place.

The empty coffee machines would be perfect in the picture and I took the other two empty coffee pots and placed them on their sides beside the machines.

But there still felt as if something was missing.

Actually two things. I would need a title as well.

I stared and stared at the scene I had built until finally inspiration hit me like a glass of cold water. I knew exactly what was missing.

I took three people out of the booths and moved them into positions around the waitress in the back, empty coffee cups held over the heads like weapons. Each person I posed with an angry expression on their face and in a posture as if they were about to beat the waitress for not having coffee.

I put an expression of fear on her face, and on the other waitress's face.

Then I stood back and again studied the work. Now it was perfect.

But I still needed a title. Maybe a title would come after I took the image? It sometimes worked that way.

I took my hand-held recorder and got it into the exact right position, where the empty coffee machine was clear, where the attack on the waitress was clear, where all the people out of coffee were clear. This one didn't need smells after all. It would do just as it was.

I quickly captured the scene and then stood and stared at the image I had recorded. If this didn't sell, nothing would. I just had to have a title.

Then suddenly it came to me. Coffee, it seemed, was an addiction for the ages, and everyone would understood my work because I tapped in on that.

I quickly titled the work in my scene recorder.

"Seattle Addiction."

And no matter how famous this made me, I would never tell a soul that it had all come about because I couldn't make even a single cup of coffee.

THE CASE OF THE PLEASANT HILLS MURDER

A Cold Poker Gang Story

USA Today *bestselling writer Dean Wesley Smith mentioned the Cold Poker Gang in his acclaimed thriller* Dead Money.

Now he introduces us for the first time to Retired-Detective Lott and the rest of the retired Las Vegas detectives who play poker, solve cold cases, and call themselves the Cold Poker Gang.

They solve cases every week, but this case becomes very personal for Retired-Detective Lott. More so than any cold case he and the Gang ever tackled before. And as with most cold cases, solutions do not come easy. And answers tend not to be what anyone hoped.

One

January, 1992
Pleasant Hills
Las Vegas, Nevada

THE AFTERNOON FELT DARK and gloomy, the wind kicking a chill through Nesto Poretz's gloved hands and light jacket as he expertly dug at the soft soil along the ridgeline with his backhoe, taking large shovelfuls of dirt quickly to one side and dumping them on a pile, then returning the big shovel for another in almost a seamless movement.

The sound of the engine a constant rumbling to him, something he was used to after all the years. Something that he sometimes missed at night, when his apartment was quiet, the kids asleep.

He loved the simple noise of a working machine. There was nothing better.

The sky was cloudy and threatening, coloring everything in the normally brown desert a dull gunmetal gray. Nesto's job, before it got dark, was to get as much of the foundation dug out for this new house as he could. He wouldn't get it all done, but enough to keep his boss happy.

Danny, a tall thin white kid stood beside the hole Nesto was digging, leaning against his shovel. Danny had far too much attitude and thought himself too good to be working this kind of job. He considered himself a real catch for any woman and loved to brag about his conquests, most of which Nesto was sure were completely made up.

For some reason the boss had hired the idiot and had assigned him to Nesto three days ago. As far as Nesto was concerned, letting Danny stand and lean on his shovel was the best place for the kid. That way he didn't screw anything up.

Nesto dumped a shovelful and swung the shovel back over the hole when suddenly Danny shouted "Stop!"

Danny ignored the hand-signals Nesto had taught him and jumped down off the edge into the hole.

Nesto got the bucket stopped just in time, shaking his head and wondering if he would have just done the world a favor not getting the bucket stopped in time. But then he would have had to live with Danny's death and that kid just wasn't worth it.

Most of the time the kid wasn't worth the air he was breathing.

The hole was only about four feet deep where Danny had jumped down and then bent over, so Nesto couldn't see him.

Suddenly Danny scrambled up the bank and out of the hole faster than if some woman was chasing him for child support. He ran about ten steps, then bent over and threw up.

Nesto watched him for a moment from his seat on the rumbling backhoe, then put the machine in reverse and backed away from the edge and shut the engine down.

The silence swarmed over him like a blanket as he climbed down.

The cold wind tried to push him back from the foundation hole he had been digging, but he moved over and around to get a better look at what had caused Danny to lose his far-too-expensive lunch.

In his ten years working backhoe, Nesto had dug up a lot of things. Some not so pleasant.

From the looks of how Danny stood, his hands on his knees, shaking his head, this was going to be one of those times.

Nesto moved around and then finally, with a deep breath of the cold afternoon air, he looked down into the hole.

A man's head and left arm were there, sticking out of the dirt.

Most of the guy's skin was gone, his eyes blank sockets, but the guy's brown hair still clung in place.

And on the wrist was a fairly new watch.

Gold watch.

Nesto had just found his third body. The two before had been old settler's skeletons. This one was far from that.

He turned for his truck to call in to dispatch to get the police coming. There was no chance he was finishing this job tomorrow.

More than likely not even next week.

The boss was not going to be happy.

Two

May 2014
Pleasant Hills
Las Vegas, Nevada

AT SIX-THIRTY, I took two bowls of Lays chips down the half flight of stairs to my poker room. I had had the poker table custom built a year ago and sized it perfectly for the area to the left side of the staircase. It could seat eight, with eight matching brown leather chairs around the table. There was a place at each seat to hold chips and a drink and a comfortable light over the table.

I loved that table and felt at home sitting at it.

I already had the chips in place and an unopened deck of cards sitting on the wet bar beside the table. It was Tuesday night and I was flat excited for another fun night of poker with the gang.

I had decorated the rest of the room in framed posters of different

Las Vegas events from the past, including one classic showing Sinatra and Martin. A large couch and two recliners filled one end of the room facing a large screen television.

I had to admit, I had spent far, far too much time in this room since my wife, Connie, died two years ago. That's why last year I had decided to completely remodel it and make it the perfect place for me to spend time.

I had made the room all mine, and Annie, my daughter, thought that was a great idea. Upstairs, for me, Connie was still there. I didn't mind that. I thought about her every day and still can't believe I managed to keep going after she died, But somehow I had, thanks to a lot of help from Annie. Now this basement was my space.

Three of the gang said they would be here tonight for the game. Sometimes we had six or seven on a Tuesday night. Most of the time we ended up with only four.

We called ourselves the "Cold Poker Gang" since we were all retired detectives and every Tuesday we played poker while we sat around and talked about cold cases.

I loved poker and I loved being a detective, so Tuesday night didn't come fast enough for me every week.

During the week, each of us would take a case and run down leads and bring the results back to the gang. Just as when we were on the force, one would take the lead on each case.

I just couldn't believe how much I looked forward to the game every week, and especially this week since the case I had lead on for the last month I had finally solved. Together, the gang had solved ten cold cases in just under a year and since we were working for free, that record of closures sure made Benson, the Chief of Detectives, happy.

There was a loud knock at the door just as I sat the chips down on the bar. I glanced at the time.

Someone was very early.

I headed back up and got to the front door as the knock came again.

Retired Detective Andor Williams stood there, a file folder in his hand and a frown on his face. It was Williams' turn to get a new case from the city for tonight, for me to take lead on. The tradition was Williams would present the case to everyone during the game.

Williams looked the oldest of all of us, with almost no hair, wrinkled face, and sloppy clothes like an old man would wear. At seventy, he was still very spry and walked like he was always late for something.

Just like what had happened to me, Williams had lost his wife two years ago, and at times it seemed to me that the gang and solving cold cases was the only thing Williams went on living for. Both of Williams' kids lived in California and he seldom talked about them. He spent far more time than anyone working on his assigned case as well as helping others with their cases.

Williams said, "Lott, good seeing you." Then he handed the file to me, and pushed past. "Figured you needed to see this before we open it to the gang."

I stared at the file in my hand. It was an official homicide folder of the Las Vegas police, with the words "copy" stamped on both sides.

Normal.

I pushed the door closed and followed Williams to the staircase and back down into the poker room. Williams took his normal seat with his back to the staircase and I took the file and went to the wet bar and opened it, spreading it out on the marble top.

It took a moment for me to finally see what I needed to see and why Williams had brought the case to me early. A murder victim had been found in January 1992 and the case never solved.

"Holy shit!" I said.

"My opinion exactly," Williams said.

I was so stunned, I didn't know what else to say.

I just kept staring at the address where they had dug up the vic, not really believing it wasn't a joke or something. The body in this cold case had been found right here.

"That's why I brought it over early," Williams said. "They found the body when they were digging this very basement twenty-two years ago. Go figure, huh? And I can tell by the look on your face no one told you when you bought the house."

I had nothing I could say.

I had had no idea. And I was pretty darned certain Connie would have never agreed to buy the place if she had known.

This was now one of the strangest cold cases I had ever seen.

Three

May 2014
Henderson
Outside of Las Vegas, Nevada

I BANGED ON the weathered screen door on the small house, knocking some paint flecks loose. Beside me Williams stood, looking stern and official. Or at least as much as he could with his rumpled suit and unshaven face.

The weather was headed toward the warm side for the day, a promise of the hot summer to come. We were about two blocks off the old Boulder Highway, in a Henderson neighborhood that had seen a far better time in the past. The houses here were small and the yards tiny, built to house casino workers coming in during the first boom in the late 1960s.

The house we were at hadn't seen a coat of paint in a decade or more and the lawn had long since turned to weeds, only slightly green now because of the wet spring we had had.

I had no idea what we would find, but this was the address we got for the dead guy's daughter.

"Yeah," a woman's voice came from inside the house, then some rustling around and the door opened.

Both of us had our guns unstrapped and ready, just in case. If there was nothing else we had learned over the years, we didn't go knocking on a door without being ready for anything to come at us.

As the big, paint-peeling door swung open, the stench of uncleaned cat boxes and stale beer hit me, turning my stomach. It was a toxic mix and I hoped like hell she wasn't going to invite us inside.

Beside me, Williams short of shook his head at the odor, giving a slight cough.

Through the dirty screen on the door, I could see an extremely obese woman in what had been a blue bathrobe that had more stains than color. She had short hair that looked greasy and a tattoo on her neck that was as faded as her bathrobe.

"Detectives Bayard Lott and Andor Williams," I said. "We're looking for Karen Rafferty."

"You found her," the woman said. She sounded like she'd smoked far, far too many cigarettes in her lifetime as well as eating far, far too much.

The Chief didn't mind us introducing ourselves as detectives as long as he didn't hear about it. With our track record of closing cold cases, he was willing to let us drop the "retired" part at times.

Williams and I both flashed our old badges as well to the woman who just looked dazed, more than likely on something even this early in the morning.

"What do you want?" she asked. "That kid of mine get into trouble again?"

"No," I said, "we're here about your father, Nixon Rafferty."

She actually seemed to take a step back from the door and her face twisted up into something so ugly, I couldn't imagine being around her for more than a few seconds.

She pulled her poor, abused robe even tighter across her large bulk and said in a very cold voice. "I don't want to ever think of that bastard again. Not ever. He ruined my life and killed my mother and my baby sister."

With that she slammed the door in our faces, sending paint chips flying into the air around us.

I looked at Williams, who just shrugged.

"More than we expected," Williams said as we turned away.

I could only smile as we headed back toward my brand new Jeep Grand Cherokee, a Christmas gift from Annie.

That response had been a lot more than I had expected. We had solved a lot of cases on a lot less.

Now at least we had something to go on.

Four

June 2014
Pleasant Hills
Las Vegas, Nevada

I TOSSED my ten-jack off-suit into the muck as a response to Williams' three-dollar raise and sat back in my leather chair. Williams usually played tight and when he raised, it was either a stone cold bluff, or he had decent cards. Ten-jack wasn't a good enough hand to test the bluff theory.

The Tuesday night game of the Cold Poker Gang had four retired detectives around the table in my basement game room. The game we always played was pure Texas Hold'em. The stakes were one-dollar small blind and two-dollar big blind with a max bet of five bucks. The worst I had gotten hurt one week was two hundred and my best night winnings had been around one hundred and fifty.

All four of us tonight were good poker players, but not professional level like my daughter, Annie, and her boyfriend, Doc Hill. They both made more money from the game than I ever wanted to think about.

All the players tonight had no real worry about money, so the stakes were good, but not enough to hurt any of us.

To my right sat Ben "The Sarge" Carson. He was a year younger than I was at sixty-two and was in the best shape of all of us since he spent so much time in a gym every day. He told us it was a great place to meet women. I tended to believe him.

He had gray hair cut perfectly, a smile that he said had cost him a fortune, and more money than any one person should have. He was the only heir to a major fortune. Except for a new sports car, he still lived as he had when on the force.

He got his nickname from being a Sergeant in the Army before retiring and becoming a cop. Over the years that I had known Sarge, the guy had gone through three wives and yet managed to have no children. Now we all kidded him about looking for wife four, but he always said no, he had too much money to risk another wife.

Outside of the game or working on a case, I never saw Sarge without a younger woman on his arm. Always a different one as well, so Sarge's plan of avoiding another commitment seemed to be working.

The fourth member of the night was Conklin. I wasn't even sure of his first name since in thirty years I had never heard Conklin called by any other name.

Conklin was the only one of us here tonight with a wife. She supported his poker and cold case hobby because "It got him out of her hair." He had a badly broken nose that hadn't healed right and looked smashed on his face, and he never seemed to smile, although he had a dry and biting sense of humor.

He was also the only one of us with an advanced college degree. He had gotten a night-class MBA years back when he had considered quitting the force to start a business. Conklin always amazed me with his ability with numbers.

Conklin called Williams' raise and, since he was dealing the hand, burnt a card and put three up on the board, face up. My ten-jack would have been even weaker since the flop had come king, five, four, all off-suit.

Williams bet three dollars again and Conklin just shook his head and folded, passing the deck of cards to Sarge for the next deal.

"So, where does the Rafferty case stand?" Conklin asked, sitting back. Every night he was the one to sort of do an inventory of the cases we were working on.

"It's just laying there like a dead, stinking fish," I said, feeling disgusted.

Beside me Williams nodded.

"The daughter said that the vic had killed her mother and her sister," I said, "but the mother and younger sister both died a few years after Rafferty went missing, both from drug overdoses."

"We got no idea what she was talking about," Williams said.

I felt slightly angry that I had to agree with Williams. This case just seemed to be going nowhere.

We had looked through all of Rafferty's bills and debts and he seemed like a poor working slob that no one had paid any attention to.

"So no luck there," Conklin said. "But when I was coming in here tonight I noticed your view, Lott."

I glanced at my flat-nosed friend. "Yeah, one of the reasons Connie and I bought this place."

Conklin nodded. "Back when Rafferty was buried up here, why would someone bury a guy they had just shot on a hill with a view?"

I glanced over at Williams. "That's a question I never thought about. Why kill a guy and then give him a view like you care about him?"

"Family," Williams said, nodding. "Rafferty was a slight drinker, but had no gambling problems and no mob connections or any other crime record. So it goes back to family or a mistress."

"We need more on the wife and younger daughter," I said, nodding. Now I suddenly felt like I had a direction with the case again.

Sarge dealt, then as he put the deck down, he said simply. "Family. If it's not sex that gets a guy killed, it's family."

"Spoken like a guy with far too much experience in both," Williams said.

"You can never have too much experience in sex," Conklin said flatly, picking up his cards and studying them as we all laughed and agreed.

But I knew there was a lot of truth in what Sarge had said. And chances are if we were going to solve the murder of the guy who had been buried right were we were playing cards, I was going to have to dig deeper into the mother and younger daughter.

I tossed away my seven-ten off-suit and sat back, sipping on my Diet Coke and thinking about the next step in the case as the others all called the blind and waited for the flop.

It didn't get any better for me than Tuesday night.

Five

June 2014
Martin Luther King Blvd
Las Vegas, Nevada

I HAD DONE ALL the searching I could online of records about the wife and the younger daughter of Rafferty. But some of the older records hadn't been loaded up to the online services, so I found myself once again downtown in the Clark County Records building, the smell of dust and cleaning solution filling the air like a musty perfume.

It felt like old home week. I couldn't begin to remember how many hours over the years before computers I had spent in this building digging through records.

I had called Williams and got him to join me, since I knew Williams loved the musty paper files and didn't trust the information on the computers. He was as old-school as they came. And sometimes that had paid off for us.

It took us about twenty minutes, but we eventually found the death certificates for both the daughter and the wife of Rafferty. Both had died of prescription drug overdoses, way before that problem was even considered a problem.

"Take a look at this," Williams said, pointing to a name of the doctor who prescribed the drug for the daughter.

I glanced at the name and then the credentials. It was a psychiatrist.

I quickly glanced at the wife's file, then nodded and slipped it over to Williams.

"Same doctor," I said, pulling out my iPad, another gift from Annie, and doing a quick search to see if the Doctor Harriet Bert was still alive. It was always a problem with cold cases, especially really old ones like this. People had a way of dying or moving out of state and making it damn hard to track.

"Alive, but retired," I said, feeling relieved as I jotted down her address. It was a house address off the strip near the university.

"A visit?" Williams asked, smiling and standing.

"A visit," I said, glancing at my watch. It was almost noon. We might actually have a chance of catching her.

It turned out she wasn't home, but had started teaching part time at the University, so we tracked her to her office on campus in one of the older buildings.

The day was growing hot and both of us were sweating when we reached the red-brick building from the parking lot.

I felt very much out of place walking down the narrow hallway toward her office as students passed us, giving us both odd looks.

"Guess not many old farts take classes here," Williams said.

"No, they think we are professors," I said.

"Yeah, us professors," Williams said, and laughed.

"Why not?" I asked, laughing as well. "We could teach kids a thing or two."

"And both of the things would be wrong and outdated," Williams said as we reached Harriet Bert's office door.

Shaking my head and trying not to laugh, I knocked and a woman's voice said we should come in.

I went in first to be met with a room full of books, floor-to-ceiling, with a matronly woman sitting behind a big, wooden desk. The place was fairly large and smelled of flowers and tea. Or a very flowery tea.

We introduced ourselves and Harriet Bert switched glasses and offered us the only two chairs facing her desk.

"We are investigating the murder of a man by the name of Nixon Rafferty," I said.

Bert looked puzzled for a moment, then said, "Excuse me for a moment."

She switched her glasses again, leaving the other pair hanging from a chain around her neck and turned to her computer. After a moment she finally nodded.

"Sorry, just had to refresh a failing memory," she said, turning back to us and again changing her glasses. "I didn't know Nixon Rafferty was killed. All I knew was that he vanished suddenly leaving his family behind. I treated all three of his family for a time."

"That's why we are here," Williams said. "Rafferty's body was dug up in 1992. He had been shot. The case was never solved."

"So you are trying to solve the cold case now?" she asked, nodding. "I like that. What can I do to help?"

"As you mentioned," I said, "you treated the entire family after the disappearance. Could you tell us when your treatment stopped?"

She nodded, switched out the glasses again and went back to her computer. Then she looked over her glasses at them. "I treated all three for over a year, working to help them get past his disappearance, but all three quit at the same time in January of 1992."

I glanced at Williams. I knew that couldn't be a coincidence. That was when the body was found.

"We would never ask you to break client confidentiality, doctor," I said, knowing I had to be very careful and walk a fine line. "But both the younger daughter and the mother died later that year from drug overdoses. The younger daughter first, then the mother. The older daughter is still alive. But on the two that are dead, is there anything you would feel comfortable telling us about."

Doctor Bert frowned and went back to studying her records. Then without looking at us she said, "I remember when they died. They had used a prescription I had given them while I was still treating them. It was no longer valid since they were no longer in my care, but they somehow made copies and altered it and filled it at a dozen different places. Police ended up shutting a few of those places down after that."

I said nothing.

She studied the record for a short time on her computer screen, then switching glasses, she turned back to us. "I can tell you that Nixon Rafferty was a pedophile. He abused his youngest daughter and the mother had huge guilt feelings about letting him do that because she discovered it and let it go on. I was doing my best to help the two that died get past that. Clearly I failed."

I nodded and stood. I knew we would get nothing more from Doctor Bert. But now some pieces were starting to fall into place.

We thanked the doctor for her time and headed through the crowds of young students to get to my car.

"Think the family did it?" Williams asked as we climbed in and I got the car started and the air conditioning going.

I nodded. "One of them did it, and I have a hunch which one."

"Youngest?" Williams asked.

"Youngest," I said, nodding. "Now, let's just figure out how to prove it."

Six

June 2014
Pleasant Hills
Las Vegas, Nevada

I SAT WATCHING the rest of the Cold Poker Gang battle over a hand. All three of them were in and Williams ended up taking it when he hit a third king on the river.

That clearly disgusted both Sarge and Conklin.

"Okay," Conklin said turning to me, "after that stupidity, how does the Rafferty murder case go?"

"Solved and closed," I said. I bowed slightly as the other three applauded.

"Williams had a lot to do with this as well," I said.

"So lay it out," Conklin said as Sarge gathered the cards and started to shuffle.

I explained how Williams and I had tracked down the psychologist on the prescriptions and she had given us the information that Rafferty had been a pedophile.

"Family?" Conklin asked.

I nodded, "But we both figured the younger daughter killed Rafferty in the act. She would have been twelve when he died and was fourteen when his body was found when they dug this basement in 1992."

"Why in the act?" Sarge asked.

"The bullet went into his mouth," Williams said, "in an upward direction and exited out of the back of his head."

"So he was on his back," I said.

"So she shot him," Sarge said. "Then the fourteen-year-old sister and mother helped bury him up here on the hill."

Conklin nodded. "Thus the view."

"Exactly," I said.

"Just ugly," Sarge said, shaking his head. "A tragedy all the way around."

"That it was," I said. "A twelve year old girl killing her own father. Doesn't get much worse than that."

"Didn't the detectives back when they found the body in 1992 make a run at the family?" Sarge asked as he started to deal out the next hand.

"They did, but had no luck," I said. "The three family members all held to their story that he had just vanished one night walking to the store for smokes. They were a complete dead end and the detectives then had nothing at all to point to them, or anyone else for that matter."

"So how did you get the older live sister to come clean now, after all this time?" Conklin asked.

"Good old-fashioned blackmail," I said, smiling.

"She has a son who's in and out of jail," Williams said.

"We got dealt some perfect cards," I said, laughing. "At the moment the son was in jail for a minor drug bust, so when they hauled the older sister, his mother, in for questioning, the detectives told her that her son would serve twenty years on the drug charge unless she told them the truth about what happened to her father."

"And the chief went for that?" Sarge asked.

I had to admit, I had been stunned when I suggested the idea and he had agreed.

"He did," I said. "The kid would have been released in a day or so, but she didn't know that. It was a pure bluff."

"And she caved to that?"

"She did," I said. "Spilled every last detail like she had been waiting twenty-four years to tell someone."

"She had," Conklin said.

"So her younger sister killed her father for what he was doing to her," Sarge said, nodding.

"And when the body was found, the guilt just overwhelmed the poor young thing," Williams said. "She could make herself believe that her father was just gone without the body and the investigation. But not after a funeral."

"Killed herself a month after the body was found," I said, "and the mother did the same the next month."

"Wow," Sarge said as he finished dealing out the cards. "What kind of deal did the older sister get?"

I shrugged. "She'll spend some time in jail for a number of charges. Chances are it won't be many since she was a minor when it all happened. And maybe she can now get some real help."

"Always an optimist," Williams said, laughing at me.

I glanced down at a pair of jacks and nodded. "Sometimes I am."

I raised three dollars and only Williams called.

"Now who's an optimist?" I asked.

"Trust me," Williams said, "these cards have a thousand percent better chance of winning this hand then that poor woman has in coming out of that family mess even slightly healthy."

And with that, I sadly had to agree. Sometimes solving old cases had their downsides.

But I still felt like a cop and it was my job, and this poker group's job, to dig up the past and solve the cases.

And even when what we found showed a true dark side of human culture, solving the case felt great.

I sat back slightly and watched Sarge put a third jack on the flop.

And somehow I managed to not smile.

It didn't get any better for me than Tuesday night with the Cold Poker Gang.

I KILLED JESSIE TOOK

USA Today *bestselling writer, Dean Wesley Smith, returns to the world of his human garbage collector. A man without a real name who prides himself in his ability to take out the garbage of society.*

After going freelance, his former employer wants to take him to the curb as well. Not only must the garbage collector finish what he started, but play the killers coming after him as well.

A twisted mystery in this second installment in the "I Killed..." series.

One

I TAKE OUT HUMAN GARBAGE. It's what I do.

Since my former employer decided that I needed to be taken out as garbage as well, I have gone freelance. It was never difficult for me to go freelance, since I had saved almost every penny of all the millions I had earned from all my garbage runs for them. My former employer never really ever knew who I was or where I was or where I was based.

I had always made sure of that.

My real name is long lost in the past. As are my real looks.

I only had contact with my former employer from a distance when getting an assignment and when reporting in that the garbage was removed. I was always paid through accounts that only existed for each job and then vanished and could not be traced back to me or any business associated with me.

My former employer didn't even know what I looked like exactly. I had made sure of that with changing looks for every assignment.

I could do little about my six-foot height, but I changed hair color, facial features, walk, and other features with simple disguises and a vast amount of training.

I am also an expert in the modern computer age. I can make an identity appear and disappear at will. I can change identities easily, and study my targets carefully.

Before being a freelance human garbage collector, I never felt any need to record my job. It was just a job, after all.

But now, as a freelancer, I have decided to record these events in a case-by-case nature.

And since my first official case on my own had actually been my last for my former employer, I have recorded it under the case title "I Killed Adam Chaser."

Granted, my former employer did transfer my standard four-point-one million to my accounts after the initial job was finished, but I considered that a freelance fee in killing the agent they sent to kill me. Seemed only a fair trade.

I unofficially call my little business "I Killed…" I could think of no name that suited "Garbage Man for Human Waste" that I liked. So simply "I Killed…" But no one would ever be able to track it under that name or any other name.

I am that good.

This, my first job after becoming a freelance human garbage man, taking out the human waste of society, I will call "I Killed Jessie Took."

The reason for that, I decided, was to track easily what each case is about. The target's original name is Jessie Took, but he went by Joe Harley in Portland, Oregon.

And I know for a fact that this case will also involve my former employer. It must.

It is the nature of my former employee, to leave nothing unfinished. I am a very unfinished business they cannot leave open.

I must be killed. I must be taken to the curb.

I welcome their involvement.

And they have presented me this Jessie Took, my first freelance case, like it's tied up in a bow, a bow they know I will not resist.

They believe that sometimes garbage men must be taken to the curb as well.

I've killed other garbage men in the past; I can do it again if they force my hand.

Which, of course, they will do.

Two

UNLIKE WHEN I WORKED for my former employer, I am fed no information on which garbage needs to be taken out. So over the last year, since the Adam Chaser case, I developed a method of searching for unsolved crimes, of criminals going free for various reasons, of simple "talk" about a person.

One series of unsolved teenage girl disappearances came to light, seeming to string across the country from Michigan to Oregon. They did not seem to be related and each remained active cases in their local areas.

But since I was looking at patterns as my former employer knew I would, the cases came together for me fairly clearly. Each girl was sixteen, each brunette, each had slight problems in school, often with minor drugs and boys.

And each had brown eyes.

Seven missing teenage girls in seven years. A trail leading to Portland, Oregon, like a neon arrow as far as I was concerned.

Right back to the same town of my first freelance case, my last working assignment that became "I Killed Adam Chaser."

That seemed to tell me that more than likely my former employer had set this up, made it clear, to attract me like a bee to a flower.

It would not matter. They could keep sending agents and I would keep helping them remove that agent from their workforce.

But before I could have that looked-forward-to meeting with another garbage man or woman, I needed to find who was taking the girls and why. I was sure my former employer already knew.

So for each girl's disappearance, I searched for the one common denominator that held that trail together. That took me almost four months of searching from my Las Vegas home near the University of Nevada.

Of course, my research could not be traced in any fashion.

I spotted a few attempts to backtrack on my traces, but they were blocked easily.

What became the clear connection in all the disappearances was a yard maintenance man who went under a different name in every town. He seemed about twenty-five, had short brown hair, a slight moustache, and dark eyes that seemed to see everything. And they looked hungry.

I could find no picture of him in any fashion where he was smiling. Even in security camera footage, stoplight security cameras, and so on.

He never smiled.

He worked for different yard maintenance firms in every city, always under different names, and always quit early in the fall to move on. Always a month before a girl disappeared.

He had been born and raised under the name Jessie Ben Took in Lansing, Michigan. Right out of high school he had started working yard maintenance and he had left two months before a popular girl from his former high school had gone missing. The reports of her disappearance never mentioned his name in any way since he was already out of town and living outside of Madison, Wisconsin.

Every fall he moved on. A month or so later a girl went missing from his former town.

It was a trail I could not miss.

And my former employers would know that if I remained freelance, I would not miss it.

So I went back to Portland, Oregon, changing identities as I traveled and setting up escape routes.

The day I finally settled into Portland was a warm early-summer day, the leaves green, and the air smelling of open restaurants baking bread. The apartment I found was in the Northwest section of Portland with a slight view down the street of the river and one of the many bridges.

The apartment had large windows and too much light. It was on the second floor of an old Victorian that had been divided into four apartments, plus a manager's apartment on the main floor.

I went in under the name Nick Benson, an engineer from Idaho brought in to work on a new building down on the riverfront. I told the woman with large sixties' gray hair who was the landlord that I would be in and out of town a great deal and not to worry. I paid her four months in advance, which she liked.

The apartment was directly across the tree-shaded street from Jessie's apartment in a small ten-apartment complex that had been built in the mid 1960s out of cinder blocks and concrete stairs.

I bugged his small two-bedroom apartment one afternoon when he was at work, filled his walls with tiny cameras that looked like fly specks so there was no place in the apartment I couldn't see.

Then I put a few cameras in my apartment as well and rented another house a quick train-ride and identity change away. The second apartment was in a complex similar to Jessie's and the apartment had a very clear method of entry that required me to climb a flight of stairs.

The cameras in Jessie's walls any agent from my former employer would recognize. They would know I was here.

The ones in my apartment in the old Victorian were far better hidden and the signals could not be traced in any fashion. I wanted to know when my former employer's agent came snooping around my apartment.

But I knew they were already here. This had been a set-up, of that there was no doubt. They were well-trained in situational death, otherwise one of them would have attempted to kill me the first moment they realized who I was.

But as I said, they would work to cover their tracks. It was the nature of the business they worked for.

I doubted my employer had yet to realize I no longer needed to follow those same rules.

In my second apartment, as one more level of protection, I rented under a corporation name the empty apartment under my second apartment. That had a number of varied exits through a back door and a couple windows. I cut a hidden escape hatch through the closet floor of my second apartment to the third apartment's closet.

Then, protected with a number of back-up plans, I went about the business of making sure that Jessie Ben Took, maintenance man from Lansing, Michigan, really was responsible for all of the disappearances of the girls.

It became clear in very short order that he was human garbage that really, really needed to be taken out. He had a notebook hidden in his apartment of pictures of all the girls. All of them were nude and he was posing with all of them.

Typical of sick humans like him, he kept trophies.

All of them were the old Kodak-style prints. And I found an old camera in his apartment as well.

I captured each of the images, then spent the next day checking that none of them had been faked, that the locations and times were accurate. I did not put it past my former employer to set up an innocent man.

But with very little research, it became clear that Jessie was far from innocent. He spent a night a week poring over that notebook and reliving sexual acts he must have performed on each girl.

So I was the major target in this game and he was just a bonus.

So I spent the next few days tracing back through his employment in a new town, searching for where the girl's body would be buried. It made sense that since he worked yard maintenance and landscape work, he would bury the girl when he was finished with her in one of his projects.

He clearly had no young girl in his apartment across from my Victorian apartment, so I started tracing him. His last victim had been a girl from Boise. I doubted she would still be alive since it had been six months since she had been taken, but there might be a chance.

I found in a quick search, under his mother's maiden name, a storage locker that had been rented outside of Portland off of I-84.

I watched the rental for a few days to make sure it was not a trap by my former employers. They were not there and he did not visit the unit at all.

So after two days I moved in so that no security camera could see me and I opened the storage unit.

She was there.

In a large wooden crate inside the unit, with high levels of soundproofing covering the inside. She wasn't dead, but she might as well have been. She would be in another day at most. He had left her tied up and gagged to starve to death.

Now I was very, very angry at my former employee. They were willing to let this young girl die just to get me.

This had to end, and end now.

Three

I LEFT, locked everything back up, and made sure I was not seen when leaving.

Then, from a secure phone, I called the police and told them where they would find the poor young girl from Boise and who she was. She would survive.

That left me only a few hours at most. Jessie wasn't good at covering his tracks and clearly would be identified and quickly arrested. So I needed to move fast and take care of my former employer's agents.

I went back to my Victorian apartment and made sure no one had been in. I knew no one would be, but better to be safe. My former employer had sat this trap up a long time in advance.

I had to admit, it was a well-done trap. And if I hadn't been expecting it, I would have walked right into it.

I set the signal to self-destruct all my cameras in Jessie's apartment and the Victorian apartment.

On the way out, carrying a suitcase with everything I would need to make my escape clean, I knocked on my landlord's door and told her that I would be gone for a few weeks on a trip to Boise.

To any other agent, that would be the signal that I was leaving and she had to act and act fast.

"I've got a package that came for you today," she said, turning away from me.

She should have been ready for me. Sloppy work.

I put a bullet in the back of her head.

Actually, she should have shot me the first moment she saw me. But my former employer had taught all its agents, including me, to play out the scene and cover tracks. She had lived, and now died, by that rule.

I glanced around. No one had seen.

My sound-suppresser was good and the shot had not been heard.

I quickly pushed her body back inside and closed the door. Her computer had cameras all over the building next door. And as I had suspected, the young guy in the apartment next to Jessie's apartment was the second agent on this job.

He was asleep in his apartment.

I sent a coded message from her computer to my former employer that said simply, "The garbage has been taken out."

That was a signal that she should be paid.

That I was dead.

I gave them an account number as was standard.

I made sure that the ten million and change she was paid was moved out of that account quickly and shuttled around so that it couldn't be traced. It would eventually land in accounts I controlled, but could not be traced back to me in Las Vegas.

She would have instantly moved the money as well if she had been a good agent.

She had been far higher paid than I had ever been. That meant she was in charge of this entire hunt for me. And that meant that more than likely there was more than just a second agent. Otherwise her pay would not have been so high.

I hadn't expected to make any money on this job, but a few extra million would make up for the extra mess I was being forced to cause.

Then I triggered her computer to self-destruct and destroy all her cameras in both buildings.

As I turned to leave, I could see that the mask over her face had been blown partially off her face by my shot. She had been far more beautiful than her disguise had played.

And far younger.

The local police were going to have a field day with this one. I wonder what happened to the actual landlady of this building.

I walked across the street and up to the location of Jessie's apartment. I knew for a fact the other agent was asleep. The two agents slept in shifts as they had been trained.

Just to be sure, I planted a few small explosive charges along the staircase. Blinding charges. In case I missed a third agent, I didn't want to be surprised and caught without a defense in this hallway.

I entered the second agent's small apartment very silently and put two bullets in him before he could even roll over.

Then I went to his computer and sent the same coded message to my former employer.

"The garbage has been taken out."

I moved another four million that was his payment to my accounts, then set his computer to self-destruct, along with all the cameras he had set up from that computer.

Two down, one to go. This was a lot of trips to the curb.

A lot of human garbage to haul.

As I stepped into the hallway, I saw Jessie coming up the stairs.

And my little voice rang out clearly.

My former employer had already killed Jessie and had replaced him with a disguised agent as bait.

Of course.

This Jessie was smiling. The original Jessie never smiled.

And this agent was pulling out a gun as he saw me.

The tiny button in my left hand instantly triggered the string explosives across the stairs and I dropped to the concrete entrance floor.

The small, but bright and violent, explosion sent the agent back as he fired and tried to catch his balance at the same time.

His shots went over me and into the old wood siding behind me. I put two in his chest and another between his eyes before he could get off a third shot.

He was dead before he hit the bottom of the stairs.

My small explosions were also designed to start a heavy-smoke fire.

I went down the stairs quickly, moving through the smoke and out into the street, my gun now hidden in my suit-coat pocket, but my hand on it.

The day was warming up by the moment and the heat on the street was more than I had noticed the first time across.

I pretended to cough and stagger to the far side of the street and the mowed lawns there, keeping my head down as neighbors came running.

"Fire," I said, pointing at the smoke now pouring out of the staircase of the building while keeping my head down and then again pretending to cough.

I had to be really, really careful in case there was a fourth agent close by.

Around me a dozen people were on their cell phones and two men were running at the building while another man was banging on apartment doors on the ground floor.

The fire I had set wouldn't spread, but they didn't know that.

"You all right, mister?" a woman asked.

I didn't want to look up, but I had to.

I stood and nodded, taking a deep breath of the warm Portland afternoon air.

The woman had a cell phone against her ear and as I looked at her and nodded, I saw a flicker of recognition cross her eyes.

She was young and I had surprised her. She did not expect to be talking with me.

Her hand went for her jacket pocket and I put one shot through my jacket pocket into her forehead.

She slumped and I caught her, pulling her over toward the shade of a nearby tree, talking to her as if she had just grown faint from the heat.

The wound in her forehead wasn't bleeding much, so I pulled her medium length hair from her wig down over her forehead and sat her down on a bus stop bench and posed her with her head between her knees, talking with her all the time as if I was trying to calm her.

I quickly slipped her gun from her pocket and put it in mine.

Then I pointed to a young guy about twenty feet away standing watching the fire, holding his bike that he clearly had been riding.

"She fainted," I shouted. "She's going to be all right. I'm going to get her meds for her. Watch her, would you?"

The guy nodded, looking at her as I turned and went toward the Victorian house with my apartment in it.

Walking quickly and still carrying my case, as if I was in a hurry to get her meds, I went inside and then through and into a back corridor. There I lost the coat and the brown hair and the slacks, switching them out for a pair of jeans and a light Levi jacket.

When I ambled out the back door I had long blonde hair flowing out of the back of a Oregon Ducks baseball cap. Any sign of Nick Benson, the former engineer from Boise, was gone.

I unlocked a used Jeep I had bought and parked a dozen blocks away as the sounds of police and fire sirens filled the afternoon air. I drove it to a Mongolian restaurant in Tigard, Oregon, about five miles outside of Portland.

I parked the Jeep down the street from the restaurant near some suburban homes and behind a new Dodge minivan that I had bought as well under yet a different name.

Then in the bathroom of the restaurant, I lost the Levi jacket and the long blonde hair and replaced it with gray hair pulled back under a plain gray baseball cap, different color contacts for my eyes, and padded shoulders in a sports jacket over the jeans.

I collapsed the small suitcase I had been carrying and put it inside a brown backpack.

I sat and ate, then paid with the credit card of my new name, Dan

Curtis. After an amazingly good meal, I climbed into the mini-van and headed for Salt Lake City, going through Bend, Oregon, and across the desert.

Salt Lake was where the identity of Dan Curtis was from.

Two days later, Dan vanished there, never to be seen or heard of again.

Driving my three-year-old Cadillac, I headed back to Las Vegas and my teaching job at the university. I was a tenured professor in prelaw and law enforcement.

And I was a garbage man on the side, between semesters.

I took out the human garbage.

And sometimes that included other garbage men.

SLEEPING WITH THE GODDESS

USA Today *bestselling writer, Dean Wesley Smith, remembers clearly the early days of dating. The fear, the dreams, and the vivid imagination.*

"Sleeping with the Goddess" takes a glance inside one special date when reality sometimes gets mixed up in a guy's mind. Especially when things on the date seem great and all girls represent a goddess.

OKAY, BAST HAD LEGS that touched the ground and extended all the way up into heaven. I knew the ground part of the equation because her heels clicked when she walked on the sidewalk beside me as we headed into the movie.

Click. Click. Click. Click. Proof the goddess walked on the earth.

The heaven part I hoped to visit later in the evening. It was a faith issue, and I wanted to be the converted.

The date had started off well, the conversation light but strained as I walked with her from her parents' suburban house down the driveway to my car. I even held the passenger door of my Bug open for her to get in.

She liked that, said she liked the car, and gave me a beaming smile with perfect white teeth.

I liked what the seat belt did to her chest, but I didn't say that of course.

Bast had been named after an Egyptian goddess, so I figured the best way to find my way into her stone chamber was to treat her like a goddess. Tonight, I would be on my best behavior. So far, so good.

She was wearing a bright blue blouse with short sleeves, a matching blue short skirt, and heels that made her almost as tall as I am.

She had pulled back her long blonde hair like she did when she was wearing her cheerleader uniform and leading the school to shout and yell for the football players. With her hair pulled back tight like that, her face seemed to stretch and she actually had a cat-like look that could melt any guy in the school.

Kind of creepy when you consider her name, Bast, was the name of the Egyptian cat goddess.

I know because I had looked it up after the second day of sitting beside her. I loved the part about Bast that she was the pleasure-loving goddess in whose honor wild parties were thrown.

However, I sure didn't look like any goddess consort. I had on my normal jeans, sweatshirt, and Reeboks. I wasn't one of the football or basketball jocks cheerleaders normally went for. My only sport was snowboarding and I did it well. In fact, with luck, I hoped to have a shot at the regional tryouts for the Olympics next spring.

We had ended up sitting next to each other in a second period English literature class. It had taken me a week just to get up the nerve to nod at her before class, and after the first nod I just sat there and sweated the entire hour.

It took me another week to say hi.

And another week to actually ask her a question. I think my first question was where she was thinking about going to college the following year. I'm not sure if I stammered or not. I hope not.

Stanford was the answer. Prelaw major.

She asked me in return and when I told her Columbia, if things worked out, she had given me my first smile.

I remember sort of melting into the chair after that smile. It had taken another two days for me to get up the nerve to talk to her again.

After that we sort of talked every day, sometimes just a hi, sometimes a few sentences. I looked forward to every word, to be honest.

Then the big day came when she even asked me my name after one class in which I had answered correctly a fairly hard Shakespeare question.

There is nothing like a beautiful girl wanting to know the name of a boy in her class. The simple question can send a boy into masturbation heaven. I was no exception to the rule.

Then when the school newspaper did the article on me trying for the Olympics, she got real friendly and we talked before and after every class, even walking twice to our next classes together. I guess having a goal beyond making the next touchdown was a little interesting to her.

A week later I finally got up the nerve to ask her out.

Or she asked me out.

I'm not really sure how the date happened, but it sort of did.

Luckily, a film we both wanted to see was opening on Friday night, so we decided that would be perfect.

And unlike what I had feared might happen, the date went very, very well.

She looked like a goddess. I looked like a snowboarder.

I made no gaffes in the car as we talked about why she wanted to go to Stanford, and managed to keep my gaze on her beautiful blue eyes instead of her beautiful blue blouse.

I bought the tickets to the show. She insisted on buying the popcorn and Diet Coke.

The movie was good. We both laughed a lot, which broke even more of the first-date tension.

After the show we went for pizza, discovering both of us liked Canadian bacon and tomatoes. Having the same taste in pizza is important.

I asked her about her family, which I found out consisted of one brother and her mother who worked. Her dad lived across town and was a college professor of ancient history, thus her name. I discovered she wanted to be a lawyer and help people.

She asked about my Olympic hopes, about me going to New York to go to college, which was a long way from a snowboard hill, and my family, which consisted of one younger sister and parents who should be divorced but didn't know it yet.

We talked for hours, working at the pizza and drinking Diet Coke, having a blast, to be honest. By the end of the conversation, my single-minded thoughts of finding goddess heaven had faded back to actually enjoying Bast's company.

I took her back to her house, parked the Bug on the street, and turned to her, suddenly realizing the tension was high again between us.

Sexual tension?

First kiss tension?

How to end a really perfect evening tension?

All of the above more than likely.

"Now this was fun," I said after we stared into each other's eyes for a few moments.

"It sure was," she said, giving me that melting smile and a wonderful laugh. "Want to do it again?"

"Sure do," I said. "Different movie though. I hate seeing the same movie twice."

Again she laughed, which was nice of her for such a lame joke.

"Deal," she said.

She started to reach for the door handle, hesitated, glancing back at me.

The moment seemed to take a lifetime. Then she turned to me, leaned toward me, used one hand to grab my sweatshirt, and pulled me into a kiss.

Now understand, I have kissed my share of girls before. Being around ski lodges certainly gives a guy like me lots of chances for meeting and finding private places to end up with girls. I hadn't lost my virginity yet, but kissing I was downright good at.

She was better.

She kissed like a goddess.

I melted and lost my mind, all at the same moment.

From that kiss on I have no idea what actually happened.

Granted, I have a memory of the events that followed, but no belief in those events.

I think what happened is that she pulled away from the kiss and said, "Let's go inside."

I asked about her mother and what would she say.

"She is not a problem," she had said, getting out and motioning for me to follow.

I don't remember my feet touching the driveway. I don't remember closing my car door. I don't remember opening her front door.

I do remember staring at her wonderful body and thinking of the smooth skin and wonderful feel of her lips.

That I remember.

We went inside, her holding my hand and pulling my stumbling body along.

I do remember stopping just inside the front door as she closed it behind me, staring. And I remember being stunned.

The inside of the house wasn't a three bedroom standard American. It looked like an Egyptian King's bedroom, with silk hanging from impossibly high ceilings, and dozens of people bowing to Bast.

As we entered her clothes seemed to change from the short skirt and blue blouse to blue Egyptian silk that shimmered around her as she walked, showing off the smooth skin of her legs, her shoulders, her neck.

Two large men came forward and bowed to her, two others fanned her with reed fans.

I remember thinking they should be fanning me instead, because I was the one that was having the heat stroke.

She directed still another two men to take me, strip me, and put me in the hot baths.

They were big guys, and I don't remember fighting them as they helped me undress.

Then after I was in the water, she slowly let the silk slide off her shoulders into a pile beside the pools.

I swear trumpets rang out somewhere in the distance.

She had the most perfect body I could have ever imagined, and as an eighteen-year-old boy, I had done some pretty good imagining. Her body was even better than anything in the men's magazines. She came down the steps into the water very, very slowly, smiling at me and clearly enjoying my stare.

I remember that we kissed again.

Then we washed each other, we kissed some more, did more washing.

Kiss on, wash off. Kiss on, wash off. I explored her body.

Finally, I think I remember that she took me by the hand and led me to the biggest bed I had ever seen, where we made love for hours, and I truly became a believer.

The first real sexual experience with anyone would do that for any boy my age, but with a goddess, it was special, real special.

We slept for hours after that. Then she had two of her slaves help me dress and send me out to my car in the driveway of the very ordinary looking suburban house, while she stood and waved at me from the front step, dressed again in her movie attire.

I was surprised it was still dark.

Now I think all that happened.

But I'm convinced it couldn't have.

More than likely she just kissed me, got out of the car, and I came to after the kiss about the point she reached the front step and turned to wave.

I turned on the car engine as she stepped inside and closed the door.

I managed to get the car out into the street and headed home, wondering about the weird power-dream one kiss could bring on.

Then I noticed it was a lot later than I had thought it was. All the way home I questioned myself if the dream had been real or not.

I still, even the next day, don't know for sure, because I'm not really sure of the power of a true goddess. And I'm sure not going to ask her between classes.

But I do know that when I got home, I had my underwear on backwards.

And I smelled like rose petals.

THE MATCH

A Poker Boy Story

Poker Boy awakes one morning in his own past, before he became a superhero in the gambling universe, before he met the love of his life, before Stan, the God of Poker, even knew Poker Boy existed.

One problem: Poker Boy remembers the next fifteen years. He belongs in 2014, not 1999. So who broke all rules against time travel and transported him into his own past? The fate of the world rested once again on finding answers. And sometimes those answers can only be found in a poker game.

One

I HAD A HUNCH that something was very, very wrong when I woke up in my own bed, in my doublewide trailer in the Oregon Coast Mountains. I know it sounds weird to say I knew something was wrong because I woke up in my own bed. Where else was I supposed to wake up, after all?

Problem being, I hadn't slept in that bed in years. Every night I normally slept with Patty Ledgerwood, aka Front Desk Girl, my girl-friend and sidekick. And she didn't much like (read that hated) my old doublewide, so we always stayed in her apartment in Las Vegas.

I didn't remember us having a fight.

And my sheets didn't smell musty from lack of use for years.

So something was very wrong.

Outside a slight rain and wind was rattling the windows and drumming on the flat roof.

In five or six months, Patty and I would have a big new mansion built on land I owned up in the mountains near here that we had designed together. But until that was finished, we stayed in her wonderful apartment in Las Vegas.

I remembered going to bed last night with her.

She had already been asleep, since I had gotten in late from a tournament at the Bellagio. I remember clearly she cuddled with me for a moment, still asleep, then rolled over.

As always, she had smelled wonderful and I remember rolling over as well, thinking I was the luckiest man alive.

Which, I had to admit, I was.

So how did I get here?

Was I sleep-teleporting or something?

I put on my clothes, which were Levis, tennis shoes, a plain dress shirt, black Fedora-like hat and black leather coat that was my uniform. I got my power from casinos, and it felt that when I had that coat and hat on I could channel the power better.

Then I jumped back to Patty's apartment.

Only I didn't jump.

I didn't go anywhere.

I just stood there in the middle of the doublewide's living room with a face that looked like I might take a crap on the green shag carpet at any moment.

Normally I just thought about where I wanted to go, concentrated, and then went there.

I tried again.

Nothing.

My old couch with a tan blanket covering it still sat there, a half-eaten tv dinner filled the center of the fake-wood coffee table, and the rain still drummed on the roof.

For some reason, my ability to teleport was shut off.

I felt a slight twisting of worry in my stomach, but there were a thousand reasons for this happening, not the least of which was a practical joke by one of the gods.

I did another quick check of the living room of my big doublewide to see if I could see anything at all different. The big box television was on as I normally left it on when here. Sort of background sounds.

I moved over into the kitchen area and checked my fridge. It was stocked, something I hadn't done in a couple years, and there were a few dirty dishes in the sink that didn't even look that crusty yet.

Whoever had done this to me had gotten the details right.

There was a carton of unopened milk in the fridge. I always kept milk there, and I went to open it for a drink to try to calm my twisting stomach. That was when I noticed the sell-by date.

June 18, 1999.

Only the milk inside was very fresh.

That date was almost a year before I was first approached by Stan to be a superhero.

I put the milk back without drinking any of it.

My stomach was now twisting a lot harder than it had a moment before. Had something happened that shifted me back in time? I had learned that time travel was possible, but very protected by the gods and not allowed. In fact, from my understanding, there were very few gods who could even do it.

Had I been sleepwalking through time? Not likely. Which left only one conclusion.

Someone had sent me back here.

But who would send me back to this date and why?

Actually I didn't know the exact date.

I went over to the television and flipped around a few channels until I hit one with a running banner.

It said the day was June 7th, 1999. It was 10:07 in the morning Pacific Daylight Time.

I dropped onto the couch and tried to remember for a moment what I was doing on this day in 1999. All I knew that in general I was a professional poker player and winning my share. Even though I lived like a broke gambler in an old doublewide trailer with furnishings decades out of date, I was already pretty rich by the early summer of 1999.

Actually very, very rich.

And I was still years from meeting Patty.

But what I had done on June 7th, 1999 was beyond me.

Finally, I had had enough. I glanced up at the ceiling and shouted "Stan, a little help?"

I have no idea why I shouted at the ceiling for my boss, Stan, the God of Poker. But I always did.

He didn't appear.

"Hey, Stan, funny joke. Now tell me what's happening?"

No Stan.

And without Stan, that meant I had no team either to help me solve this.

I stood and headed for the front door. I needed to get to a casino and the closest one was my home casino, Spirit Winds, about a mile away.

I opened the door not knowing what to expect.

The old black Thunderbird that I had sold in 2010 was sitting out front in the gravel driveway where I always used to park. The doublewide was tucked in under some tall pine and the rain was dripping through the trees.

I took the keys off the hook beside the front door where I always left them and went out.

The Thunderbird started right up. I let it warm up a little and checked my wallet. I had just under five hundred, which was a pretty normal amount for me to carry at that point in time. Even my 1999 driver's license was current.

As I approached the big casino, I could see that the new additions had not yet been added.

I really was in 1999.

And totally alone once again.

Two

MY STOMACH WAS TWISTING like a bad pretzel under a carnival vender's heat lamp. I was going to need some food and time to think. And some power from the casino.

I parked in my normal spot around to the side of the big building and headed inside, letting the power of the casino fill me. I flat loved walking into casinos. They felt like my home and I could always feel the power they gave me, even before I had become a superhero.

The casino power calmed me as I strode toward the buffet in its old location across from the front door.

Then suddenly it dawned on me that maybe the reason I couldn't teleport to Patty's apartment was because it wasn't there yet. It didn't get built until 2004 and her apartment was on the fourteenth floor.

Damn this time travel stuff could give a guy a headache.

I quickly turned and went into the men's restroom. No one was in there.

Then I thought of the front room of my trailer and jumped there.

It worked.

Worked fine, actually.

I clicked off the television I had left on when I left a few minutes earlier, feeling very, very relieved that I still had my powers.

I wasn't losing my mind completely.

I jumped back to the casino's men's room and resumed my journey to the buffet for breakfast. Somehow I needed to figure out why I was here, who had sent me here, and how to get back to 2014.

And without my team, I had no idea how to even start doing that.

What worried me even more was that someone had done this to get me out of the way. If I disappeared into the past, out of contact, my team might not be able to stop what danger might be happening in 2014.

I paid for breakfast and asked for a table against the wall. As the woman seated me and took my orange juice order, I glanced around at the few people eating in the buffet. I didn't know a one of them. Or at least I didn't remember any of them.

And none of them seemed to be giving me any strange looks.

I filled my plate with some ham, scrambled eggs, and a piece of toast and sat down with my back to the wall. No one said hello or even gave me a second glance.

I took myself out of time, freezing everyone around me. It felt like I stopped time, but I really didn't. I just stepped into a bubble between instants of time.

The sounds from the kitchen and the casino floor vanished, leaving me in complete silence.

The stepping between instants of time power was one of my most favorite powers. Right up there next to teleportation.

I took a bite of the eggs, then the ham, letting any of the gods who might be paying attention figure out there was a time bubble here that no one knew about. I knew these things were fairly easy to see for most gods.

After a full minute, I once again said, "Stan! Calling Stan, the God of Poker."

I imagined him clearly.

He appeared in front of me, frowning, not something I normally saw on my boss's face. The guy had the best poker face of anyone I had ever met. He was dressed as he always did, in tan slacks, a tan shirt, a plain button-down sweater and loafers. His short hair made him the plainest person I had ever met.

He glanced around at the time bubble, then back at me.

"How did you do this? And who are you?"

"My name is Poker Boy," I said. "And you recruit me out of this casino to be a superhero in about a year. You taught me how to do this a few years later."

He opened his mouth and shut it.

"I somehow got pulled here from 2014. I have no idea how or why."

"Time travel is not allowed," he said.

"I know," I said. "You want to tell the person who did this to me?"

He opened his mouth, then shut it again without saying a word. I knew how he was feeling. Time travel was a scary thing and even my telling him as much as I had might change history. But I had to take that chance.

I indicated that he sit down and he did in the chair across from me.

"I am figuring that in the future someone needed me out of the way," I said. "So who, among the gods, could do this? Trap me back here? More than likely Laverne, but she wouldn't do this, so who else?"

He started to answer, but I stopped him. "I don't want to know. We need to be careful. I just need you and Laverne to figure this out and then tell me how I get back to 2014 without going through the last, or next, as the case might be, 15 years."

He nodded and vanished.

I moved myself back into the flow of time and the sounds came crashing back around me. Then I went to work on my breakfast again. When I got back to my own time, I'd ask Stan about this one. I had a hunch he was going to remember more about this day than I did at this moment.

I didn't want to think about where the real me was at this moment.

At least I hadn't woken up this morning next to myself. That might have been a tough thing to explain.

But my car had been in front of my trailer. So if I hadn't been home, exactly where was the other me?

Then I had the worst thought of the morning.

Maybe the old me had switched places with me in the future.

"Oh, I'm sorry, Patty," I said out loud, shaking my head and smiling at that idea.

"You should be," a voice said beside me.

Suddenly I was back out of time, the noise of the casino and buffet gone, and Stan was sitting across from me, smiling.

And Patty was sitting beside me, giving me her pretend angry look.

She kissed me before I had time to even say anything.

And let me say, after thinking I was alone, stuck in the past, that kiss felt wonderful, even better than normal, which was going some with kissing Patty.

Three

STAN CLEARED HIS THROAT. "Sorry to break this up," he said, "but I'll be back in about one minute and we have to be very careful this is not seen."

"The past you?" I asked.

Stan nodded.

"And you have the other me in a time bubble waiting somewhere for this to finish up?"

"Got it," Stan said.

"You were cute," Patty said, smiling at me.

"Am I going to need counseling after waking up with an older woman?" I asked her, smiling.

She whacked me and laughed. "You might."

I turned to Stan, my Stan from the future. "So what do I do?"

"I can't tell you a thing," Stan said. "At least not at this point. It has to play out. And it concerns this time."

"Isn't this part of it playing out?" I asked.

"All we can say at the moment," Stan said, shaking his head.

"Watch yourself there as well," I said. "This might be to get me out of the way."

"Good thinking," Stan said.

But I could tell he didn't give it a second thought. So this had nothing to do with a threat in 2014. It was completely about something here in 1999.

"See you in about fifteen years," Patty said, kissing me again.

"Be nice to the other me," I said.

She winked. "Oh, I will."

Then they were both gone and the time bubble was gone. The sounds of the buffet came crashing back in.

I sipped on the last of my orange juice, thinking about her last joke. I sure couldn't be jealous of my girlfriend spending time with me, even though it wasn't really me. At least not the me of now.

I was pretty sure, from my memory, which seemed oddly blank for this time period, I hadn't been allowed to remember what had happened.

A moment later another time bubble formed around me, plunging me back into silence and the young Stan appeared. Actually, he looked exactly like the Stan in fifteen years. I even think he was dressed in the same sweater and slacks.

"The other you is in your time in the future," Stan said, sitting down.

Around us everyone remained frozen, some in stride, others with a mouthful of food.

"I know," I said and he looked surprised, again losing his normal poker face.

He started to ask a question, but I waved him off.

"Only thing that could happen. I can't think of one reason I would be brought back in time."

"To play poker," Stan said.

Now it was my turn to be surprised. "Not something you could handle. You are as good as I am, if not better."

"I am told I am not," Stan said.

Again I was surprised.

"Laverne switched you out last night," Stan said. "The window was so tight for the transfer that she did not have time to warn you. She sends her apologies."

"Window?" I asked, getting more confused by the moment.

Stan nodded. "The entity who is setting this up needs to think you are not a superhero yet. When Laverne learned of what was to happen, she only had a few seconds to act."

"I'm to play this entity?" I'd done that a few times, the most memorable being an alien who looked like a snake. Actually, it was the same snake alien who messed up the Garden of Eden.

"No," Stan said. "You are to play another professional poker player."

Now I was getting very, very worried. And not about playing another professional poker player, but about the stakes. This was a lot of trouble to go through to set up a friendly game. And clearly Laverne was worried about it as well.

"So what kind of alien invasion is this going to stop if I win?"

Stan actually laughed. "Don't I wish?"

Now I was beyond worried.

"If I lose the world ends?" I asked.

Again Stan just laughed and shook his head. "Wow, you develop a wild ego, don't you? I hope your poker is as good as the ego."

"Better," I said. "So what am I playing for?"

"My job," Stan said.

I kind of opened and then closed my mouth.

"So you are actually playing for your job as well," Stan said, half laughing. "Since I hire you."

All I could do was sit there and think over all of the times my team and I rescued the entire planet. I really was playing for everything. The survival of the entire world. But Stan, this Stan, would have no way of knowing that.

And I didn't dare tell him.

No wonder Laverne had sent me back here.

"So Bernice, the God of Keno, is the entity that set this up?" I asked.

It was Stan's turn to open his mouth, then shut it. He nodded.

"And a lot of betting is going on among gods right now. Correct?"

Again Stan nodded.

"Bernice makes a run at me a few years after you hire me to get your job that way. She tried using all her 'charms' on me and failed."

"Wow, you turned down those looks?" Stan said.

Model looks, a soft voice, and huge breasts didn't much do it for me. And her laugh sounded more like a baying donkey anyway. She was the best-looking of all the gods in classical beauty, and I didn't blame her for wanting to get out of the dead-end world of Keno. Only problem was, she had the brains of a Keno player.

As poker players like to joke, a Keno player is a gambler who has lost the will to live.

Why she kept making runs at Stan's job was beyond me. But if she got it this time, she would never hire me and the world would end at any number of different points in the next fifteen years when me and my team were not together to save it.

I was going to have to win this.

One way or another.

THE LADY AND THE SEEDERS

A Seeders Universe Story

About a year ago I had an assignment from editor John Helfers to write a story for his Fiction River: How to Save the World *anthology. Now understand, I am one of the executive editors on the Fiction River line of anthologies. But the editors of each volume have the final call on the stories in each volume (within reason).*

John had been pretty clear on what he wanted, but I had written "The Lady and the Seeders" a month before, starting it from the title and hadn't done anything with it. And it was about saving the world, after all. So I sent it to John just to see if he was going to expand out his directions enough to include it.

He wasn't. He liked the story, though, and Kris liked the story, and I was kind of fond of it as well. But in his rejection letter to me, he said it felt like a novel.

Now, as an editor, I say that to writers at times myself. Often frustrating to the poor writer, but in this case, John was right. It did feel like a plot of a novel. Sort of. So I put the story away and as I started into this Smith's Monthly, *I decided to write the novel from the short story.*

It's called Against Time *and it was in* Smith's Monthly #3.

There are tiny parts of the story in the novel, and characters have shifted around, but the core of the book is similar to the short story. So here in this fourth issue, I thought it would be fun and interesting to readers to show the short story that started the novel you read last month.

Enjoy.

One

I SAT IN MY BIG BLACK INERTIA CHAIR, holding on for dear life as we came from deep space way too hot and directly into orbit insertion around a big, green-and-blue Earth-like planet we had named N-21-7. I had no doubt my fingers were going to have to be pried from the soft foam of the armrests and it tasted like my stomach might revolt from the sharp garlic on artichoke pizza I had baked us for lunch.

Doc, sitting to my right in his inertia chair, had us braking like crazy to hold the orbit as the features of the planet flashed by far, far too fast for me to even catch a glimpse. You would have thought we had someone with damn big guns on our ass.

Doc's fingers were flying over his control panel. My job was to watch for anything in front of us in orbit, but as fast as Doc had us braking, our orbital trajectory just kept changing, so I had no clue what was coming up, let alone be able to watch for anything.

We might hit something before we even had time to blink, and if the object we plowed into was too large, our screens might not block it.

This stunt was all my skinny partner's idea. Doc wanted to test out a new theory. He wanted to see how close to a planet we could drop out of a trans-tunnel and still control slowing into an orbit. He convinced me to give it a try by saying, "Just never know when it might come in handy in the future."

I was big on being prepared for just damn near anything, and we had been chased more than once in the last few years of roaming around through space. And more than likely it would happen again. Besides, I figured that if we didn't plow into something large, the worst that would happen was that we would just sling off the orbit like a flea off a dog's back and then have to backtrack.

Doc was convinced that wasn't going to happen, and he tried to show me the math. I nodded like I always do when he gets into the math on anything concerning orbits and trans-tunnel speeds and finally he stopped and said, "You'll see. It will work."

"Just don't hit the damn planet square on."

"No worries, Skip," he had said.

And that always made me worry. Especially when he called me "Skip" which was short for "Skipper." He never did that unless he was worried as well. My actual name was Fisher, Vardis Fisher, but everyone called me Fisher. I owned *The Lady*, as I called this deep space exploration ship.

Most of the time Doc just called her "The Ship."

We had built her in two years in a huge warehouse on my parent's estate just north of our hometown, right after we both finally finished with far too many advanced degrees in college.

I had the family money in my trust, more than enough, actually, to build a couple ships. And I had patents on a dozen devices I had invented that drew energy from dark matter.

Doc had the idea for the gravity drive that allowed us to not only just float out of a gravity well, but jump long distances very quickly in what Doc called "Trans-Tunnel Flight."

Basically it was a form of time-bending warp drive, but when we were in it, space looked like it had become a tunnel, so Doc named it the "Trans-Tunnel Drive."

"Better than "Warp Drive" he had said.

In the planning stage, we decided to make the ship really huge and really cool, right out of a 1950's science fiction movie. We even had painted it silver and put fins like a nifty plane and a pointed nose on it so it looked like a cross between a very fast plane and an old rocket ship. The fins were worthless unless in the atmosphere if the drive went out, and the pointed nose housed nothing but sensors.

We each had huge five-room suites on board, since the ship was the size of a hotel that flew. It was so big, there were parts of this ship I hadn't been in for over a year.

It actually didn't need to be this big, but both Doc and I had figured we never knew what we might run into out in space, or how much room we might need, or who might be riding along. The actual engine itself took up the room of a small closet and a large warehouse area was filled with many, many spare parts. The rest was a game room, an exercise room, a small gym, a massive kitchen with a dozen freezers, and numbers of spare bedrooms for a future crew or guests. So far, those guest rooms had not been used.

Before we took off, we had stocked more food than we would be able to eat in five years, even though, from darned-near-anywhere in this area of the galaxy, we could jump back to earth in a matter of a day or two.

Food is my passion. Somewhere back in college, after getting my first doctorate, I got close to three hundred pounds on my five-foot-ten inch frame. Back then people said Doc and I looked like the old comedy team of Laurel and Hardy, but I was larger back then than Hardy ever got.

And I loved cooking. Especially really rich foods. But a couple doctors told me that if I didn't lose some weight, I was going to have to cut down on many of the dishes I loved to cook.

So I went exercise crazy. Right before we left, I had run in my tenth marathon and I had been training for an Iron Man competition. I now weighed just under one-seventy and that was all muscle. And I could eat anything I damn well wanted.

Somehow, Doc ate everything I served him with relish and never gained a pound and spent only a minor amount of time in the gym, usually when he wanted to talk to me about something and knew I was a captive audience while in an exercise routine.

I didn't feel right if I didn't exercise, just as I didn't feel right when I didn't eat decent food.

One of the most enjoyable aspects of this exploring around space was discovering new types of food and ways of cooking it. I was stock-piling the recipes with hopes of doing a number of cookbooks when we got back to Earth.

I could spend two or three hours a day in the kitchen just testing new foods and writing it all down.

I doubted anyone would give my books any credit, just as they didn't give my energy inventions even a second look. The power for everything on this ship and Doc's drive came from the energy floating around between matter and dark matter.

For some reason I had the ability to understand when something hidden was between two obvious things. I had perfected the idea of using the energy between the two states of matter while in school and applied for patents, but no professor would let me write it as a thesis. No one really gave my ideas any credit at all, actually, just as they didn't give Doc's trans-tunnel drive and anti-gravity work anything but laughter.

If they could only see us now.

Finally, Doc had us slowed enough that the orbit we had settled into seemed stable, even though we were still braking.

"Told you it would work," Doc said, smiling at me, his thin face twisted into mostly bright white teeth and wide blue eyes.

I just shook my head and worked my fingers off the armrests of my chair. "Only emergencies," I said as my stomach started to settle.

"Exactly," he said, nodding and going back to continuing to brake us into a stable orbit. "At some point I hope to figure out how we can come out of a trans-tunnel without forward speed. It should be possible."

"Make that a priority," I said.

Suddenly the warning lights on my heads-up panel flashed into a display that would do a Christmas tree proud.

The orbit we had dropped into had us hitting a large orbiting object in about five seconds.

I kicked off Doc's controls and cut the braking, which allowed us to move out higher away from the planet. On my screen our orbit around the planet changed from a nice circular pattern into a big egg-shaped elliptical orbit.

We flashed past what looked like an orbiting station far too fast to get a good look at it.

And far too close for my stomach to be happy. I had long ago lost the desire for near-misses on anything. And if we had hit it, we would have put a very, very large hole in it. Our screens would have kept us safe, but the station and everyone on it would have been in trouble.

"Wow, good catch, Fisher," Doc said. "Looks like we have a space-faring culture on this planet."

"Great, just great," I said. "Someone to chase us again after we almost destroyed their space station."

Doc laughed. "Yeah, we have a way of making an entrance, don't we?"

Two

AS DOC BROUGHT US AROUND the planet again and worked to match the orbit of the space station, I scanned the planet. It felt a little like scanning Earth from a low orbit. Evidence of human activity everywhere, large, sprawling cities on all of its major continents, and thousands of roads and smaller cities and towns.

It looked the same as many of the Earth-type planets we had visited. Humans had clearly been seeded on every Goldilocks zone planet that we had come to at some point in the distant past. We had run across no aliens, but humans were everywhere. At least in the small area of the Milky Way Galaxy we had explored.

At last count, we had found over two hundred Earth-like planets and every darned one of them had either had human life on them at one point or still did have thriving civilizations.

And not many of them seemed very far beyond or behind Earth's level, as if they had all started at the same time in history.

Very, very strange and it had bothered us both for the first fifty or so planets, but now we were growing used to the idea.

The human civilization on the planet below also seemed to be around Earth's level of growth and expansion.

But as we went around the dark side in our orbit, I noticed one major problem: Nothing was moving.

And the planet was slowly dropping silent and dark. Only basic recorded sounds were coming from the surface.

In very short order it would be ghostly silent. And very, very dark.

"Doc, we have a problem," I said.

"They can't be coming after us already," he said, not looking up from his board as he brought *The Lady* up slowly on the orbiting space station. "We missed them, didn't we?"

"No one is coming after us," I said.

"That's good," he said, still not looking up. "So what's the problem?"

My fingers were moving as fast as I could get them to move over my controls to confirm what I feared.

All the readings came up the same.

"Everyone down there is dead."

At that, he looked up.

Three

WE DID TEN ORBITS over the next few hours, recording and studying everything we could. There was no doubt the planet below us was just flat dead. Actually, the planet was fine, but all the humans and a bunch of animal life had died very, very suddenly.

And very recently.

There were numbers of smaller animals and some larger ones still alive, but human bodies lay everywhere, in every building, in every street.

Something had killed everyone on the planet and it had done it quickly, where they stood, as they walked, as they drove cars that looked frighteningly like cars from Earth.

"You see anyone alive?" I finally asked Doc.

"Not a one," he said, his voice unnaturally soft.

He looked over at me, his eyes looking as haunted as I had ever seen them. We had run into a couple of Earth-like planets with no humans and only signs of a civilization in the distant past. That was one thing, almost a scientific curiosity as to what happened.

But it was a different thing when you could see human bodies littering the streets and filling the buildings.

Recently dead human bodies.

Millions and millions of them.

A vastly different thing.

And what worried me more than anything else was that this could happen to Earth. We somehow needed to find out what happened here.

"The station," I said.

He nodded. After this many years together, we often didn't have to finish sentences or thoughts.

We both knew that the instruments there might give us some sort of understanding of what had killed the population of this planet.

His fingers again flew over the control board, bringing us even closer in to match the orbit of the large space station.

I was feeling stunned and not really looking forward to going into that station when suddenly space around the planet was filled with a hundred huge ships.

They just appeared out of nowhere and at a dead stop. They made *The Lady* look like a kids ship in a bathtub compared to an aircraft carrier.

"What the…" I said, pushing back in my chair as if I needed to get farther away from those clearly alien monster ships.

Doc glanced up and jerked, also pushing back.

Then suddenly, on my sensors, I started reading humans again on the planet below.

Some alone, some scattered in groups.

I pointed to the readings and tapped Doc who glanced at it and nodded.

"They are transporting humans to the planet below," he said. "Looks like we found our seeders."

"We are not the originals," a voice said clearly inside the control room of *The Lady*. Only it wasn't my voice or Doc's.

Then everything around us shimmered for a moment and stabilized again.

The Lady was no longer floating in space near an empty space station. It was now seemingly sitting on a huge landing dock inside another ship.

"Oh, man," I said, trying to keep the last bit of control I had. Somehow I managed to not scream and run to the back of the ship.

"Now what are we going to do?" I asked.

Doc shook his head slowly, clearly as shaken as I had ever seen him before.

Then he turned to me and with a half-smile said, "Go and say hello?"

Four

WE DID SOME QUICK CHECKING and the atmosphere outside the ship in the huge space dock was normal, no bad things in it that could kill us. And the gravity seemed to be Earth-normal as well.

Beyond that, we couldn't tell much of anything about the ship around us past what we could see in the huge room. The dock had to be as large as a football stadium and could have easily held three or four ships The Lady's size.

We tested, but every control we had was locked down solid and our engines were offline. We were going nowhere under our own power.

"You ready, Skip?" Doc asked, standing and pretending to stretch like he was relaxed about meeting the owners of these huge ships.

I just shook my head and stood as well. "Seems like we have no choice, doesn't it?"

A good minute later we were standing on the deck looking around. The sides of the room seem to vanish in the distance and I was clearly wrong. This room could hold twenty ships the size of ours, and have room between them all.

And we thought we had built a large ship when we built the Lady. Everything in space was relative it seemed.

Then, just as the first time we were grabbed, everything shimmered and we found ourselves in a meeting room with tables full of meats and vegetables and breads that that looked like they had been worked over by starving hordes.

I turned slowly around, surveying the large meeting room. The place was littered with a bunch of blankets and chairs and cots. One wall was filled with a huge view port that looked down on the greens and blues and whites of the planet below.

"Looks like we are late for the party," Doc said.

"If you had come to this planet ten minutes earlier," a voice said from behind us, "you more than likely would have been as dead as most of those on the planet below."

Doc and I spun around to see a man about my height and weight walking toward us, smiling. He had brown hair, wore jeans and a green short-sleeved shirt tucked into his pants. He looked as normal and as human as anyone from Earth.

And as far as I could tell, he was speaking perfect English. We had met a few human cultures that had perfected some sort of translation devices that just made it sound like they were speaking English. But this was even more advanced. His lips seemed to match what he was saying.

Considering the size of this ship we were in, I think I would have been less stunned if an alien had joined us spouting six arms and a beak and squeaking our national anthem.

He extended his hand for me to shake. "I'm Benson."

"Fisher," I said, carefully shaking his hand back.

It felt as normal as any human handshake, which bothered me even more.

"Doc," my stunned partner said softly as he shook Benson's hand next.

"So you are the two explorers we've been hearing about," Benson said, smiling. "I understand you have had some adventures."

"A few," I said, even more shocked that anyone had followed us around this area of space. Granted, it was a tiny area in comparison to the entire Milky Way Galaxy, but we had still covered a lot of light years and visited a few hundred Earth-like planets. And tracking us through open trans-tunnel space wasn't like following footprints in the mud. Or at least I didn't think it was.

"So where are you two from?" Benson asked.

"Earth." I gave him the answer I knew would make him smile and at the same time give him no information at all, since most of the human planets we had visited had called their planets Earth. In fact, every one of them had.

He did smile. "I don't blame you for not wanting to tell me. How about I show you around and tell you what we are doing and then maybe you'll feel more like talking. I find it fascinating that a human culture in this area has advanced as far as you have."

I almost told him that the rest of our planet hadn't just yet, but instead just nodded and said, "Lead the way. But first off, what happened down there?"

I pointed at the planet that could be seen out of a large view port on one side of the room.

Benson tapped something on his wrist and in the air near us an image of the Milky Way Galaxy came into being, spinning in the air.

Impressive three-dimensional image.

Then like focusing in, the view shifted down to this spiral arm of the galaxy and then to this small section of space. There had to be five hundred suns represented by nothing more than bright colored lights floating in the air.

One light was suddenly circled in the air by a red ring.

"An explosion in this sun caused rays of extreme electro-magnetic energy to be sent out into space."

From the circled star a number of white rays seemed to expand outward. Benson went on. "By the time we noticed the explosion and calculated the frequency of the energy and then traced its path, we were too late to get here to save the people of this planet."

"EMP blast killed them where they stood," Doc said, nodding. "The right frequency would short circuit human brains like that."

Benson nodded. "About three million of the population survived by accidentally being in different forms of shelters or underground or inside something that shielded them. They didn't know it was coming.

Then I understood finally what we had seen. "But there was a second blast of energy following the first."

Benson nodded. "We got here ahead of that with a large enough fleet and got the survivors out of the way. What you witnessed was us putting them back."

"We arrived right behind the second wave?" Doc asked.

"About two minutes after it passed," Benson said. "Your shielding might have sheltered you, but it might not have either. Before you leave we will help you strengthen that shielding some for the future."

I looked at Benson and then nodded. "Thanks."

"So you go around rescuing planets full of humans?" Doc asked.

Benson shook his head sadly. "First time. But after this we will be more vigilant. Millions died down there before we got here."

He seemed actually deeply affected by that, so I tried to change the subject.

"So you know who seeded humans on so many planets in this area of the galaxy?" I asked.

"In every area of the galaxy," he said so matter-of-factly that it bothered me. "There are hundreds and hundreds of thousands of human civilizations in different stages of development in the galaxy. And no one knows much about the people or race who did it except that it took them over fifty thousand years to complete the task."

"Your planet was seeded as well?" Doc asked. "How come you are more advanced than any we have seen?"

"We were all seeded," he said, nodding. Again the floating map of the Milky Way Galaxy came into being in the air beside us. "My home planet is there, also called Earth."

A circle appeared around a dot a third of the way around the galaxy. Then another appeared around a dot I knew to be the sun we were orbiting.

"We are here at the moment," Benson said. "My area of the galaxy was seemingly seeded first, so civilizations that survived in that area are the most advanced. This arm of the galaxy was next, and as you move around in a clockwise direction, each human civilization gets more primitive."

"Wow," was all I could say.

Benson went on. "Our area of the galaxy has formed a large organization of aligned planets and about fifty worlds work together. That's why we could mount such a large fleet on such short notice."

"And no alien life at all?" Doc asked.

"Nothing above basic animal level," Benson said. "The Seeders, as we call them, not only seeded humans, but all the plant and animal life it would take to sustain human civilizations in the growth years."

"All the same on every planet?" Doc asked.

"All the same. Exactly."

I stood there shaking my head and just staring at the image of the galaxy floating in the empty meeting room air. I remembered how stunned I had felt every time we came across another human civilization during our first year exploring. But after a while I had just come to expect it.

Now I was feeling that same feeling again. It was just too much to grasp.

Humans always thought we were alone in the galaxy. It seems we were. But not in the way people back home might think.

Finally I shook my head and glanced at Benson, who looked almost haunted as he stared out the view port at the planet below. For some reason he clearly felt responsible for all those deaths.

I decided that our only hope in learning even more from Benson and his people was to confide in him.

"Could you focus this image in again to this area of space?" I asked, pointing to the floating galaxy.

He nodded and the floating image focused down and I pointed to a yellow star about sixty light years from this sun. "That's our Earth. And we are the only two that have this kind of technology at the moment."

Benson nodded. "I figured as much," he said. "On a couple of the planets in our area single explorers were the first out between the stars as well."

"So we are the first in this area of space," Doc said.

Benson nodded. "But after some of your visits to a few of the planets, I have a hunch those won't be far behind now that they know it's possible."

How in the world had he traced us? I was about to ask, but Doc got a question in first.

"So is your drive the same technology as ours?" Doc asked as I turned to stare back out at the damaged planet below.

Out of the corner of my eye I saw Benson shrug. "Just more advanced, but the same principles. If you want, I'll get some of our scientists to explain some of it to you?"

"You'd do that?" I asked, turning to Benson. I was again as stunned as Doc looked.

"Why not?" Benson asked. "We're all out here together. If we can't help other human civilizations, what's the point?"

Doc opened his mouth, but nothing came out. He was like a kid that had just been offered everything for free in a candy store.

I just shook my head and turned back to the view port. "So how do we help all those people down there?"

"We can't do much," Benson said. "At least not right now. Not until they get through the rebuilding stage, which the experts tell me is going to take a few hundred years at least."

"They have enough population to survive?" I asked.

Benson nodded. "More than enough. The Seeders only put a hundred and forty-four thousand humans on every planet and all but a few populations managed to keep going. There's almost three million alive down there still."

That exact number bothered me as well. A lot about this was bothering me, but I was in such shock, nothing was fitting together.

"You saved millions," Doc said. "That's impressive."

"And we didn't save many millions more," Benson said, his voice soft. "But the one thing we know about humans, we survive. And they will as well. The Seeders made sure we all had that trait."

Five

WE SPENT THE NEXT two months on the big ship, getting *The Lady* refitted with the most advanced technology and screens. Doc was like a kid let loose with a million new toys. He was soaking in more information than I could ever imagine and said that *The Lady* would be the fastest thing in the galaxy when he got finished with it. And the safest.

I was happy to hear that second part.

At first I spent about half my time with him learning everything I could about our new upgrades, especially the ones that were in my areas of expertise. The rest of the time I explored Benson's vast ship that he called *The R-12*. He said it was so new, rushed into service for the big evacuation, that it hadn't been officially named yet.

It turned out Benson was actually the captain of the thing. But it seemed the big ships of his world were run more like huge corporations and he was the Chairman of the Board. Everyone called him "Mr. Chairman" instead of Captain.

Their corporate system sure seemed to work. There had to be a thousand people on board of all ages and sizes. And many had families, including newborn babies.

"Nice thing about space," Benson said one day when I commented on the size of the ship while sitting in his office. "Materials are plentiful in space, power is limitless, and size is easy."

At first, after the second day we were on Benson's ship, there were still four of the original hundreds of the big ships in orbit around the planet. But as the month wore on the other three ships left when it became clear that there just wasn't anything more anyone could do to help the people on the planet. Those people down there were starting over in the bones of their own civilization. But it was clear even after a month that they would make it.

Benson said his ship had been picked to remain in orbit watching them for at least six months. He said it gave him and his crew time to settle in to their new ship.

At the beginning of the second month, I finally decided to flat ask Benson a question that had haunted me since we had been on board.

"Has anyone ever gone looking for the Seeders?"

He laughed. "Just about every day from every planet out there that has figured out space travel."

"And no trace?"

"Not one item left behind by the Seeders. Nothing. They seeded the galaxy with humans and plants and animal life that took over on each Earth-like planet in the Goldilocks zone of each sun and then seemingly vanished."

He tapped what I had come to learn was a form of computer panel on his desk, then scribbled something on a note pad that everyone on the ship seemed to have and leave around like paper. He then handed the pad to me.

"Doctor Jenny Sins, the top scientist in the department focused on the Seeders search. Go talk with her. Tell her I sent you."

"You have an entire department on the ship for this?"

"Every ship does. The question you asked is that important to all of us. We all know how the universe started. That's just science. None of us have a clue how we got here. Or for that matter, why?"

Six

I WAS STUNNED when I entered the Seeder Research area of Benson's big ship. There had to be fifty people working in the large room at different stations. I had no idea what they might be doing.

An elderly man with white hair and a formally white lab coat that seemed smeared with some sort of strawberry jam sat at the first desk closest to the entrance. He glanced up and then smiled with a perfect set of teeth. The smile made his face turn into a mass of loose flesh and wrinkles. "You're one of the explorers from this sector, aren't you?"

"I am. Doctor Vardis Fisher," I said, extending my hand. "But everyone just calls me Fisher."

The older man took my hand and shook it, but before he could say anything a woman's voice behind me said, "Well, Doctor Fisher, The Chairman warned me you would be coming."

I turned around to face one of the most beautiful woman I could have ever imagined wearing a white lab coat. And trust me, over the years I had imagined some pretty amazing women in white lab coats. Never met one, but imagined many.

"I'm Doctor Jenny Sins," she said, extending her hand and smiling and melting me down even more. The smile reached her pretty green eyes and made her seem radiant. She had long brown hair pulled back into a ponytail, and seemed to be about my height.

And she was my age as far as I could tell. I was far, far, far from an expert on anything to do with women. Most of them over the years had just ignored me, and to be honest, most of the time I had been too busy with research and work to pay much attention to them in return.

That didn't mean I didn't want a relationship some day. It just had never come to the top of the priority list.

I took her hand and managed to choke out that I was pleased to meet her.

More pleased than she would want to know I imagine.

She held my hand for a few seconds too long while she stared into my eyes, then nodded and let go and turned away. "Let me show you what we do here."

Somehow, following her and her flowing brown hair and white lab coat, I managed to pull myself back together a little. But for a climate-controlled ship, it was sure hot in this Seeder Research lab.

After introducing me to three others, we finally ended up in a large open office built into one wall of the large room. It was clearly her office and from it she could pretty much see the entire room.

She went around and sat behind a large desk that had seemed to have grown out of the floor. She indicated I should take the chair across the desk from her, which I gladly did. Anything at that point to stay talking with her.

She smiled at me again and once again the room got far too hot for normal climate control.

"Well, Doctor Fisher, ask me anything and I'll see what I can tell you."

"It's just Fisher," I said.

She smiled again. "Jenny."

I think I smiled in return and then tried to gather my wits enough to ask something logical about the Seeders.

"So is it clear where they started and where they stopped?"

She nodded and with a few quick taps on a control panel on her desk, an image of the Milky Way Galaxy appeared on the wall to the right.

"They started in this area," she said, and on the map an arrow appeared pointing at some stars on the outer edge of one of the spiral arms of the galaxy.

"They went around the galaxy clockwise, working inward and then outward, and ended in this area."

Again on the image of the galaxy another arrow appeared near the edge of the galaxy.

"Looks like they came into the galaxy," I said, "did their work, and then left."

She nodded. "Sure seems that way."

"How far into the core of the galaxy did they push?"

"Only as far in as human population could stand the radiation levels," she said. "But very few of those civilizations in close have survived for very long. Just too much going on that causes planet-wide destruction."

"Like what we saw below," I said.

"At a vastly more frequent and violent scale," she said. "The closer to the core of this galaxy, the nastier it gets for human life."

"So where do you think they went?"

"Andromeda Galaxy," she said without hesitation.

The map of the galaxy shrunk down to the size of a small dinner plate on the wall allowing the closest neighboring galaxies to be shown. "Looks like they came in from the Large Magellanec Cloud and then headed to Andromeda and all of its satellite galaxies."

I had to admit that it looked that way.

"Anyone go after them?"

"Not that I know of," she said. "Our ships don't have the speed to cross that much distance in a time that would allow us to catch them, even if we were sure where they were headed."

"So how did they do it?" I asked. "Are we all genetically the same? Everyone on every planet?"

"We all started from the same basic gene pool," she said. "And no degradation over time. Every planet's human and animal population started with the same genes, the same diversity, the same numbers. One hundred and forty-four thousand."

There was that number again. I just couldn't seem to make any logical sense out of any of this. There was something very clear I was missing. I knew that feeling. I just had to find what was between the obvious.

"Did they grow our ancestors or something?"

She shrugged. "Lots of theories on that. But what we do know is that it took them six major visits to each planet to accomplish what they did.

"Six?"

She nodded. "On the first visit they shoved some asteroid or something large into every planet that caused a vast extinction event of most of the animal and plant life that was natural to the planet."

"You're kidding?"

She shook her head no. "On the next four visits they covered each planet with new plants at first and then stages of animal life that quickly took over, including early primates."

"How long between that last animal seeding and the introduction of humans?"

"About three thousand years," she said, not even breaking into a smile.

I shook my head. "That is so against all science I know that it's scary."

She nodded. "We are convinced they also seeded historical evidence on every planet of both human, plant, and animal history."

I started to open my mouth to object, then realized where I was sitting and that I was talking to a beautiful human scientist I was very attracted to on a spaceship light years from my home and even farther from her home.

Historical evidence could be planted. Sitting here was very real and hard to discount.

I closed my mouth and just sat there.

"Hard to get a grasp on it all, isn't it?"

I laughed. "I imagine you grew up with this knowledge. I've just been coming to grips with it over the last two years that we have been out here exploring."

"That would be difficult," she said, a look of worry suddenly in her green eyes.

"I'm sure I'll come to terms with it," I said, even though I wasn't so sure. "So how long do you think the Seeders were in this galaxy?"

"Only about fifty thousand years," she said.

That number made no sense to me. "How many planets did they do this to?"

She shrugged. No firm count. "Maybe upward of a million. No one really knows."

"In fifty thousand years? Holy smokes, how many Seeders were there?"

She shrugged. "No one knows that either, but they just finished about five thousand years ago as far as we can tell."

That stunned me even more.

"How long have the races in your sector been in space?"

"About two thousand years," she said. "We just missed them."

"And they didn't leave a trace?" I asked, stunned at what she had told me.

"Just us," she said. "Just us."

Seven

I SPENT A LARGE AMOUNT of time over the next few weeks with Jenny, not only learning more about the Seeders, but about her as well.

She was single, had been married once and divorced when she left for space on this rescue mission. She liked my sense of humor and she loved my cooking. Luckily she was also an exercise buff.

She also made a room heat up around me with a single touch of her hand on my arm. I was smitten, of that there was no doubt. And surprisingly, she seemed to like me in return.

During that time Doc had also met a woman named Xin in the

engineering department. He had been spending a lot of time with her as well.

She was as tall and as thin as he was. She had bright brown eyes, dark skin, and a set of white teeth that could light up the blackest of nights when she smiled.

At the start of our third month on the big ship, I cooked the two of them dinner on The Lady. Jenny had to work to finish an experiment and get in her exercise, but she made me promise to save her leftovers.

Most of the conversation was about the new drive they were working on together. Even with my science background, I only understood about half of what they were talking about. Xin was as smart as Doc and they clearly spoke on their own level, sometimes only in half-sentences.

Clearly Doc had been soaking up all the technology of a civilization a thousand years ahead of us and having no problems at all. In fact, it seemed, he was helping advance it.

Somewhere in that conversation I asked Doc about The Lady's new speed. Both Doc and Xin lit up like high school kids getting to talk about their favorite science fair project.

"It seemed that because of The Lady's small size," Doc said, "compared to the huge ships like the one serving as our host, it is possible to go faster. Much faster."

"The size of the large ships takes too much energy to drive it forward through a trans-tunnel conduit," Xin said, smiling at me with those bright teeth.

Doc and Xin had come up with what seemed like a brand new idea of putting a trans-tunnel drive conduit through space inside of an already opened trans-tunnel conduit.

In other words, we would jump like we normally did and then while in transit open up another trans-tunnel conduit inside the original and jump again to increase our speed by some factor.

Doc and Xin were leading a research team on the idea and it seemed likely it could increase speeds to levels I didn't want to much think about. Doc and Xin both said The Chairman was behind them all the way and had been diverting resources to their new department.

"So how fast could we get home?" I asked.

I knew by our old drive that the time was about thirty hours from this place in space. We really didn't have much to go home for at this point except to report into parents that thought we were on a remote research station for a few years and out of touch.

"Six hours," Doc said, smiling.

"Six hours? That's a lot faster than thirty."

Doc smiled. "And if we can figure out a few more details, we might be able to open up many, many trans-tunnel conduits inside each other. If we figure that out we could be home from here in minutes."

"Wow," I said.

Then the two of them went off into the details and I was soon completely lost.

I picked at the peach cobbler I had made for dessert while I half listened and half watched them talk.

Then, suddenly, out of the blue, what had been eating at me since we came aboard finally came to the surface like a dolphin jumping.

"Culture," I said out loud.

Suddenly I could see all the details right there between the pieces of information just as I had found all the energy between matter and dark matter.

Both Doc and Xin stopped talking and looked at me with almost identical puzzled frowns.

"Xin, what planet are you from?"

"We called it Earth like most every other human planet."

I nodded. "And Jenny is from an Earth as well."

"So?" Doc asked. "Common term in all languages."

"Xin, your culture is pretty much capitalistic and democratic, right?"

She nodded, frowning.

"As is most of our planet and all of Jenny's and most of all of the planets we visited."

Now Doc clearly saw where I was heading. And he was frowning.

"How is that similar growth possible," he asked, "when one-hundred-and-forty-four-thousand humans were planted at a caveman level and left to develop over centuries?"

"It's not," I said, "without guidance."

"And who did the guiding?" Xin asked, frowning as well.

"The Seeders," I said, smiling and shaking my head at how really, really simple it was. "They're still here."

"So how come there is no evidence of them anywhere?" Xin asked, her frown covering her entire face. Clearly I was questioning something she didn't like to look at too closely.

"Oh, there is," I said, standing. "We're just not looking in the right places. Sort of like finding energy where there isn't supposed to be any."

I headed out the airlock and into the big hanger. I had to talk with Jenny.

Behind me I heard Doc shout. "Thanks for dinner!"

Eight

I PAGED JENNY once I got off the landing deck and she agreed to meet me in her office.

She showed up only a minute behind me, her hair pulled back and a white towel draped over her shoulder. She was dressed in her exercise clothes, a gray tee-shirt under a dark sweatshirt. She had on sweat pants as well and tennis shoes and still looked like she had a slight sheen of sweat on her neck.

She looked even more stunning that way than in her white lab coat.

"How was your dinner with Doc and Xin?"

"Over my head, mostly," I said, laughing. "Those two are really making some trans-tunnel breakthroughs with speed."

"How much speed?" she asked, suddenly very interested.

"They tell me that it could be factors of thousands of times faster," I said. "Maybe more."

"You're serious?" she asked, leaning forward.

I knew exactly what she was thinking. With that kind of speed, it would be possible to follow the Seeders.

"We can talk to them later," I said. "But they seem sure and The Chairman is backing them with a department full of help."

"Wow," she said softly, leaning back and wiping off her face with the towel.

"But we may not need that kind of speed to actually talk with the Seeders," I said.

Now she put the towel aside and leaned forward. "Too much to drink or just a new theory?"

"Nothing to drink and not so much a theory," I said, smiling at her.

"More just observed facts that the Seeders, at least some of them, never left."

She just shook her head. "Then where are they?"

"Right here. We're Seeders. Or we will be when we get a little more advanced."

She shook her head. "That theory has been considered and discarded a number of times over the years."

"No hard evidence, right?" I asked.

She nodded.

Even though your culture has pretty much invented everything needed to be a seeder. And you built ships that held over three million humans on short notice."

Again she nodded, a little more slowly.

"Looking for Seeders seems to have always been an outwardly directed hunt. But all of us looking didn't know where to look. One of my specialties is being able to see things where there isn't supposed to be anything."

"So what evidence have we all missed for a thousand years of studying this?"

I could tell I was on the edge of insulting her, but I kept on.

"Assume the Seeders are humans just like us. Any evidence would be human evidence."

"We've thought of that," she said. "I can give you some of the papers discounting those theories."

"Written by Seeders, of course," I said, smiling at her frown.

Then not giving her a chance to go on, I said, "Just look at the cultures. Now I know math, and I wouldn't want to even try to calculate the chance that every culture on every Earth-like planet would become over centuries of war and fighting democracy and capitalism based. Or that every planet would develop along the same exact lines and at the same speed."

"They were directed and helped," she said. "That's your theory?"

I laughed. "It's the only thing that explains anything I've seen in the last two years. They are still here and still helping and you've met them."

"And just how are you so certain of that?" she asked, clearly upset.

"Because I've met one as well."

I glanced up at the ceiling and said just slightly louder, "Am I correct, Mr. Chairman?"

At that moment Benson shimmered into view, pulled over a chair and sat down next to me.

"What gave me away?" he asked, smiling and ignoring the completely shocked look on Jenny's face. Her mouth was opening and closing and nothing was coming out, sort of how I felt when I first met her.

"A couple of slips," I said. "You knew about me and Doc ahead of time."

He laughed. "I had hoped you had missed that. Not sure what I was thinking on that."

"And the look in your eyes when you looked at the planet below. It was a personal failure to you."

He nodded, his eyes again filled with sadness. "It was. This area of the region is mine to watch and I just couldn't mount a rescue operation fast enough, get the right people on advanced enough planets involved quick enough, get them here fast enough. At least we saved some of those poor souls."

"How long ahead did you know what was going to happen?" I asked, my voice respectful.

"A good three hundred years," he said, his voice soft.

Then he looked directly at me and shook his head. "I knew from the moment you two started building your ship that you would be problems."

I laughed. "Your secret is safe with us. But I'm betting the problem is Doc and Xin, right?"

He nodded. "They are a rare combination and very advanced. This galaxy isn't supposed to develop that kind of speed for another two thousand years. It's about then we'll be needing help in Andromeda."

"Can't use a little help a little earlier?" I asked.

He laughed. "Seems like we're going to get it even if we don't need it, huh? But before then, we could use a little help here in the Milky Way. There are a lot of wars going on right now on the developing planets. And there's only so many of us to go around who stayed behind to help here."

"So how long until you teach us that teleportation trick and the long age secret?"

"You agree to become a Seeder and it might be a lot sooner than later," he said, smiling.

With that he smiled at Jenny's open mouth and stood. "I'll let you explain what just happened to Jenny," he said. "I've got a war to try to stop about fifty light years from here. We can talk tomorrow if you want."

With that he vanished.

I turned to face Jenny and her shocked expression. "I told you that you had met some Seeders."

"But..."

"That's all right," I said, laughing. "Let's go find you a shower and some dinner and we can talk about being recruited by the Seeders."

She let me lead her back toward her apartment without saying a word the entire way. I knew what it was like to have my entire world-view shaken up.

Visiting Earth-like planet after Earth-like planet had done that to me.

Watching Benson and his people save an entire planet of people had done that.

And meeting Jenny had done that to me as well.

She would recover, just as I had done, as soon as she realized that what she had searched for her entire life had always been right there in front of her.

IF SEX IS ALL A DREAM, THEN WHO CLEANS UP THE MESS

USA Today *bestselling writer turns science fiction on its head with a strange sexual journey through space.*

It seemed like such a simple cargo run between systems for Sabrina and her husband. No passengers, lots of great alone-time for a couple in love to enjoy each other. What more could they ask for?

But then the cargo rebelled. And you thought sex caused a mess before.

(Note: This story appeared once before in an anthology from a company that went out of business when the book appeared and only authors in the book saw the story. But I liked this story, so here it is again. This does have sexual content.)

SABRINA KNEW she was dreaming when the vast green ocean of smooth water that covered the blue planet rippled like someone had dropped a stone in it, obscuring her reflection, turning her from a young woman to one with wrinkles and shimmering skin. Then the ripples sucked back in on themselves, as they can only do in a dream, and the ocean became smooth again, showing her almost-true face in the reflection as she drifted through the air.

She had long hair in this dream, not short and cut tight against her scalp like she had kept it for the last four years. And her nose was shorter, just like she'd always wished.

And her hips were narrower.

And she was naked.

And hungry.

She could see fish swimming down under the water, smiling up at her with the face of her old history teacher back in college on Earth. She could eat one of them, but she doubted they would taste very good, since she had always hated his classes.

Ahead she could see a small island, with two large trees and a man standing under one tree. The next instant she stood beside him under the other tree, the shade making her nipples hard and goose-bumps form on her arms. The man was her husband, Lyman, and he was naked as well. He was taller than her, and looked even more handsome than she thought he looked normally. His blue eyes seemed to shine with extra light, and his dark hair blew in the breeze.

She realized she was hungry for him, not food.

"Sabrina," he said, "you're naked and dreaming and thinking about sex and I like your hair longer and your nose shorter."

"I know," she said as a giant fish six feet long flopped up on the shore between them. Instantly it started to smell foul, as if rotting and burning at the same time.

It stared at her with one fish-eye, as if daring her to get near it, to get past it to be near her husband. She tried.

And tried.

But no matter how hard she wanted sex with her husband, she couldn't get past the smell to be near him, to touch his body, to feel him inside her, to let him touch her shorter nose.

The stench became like a cloud, filling the air, choking her, forcing her to her knees. This was quickly becoming a nightmare, not a dream. She had to wake up.

Like swimming for the surface of a deep ocean, she fought to come out of the sleep. She blinked and opened her eyes, staring at the ceiling over her bed. Thank heavens she was awake.

But the smell was still there.

Rotting fish and burning trash.

"What...?"

She tried to push the dream back and clear the sleep from her head. She was in their private cabin on board their charter ship, the *Sweet Adele.* They were on a five day run to the colony on Daring Three.

No passengers this time, just three plastic crates of cargo. High paying cargo, but cargo.

They were the only two on board, but if there had been a major problem with the ship, or a fire on board, the alarms would have ripped her from the bed. Clearly the ship's sensors didn't think the smell was a major problem.

Lyman was beside her, tossing and turning as if in a nightmare. He had kicked the covers down to a point just below his waist, exposing his firm stomach, hard chest, and just a hint of pubic hair. She liked making love right after they woke up. And over the last four days of this trip, they had made love a lot. But just like in her dream, that smell wasn't going to allow her to pull that blanket even lower at the moment.

She grabbed his shoulder and shook him. "Lyman! Wake up. We have a problem."

He didn't want to come awake.

"Lyman!" She shook him really hard that time. "We have a problem!"

He jerked and opened his green eyes. "Wow, that was a weird dream..." Suddenly he sat up. "What's that smell?"

"That's the problem," she said.

By the time he had on his pants and shoes, she had put on a halter top, a pair of shorts, and her shoes and was headed out the door. In the main corridor that ran the length of their thin, long ship, the smell was even worse. It choked her and she covered her nose in a useless defense.

"Has to be coming from the cargo," Lyman said.

She turned and headed for the cargo bay with Lyman right beside her. With every step it felt as if she was climbing a steeper and steeper slope, slick with slime and goo. The air seemed to get thicker and thicker, holding her back.

Finally she stopped and leaned against the bulkhead, not wanting to breathe in any more of the foulness that surrounded her. The cargo bay door was still a good twenty paces ahead.

Lyman stopped beside her, his face white and sick-looking.

"What do you think is holding us back?" she asked, barely managing to keep the snack she had eaten before going to bed in her stomach. The smell was so bad now, it was as if she had put her head inside a rotting fish, and then stuck pieces of it up her nose.

"I have no idea," he said. "Let's get back to the control room."

She nodded. They had access to the security cameras there, as well as environmental suits. Together they turned around and headed away from the cargo bay.

Suddenly it seemed as if the air was pushing them, helping them move faster and faster down the corridor, as if they were in a strong river and the current was rushing them toward something. It was the strangest thing she had ever felt.

By the time they reached the control room at the other end of the *Sweet Adele's* long central corridor, the smell was very weak, the intensity of it gone from everything but memory. There was no way she would ever forget that smell. She may never eat another fish as long as she lived.

Lyman shut the door to the control room behind him, clearly hoping to keep the smell out. She doubted that would work. The control room was as comfortable to her as her living room in her parents' home when growing up. Over the past five years she and Lyman had made the *Sweet Adele* their home, making hundreds of runs in this area of space, ferrying passengers and cargo. And lots of strange things had happened, but never anything like this.

Usually they took on up to a dozen passengers, ferrying them from the Bank System to the interstellar jump hub in the Dawson System. But two days ago a man named Garren Fore had hired them to take three large crates to Daring Three, a small, out-of-the-way colony world. He had paid full price for the ship, and added a nice bonus for on-time delivery.

He had demanded that no passengers be taken, as if anyone was in a rush to go to Daring Three anyway. He just wanted the three crates to be the only thing aboard and was willing to pay for it, which had been fine with Sabrina and Lyman. They had both figured to spend the time catching up on work and making love. And for the first four days, they had done just that. It had been wonderful. Now it seemed their cargo wasn't going to be so trouble-free as they expected.

Lyman moved over to the communications panel and punched up the security images of the cargo bay. The three crates were no longer secured ten paces apart. Somehow, they had moved together and merged, as if they had always been one unit.

A pool of liquid covered the floor around them. The same color as the ocean in her dream. The thought made her shudder.

The rest of the cargo bay looked as if it had been sprayed with slime-like paste. It was going to take a long time to clean up that mess.

"How did they get like that?" She asked, staring at the three crates. Only she and Lyman were on this ship, yet something had moved those crates together.

"I have no idea," Lyman said. He flicked through five different images of the crates, looking at them from all sides. They seemed to be the standard, hard plastic crates used to ship everything from food to medical supplies. Except now they were fused together somehow, the hard plastic melted and reformed.

And there was no telling what was going to happen next. Maybe they should have been just a little more insistent on knowing what was in those crates before they started. But the money Fore had offered had been so good, it just didn't seem important enough to push the issue.

The smell in the room was starting to get worse. Clearly they were running out of time.

Lyman moved over and put the environmental controls on higher pressure for the control room. That would help keep the airflow moving outward from them. But she doubted that would do much good, either. It wouldn't be long until the entire ship was contaminated. They had to do something and do it quickly. But what? Against what? A smell?

Sabrina laughed at the thought. She moved to the communications panel and opened a channel to the communications hub on Banks Two. She knew it would be a very costly expense. Any sub-space conversation costs a lot per second, but this seemed to be the time to spend the money. Besides, Fore was going to pay for it if she had her way.

After the standard ten second jump-lag setting up the link, the officer on duty appeared on the screen. "Channel open and tied in. Go ahead *Sweet Adele*."

"We need to make an emergency call to a Mr. Garren Fore." She gave the officer Fore's communication link information and waited as the screen went blank.

Lyman moved over beside her and stood with his hand on her shoulder. Clearly he agreed with what she was doing. As far as she could see, they had no other choice. They had to know what was in those crates, so they could figure out a way to fight what was happening.

When Fore's weathered and wrinkled face appeared on the screen and saw her, he actually paled and swallowed. "Is there a problem with my cargo?"

"You tell me," she said, sending him the image of the cargo bay and the three fused crates. Then she said, "We can't get near them for some reason, and the smell is enough to choke a pig."

Fore looked almost angry, not at her, but clearly at himself. "This wasn't supposed to have happened."

"No kidding," Sabrina said. "So how about starting from the beginning and tell us exactly what is in those crates and what is happening."

Fore nodded. "Ever hear of Pelagic Prime?"

She nodded and glanced up at Lyman, who clearly had also heard of the planet.

"The water-world in the Bella System," Sabrina said.

"What is in the crates are a dozen Elucidations from Pelagic Prime," Fore said.

"Fish?" Sabrina asked. The idea stunned her.

"Very special fish," Fore said. "Telepathic fish for a scientist on Daring Three."

"Telepathic fish?" Sabrina almost laughed, but somehow managed to contain it. Around them the smell was getting worse.

"So what's going on in our cargo bay?" Lyman asked, leaning down beside her so his face was captured on the com-link camera.

"The Elucidations are mating," Fore said simply. "This wasn't supposed to start for another ten days."

"Wonderful," Sabrina said. "Smelly fish sex."

Fore said nothing.

"And they have the power to fuse plastic and hold us away?" Lyman asked.

"They do," Fore said. "Their telepathic and telekinetic abilities are fantastic when they are mating."

"Nothing gets in the way of their having sex, huh?" Sabrina said, not really wanting to believe what Fore was telling her.

"Basically, yes," Fore said. "It developed as a necessity on their home world. Their power is what we are trying to study."

"But they jumped the gun," Lyman said, "on the mating part."

"And smelled up our ship," Sabrina said.

"Your ship will survive," Fore said. "I'm more worried about you two."

"You want to explain what you mean by that?" Lyman said, his voice cold and angry.

Fore nodded. "In a short time the odor will overcome you. You will either suffocate or fall into a very, very deep sleep from which you will never wake up."

"So we just dump the cargo bay into space," Lyman said.

Sabrina agreed.

"Have you tried that yet?" Fore said.

"No, but I'm thinking we should."

"It won't work," Fore said. "Take a look at the images from the cargo bay. See the slime covering everything. That's a protective cocoon the fish create around themselves during this time. Blowing the cargo hatch would do no good, since that slime layer will hold them in place."

"Wonderful," Lyman said, staring at the screen and the image of their messed-up cargo bay.

"And how were your people on Daring Three going to deal with this problem?" Sabrina asked.

"They are prepared with environmental suits capable of keeping all outside influences out."

She glanced over at Lyman, who caught where she was going.

"We have a full environmental suite on this ship," Lyman said, "built for passengers who couldn't mingle with our normal air. Would that help?"

"Completely self-contained?" Fore asked.

"Completely," Lyman said.

They had added in the suite in case they needed to transport any medical patients. They hadn't had to use it yet other than as a normal passenger room.

"It would keep you alive for a while," Fore said.

"We can program the auto-pilot to take up a standard orbit when reaching Daring Three," Lyman said. "Can your people take care of your cargo at that point?"

"We can," Fore said, "if you give me the information on how to open your cargo bay doors from the outside when your ship arrives. My people will be able to remove the Elucidations to a safe place."

Sabrina felt even more shivers run up her back. "And just what are we going to be doing in the mean time?"

"Sleeping," Fore said, his dark eyes not blinking.

"And why would we be doing that?" Lyman asked.

"Because you will have no choice," he said.

"Oh," she said.

"How much time do we have?"

"Can you smell anything?"

"Yes," she said. Clearly Lyman's attempt to set up a counter-flow of air out of the control room wasn't doing much good.

"The effects of the Elucidation mating spreads as time goes on," Fore said, "and becomes far more intense. The quicker you get into that suite, the more chance you have of survival."

Sabrina had a very clear memory of trying to push toward the cargo bay in that smell. Fore clearly knew what they were dealing with. And there would be time later for making her believe there was such a thing as telepathic fish.

"Got it," Lyman said.

They both set to work as each minute the smell grew more and more intense.

It took Lyman ten minutes to completely program the auto-pilot for the approach and orbit of Daring Three, then place a back-up program in the computer, plus send Fore the details of how to override all ship's systems if necessary.

While he was doing that, Sabrina was giving Fore the codes for entering the cargo bay area from the outside, as well as three other hatches, and then she scrounged together some medical supplies and extra food for the environmental room.

The smell was choking the corridor outside the control room when fifteen minutes later Lyman shut and secured the double airlock door to the environmental room, locking them inside.

She sat down on the bed and looked around the small cabin. There was a closet, a sink and bathroom area, a dresser built into the wall, and a large bed. She could almost imagine the sound of the environmental systems behind the wall to the right recycling all their air. They were going to have to be in here for the next twenty-seven hours while the *Sweet Adele* set its own orbit around Daring Three and strangers boarded her and took off the fused crates.

In her entire life she had never felt so helpless.

Lyman moved over and sat down beside her. "Jailed on our own ship."

"Yeah," she said. "And by telepathic alien fish with bad body odor."

"And too much sex drive," he said, smiling at her.

"There can never be too much sex drive," she said.

"Why'd I know you'd say that?" Lyman said, putting his arm around her and holding her.

His body felt wonderful holding her. Until that moment she had not realized just how much this situation had scared her. For some reason, even jailed on their own ship, when in his arms she felt secure. And safe.

They sat like that for a few moments, then Lyman pulled away and headed for the bathroom. She stretched out on the bed, staring at the ceiling. The next twenty-seven hours were going to crawl by, that was for sure. She just didn't believe that they would be forced to sleep the entire way.

A few moments later Lyman lay down beside her and she snuggled against him.

"What are we going to do for twenty-seven hours?" she asked.

"Oh, I have a few ideas," he said, squeezing her, "for at least as long as we are awake."

She smiled at him, then kissed him hard to let him know she liked at least one of his ideas. And if this kept up, she planned on being awake the entire time.

Then she snuggled against him, feeling safe.

She closed her eyes, trying to make herself relax.

A moment later she was asleep.

And dreaming again.

This time she was alone in her dream, back on the island in the middle of the vast green ocean. There was no smell, no fish, and no Lyman. Just water and sand and palm trees.

She moved to the edge of the water, looking down at her reflection in the glass-like surface. She was naked. Again her hair was long, her waist narrower, and her nose shorter. When they got out of this fish mess, she was going to have to grow her hair long. Clearly these dreams were telling her she wanted it that way.

There wasn't much she could do about her hips though. Or her nose.

"Nice ass."

She turned around to see Lyman standing naked behind her.

"You fell asleep as well?"

"Seems that way," he said. He glanced around. "I like this island better without the smelly fish."

"Yeah, me too," she said, moving up to him and pressing her naked body against his.

If this was a dream, it was the best-feeling dream she had ever had. His body hardened against her, his skin seemed to almost melt into hers. Every inch of her skin felt alive under his touch.

His hand went to her breasts, stroking them, making them feel wanted and cared for, then moved to her crotch.

At his first touch the orgasm overwhelmed her as she lost herself in the movement of his fingers.

Back and forth, back and forth.

The orgasm was small and sharp and wonderful, like a sampling taste before a big meal.

Behind them the waves started to roll up on the beach, lapping at the sand, matching the movements of his hand and the pulses of her orgasm.

After her mind cleared, she kissed him hard, letting him hold her up as the ocean calmed.

Then she took him by the hand and led him back toward one of the palm trees where a blanket lay covering the sand. Even in her dreams she was being practical not wanting sand in places where sand shouldn't be.

She pushed him down on the blanket and started kissing him, first on his lips, then his neck, then his chest, then his stomach, then his hard penis.

Above them the clouds rolled over, rumbling and boiling like angry watchers as she brought him, and herself, nearer and nearer.

After what seemed like only a few moments, yet at the same time was just the right amount of foreplay, a full hurricane pounded down on the island, whipping the waves up over them, snapping off the palm trees, yet never touching them on the blanket.

She could feel he was about to come, so she intensified her actions with her mouth on him, and her own hand on herself.

As his first explosion filled her, she had her second orgasm.

The wind picked up the island, spinning it through the air over the ocean as wave-after-wave of orgasm shook them both.

On the blanket she could feel nothing but the pleasure of her own orgasm, and her husband's pulsing hardness.

The moment seemed to last for hours and hours, all wrapped into the seconds, confused as all time is in dreams.

Finally the island dropped back to the water and she crawled up and lay beside him, stroking his chest softly. He held her, not letting her go, making her feel safe and warm and cared for.

"I like this dream," she said to him.

"I like to dream with you," he said.

He rolled her over on her back and knelt between her legs. The waves on the ocean around them had just begun to calm when he slid inside her, pushing her down into the blanket and sand with all his weight.

Suddenly a massive wave crashed over them both as she lost herself in the feel of his hardness inside her.

He filled her with life, with energy, with desire.

The wave pulled them off the island and under the water, letting them float to the soft ocean floor as he kept pushing into her, then pulling almost all the way out, then pushing in again.

Above them the storm raged, but the ocean protected them, made them feel safe and secure and together as they made love.

She could feel her husband's movements getting more insistent, and at the same time another orgasm was building for her as well.

Under them the floor of the ocean pushed them upward, closer to the storm raging just above the surface.

Lyman moved faster and faster, pumping into her.

She met his every thrust, pushing back, harder and harder.

Until finally she was coming again, even harder and more intensely than before.

The ocean bottom shoved them into the storm, thrusting them into the air, up through the clouds, and into the intense blackness of space.

The pulsing of her orgasm matched Lyman's.

All the stars around them pulsed with her orgasm.

Bright.

Dim.

Bright.

Dim.

The orgasm lasted and lasted, seemingly for all time.

Galaxies crashed, and then were reborn around them.

Stars went nova, new systems were formed.

Finally, as the universe cooled and their orgasms faded, they spun back toward the ocean planet. They dropped onto the island, landing on the beach, on the blanket next to the calming ocean.

She looked up into her husband's face and had nothing to say. What could you say after sex so great that the Big Bang paled in comparison?

He moved off her and lay down on the blanket. "That was nice."

"Nice?" she asked, looking over at his smiling face. He was clearly teasing her.

"You want to see nice, try this," she said. She climbed on him, straddling his hard penis, letting it sink inside her once again, only this time she was in control. And she would take him to parts of the universe neither of them could ever imagine, even in this dream.

She started to move on him, her gaze locked on his, when suddenly he vanished.

She was empty, kneeling on the blanket.

"Lyman!" she shouted, the panic filling her heart.

"Sabrina!"

She could hear his voice, but it seemed like it came from a long distance away.

She stood and looked out over the glass-calm surface of the ocean. Why had he left her? Where had he gone?

"Sabrina!"

His voice carried over the water.

"Wake up!"

The ground shook and then she realized the dream was about to end. She didn't want it to end, but she had to see what Lyman wanted. Then they could come back. They had plenty of time before they reached Daring Three.

With that thought she opened her eyes.

Lyman was staring down at her, smiling. Beside him stood a strange man she didn't know wearing a protective suit of bright silver.

"Good," the man said. "She's going to be all right." He turned and keyed in a com-link. "All clear."

"Am I still dreaming?" she asked, her throat dry.

"No, you're not," the man said, smiling at her.

"We're in orbit over Daring Three," Lyman said. "We made it!"

"And the fish?" she said, sitting up with Lyman's help. Every muscle in her body seemed to ache.

"Being taken off the ship now," he said. "But we had to be awake to make sure we weren't taken with them."

"Taken with them?" she asked.

The man nodded. "I'm sure Mr. Fore will explain it to you when he arrives. Something about your minds being lost."

"Nice of him to mention that possibility," she said.

The guy in the silver suit laughed.

"So we were asleep and dreaming for twenty-seven hours?" She couldn't believe that was possible.

"Yeah," Lyman said. "Strange, huh? But wonderful." He smiled at her, a twinkle in his eye. Clearly he had had the same dream.

She could still feel the beach, the wonderful sex, the exploding orgasms. She leaned in and kissed her husband as hard as she could. She wanted him to crawl up inside her, to take them both back to the dream.

He kissed her back, hard and passionately, the real feeling of him now even more wonderful than the dream.

The man in the silver suit laughed. "I'll excuse myself now," he said. "The effect of the dream will fade with time."

Lyman broke the kiss and turned to the man standing in the door-way. "How long?"

"A few hours," the man said.

"Time enough," Lyman said.

She couldn't agree more. "Pull that door closed behind you."

The man in silver nodded. "Will do. Just no sleeping until we get the Elucidations to the surface."

They both laughed.

"Trust me," she said. "Sleeping is the farthest thing from our minds."

As the man in the silver suit pulled the door closed, she turned back to her husband and gave him a long, hard, kiss that was the start of a wonderful adventure in sex, time, and space.

Two hours later, as they lay there in each other's arms, she asked, "You ever thought of getting an aquarium for the ship?"

His laughter started them both all over again.

LOVE WITH THE PROPER NAPKIN

As two of the other stories in this issue, this story had a short flash of a previous life in a small newspaper magazine that died right after this story was published and very few people saw the issue or the story.

And since the story fits the theme of this issue perfectly, I wanted to bring it back to life here.

In romance terms, this is a "meet-cute" story. The alien helps.

HELLO, SERIOUS AND BEAUTIFUL woman across the bar.

The drink is my treat and the bartender will point me out. Remember that old joke about an alien being a piece of paper and the paper is making love to your fingers? Well, it just came true for you. Honest.

Don't laugh.

The bar napkin that this message is written on is an alien called a Roggen. It snuck into the human area through the supply section of the hotel here on the station. It has the ability to split itself into thousands of little bar napkins as a disguise to watch and study humans. At this very moment it is making love to your fingers and I can tell from clear across the bar you are enjoying it.

Have fun,

Anna
ps...hope you enjoy the drink.

———

Dear Anna,

Thank you for the drink and introducing me to these great little aliens. What planet did you say they were from? I'd love to go there some day.

Enjoying the feel,
Carla

———

Dear Carla,

The alien this is written on says your name is beautiful.

The alien said the sun their planet circles is called BAC 151. Damned if I know where that is.

He said he revealed himself to only a few of us so as to not cause too much commotion around the human section of the hotel. He also likes the beautiful dress you are wearing and I agree with him.

Trying not to stare,
Anna

———

Dear Anna,

What do you suppose would happen to the poor alien if I stuck him down the front of my dress? Can he turn himself into anything???? Oh, the possibilities are endless.

Thank you for the nice compliment and I hope you enjoy the drink in return.

Staring back,
Carla

ps...don't you think the bartender is going to mind passing all these notes back and forth?

———

Dear Carla,

The bartender loves it. I'm giving the poor kid twenty hotel credits every time. He'll deliver notes until doomsday for that.

By the way, the alien says doomsday for this hotel isn't for a few thousand years. Good to know, huh?

Notice the guy next to me. He thinks I'm weird because I talk to bar napkins. He should talk. His cologne smells like it was scraped off a well-used saddle.

Holding my breath and trying not to laugh,

Anna

ps...is that an empty stool there beside you?

———

Dear Anna,

I don't think you're weird. In fact, I kind of like what the bar napkins are doing to my fingers. Would you call it "paper sex?" Just the thought has me hot.

I'm afraid the seat next to me is taken by my current date, who happens to be off talking to some friends about something boring like rebuilding a cargo ship or something stupid like that. At least he doesn't make me sit and listen to it.

Stroking the alien,

Carla

———

Dear Carla,

Did you see that guy who just asked me to dance? God, what are they letting into the hotel these days? Some of these humans belong over in the other sections, I am sure.

The alien told me the guy only wanted to chew on my panties. I guess the alien can read minds or something like that.

He told me the guy next to me wants to do something kinky with ropes. Can you believe that?

Ask your alien a question. Go ahead. He'll tell you inside your head. No one will hear.

Go ahead and try it,

Anna

———

Dear Anna,

My God, you were right. I damn near fell off my stool.

I asked the napkin what your last name was and this little voice inside my ear said "Hartzell." Is that right????

Then I got afraid to write on one of them and the napkin said to go ahead. He said he loved it. I thought I had seen everything the galaxy had to offer. I guess not.

Gone completely nuts,

Carla

———

Carla,

I was watching and laughing.

Yes, my last name is Hartzell. The alien says you want to know if I'm a lesbian. I'm bi, just like you. (The alien told me...no secrets with these little white things around, huh?) Is this place getting crowded and loud or what?

Is your boyfriend ever coming back? I want to see this guy.

Waiting and drooling,

Anna

———

Anna,

The napkin says the fool who is my date (or I am the fool for being his) is over at a table by the dance floor talking to a young woman named Brenda Dare. The napkin says this Brenda is totally drunk, has already spilled two drinks and my date is staring down her dress.

I think he deserves her.

What do you think?

Annoyed,

Carla

ps...this alien napkin says my now ex-date hopes to get both me and Brenda in bed together. Hah! What a joker he is.

———

Carla,

How about me? In bed, that is?

How's that for forward?

The alien said my skin temperature went up a half degree just writing that first line. See what you do to me from clear across the bar. Damn, I wish these napkins were bigger and this bar not so crowded.

Wondering what your voice sounds like,

Anna

ps...the alien said he would be happy to be any size I wanted. Too bad I can't find a man that flexible.

———

Anna,

Why don't you come on over? If that jerk of a date returns, I'll tell him to take a walk out an airlock without a suit.

And bring as many of those napkins as you can. This alien told me that with enough of his old self in one place, he could reform quickly into something that just might please both of us. He showed me an image of what he would look like and I agree.

Stuffing napkins in my purse and pockets,

Carla

———

Carla

On my way.

I tipped the bartender a hundred credits to deliver this last note and let us take as many napkins as we can carry. The alien showed me the same image and I damn near melted off my stool. What do you say we head for somewhere much quieter and far less crowded, such as my room?

Almost too excited to walk,

Anna

ps...the alien told me that the more napkins we take, the bigger he will be able to reform. I've got an armload. How about you?

STAND FOR HOME

A Thunder Mountain Story

Keeping with the theme of this issue for the short stories, I wrote this western for an anthology that got no distribution. No one saw it. Plus I wrote it as a partial collaboration with another writer under a pen name.

With the permission of the other author, who had only added in the sex scenes, I removed the sex scenes, reverting the story back to my original draft which I was pretty proud of, to be honest.

So now, because of this magazine, I get to give this story, in its original form, a new life.

Cora and her husband, Harold, fight for their lives in the rough lands of the western wilderness. A story of survival and defending your home and family.

And as a side note, this story takes place in the same setting as my novels Thunder Mountain and Monumental Summit. In fact, both the reminiscences from Viola Lamb, a real pioneer, and the story opening, takes place on the Roosevelt side of the very real Monumental Summit.

"...it was while going up Elk Summit that Barney McGill died. He sat right down on his toboggan and died from sheer exhaustion, and three men were killed in a snow slide just two days before we went over. I saw their supplies beside the trail."

From the reminiscences of Viola Lamb
Thunder Mountain Gold Rush
Idaho, June, 1902

One

THE SOUND OF THE HORSES splashing through the cold, rushing stream echoed off the tall mountain walls and massive pine trees.

Cora Danials patted the neck of her gray mount and kept the solid old mare following the white packhorse being led by her husband, Harold. Through habit born from weeks of practice, she started to turn to make sure that the packhorse she was leading made it through the stream, then remembered that horse had gone off the edge of the trail just over the summit earlier this morning.

She shuddered and forced herself to take a deep breath as the scene again flashed through thoughts. It had been like a nightmare happening in slow motion.

The big, black beast slipped, tried to catch its footing on the snow-covered trail, then slipped again, dropping to its knees. The heavy packs seemed to pull it over the edge as it struggled to climb to its feet.

Finally, it just toppled over the edge, the look of panic and terror filling its round eyes.

She had only been five steps away, leading her own horse, but Harold said she could have done nothing to save the creature. The sound of the massive beast rolling and crashing through the brush for a thousand feet below them had been more than she could take. She had simply dropped to the snow and sobbed.

There was no getting to the supplies that had been on that horse. Somehow after a few minutes she had managed to go on, one step at a time, the fear of falling off the side of the mountain squeezing her chest every foot of the way.

Now, finally, they had reached the wide, safe valley floor. More than anything she wanted to stop, rest her back, wash her face in the snow-melt water, but she said nothing. Before crossing the stream Harold had said they had two more miles yet to go before stopping for the night. And since Harold was leading the four of them to the gold mining town of Roosevelt, no on argued.

Besides, the other two worked for Harold. He had hired them and their packhorses to get all the extra supplies into the Roosevelt area. He was to be the area's first postmaster. And, of course, he hoped to do a little prospecting on the side as well.

She wasn't sure exactly what she was expected to do when they got there. All Harold had told her was that the area was rugged and that he would need her help.

They crossed into a clearing, and the sun directly overhead warmed her back. She could have never imagined that a land could be so downright inhospitable and beautiful as this Thunder Mountain area. The snow-covered ridges and peaks towered so far over her head on both sides that she sometimes imagined that any moment the mountainside might simply fall and cover them all. Growing up on the rolling hills of the Midwest, she had never thought about real mountains. And now actually being in them terrified her more than she wanted Harold to know.

The meadow they were crossing for the moment felt safe and inviting, pushing back the memory of coming over the summit. How they had managed she had no idea. That had been the worst part of the trip so far. Much more frightening than swimming the horses across the angry Payette River, or wading through the mud that was called a trail above Warren. Now this valley floor and beautiful meadow was much better. And if Harold was right, the boomtown of Roosevelt was only ten miles farther on.

"Yo!" The shout came from behind her. "Hold up!"

She glanced around to see Danny, the youngest member of their four-person party, jump down off his horse and move into the brush. He was followed a moment later by Al. She hadn't trusted Danny and Al from the moment Harold had told her he had hired them. Danny seemed to always have a smirk on his boyish face, and Al had mean, dark eyes that seemed to spend far more time staring at her then was proper.

"Now what are they up to?" Harold asked. He dropped off his horse and headed back past her. Harold seemed at home in these mountains, which surprised her. He wasn't a big man, at only five-six, but he was strong and had a level nature and a wonderful smile. She had wished a number of times over the last few weeks that Danny and Al hadn't been along, so she and Harold could have enjoyed a naked swim in one of the lakes they had passed, or made love under the stars. But with two men she didn't trust so close, that hadn't happened, and she was frustrated more than she wanted to admit.

"Stay in the saddle and I'll find out what's going on," Harold said as moved past her.

She nodded, even though she had no intention of staying on this mount one moment longer then necessary. As he disappeared into the brush near the creek to follow the others, her stomach suddenly twisted into a tight knot.

Something was wrong, she could feel it.

Very wrong.

She slipped down off the horse, feeling the tight muscles in her shoulders and strain in her back. Stretching those aches was a welcome feeling after the hours of riding. She pulled her saddle rifle out of its holster and quickly checked it to make sure it was loaded.

Then moving as silently as she could while making sure her skirt didn't catch on anything, she crossed the fifty paces through the grass and brush in the meadow toward the shade of the trees. If something was going wrong, she was going to be ready. And if not, standing in the shade would be much better than sitting on the horse in the sun.

There was still no sign of the three men when she reached the dark area under a massive pine tree. Even the trees in these mountains seemed to tower into the air higher than she could have ever imagined. Nothing was small about this country.

She watched and waited, staring at the spot across the open area where Harold had disappeared, trying to calm the little voice in her head that said something was wrong. But with each passing second, the voice just got louder and louder.

Then finally she saw movement in the brush. Harold appeared first, followed closely by Danny and then Al.

She was about to let out the breath she'd been holding when she realized Danny was too close behind Harold. And Harold's sidearm was missing out of his holster on his hip.

She stepped back behind the tree and deeper into the dark shadows so they couldn't see her.

"Damn," Al said, his voice carrying over the open meadow, "where'd she go?"

"Call her," Danny said to Harold, his voice mean and nasty-sounding.

"So you can kill us both?" Harold said.

"You'll die this instant if you don't call her," Danny said.

She could hear Harold grunt in pain as Danny jabbed him with the gun.

She felt as if someone had slammed a fist into her stomach and knocked every bit of the wind out of her. She had never trusted those two, and now she knew why. They were going to kill her and Harold and take their supplies, more than likely to stake their own mining claim.

"Cora!" Harold shouted.

Cora glanced around. Behind her the brush was thick and the hillside was only a few hundred paces through it. The walls of this very narrow valley were so steep that there was no way out. She either had to go up or down the narrow valley along the stream. Going down was the little town of Roosevelt, but that was too far to get help quickly. Besides, she couldn't run and leave Harold with those two. He would be dead and buried before she could make the ten miles to Roosevelt and the ten miles back. And that was assuming there would even be help in Roosevelt. Harold had told her that often these boomtowns didn't have much law.

She had felt alone since they left Boise, and now that feeling was even more overwhelming. At this moment their lives depended on what she did next.

She brought her rifle up past the edge of the tree, holding it steady on the rough bark of the trunk. She had Al in her sights about three steps to Harold and Danny's right. Her only hope was to shoot Al. With luck that would startle Danny enough to give Harold a chance to escape.

She took a deep breath, as Harold had taught her to do in his hours of making her practice firing this rifle. She had complained when they were doing it, but all he had said was, "You never know when you will need to know how to fire a rifle in the mountains. Better to be prepared than sorry."

How right he had been, but she had a hunch he'd been thinking more about her shooting a bear or moose than a human.

"Cora?" Harold shouted again as Danny jammed the gun in his back.

It was clear they weren't going to wait much longer. They might decide to just shoot Harold and come looking for her.

Al turned so that his chest was facing her directly on.

The little voice in her head shouted, Don't think, just do it!

She fired.

The shot was much, much louder than she had expected under the trees.

Al spun to his right and slammed into the dirt of the trail. She couldn't believe it!

She had hit him!

Harold reacted instantly, twisting to the right and smashing into Danny.

Danny stumbled and went down as Harold turned and ran toward her.

She cocked another shell into the chamber and fired past him, her not-so-carefully-aimed shot kicking up dust beside where Al was fighting to climb to his feet.

Danny started to take aim at her husband's back.

She fired again, past Harold at Danny.

The bullet kicked dirt up on Danny as the bullet tore into the ground beside him.

Danny fired but missed Harold.

She fired again, moving her aim up slightly.

Again she missed, but not by much. The shot ripped a hole in Danny's sleeve.

Danny scrambled for the brush, firing wildly at Harold, but clearly missing. One bullet smashed into a branch over her head. She fired back, again sending dirt spraying up on Danny.

Harold reached her just as Al, holding a bleeding arm, managed to stand and stagger after Danny.

Breathless, Harold ran in behind the massive tree beside her and they hugged like it had been a year since they had seen each other. Never, in the years they had been together did Harold feel so good against her. She didn't want to ever let go.

He kissed her long and hard, then looked at her directly. In the five years they had been together, she had never seen Harold gaze at her with such pride and admiration. He gave her strength she didn't even know she had.

"Now what do we do?" she asked.

He nodded at the meadow. "We get the horses."

"Why not just head for Roosevelt and get help?"

He shook his head. "In this country, those supplies are everything.

There's no place in Roosevelt to replace them, even if we had the money."

They peered around the tree. She could see all seven horses were still standing in the open meadow, their supplies still in place. The gunfire hadn't seemed to bother the horses at all.

"You're not going back out there?" she asked, not believing that Harold would risk his life like that.

"I have to," he said, matter-of-fact.

She offered him the rifle, but he shook his head. "You're doing fine. I need you to cover me. How many shots do you have left?"

She thought for a moment, then said "Five."

"Use them carefully," he said, "and make them count."

He looked at her and she knew exactly what he meant. Kill Danny or Al if she had to.

She nodded.

"They'll come at us from the upper side of the valley," he said, pointing to the brush and trees to her left. "Watch there and I'll see if I can get my rifle and the horses. When I reach them, start moving down along the edge of the meadow and I'll join you near that big tree."

He pointed to a large pine at the lower end of the meadow and she nodded.

Without another word he ducked and moved back out into the meadow, staying low enough to almost be crawling through the grass and brush.

She held her breath and waited for the first shot to ring out, but only the sound of water rushing over rocks filled the valley.

She moved into a position where she could both watch what Harold was doing and at the same time the brush where Al and Danny had gone.

It seemed to take an eternity, but finally Harold reached his horse and stood, pulling his rifle from its scabbard in one quick motion before ducking back down.

She instantly felt better, with both of them now armed. Harold was a much, much better shot than she was.

She moved away from the massive tree trunk that had been her shelter and ran toward the next large pine as Harold started the horses walking slowly forward. Four mounts followed Harold's lead horse, but the other two just stood, grazing on the grass. She was glad that Harold made no move to go back and get them.

Ten running paces and she reached the shelter of the next pine. She paused to catch her breath and listen.

Nothing but the sounds of the stream and the distant cry of a bird.

She was about to step into the open again when a bullet smashed into the trunk of the tree just over hear head, sending bark everywhere. A piece hit her neck as she ducked. An instant later the sound of the shot filled every sense she had.

They had moved around and got almost even with her along the valley wall. She could barely see them on the other side of the thick brush.

She scrambled away from the pine as another shot cut through the air, followed by the sound of Danny laughing.

"Shut up and kill her," Al shouted as another shot kicked up dirt just in front of her.

She got to the shelter of another pine, brought her rifle up and aimed at the only piece of color she could see through the brush; a red patch on Danny's shirt.

Her shot cut through the air at the same time Danny fired.

Danny's shot snapped her skirt around her legs.

Her shot sent both Danny and Al scrambling for cover.

Behind her Harold had the five horses tied together and was leading them at a fast walk toward the tree.

She fired once more at a flash of color in the brush and heard Al swear in response.

With that she turned and ran, moving out into the open and across the lower corner of the meadow. She hoped that Danny and Al were so deep in the brush that by the time they got through it, she would be back with Harold.

Harold had the horses into the trees and she was about to join him when another shot rang out from behind and a bullet passed so close to her ear she felt the heat of it.

Harold returned fire, repeating round after round as she staggered past him and to the safety of a large pine tree.

"You all right?" Harold asked as he continued to fire one shot after another into the brush where Al and Danny were.

"Fine," she said.

"Grab my horse and start down the trail," he said. "I'll keep them pinned down and give you a few minutes head start."

She didn't like the sound of that, but didn't argue.

As Harold reloaded and kept firing, she yanked his horse into motion, giving the other four horses a moment to get up to speed, she started down the trail, working the speed up to a run. She forced herself to ignore the shooting going on behind her and focus on where she was putting each step on the rough trail. The last thing they needed was for her to fall and twist an ankle or get trampled by the horses.

For what seemed like an eternity she kept going, pushing herself as her lungs burnt for breath in the thin, mountain air. Each step was a success, each shot behind her twisted her heart. Harold was back there in a fight and she was running away. Yet she knew that wasn't the case. She was saving what future they had in these mountains.

Suddenly the firing stopped.

The valley now echoed only with the thuds of the horse's hooves on the dirt and her heavy breathing.

She pushed on, her skirt held high in one hand, her other hand pulling on the horse. She had no idea how far she needed to go, but if she had to, she'd run all the way to Roosevelt.

Suddenly the sound of Harold's rifle filled the air again. Five, then six shots, the sound echoing between the tall peaks and fading.

She knew what he'd done. He'd stopped firing, letting them think he'd moved on. And then when they moved, he opened up on them again. It would slow them down some, if he hadn't killed them.

Again the silence of the valley replaced the echoing gunfire.

One foot in front of the other. Running as fast as she dared but not so fast that Harold couldn't catch her easily.

She figured she had gone at least two miles when she finally heard over her own labored breathing the words she'd been hoping to hear.

"Cora, slow up!"

She slowed and stopped, then turned to see Harold running down the trail, rifle in hand. He was also winded, but otherwise looked unhurt.

She hugged him, both of them too winded to even try to speak at first. Even with both of them covered in grime and sweat, he felt wonderful and she again didn't want to let him go.

Finally she leaned back and looked him in the eye. "Can we make Roosevelt?"

"Not before dark with pack horses," he said. "You were moving them just about as fast as they could move. Danny and Al both have their own mounts and could catch us easily, even with Al hurt."

"So what do we do?" she asked, the fear twisting her stomach even tighter than it had before. Getting into another gunfight with those two was not what she wanted.

"We hide the supplies and horses for the night," Harold said, "then tomorrow go for help on foot."

"Hide them?" She glanced at the steep walls of the valley twenty paces to her left and the just-as-steep walls of the other side of the valley a hundred paces away. This valley was like being in a narrow hallway. There was no place to hide anything.

"There's a worked-out mine about a mile ahead up a side canyon," he said. "We'll be safe there for the night."

She looked at her husband, clearly showing the shock she was feeling. "How do you know that?"

He laughed and took the lead of his horse from her hand. "I bought it while we were in Boise," he said. "I wanted to surprise you."

"Well, you did," she said.

Harold just laughed softly and gave her a hug.

It took them less than fifteen minutes to get to the place where a faint trail led off up the canyon. Harold pointed it out, but then kept going on forward on the main trail toward Roosevelt. Finally another hundred paces ahead, where the trail crossed the stream he led the horses through, then doubled them back into the water and headed back upstream.

Core knew what he was doing right away. He was trying to let Danny and Al, who wouldn't be that far behind them, think they had kept going down toward Roosevelt.

Since it was getting late in the day and the sun had already vanished behind the tall mountains above them, by the time Danny and Al discovered they hadn't kept going, it would be getting too dark to backtrack. Right at that moment she was even prouder of her husband than she had been before.

The mine was about a half mile up a very steep-walled side canyon. There was a small, windowless log cabin, clearly not more than a few years old, built against one rock wall, and mine tailings scattered down the hill toward the small creek that wound through the bottom. The cabin sat up high enough to give a very clear view of anything below.

"What's farther up the canyon?" she asked as they dismounted on the flat area in front of the cabin.

"The guy who sold me this claim told me it was too steep to climb," Harold said. "No way out."

She looked at the cabin and then back down the narrow valley. "I was afraid you were going to say that."

"Don't worry," he said. "We can defend this place if we have to." He pointed up the steep hill above the canyon. "They can't come at us from that direction, so the only way to get up to this cabin is the way we came. And with us on the high ground here, they'd be fools to try it."

"So where's the mine?" she asked. She could see all the rock tailings that had been dug out of the hill, and the small log cabin, but no mine opening.

Harold moved over to the large main door and pushed it open, then pointed inside at the blackness.

"That's the opening to the mine?"

He nodded. "Hold on to the horses for a moment and let me see what we have."

She pulled her rifle from its saddle holster again and made sure it was fully loaded, keeping an eye back down the quickly darkening small canyon while holding onto Harold's horse.

The sounds of the stream were faint here, and only the cry of a hawk circling overhead disturbed the intense quiet.

After what seemed like an eternity, Harold came back out and took his horse from her, telling her to stand guard. He then led the horse toward the door, stopping just outside. He unstrapped the packs and pulled them off to one side, then led the horse into the cabin. The sound of the hooves on the board floor echoed louder than she wanted any sound to be from them.

She moved over and sat down on a large rock, intently studying the brush and trees below the cabin, expecting to see movement at any time.

Nothing.

It was almost completely dark by the time Harold got the last horse inside and the packs pulled inside as well.

"I'll watch the trail," he said. "Go take a look at our place, but close the door so the light doesn't show."

"Four sweaty horses in the house," she said. "You sure know how to make a home attractive to a woman."

He laughed. "I do my best."

She was surprised when she got inside the cabin. It was a large room, with a table and counter on the left side that served as a kitchen area. A large bed filled the right wall. The space was lit by a warm, orange light from a lantern sitting on the table. On the wall directly across from the main door was another large door, slightly closed. She opened it to see the mine tunnel disappearing off into the mountain. The horses were tied in a line in the rock and wood shaft, facing her. Each had some grain and water and they seemed happy enough for the moment.

She glanced around the cabin again. It felt warm and cozy and safe. She liked it at once.

Back outside in the dark it took a moment for her eyes to adjust, then she moved over and sat down beside Harold on the large rock overlooking the small, narrow canyon. "So what happens now?"

"We get a good night's sleep," he said, putting his arm around her and pulling her close.

It felt good. "What about Danny and Al?"

"This is a pretty hidden canyon, and I doubt they even know it's up here," he said. "Plus, another half hour and there won't be any moving around in the brush. Too dark"

"Plus Al's hurt," she said, thinking about how she had shot him. She didn't regret doing it at all. She just wished she had killed him.

"Yeah," Harold said. "And I think I winged Danny as well."

"Good," she said. "And in the morning?"

"We deal with them."

She didn't like the sounds of that, but had no other plan at all.

They sat there in the dark, watching and listening, Harold's arm around her, holding her. Even with two men chasing them, right then she felt safer than she had since they left the midwest. She was going to love this little canyon, she knew. But first they were going to have to defend it.

Two

THE NEXT MORNING, when it was just barely light enough to see the edge of the rock area in front of the cabin, Harold gave her a hug and they went out in front of the cabin to get ready.

Even with him beside her she had never felt so alone. There was something about these mountains that just made a person feel small. Yet behind her she had something to defend and she was going to do it in any way possible. Last night they had made that cabin their home, and she wasn't going to let anyone take that home from her if she had anything to say about it.

She had on her coat and gloves and she had put a blanket on the ground near the cover of the big rock she had sat on the night before. From the blanket she had a clear view of the narrow canyon, but anyone coming up would have a hard time spotting her.

Harold was about ten steps to her left, also lying down.

She had her saddle rifle and extra shots, plus an extra thirty-thirty Harold had bought. Both rifles were loaded and ready. Harold had his rifle and his sidearm. It was going to take a lot to get past them.

Harold had said that if Danny and Al were smart, they would take the two horses they had, and the supplies on them, and get out of the valley at first light. But she didn't think Danny and Al were the type to run. Especially with a woman getting the best of them yesterday. She knew they were coming. It was only a matter of when.

The sun still hadn't quite reached the valley floor yet when she heard them coming long before she saw them. Danny's voice echoed up the small canyon, and the sound of brush cracking on the trail was like small shots.

She forced herself to stay as low as she could, keeping the rifle focused on where the trail came out of the trees and brush about a hundred paces below the mine tailings where she lay. The rifle felt comfortable against her shoulder and this time when she fired there were going to be no doubts at all.

Danny appeared first, on his horse, staring up through the shadows at the cabin and mine tailings. She knew he couldn't see her if she didn't move.

She took a deep breath and made herself wait while Danny got farther into the open.

"Take Danny, I'll take Al," Harold whispered just loud enough for her to hear.

Danny stopped and Al appeared, his arm wrapped in a white cloth that had a large red spot on it. Danny had a cloth wrapped around one shoulder as well, which must have been where Harold hit him.

They both stopped and stared up at the cabin, staying on their horses.

"You think they're up there?" Al asked, his voice carrying.

She took a deep breath, focused all her attention on Danny's chest, aimed slightly high to adjust for firing downhill, just as Harold had taught her, and fired.

Harold fired an instant behind her.

The sound of the shots filled the canyon and Danny flipped over backwards off his horse.

Al spun to his left and also fell off his horse.

She reloaded and fired again at Danny as he hit the ground. Her second shot missed, kicking up dirt near his head, but her third shot caught him square in the shoulder, the sound a thickening thud mixed with the echoes.

Harold had also fired twice more.

The sound of the shots echoed into the distance and then was replaced by the silence of the canyon. Both horses had moved off twenty paces and stopped. The two men lay there in the rocks and dirt, neither moving. Danny looked dead, twisted in an unnatural way, his neck sideways and his head turned too far to the side. If her shots hadn't killed him, it looked like the fall had.

Al she wasn't so sure about. If he moved, she and Harold were both going to fire again, since Al still had his rifle right near him.

They waited, trying to see any movement at all from either of them. The silence was almost too much to stand.

Finally, after what seemed like half a day, just as the sun was starting to reach the two bodies, Harold said, "Let's take a look."

Keeping her rifle cocked and ready, she moved down the slope beside her husband, easing up on the two men who had tried to kill them.

She had been right about Danny. He was dead as dead could be, his neck twisted like a chicken's. Harold checked closer to make sure Al was dead. He was. It looked as if his shot caught him right under the arm and plowed into his chest.

She let out a deep sigh and hugged Harold. For the moment they were safe and for the first time on this trip that felt wonderful.

Three

IT TOOK THEM the next hour to unpack Danny and Al's horses,

then hook rope around the dead men's arms and have their horses drag them up the canyon.

There Harold spotted a sharp rock outcropping and they stacked the two bodies there. Then Harold went back and got a stick of dynamite. He lit it and tossed it into the rocks above the two.

The explosion did exactly what he had planned it would do. The rockslide buried them so deep no animal would ever find them.

An hour after that they had carried water up to the cabin and she had started some boiling for washing. It was going to take her a long time to wash off the grime from those two, and even longer to push the memory back.

When Harold came in, she turned to him. "Think anyone will miss them?"

Harold stepped up and held her tightly. "You heard the stories in Boise. If a local didn't show up to winter there, people thought the mountains got him."

Cora nodded and walked with Harold back outside. The air was warm and the faint sounds of the stream were a nice background. It calmed her instead of scaring her.

She looked up at the peaks while holding onto the man she loved more than anything. The mountains had nearly got her. If Harold hadn't taught her how to use that rifle, if she hadn't had a strong will to survive, she might have slipped off that trail like that horse, or let those two men shoot her.

Harold was worth fighting for. This new home was worth fighting for. She knew that now. A home was never worth much unless you stood and defended it.

"Regrets?" Harold asked, sounding very worried.

She hugged him and then kissed him hard. "No, I'd do it all over again if I had to."

He sighed in relief and buried his face in her hair. "Can I ask why not?"

She laughed and kissed him again. "I have you and I have all this."

She gestured toward the fantastically beautiful tall mountains towering over them. "That's more than I could have ever hoped for."

He looked at her for a moment, as if her words had surprised him. Then he bent down and kissed her, gently, as if it were the first time.

Which, in a way, it was.

THAT LOST RIDDLE

A Poker Boy Story

Since this issue has all sorts of new features in it, including some sex in science fiction, I figured why not continue to be strange. So I have decided to include my Fiction River stories, one per issue, until I catch up to Fiction River. From that point, it will be one every other month.

I am proud of the stories I had in Fiction River and I wanted them to be here as well as the months go along. "The Lost Riddle" came from the very first volume, Fiction River: Unnatural Worlds.

Poker Boy finds himself taken by his boss, Stan the God of Poker, to Reno on a surprise mission for the team of superheroes. But little did they know that the puzzle wasn't the mission, but something far stranger.

OUT OF THIN AIR I heard Stan, the God of Poker say, "Knock, knock."

It wasn't a bad joke. It was how he asked to come into my private doublewide trailer up in the woods in Oregon. It seems that when Stan teleported, he couldn't just drop in outside and then use the door to actually knock on. But he was a God, and my boss, so I supposed he could do just about anything he wanted, even make bad "knock-knock" sounds in thin air in my living room. I was only Poker Boy, a lowly superhero. Not much I could say about it.

I pushed aside the cold fried chicken I had been eating while sitting on my old green couch and watching the evening news out of Portland. "Come on down."

Stan appeared beside my couch and glanced around, shaking his head. He always did that when he came here. He just didn't understand why someone with as much money as I had (and as many superpowers) would keep an old, 1970s-furnished doublewide trailer in the Oregon Coastal Mountains, even if it was within a half mile of a casino.

It was the green couch and chair and shag carpet that did it for most people, not counting the fake wood paneling on the wall. I figured if I waited long enough the styles would come around.

The last time Stan had come here he suggested I put a felt painting of dogs playing poker on the wall. I was considering it.

My girlfriend and sidekick, Patty Ledgerwood, aka Front Desk Girl, couldn't figure out why I liked this place either, now that she knew how much money I really did have. I discovered I had a vast amount when Patty made me go through it and lay it all out for her. I hadn't bothered to total it in a decade. I just kept adding to it.

Even though I could afford a couple dozen mansions, I liked this old place, even though Patty said it smelled of faint mold and pine trees. It reminded me of my early days as a poker player and superhero. The old furniture and funky smell sort of kept me grounded. I said that to Patty once and she just shook her head and muttered something about how the place kept me actually in the dirt.

Needless to say, we spent most nights in her wonderful and very large apartment in Las Vegas, furnished with the best and most modern furniture, thick carpet, and views of Las Vegas that were tough to beat.

I usually only came up here while she was working and I was waiting for a tournament to start. Instantly jumping from Las Vegas to the mountains of Oregon was one of the many advantages of being able to teleport.

Stan didn't say anything after his disgusted look at my place. He was wearing his standard tan sweater, tan slacks, and loafers. He looked so nondescript, he could blend in anywhere and no one would notice him. I had a hunch if he stood in my trailer long enough, his sweater and slacks would turn 1970s green.

I took one more bite of the cold chicken leg, then stood and headed for the coat hanger beside the front door to get my black leather coat and black fedora-like hat. They were my superhero uniform that helped make me Poker Boy.

Stan only came here to get me when something was going wrong somewhere. Never a good sign. So the coat and hat were going to be needed for something very soon.

"So where to?" I asked as I slipped on my coat.

"You look like you need a drink," he said.

"What?" He knew I didn't drink. Never had and I sure couldn't see myself starting now.

I was about to say something about going back to my chicken and news when Stan jumped us to position beside a large white-marble pillar with people walking by. There were slot machines and a nearby restaurant. I could feel the power from the casino around us flowing into me.

The air smelled of prime rib and faint cigarette smoke. It took me only a second before I realized we were on the second floor, the mezzanine level, of the Eldorado Hotel and Casino in downtown Reno, Nevada.

To my left along the interior mall-like area was the Silver Legacy Hotel and Casino and beyond that the Circus Circus Hotel and Casino.

This interior mall area stretched for a very long three blocks and must have a couple dozen restaurants, shops and gift stores along its wide corridor. It was a nice place considering Reno's weather in the winter, allowing people to move between the three casinos without ever going outside.

I had always liked this interior mall and the feel of it. Some people said it reminded them of a huge cruise ship, only without ocean views and people getting seasick.

I glanced around. No one had noticed our arrival so I figured Stan had jumped us into a blind camera area.

"Back with your girlfriend in a moment," Stan said and vanished, leaving me alone.

I had no idea what the problem was, or why we were in Reno, but if he was going for Patty when she was still at work, I knew it couldn't be good.

I stepped away from the stone pillar and let my poker senses take in everything around me. A few people upset at losing, and one couple went past not happy, headed for the Silver Legacy. I caught part of a conversation about how the guy was angry with his wife flirting with another man. He was telling her so in no uncertain terms. It wasn't hard to miss, even without extra poker senses.

But I could sense nothing that would cause Stan to jump us to Reno and into the Eldorado.

Across from me was a brewpub full of younger patrons laughing and drinking. I'm not sure exactly when I started thinking of adults around age thirty as younger, but I did. Since I have been told that as a superhero, I have basically stopped aging at thirty even though I am over forty, I have no idea how jaded I was going to get by the time I reached one hundred.

Or two-hundred-plus like Patty. She still hadn't told me her real age. She just shook her head and said it didn't matter every time I asked. She didn't look a day over thirty either, but knowing there might be a few hundred years in age difference sometimes actually bothered me.

I felt a hand on my shoulder and the calming sense of Patty's touch. That was one of her super powers and I loved it.

And her. More than I wanted to admit to myself at times. We just fit together in seemingly every sense.

I turned around to look into her beautiful brown and very worried eyes. She was still dressed in the uniform of the MGM Grand Hotel front desk. A black skirt, white blouse and MGM dark vest with their hotel emblem on the right side.

Her long brown hair was pulled back tight as she kept it while working.

"Any idea what's going on?"

I shook my head, keeping my poker senses on full. I didn't quite have a "Spider-Sense" like Spider-Man did in the comics, but I had a pretty good ability to know when danger was approaching and right now I could feel nothing.

"Where is Stan?" I asked.

"He went to get Screamer," she said.

"This can't be good," I said.

She nodded.

A moment later Stan appeared next to the stone column in the dead camera area. Screamer was with him looking just as puzzled.

Screamer had the ability to touch someone and get into their mind and their thoughts. He didn't have a distinctive look, more like Stan with the ability to blend into just about anywhere. He usually wore old jeans and a sweatshirt with the UNLV logo on it and tonight was no exception.

Screamer had gotten his name from his ability to put images into other people's heads. He often worked for the police and could put images so bad and so real into a suspect's mind that he could make the most hardened criminal scream. What he did could never stand up in a court, but he had solved a lot of crimes over the years.

And he had helped this team save the world a few times as well.

"All right," Stan said. "Let's go."

He turned toward the short staircase leading down around an ornate fountain and into another section of the Eldorado Hotel and Casino mezzanine level.

"What are we doing here?" Screamer asked a moment before I could.

"Going for a drink," Stan said, his voice almost lost in the sounds of the multiple fountains.

Patty just shook her head and I followed them, keeping every sense I had on full alert. And that was a lot of senses, so many in fact I hadn't named them all. But the one right now I was trusting the most was my danger awareness sense.

And it was flat coming up blank.

We went past a gift shop, down another short flight of stairs, and toward what looked to be a combination bakery counter, restaurant on the right, and bar in the back on the left, tucked against the wall.

Suddenly Patty said, "Sherri."

Her uniform morphed into a black dress, her hair flowed into a perfect shape around her head, and black high heels replaced her tennis shoes she wore while working.

All in the space of one step.

I had no idea she could do that.

None at all.

And we'd been together now for a few years. If we survived what-ever we were facing, we were going to need to have a talk about her powers.

"Oh, no," Screamer said as Stan headed toward the bar past the huge counter full of very tasty-looking pies and cakes and cinnamon rolls coated an inch deep in white frosting. The entire area smelled of fresh bread, making my stomach rumble and me wish I had taken a few more bites of that cold chicken.

"Come on, Stan, why?" Screamer asked.

Stan said nothing. Just kept walking.

Stan reached the bar and pulled up a barstool. Screamer sat on his left, Patty took the spot on his right, and I took the spot next to Patty.

I could still sense absolutely nothing wrong, but from Patty's sudden change and Screamer's comment, they were clearly sensing something I wasn't.

And that scared me more than I wanted to admit.

We sat there in silence with the sounds of the distant casino echoing faintly in the background. It must have only been a few seconds, but it felt like an eternity.

The bar was a normal wood bar, pretty wide, and even though it looked rustic, it was polished as smooth as glass. We were the only customers sitting at it. There were three empty stools to my right. It felt really, really strange to be sitting at a bar. I just never did this.

Bottles of varied booze lined the ornate back bar, blocking most of a mirror that made the area seem bigger. The top of the back bar was also a rustic ornate wood as were all the decorations on both sides of it.

This kind of bar could have been in any one of a thousand places. It actually seemed a little out of place with all the desserts in a huge counter ten paces behind us. It felt like it belonged more in an Old West saloon in a movie. A long ways from the smell of baking bread and ringing modern slot machines.

I was about to say something when a door into a back room swung open and a stunning woman emerged carrying a few bottles of vodka. She wore tan slacks, a white short-sleeve blouse, and an apron with the Eldorado Hotel logo on it. Her pitch-black hair was pulled back tight and I caught a glimpse of a dark tattoo on her shoulder and upper arm.

And she might have been one of the most beautiful women I had ever seen.

"Hey, Stan," she said, smiling in a way that could knock down just about anyone with its radiance.

Now my warning senses were going off and going off strong. If she was sitting across from me in a poker tournament, I would be very, very careful even being in a hand with her. She had power. More than likely she was a superhero or maybe a god.

But I caught no threat at all of danger from her. Just warnings about her power.

Stan nodded and didn't return the smile. "Sherri," was all he said.

She put down the bottles, wiped her hands on a white bar towel and slipped a bar napkin in front of Stan.

"Great seeing you," she said. "I suppose Mom sent you and your team here."

"She did," Stan said, again nodding.

"Well, I appreciate you coming," she said, smiling. "Thanks."

I wanted to shout out *"Mom?"* but then realized the only woman who could order Stan, the God of Poker around, was Laverne, Lady Luck herself. I now had a hunch suddenly who I was facing. I hadn't known going into a previous mission that Lady Luck had a daughter, so I suppose it shouldn't surprise me that she had two.

Or more for all I knew.

When this was over, I really needed to ask some very pointed questions about the family trees of some of my bosses.

Sherri put a bar napkin in front of Screamer, the smile turning a little sad on her face.

"I miss you," she said.

He only nodded just slightly, his gaze holding hers.

She missed him?

What in the world was going on? If this Sherri was Lady Luck's daughter, having both Stan and Screamer have strange reactions to her didn't seem like much of a good start to whatever we were facing here.

She shrugged and moved to a spot in front of Patty. She slid a napkin in front of her and smiled, the smile actually reaching her eyes. "Patty Ledgerwood I presume. I've heard so many good things about you and your work. You look stunning."

Patty smiled, blushed, and said nothing.

Sherri slid a napkin in front of me, her smile turning to something I couldn't read.

"So this is the famous Poker Boy I've been hearing so much about."

I kept my poker face and only nodded slightly.

She laughed. "You people sure aren't much for idle conversation, are you?"

"We're here," Stan said, his voice very controlled. "I don't understand why you are here, or what you need from us."

"I work here," she said, smiling. "I have now for about four years.

Moved here from the Atlantis Casino. I worked there for ten years. Remember?"

She looked at Screamer and he just nodded.

She went on. "The management here keep offering to make me a bar manager, but I like keeping my hand in the drinks and talking with the customers."

Even though Stan had the best poker face that existed, I could tell he was surprised by that. If this was Lady Luck's daughter, I was surprised as well.

"And I didn't ask you to come here," Sherri said. "That was Mom's idea. She said you four might be able to help me with my lost riddle."

Stan said nothing, Screamer just shook his head, and Patty just smiled softly and stared at her.

Wow, was there a lot of history between these four. Clearly it had all happened long before I was born. And since Stan had been married to one of Lady Luck's daughters, more than likely he wasn't pleased to see this one either. So it looked like this was going to be up to me to figure out what she was talking about.

"So what's the riddle that your mom thought we could help you solve?" I asked. "And I assume I am talking with a daughter of Lady Luck. Correct?"

"Sherri," she said, giving me that beaming smile that I had no doubt melted some of the icing off a cinnamon role in the case behind me.

"The Queen of Clubs," Screamer said, his voice soft.

"Dear husband," Sherri said, a slight touch of hurt going to her eyes, even though she kept smiling. "You used to not like anyone calling me that name."

I was trying to deal with the fact that Screamer had been married to Lady Luck's second daughter at one point. Now all I had to do was figure out why Patty had a problem with her and I might have a clue what was happening.

"So the riddle?" I asked, pulling her attention back to me. "What's so important about it?"

"It's lost," Sherri said over her shoulder to me as she moved fluidly down the bar to pour some drinks for a waitress that had come up to the waitress station in front of a bar well.

Sherri seemed to move faster than anyone I had ever seen, yet the waitress never once looked up. After only a moment, which I guessed had something to do with her slipping slightly out of time to do the drinks, she came back toward us wiping her hands on a bar towel. "Can I get any of you a drink?"

My three teammates sat silently, so I said, "Sure. Bloody Mary mix with no vodka."

"Celery?" she asked as she moved to the well again.

"Nope," I said.

As she finished my virgin drink, I studied her. Not one sense of danger, nothing from her, and she wasn't blocking me in any way. In fact, I wasn't getting that much sense that she actually had many powers at all, even though I assumed she was a god. Could it be that Lady Luck's daughter was only a superhero like I was? That didn't seem possible.

As she put the drink on my bar napkin and again wiped off her hands, I asked her a simple question. "What's so important about finding or solving the riddle?"

"It will lead me to a second key holding the Four Faces of Janus."

"Oh," was all I said.

Stan just shook his head.

Screamer sort of snorted in disgust and Patty again didn't move.

We had already gone into Elysium, the capital of the ancient race of the Titans, to rescue Sherri's sister, Helen the Queen of Hearts, who had gone there to get one of the keys that held the Four Faces of Janus.

Supposedly, legend says that when the four keys are combined, they will open the time lock and allow the Titans to return to their rightful place in time and space. Or something like that. Mythology and facts were sometimes hard to tell apart for me these days. I really, really needed to ask more questions about all this.

One thing I did know, the Titans' major city existed in the same location as Las Vegas, only many, many eons in the future. So their coming back to this time would be a pretty large problem that I doubted anyone wanted to face.

"Are all your sisters looking for a key?" Stan asked.

"Sure," Sherri said. "It's sort of a hobby for all four of us. We're giving the keys to Mom for safekeeping when we find them. We have no intention of bringing them together, especially after seeing the wonderful city the Titans are living in."

"And you four have only found the one key, right?" I asked, trying not to be too stunned at Lady Luck having four daughters. I really,

really, really needed to talk with someone about who had been married to whom and who was a child of whom.

"Just the key that you four helped my sister return with from Elysium," Sherri said, "although I feel that if I could find the lost riddle, I would be able to retrieve the second one."

Her bright smile had now vanished and she was clearly thinking about her problem. And I had zero idea what she was talking about when she said a "lost riddle" and my glowering team was sure no help at the moment.

"How can a riddle be lost?" I asked, slightly fearful I was walking into some trap.

Sherri just shrugged. "Lost in time, maybe. Never written down. Lots of ways a riddle can be lost."

"So it's just called "The Lost Riddle?" I asked.

She nodded.

Now all four of us were just looking at her as she headed back down the bar to the right to serve drinks to another waitress who had arrived at the station there.

"Someone want to tell me what's going on?" I asked.

"I think she's finally lost it," Screamer said, shaking his head sadly.

"She's fantastically beautiful," Patty said. "More than I even remember."

I stared at my girlfriend for a moment, realizing she hadn't been mad at Sherri, she had just been in some sort of fan-girl state with her.

"She's serious, all right," Stan said. "And she's as sharp as she ever was, trust me."

"So why do you hate her so much?" I asked Stan.

He laughed, softly, something I rarely heard him do. "I don't hate her. My wife, her sister, thought I fell in love with Sherri and caused all sorts of problems that led to me leaving Helen."

"You didn't?" I asked. "Fall in love with Sherri, that is?"

Again Stan just laughed. "I don't even really know her, to be honest. And Sherri's been married to Screamer here for a very long time."

"Over two hundred years," Screamer said.

"And she left you?" I asked.

"No, I left her," he said. "When I acquired this new power and could read all her thoughts every time I touched her. Staying together wasn't fair to either of us until we figured out how to deal with it all. We never got a divorce. It's been ten years now."

"So you are still married?" Patty asked, looking at Screamer, who nodded.

"Oh," was all I could say again. I had been working with this team now for some time and seen the inside of Screamer's mind more than I wanted to think about, and he had kept all this blocked from me. Clearly he had gotten pretty good at walling off parts of his own thoughts.

"She's so beautiful," Patty said, almost sighing. "We have to help her."

Now both Stan and I were shaking our heads at my girlfriend. Everything was screwy about this assignment and it was making me slightly annoyed. No one was in danger, I wasn't saving anyone, not even a dog, and I wasn't playing in a poker tournament. So far all I could see was a complete waste of a perfectly good evening.

Sherri again came back to a place in front of us. "Will you help me?"

"A couple more questions," I said. "So you need this riddle to find the Janus key?"

She shook her head. "I know where the key is at."

"So why do you need the lost riddle?" I asked, almost afraid of the answer.

"Stan," Sherri said, smiling at my boss, "If you wouldn't mind taking us all out of time for a moment, I'll answer Poker Boy's question."

He shrugged and an instant later the sounds of the casino stopped around us. And so did everyone and everything else.

I loved being able to step between an instant of time. One of my abilities was also to take myself and others out of the natural time flow. But Stan was a ton better at it and wouldn't have to strain to hold this for hours.

Sherri pointed to a place in the air behind her and an image like a three-dimensional movie appeared.

"That's new," Screamer said, looking puzzled.

"Learned it from you, actually," Sherri said, smiling at her husband. "It's a projection from my mind."

"I can't do that," Screamer said.

Sherri looked almost longingly at her husband. "We both have our new powers. I would love to talk later."

I was starting to get the clear understanding that she wasn't a god, but only a superhero like three of us at the bar. And she was learning new superpowers as she went along just as all superheroes did.

She turned back to the image she was projecting in the air as everyone in the casino remained frozen in their instant of time around us.

The image showed what looked like an old ghost town from a height of about a thousand feet in the air.

"Virginia City," Sherrie said. "South and slightly east of here."

The view came down and focused on some old buildings, then flew inside like a bird going through a wall. "Yellow Jacket Mine," she said. "Part of what most people think of as the Comstock Lode."

The traveling view of the image floating in the air went straight down, under some water and finally came into a flooded huge cave.

Sherri went on narrating the tour that was coming from her own mind. "The Yellow Jacket Mine broke into this huge cave and couldn't contain the flooding and had to retreat. No pump could ever clear it. It's over three thousand feet under Virginia City and the water temperature is over one hundred and fifty degrees."

At the bottom of the huge cave was a stone stand with a clear glass bubble covering it and protecting what looked like a very old key from the water.

"That's the second Janus key," Sherri said, her voice wispy.

"Why couldn't these stupid keys ever be hidden above ground?" I asked, shaking my head. My warning senses were going off big time just looking at that key so far down underground and underwater.

"So why the lost riddle?" Patty asked, the spell of Sherri's beauty clearly now broken by the little tour underground.

The image of the submerged cave vanished and Sherri just shrugged. "Not a clue what the riddle does," she said. "Or even what it is or why it's lost. I just know it's attached to this key in some fashion. And we don't dare touch the key until we understand what the riddle is all about."

I just shook my head. "This is a very strange hobby you and your sisters have."

Sherri laughed high and light. "Don't you think I know that? But after you guys helped my sister get the first one, Mom thinks it would be a good idea to get all four of them and get them really protected. So she's trying to help us."

I didn't want to say that having a key three thousand feet underground in one-hundred-and-sixty degree water wasn't already pretty protected, but what did I know? Lady Luck thought this was important for some reason. And she was Stan's boss and Stan was my boss, so by that reasoning I thought this important as well.

Stan let us slip back into the normal stream of time and the noise from the restaurant and distant casino slammed back into use like a tidal wave. And the wonderful smells from the restaurant came back as well, making my stomach rumble again.

"Okay," I said, trying to grab onto something that made sense in all this. "Tell me when I get this wrong."

Stan and Patty nodded and Sherri and Screamer just sort of looked at each other.

I ignored them and started trying to check off what I knew. "The four keys each have one side of the face of Janus on them. Right?"

Sherri and Stan both nodded.

"Apart they keep the doors locked, the Titans in the future, and the war between the Gods and the Titans stopped," Sherri said.

"Got that," I said. "And no one wants to start that war again."

"Exactly," Stan said.

"Does this Janus still exist?"

"No," Sherri and Stan said at the same time. They clearly did not like that question and I made a note to ask what happened to him at a later date.

"So why would anyone associate a riddle with a key?" I asked. "And then lose all record of the riddle? I've only been around this superhero and god world for a short ten or so years and I've come to realize that all you folks have very long memories."

"Good question," Stan said. "But the battle between the Gods and the Titans was long before any of our times. Long before Atlantis."

I nodded to that. I still have never asked exactly how many years all this stretched back. Another question for another time in my history lesson.

I leaned back and just stared up at the back bar. No one else said a word and Sherri moved back down the bar to serve another waitress with a tray full of dirty glasses and a long order of fresh drinks.

I tried to ignore my rumbling stomach and my desire for a cinnamon roll and just think.

On the back bar were a number of bottles of Jack Daniels, all with different colors and added names on the labels.

There were other bottles of the same brand, but different types back there as well. I stared at that for a moment and then it suddenly hit me what we were dealing with.

Being able to put things that made no sense together to make sense was one of my super powers, it seemed, and if I was right, I had just done it again.

"Stan, could you call Laverne to come and help us?"

He nodded and a moment later, without him moving, Lady Luck appeared, taking the empty stool to my right.

In my fondest dreams as a poker player, it never would have occurred to me that I would be sitting at a bar with Lady Luck herself.

Sherri finished the orders and came down the bar as her mother appeared.

"You want your usual, Mom?" she asked, smiling. Clearly the two of them had a good relationship.

"Later, honey," Lady Luck said. "First I want to hear what Poker Boy has to say about all this."

For the first time in a long time I wished I actually drank. I had a hunch I could use one right now. I took a deep breath and turned toward one of the most powerful gods that existed and asked the question I needed to ask.

"Do the keys have names besides one, two, three, and four?"

Lady Luck looked at me for a moment, then laughed and said, "I don't know, but I know who to ask."

She vanished.

I decided I could breathe again. It felt good.

I took a sip out of my Virgin Bloody Mary as Patty touched my leg and sent a calming sense through me.

"You think the key might have a name?" Sherri asked, clearly puzzled.

Stan just smiled and Screamer sort of smiled. They had seen me ask these kind of questions before that got right to the heart of a problem.

"Just an idea," I said.

It seemed like forever, but then suddenly Lady Luck was again sitting at the bar beside me.

And she was laughing.

"The one you all retrieved from the Titan's city under Vegas was called *Mystery*. The two that have not been found yet are called *Enigma* and *Dilemma*."

Then Lady Luck smiled at Sherri. "The one you found, dear daughter, is called *Riddle*."

Sherri clapped her hands together and did a little dance as she laughed and smiled. "It's not protected!"

"I'll get it," Lady Luck said, smiling at the joy her daughter felt.

She vanished and then a moment later reappeared holding the key that had been under three thousand feet of Earth and very hot water. She wasn't wet at all.

She started to hand the key to her daughter who held her hands up. "I don't want to touch it. Just get it safe and sound."

"I will," Lady Luck said.

Then she turned to me. "Once again, Poker Boy, thank you. And to your team as well for taking the time to help with this."

It never got old having Lady Luck thank me for helping her.

Never.

Then Lady Luck looked down the bar at Screamer and smiled. "Talk to your wife. If you two got back together, she'd make a great addition to this team."

"Mom!" Sherri said, but Lady Luck was already gone.

For the first time Stan really laughed. And hard. And that also was a rare thing as well for the God of Poker.

"Great seeing you again, Sherri," Stan said. "And listen to your mother. We could use you." Then he vanished.

Sherri actually blushed.

Patty smiled at Sherri and then at Screamer and touched my leg. "Come on, I'm dressed up and I think I need to do some dancing."

"Dancing?" I asked, looking at her. In all our time together she had never told me she liked to dance. Ever.

She winked at me and squeezed my leg just a little higher and I got the message. "Oh! *Dancing*."

A moment later we were in the living room of her apartment in Las Vegas, leaving Sherri and her husband alone in a crowded casino in Reno.

"Wasn't she beautiful?" Patty asked as she headed for her bedroom.

"Sherri?" I asked. "She was all right, but not as beautiful as you by a long ways."

"You sure know how to say the exact right things," Patty said.

She looked back over her shoulder at me and smiled a "dancing smile" as her dress vanished, leaving her totally naked and me totally speechless.

NEIGHBORHOODS

'Neighborhoods' got started one night when I was watching the Mayor of Chicago talk about how they were going to stop the violence. Then, in the same newscast, the Congress of this country couldn't even pass a simple gun registration bill. So, I had the thought that the only way to save the kids was to either get them out of the neighborhood or make their neighborhood bulletproof. I have a five-year degree in architecture, so I used that background to design a building that would work for security, schools, power, green living, and support the people living there without creating even more Projects that had failed in the past.

Then, to give the people a decent chance to make it, they had to have their homes paid for completely, so their money went to education and food, and so much more. So I used the idea of crowdsourcing both the initial investors behind the scenes and out front for the actual purchase of the apartments built like modular homes.

Scary fact is that this would work, even though it seems like science fiction at the moment. Especially with a couple of floors as wind tunnels and solar on the sides. This would be a money-generating building without any rents, or just low tenant fees.

May 2016

THE NEWS COMING over the big screen television made Big Ed's Bordeaux turn almost bitter to his taste. He set the glass aside in disgust and kept watching.

Heat shimmered outside the cool, air-conditioned comfort of his recreation room in his penthouse apartment. Around the apartment the city of Chicago spread out, stretching along the lake in both directions as far as anyone could see.

Big Ed sat in his big leather chair, especially designed for his six-four height, his feet up, his slippers kicked off, as he watched the Chicago evening news, watched the carnage of innocent children being killed.

Nothing seemed right. Everything in the world felt off, out of kilter for him and this city he loved. Outside, all over the city, all over the world, everything seemed to be coming apart.

Guns couldn't be controlled, kids died in the streets every night, and the summer was predicted to only get hotter. And heat meant more innocent people dead.

It made him angry, sad, and disgusted.

Something had to be done, but not a soul could figure out what that should be.

All anyone could do was watch.

He tried another sip of his wine. The bottle had cost him almost seven hundred dollars, yet the flavor he had savored a few minutes before now twisted his stomach as story after story flowed across the screen in front of him.

Like most nights, the mayor came on, vowing to stop the violence, but he had been saying that now for years and he hadn't managed to do a thing about it. It just got worse.

Not one person knew what could be done. No one had any ideas at all. And Big Ed had no doubt that if this continued here and in the other cities around the country, the world would soon follow.

Something had to be done, but here he sat, comfortable in his large apartment above Lakeshore Drive, watching just like a regular person watched a baseball game from the stands as others struggled with the problem and failed over and over.

Big Ed considered himself anything but regular. Just the idea of "being regular" made him angry. So far in his life, he had proven he was far, far from regular. A self-made millionaire, he prided himself in being unique in everything he did.

Even in casual evening clothing, he looked elegant. No one ever caught him messed up or even underdressed in the slightest. He took pride in that, and the art collection that covered his walls, and the collections of books and magazines stored in special rooms throughout the penthouse.

He took pride in being able to help artists establish themselves, help start-up companies get going, support the right charities and projects to make the world better.

A perfect dresser, a collector of fine art and books, wealthy beyond his dreams, his life should have been full. He should have felt satisfied.

Yet now, sitting here in the luxury of his apartment, he felt empty and helpless. On this hot evening, he could do nothing but sit and watch the news once again report the latest sad death of some child with real promise, gunned down without a reason.

Behind him, the door to the media room banged open. He didn't bother to turn around. It could only be one person, his good friend and attorney, Carl.

Carl dropped into the overstuffed leather chair beside him. Carl was just about as opposite to Big Ed as any person could get. He normally never got out of jeans and a dress shirt with rolled-up sleeves. His dark hair seemed to never be combed and was always too long. Always.

Big Ed always looked dapper and perfectly dressed compared to Carl. Yet Big Ed admired Carl for his intense brain and drive and ambition. The two had been friends for decades, and their tastes in women and art were the same.

Carl was the only one allowed to come into Big Ed's private media area without even knocking. They were that close.

"Someone's got to do something about this," Carl said, pointing to the news.

"I've been sitting here thinking the same thing," Big Ed said. "But what?"

Carl only shrugged as Big Ed once again tried his wine, then pushed it away in disgust. Nothing was going to seem right, taste right, *feel* right from this moment forward. Not until he tried to solve the violence problem this city (and every city in the country) faced every single day.

He was tired of being just a normal person who sat and watched.

Disgusted, he clicked off the news and stood, heading toward his office that occupied one corner of the entire floor of the building.

Over his shoulder, he said to his best friend. "Come on, we've got a city to save."

"Oh, oh," Carl said. "Here we go."

Big Ed just smiled as he kept striding toward his office. Every time Carl said that about one of his hare-brained ideas in the past, they had worked just fine. But right now Big Ed just wished he had an idea.

Any idea.

No matter how crazy it might seem, any idea was better than sitting there, watching children die, and doing nothing.

June 2016

One month later, Carl finally uttered the words Big Ed had been expecting. "You can't do that."

"Sure I can," Big Ed said, smiling at his friend who had already downed two bottles of water since coming into Big Ed's climate-controlled office twenty minutes before. Outside it was another one of those days, with temperatures coming close to a hundred and the humidity at the same level. The city was bracing for yet another night of violence, while at the same time trying to get people to cooling shelters where possible.

Sweat dripped off Carl's face, and his t-shirt was stained.

"A brutal Chicago summer day," was what one newscaster called it.

"No, this time you really can't," Carl said. "I know how much money you have, and it's not enough to even build one of those complexes. In fact, just starting it would break you, and you'd be out on the streets. Then I'd have to house and feed you, and your tastes are a tad bit beyond my budget."

Carl pointed at the very rough building model taking up the middle of the room. Actually, it was four buildings reaching forty stories into the air. Each one covered four city blocks, and was connected every ten levels over the streets by corridors.

When it was done, it would be completely self-contained and would furnish its own power, heat, water, everything. Nothing would be on the two lower floors, but restaurants and shops would be included on third and fourth floors.

Big Ed had worked with an entire firm of architects over the last two weeks, ever since he'd woken up with this idea in the middle of the night. The model of the prototype alone, in rough form, had already cost him just under twenty thousand to be rushed to this point. But seeing even the rough model, he now knew it would work.

He stared at the model for a moment, then turned to Carl. "You got the investors lined up for the engineering companies?"

"Four brand new engineering companies are incorporated and off the ground," Carl said. "Investors are coming a little slower. You're going to need to talk with some of them, give them the old presentation of whatever this is going to be."

"Oh, I will," Big Ed said, smiling. "They hear the possibility of exclusive patents and long-term sales income, and they'll be on board and pouring in money, no problem at all."

Carl snorted and said nothing.

Big Ed knew that reaction from his friend. A "I'll believe it when I see it" reaction. It was typical from Carl—but Big Ed had always delivered in the past. "How about the land companies?" he asked.

"All set up," Carl said. "Investors are coming a little easier into those because there's land under their investments. Not good land, but land."

"It will be great land in time," Big Ed said, pointing at the model of the large four-building complex. "How soon can we have the first four-block site under wraps?"

Carl shrugged. "We got top realtors on it as I speak. Maybe a month for the first full four-block site."

Big Ed nodded. "Hold off on any of the old factory grounds that will take major EPA cleanup, since they'll take some time. But try to have a few new corporations ready to buy those up when you can. We want every possible block of land we can get on the South Side."

Carl again only nodded and took another long drink of his water. Then he said, "Getting you in as an investor on these companies is not cheap. I'm buying in as well, and we're both in a few million at this point as minor investors. But that's going to go up as I set up more and more companies."

"By the time it's all said and done, I don't plan on us spending much of our own money on each complex," Big Ed said. "And that money should be returned in time if we do this right. Who knows, we might even make a profit."

"What else?" Carl said, laughing.

"And after we get the first couple complexes up and people see how this will work, others will want to buy in. I promise you that."

Carl snorted again, shook his head, and dropped down into an office chair. He put his tennis shoes on the coffee table and took another long drink of water from the bottle.

"So, explain it to me," he said. "Because I sure can't see how you'll build a complex of forty-story buildings without more millions than you and I could scrape together on a good day."

"We get investors to only build the frame and utility cores," Bid Ed said, smiling. "Like a big shell of a building with the public and business areas in place."

"That alone is going to take some major investors," Carl said, shaking his head, "to even get that far."

"Not the way this will be designed," Big Ed said, smiling. "Investors in green energy, green living, are going to be jumping at the chance to toss money at the building when they see the plans."

"So why only build the core structure?" Carl said. "Why not build the entire thing, walls, apartments, and all?"

"Because," Big Ed said, smiling and staring at the model, "we want the people on the streets to have their own place to live, a place that is safe. And it needs to be paid for as well, otherwise this won't work."

He walked over and took out a square from one side around the thirtieth floor and held it up for Carl to see. "Modular construction."

And then Big Ed showed Carl everything he was planning. Slowly and carefully, as much for Carl as for himself, working to see if in his explanation he could find even one thing that might stop this idea.

And after an hour of talking and Carl asking questions, Big Ed couldn't think of one major problem that would stop his idea.

Neither could Carl.

September 2016

Big Ed was feeling the excitement. Things were getting closer and closer.

They'd had their share of problems in the last two months, all the while keeping the idea tightly under wraps.

Zoning had been a huge issue, and if this had been any other city and any other area of the city, the politics might have gotten in the way. But Big Ed knew who to get on the side of the building to move things along, who to get to approve permits, who to get to just look the other way. He bribed no one, but he made sure that the violence in the streets and the deaths that still happened every day would be blamed on anyone who didn't support this project.

And when that hadn't worked, Carl and his massive firm of lawyers had swooped in and just plain overwhelmed anyone who wanted to stop the plan with more paperwork and filings and suits than anyone could possibly handle.

Just over two months after explaining it all to Carl, the architects had delivered their full model to Big Ed's office in his penthouse.

On any new idea that came out of the design and engineering sections of the buildings, Carl had filed patents for Big Ed and all the investors of the varied companies.

There were now more than sixty patents pending for various ideas developed in the buildings, the electrical systems, the wind tunnels, the solar arrays, the water systems, and the rest. These would be buildings like no other buildings in existence, and that took new inventions along the way to accomplish.

Big Ed had no doubt that if this worked, he and Carl and the investors would be very rich just from a few of those inventions.

Outside, the early fall weather was giving the city a break from the hot nights of violence, with a touch of chill in the night wind off the lake. But it was only early September, and there were still many hot nights remaining before they were through this summer of death.

And the newscasts made it clear that the violence still continued.

Through more than fifty holding companies and more investors than Big Ed wanted to ever think about, Carl had bought enough square blocks of the city to hold twenty-five of the four-block square complexes. All but two had the zoning worked out. Six were on the sites of old steel mills and factories, so they had cleanup issues that would take a year or more, but those would be ready in time if this first complex worked as planned.

And Carl had the multiple corporate structures together for the next steps in the process. The important step, as far as Big Ed was concerned.

During the last two months, another of their companies, again with the help of start-up capital and investors, had bought and refurbished an entire manufacturing plant on the lower South Side. It was being retooled right now, with production starting within another month.

It was so exciting to be so close to getting started, Big Ed almost couldn't sleep. And that was very rare for him. Normally, things didn't bother him much. But this project was different, very different. He was risking everything on this, and he knew it.

He and Carl stood staring at the model delivered by the architects.

"It sure doesn't look like much," Carl said, shaking his head.

Big Ed had to agree. It didn't look like much at all. Just skeletons of four buildings. The third and fourth floors of all four buildings were connected over the streets, then again on the tenth and eleventh floors, then again on the twenty and twenty-first floors, and then on the top five floors.

Those connected floors were solid and had walls on the outside so he and Carl couldn't look inside the model. But the rest of the building looked unfinished. Plus with no structure but pillars and a central utility core, all four buildings looked like they were sitting on two-story-high stilts. The entire thing was just massive framework and utility areas and elevators and staircases. You could see completely through any open floor.

"You have the contracts for the tenants done?" Big Ed asked, staring at the model.

"They'll be on your desk by the end of the week," Carl said, "and we can go over them. My office is double-checking them now, assuming the funding works."

"Will the contracts stand up to challenge?" Big Ed asked, never taking his eyes from the model.

"They will," Carl said. "And all the security regulations have been researched and opinions given. We're clear under the Jobs Act. And all zoning restrictions have long since been cleared as well on all the sites." Big Ed didn't hear a moment of hesitation in that answer, so he nodded and turned to his friend. "Construction on Complex A starts in four weeks. Still think we can keep a lid on this once we start building? A lot of people now know what we're doing."

"All we can do is try," Carl said, shrugging. "But not that many have the full picture yet. We have all the land purchases well hidden under layers of companies, and the production plant ownership is so deep, no one is going to trace it to you or me or anyone connected to any of these sites. Besides, this idea's so crazy, who's going to believe it, anyway?"

Big Ed laughed and went back to staring at the ugly frame of the model. Carl did have a point.

Crowdsourcing a building to save the world was just flat crazy.

April 2017

In the end, it cost Big Ed just under sixteen million of his own money to design and build Complex A and invest in all the various companies involved. A minor amount compared to the total cost of the four-building structure. Yet it had strained him financially and if this didn't work, he was going to be back looking for a job.

No one really had paid much attention to a massive construction project going on in a burnt-out neighborhood on the South Side of Chicago until all four buildings started to climb above ten stories in their framework. And the third and fourth floors of all four buildings were connected over the streets below forming two-block-long tunnels. That was hard to ignore by even a press used to ignoring events on the South Side.

And when people noticed, reporters starting digging into the construction and the project.

But they learned little. Carl and his team had everything covered and blocked. And none of the investors were talking, which surprised both Carl and Big Ed. It seems the people who had tossed money at one stage or another of this project believed in it as much as they did.

The four buildings reached their full height of forty floors with the news doing weekly reports on them and adding nothing new. The plans were on file with the city, but all the plans showed could be seen from the street, for the most part.

They were called the "Buildings of Mystery" by the press. Big Ed and Carl and the hundreds of investors in the various projects just called it all Complex A.

Now, Big Ed stood with his friend Carl in his media room in his penthouse apartment, again staring at the television that had forced him into action the year before. Carl stood beside him. Both of them just stared at the screen, hardly moving.

The press conference was about to start about Complex A. It would be now or never. Were they both going to be broke and laughed at for building a massive eyesore, or maybe, just maybe, had they done something that actually might help save the city—and the world?

This was the turning point.

The smiling man who walked onto the stage and faced the cameras was Devon Conrad, the president of the board of directors for the Complex A corporation, named simply Complex A Incorporated. Big Ed and Carl had helped put him in place not only for his passion for the project, but his ability to speak to the media.

They had booked the big and plush Hilton Chicago Grand Ballroom for the press conference, and set the stage perfectly to showcase something of this size.

Devon turned to face the cameras with a smile that seemed to be reassuring instead of condescending. He stood six feet tall and had the square jaw of a superhero. His dark silk suit shouted that he was a man with more money to spend than he knew what to do with.

In reality, Devon was personally rich, and he'd been an investor in a number of the companies before Carl and Big Ed offered him the front position on Complex A. Now, like Big Ed and Carl, he had money in all the companies.

Devon and Carl and Big Ed had gone over every word of Devon's speech and planned out where they thought there would be troubles. Devon was as prepared for this as he could be.

Devon started the conference with all the basic thank-yous that the press had come to expect, then made a motion and a drape moved back beside him to expose the model of Complex A.

Big Ed's stomach twisted.

Carl said, "That thing is truly ugly, you know."

Big Ed said nothing. To him it was a thing of beauty, a thing of his dreams.

The model looked exactly as the four buildings did from the street. Four building frames connected on varied floors over the streets. Big Ed had to admit, it did look half-finished to the normal eye. But he hoped the world would love the look as much as he did when this press conference was finished.

Then Devon started to talk about the violence on the streets, the children dying for no reasons, and behind him on a huge screen images from newscasts flashed past, detailing out quickly what everyone already knew: The streets were not safe for a normal family to live and raise children. Period.

"So how does a building complex like this help the crime issue in this and other cities?" Devon asked as the news feed stopped.

He paused for perfect effect. "In Complex A, we give families a completely safe place to live, to raise their children, to shop, to work, and have their children go to school. All without fear."

There was a murmuring among the reporters, looking first at Devon and then at the framework of the four buildings.

Devon smiled and moved a step over to the model. "Notice how the building is up on its frame with nothing on the two ground floors but the central core?"

He tapped the empty space on the lower two floors and a knocking sound echoed over the quiet. "There will be bulletproof glass all the way around the base of each building. The only way into each building complex will be through a series of doors leading to a security station in the center of one building. No guns or drugs will be allowed in any building. Everyone entering the buildings will be scanned and searched. No exceptions."

Again the crowd of reporters started to erupt, but he held his hands up for silence and surprisingly to Big Ed, they honored him. Devon was good, of that there was no doubt.

Devon pointed to the two floors that spread through all four buildings and were closed in except for windows. "On the third floor will be grocery stores, clothing stores, and a few restaurants. The fourth floor will contain schools for all levels, from preschool through high school. The residents of the four buildings will be offered jobs in all aspects of the businesses and schools on the two floors and they will be paid fair wages."

Devon pushed on before anyone could interrupt. Big Ed and Carl and Devon knew this was a critical point. Devon had to keep going now, or all was lost.

Devon pointed to the next two series of closed-in floors going upward. "These will contain community areas, indoor parks, playgrounds, and so on."

"Then he pointed at the top five closed-in floors. "Of course the roof will be open park area and gardens, but the five floors below will be hydroponic gardens watered by cured wastewater in each building.

Each building will grow more than enough fresh food for all residents year-round and be able to sell the extra to local markets for a profit."

"Don't stop now," Big Ed whispered to the big screen and Carl only nodded.

Before the reporters could break in, Devon pushed forward. "The third floor from the top will be laced with wind turbines and electrical storage areas. Since the wind in Chicago seems to always blow one way or another, there are over three hundred various sized electrical turbines that will generate electricity around the clock."

Big Ed could tell that Devon now had the full attention of the reporters trying to grasp an entire floor of electrical-generating wind turbines.

"On all areas of all four buildings," Devon said, gesturing to the outside areas, "that get sunshine at any time of the year, the sidings are designed to be solar panels gathering electrical energy. Between wind and solar, each building will generate so much power, it will not only supply all the energy needs of the residents, but each complex will sell power back to the main grid. Each building will sustain itself from the power sold and make a profit after city and land taxes—"

The room exploded in a thousand questions being shouted all at once.

Big Ed glanced at Carl.

Carl smiled. "Here we go. The key to all this is now. We're either going to save this city or go broke very quickly."

Big Ed just nodded, almost afraid to speak. He wanted to sit down, to make himself relax, but he just couldn't do it. Everything turned on what Devon was going to say next.

So he just stood and stared at the screen, his hands at his sides.

The reporters were shouting, but Devon just stood and smiled, holding up his hands for silence. When he could finally be heard he said, "I'll answer all your questions shortly, and we have packets with all the details to hand out to everyone to make sure all facts are correct. But…you haven't heard the best part yet."

The reporters all fell silent.

Devon smiled and pointed at the model. "Aren't you wondering why the building is nothing but a frame?"

His question sort of just hung there.

Big Ed had hoped for that exact reaction.

Devon took a square block from under the podium and held it up for everyone to see.

"This is a modular, three-thousand-square-foot apartment," he said. "It can be designed to contain two, three, four, or five bedrooms. It will have two and a half baths and a large kitchen and dining area. There are many designs to choose from for each one."

On the screen behind him, suddenly different apartments floated in and over each other showing living rooms, modern kitchens, bedrooms, family rooms, and so on in many varied colors.

Devon smiled. "These apartments are the size of apartments many of the rich people of our fair city live in."

He walked over to the model and slid the apartment block into one side of the building. It clicked into place.

Then Devon turned to the camera, looking suddenly very serious.

"Each apartment will be completely owned by a family. They will pay no electricity, no house payment, and if they choose to work so many hours in the shops or restaurants or schools or security or gardens or utility areas of the building, they will not even pay tenant's fees."

Before anyone could shout a question, Devon went on. "Their families will be completely safe inside their homes. All windows are bulletproof, as are all exterior walls. Each apartment will have a view. There are no halls in this complex. Each apartment opens onto a large open public area in the center of each floor. The apartments are only positioned around the outside of each floor."

The room started to erupt one more time, but Devon used the command in his voice to silence it. "Please hold on for one more important fact."

Right there, Big Ed knew he and Carl had picked the right man for the job.

"Each apartment unit for all of Complex A is in the first stages of production, built by a plant right here in Chicago. Each apartment will be modular construction, built in the factory to save costs, and then raised into place by cranes. But before we can get a family moved in, the family must first buy the apartment. Of course, we know the families that need protection from the violence of the streets are the families that can least afford to move. And our desire is that every apartment be paid off completely on the day that every family moves in."

Devon stared at the reporters. Then smiled again.

"We have over two hundred families signed up to move in now, with hundreds and hundreds more in the process. Complex A can hold around six hundred families. But each of those families need help, help from everyone out there who wants to see kids grow up without being shot, to live free of violence, to get top educations, and live to be productive citizens of this wonderful city."

Devon smiled. "The apartments are going to be sold at cost to each family with no profit at any step. Let me repeat that. No profit at any step will come from the sale of the apartments to the families."

He paused again for a moment, then went on. "And with the modular construction, the costs are very low. Some families have agreed to sell their homes for payment on an apartment, others who are only renting have no way to pay for an apartment. And that's where we all can help."

Again Devon got serious.

Big Ed waited for it, wondering if this was going to work or not, his stomach so cramped up he felt like he was going to be sick.

Devon looked into the camera. "Each family approved for an apartment in Complex A has been set up on Crowdsourcing Help to help fund the apartment."

On the screen behind him, a URL address appeared in large letters for the site they had created just for this project.

"There are videos and background information on each family on each project. All the details are there. Also each family has a donation fund set up at all local banks to help as well. Any extra money raised will be moved to another family. No one will make a profit from the funds donated."

Again, Devon paused and the reporters, shocked to their cores, all stood there silently, letting him finish. "For years we've all wondered how to save the children and innocents of this city. Now we have a way to not just sit in front of the televisions and wish we could do something. Now we can actually do something."

He stared directly into the camera as if talking to everyone watching. "You can help a family get into a self-sustaining apartment and into a new and safe life, with great schools and great jobs. But many need your support."

Devon looked around the shocked room. Then he really hit them with the final punch. "Over the next two years we will build at least two dozen more exactly like Complex A on the South Side of Chicago. All will be four-building-construction, all holding around six hundred families per complex."

On the screen behind him was an artist's rendering of the South Side of Chicago with towering complexes going off into the distance surrounded by green parks and wide roads. It looked almost like a scene from a science fiction novel instead of something that could happen in just a few years.

"The land has been purchased and the plans are under way for all of the new complexes. The buildings alone will supply over one third of all the power needs for the entire city."

Devon let that sink in, then hit them with his final punch. "In the very near future, families in this city who used to be afraid to walk outside their own home will live in safety, their children will go to great schools, and well-paying jobs will be available to anyone in the building in all areas of life."

Devon smiled. "Before I take any questions, I want to make one thing very, very clear. The residents of each building can come and go as they see fit, go to school where they want, move if they want. But no drugs or guns will ever be allowed in any of these buildings. At least the children in each building can play in safety, go to school in safety, and the entire family can live and work in safety if they so choose."

Devon took a deep breath and looked sad and intense at the same time. "Maybe the day will come when the citizens of this fine city can turn on the news and not have to watch a story of an innocent child being killed. So please, support a family or two or a dozen, depending on what you can afford. The families of this city want to move to safety into buildings being built right in their own neighborhoods. They just need your help. Every dollar helps."

Then he nodded and smiled at the camera. "Now I will be happy to take any questions."

The conference room exploded.

Big Ed muted the television and dropped into his chair, trying to catch his breath. There were going to be a lot of people who hated this idea. But in time, he could imagine many neighborhoods between the tall buildings being parks and open lands instead of war zones. The families who wanted to sell their homes were selling homes to corporations who would hold the homes and in time clear the land for parks.

It was going to take time, but this was a new century. No one said that they couldn't invent a new meaning for the word *neighborhood*.

Carl started pacing, the phone to his ear. Then suddenly he laughed sort of high and insane-like and hung up.

He sat down in the chair beside Big Ed, stretched out and stared at the ceiling, smiling.

"What was that all about?" Big Ed asked, staring at his friend. He had never, in all the years of their friendship, heard Carl make that noise.

"Break out a bottle of the best and most expensive wine you got," Carl said, his eyes closed as he shook his head slowly from side-to-side.

"Why?" Big Ed asked.

"Because in the first two minutes after we announced, forty of the family Crowdsource accounts got completely funded. At this rate, the first building will be funded completely by tomorrow. And by the end of the week, we might have Complex B. funded as well."

All Big Ed could do was smile. He sat back and stared at the screen where a year before he had watched children dying, and wondered what he could do to stop it.

Now six hundred families would be moving to safety very, very soon. And after that another six hundred.

They hadn't saved the entire world, but it was a start.

A damn good start.

REMEMBER

Back in 2009, I got one of those letters you can only dream about as a writer. Robert E. Vardeman and Joan Spicci Saberhagen were editing a book of original stories based on a book by Joan's late husband, Fred Saberhagen. Fred was a great guy, and a great writer and his early death was a shock to us all.

And I was always a major fan of his work, so getting a chance to write in one of his worlds just had me jumping up and down. Then Bob told me what book of Fred's they wanted to extend new stories from and I got even more excited.

Fred had written a book called Mask of the Sun, *a short novel that was a stunner in world-building and storytelling. In essence, Fred came up with a world where the Spanish were defeated by the Incas and the Aztecs and now they were world powers, filling all of Central America and South America. And they were at war, of course.*

A war that stretched through time and alternate realities.

If you have not read Mask of the Sun, *you can find it along with this story and others in a book called* Golden Reflections. *Trust me, it will be worth your time to find and read. Plus in* Golden Reflections, *which came out in 2010, you can find the full novel, plus this story, plus six others, including stories by Harry Turtledove, David Weber, Walter John Williams and others.*

All set in the world of Mask of the Sun.

This story came about because in the Mask of the Sun *novel, I noticed that Fred had one paragraph where a character (shifted to this alternate universe) was happy to see that the United States was still in existence. I instantly thought, "Wow, that means they fought at the Alamo against the Aztecs. How cool!"*

And thus the following story.

I wanted to bring this story back here because I love this story and am proud of it and not many people ever saw it, and I loved Fred Saberhagen's work and wanted to point Fred's work out to fans in this new world.

Based with permission on the Fred Saberhagen novel, Mask of the Sun

One

February 23, 1836
Bexar, Republic of Texas

"INCOMING!" a voice shouted from behind Dennis Holcomb as the muzzle flash from the Aztec cannon cut through the darkness, followed a moment later by the explosion of sound echoing over the mission. The cannon sat on a small rise built in the center of Bexar, one of two in that location.

Around him other men ducked for cover behind the two-foot-thick west wall of the Alamo, spread out on the roofs of the officer's quarters. Holcomb held his position on the wall, his night glasses allowing him to see clearly the three Aztec warriors already starting to reload the cannon.

Behind them stood another Aztec warrior wearing a thin headdress and a wide robe. From what Holcomb had learned over the last week of studying the Aztec society, the warrior looked to be a member of the Arrow clan. That meant he was in charge of the other warriors working the cannons.

The Aztec had less than a second to live. He just didn't know it. Holcomb already had the wind figured, had the distance figured to exactly 865 feet. He was ready, had his target in his sights.

As the shell exploded at the base of the wall of the Alamo mission twenty feet down to the left from his position, he fired under the covering sound, knocking the Aztec leader off the mound.

Holcomb then moved quickly, still covered by the echoing thunder of the cannon shot impact. He moved the gun sight to the second mound with another Aztec cannon twenty yards to the right of the first one. He picked the Arrow clan warrior clearly in charge standing behind the three working on the cannon, and shot, knocking him over backwards before his men even had a chance to fire that cannon.

No other person behind the Alamo wall heard his shots because of the explosion of the shell and the silence technology on the gun.

Beside him Berg DeWitt patted him lightly on the shoulder. "Nice shooting."

"Old skills come back quick," Holcomb said. "Two down, four or five thousand more Aztecs to go."

"Yeah, going to be nothing to it," DeWitt laughed, staring through night-scope binoculars at the cannons. "Just like Nam."

"We lost that war, remember?" Holcomb said, watching through the night scope on his glasses as the Aztec warriors scrambled around the cannons, pulling their dead leaders away from the mounds, leaving the cannons unattended.

"So we make up for that here," DeWitt said, focusing over the thick wall into the dark.

Holcomb glanced at the Vietnam vet beside him. DeWitt was a tall guy, maybe six-two, and he had arms on him that could bench press more than Holcomb wanted to think about. The guy had military short hair and intense green eyes. He was originally from Montana and had served in Nam for two terms leading right up to the end of the war.

He and DeWitt were both dressed as frontiersmen of the time, in soft deerskin jackets, cloth pants and heavy boots. They both had on a poncho-like gray cloth against the chill of the night.

Along the top of the Alamo wall, the Texans and other fighters got back into position as the dust from the explosion drifted on the cool evening breeze, rifles poised and aiming into the pitch darkness of the night. Halfway down the west wall, Davy Crockett stood, staring into the blackness.

Holcomb just shook his head and looked away. The real Davy Crockett looked nothing like Fess Parker, the actor who had played him on television when Holcomb was a kid.

The real Davy Crockett was short. That had been a real disappointment.

Two

May 18, 1981
Portland, Oregon, USA

HOLCOMB SAT on the park bench staring out over the calm waters of the Willamette River, not really paying any attention to those walking the path behind him or the boats floating past on the river. The day had turned warm and brought hundreds out of their homes and offices to enjoy the afternoon sunshine and beautiful spring day along the waterfront.

Holcomb hadn't noticed any of it. He had just come from a doctor. All he could remember now from the conversation was the word "Cancer" and "two months to live."

It didn't seem real, but it had been the third opinion, the third doctor, actually. He hadn't trusted the first two, hadn't believed them. But now it seemed there was no doubt. He was dying and there wasn't a damn thing anyone could do about it.

A young woman laughed, the sound high and light, floating on the soft breeze. Before learning of the cancer, he would have sat here, watching her, enjoying the sun and the afternoon. He had spent many a warm afternoon on this bench, and even knew some of the nearby shop owners by name. This bench, beside this path in the narrow park along the river, had been his favorite place in the city. He called it his spot, and anyone he dated or his few friends at work knew where to find him on nice days. And Portland, in the spring and summer and fall, had a lot of nice days.

Now, the sound of someone laughing just annoyed him. How could anyone be enjoying a day like today? He had just been given a death sentence. There was nothing worth laughing about today. He stood and, without a look at the beautiful calm river or the park around him, turned and headed back into the center of the city.

His apartment was on the third floor of an old converted hotel six blocks from the river and he didn't notice the walk, other than the few times he bumped into someone. All he could think about was dying. He had faced enemy fire a lot of times in Nam, had killed more than his share of the enemy, but never in all that time had he worried much about dying. Now that death faced him, like a train coming head on, he didn't know how to deal with it.

It just made him mad, actually.

One thing for certain, he had no intention of going the way the first doctor at the VA had described, sitting in a hospice the last few weeks, medicated so that he wouldn't feel the pain. He had bought a pistol after that little talk just for the occasion and now, with a solid third opinion, there sure didn't seem to be any reason to put off the end. He would face it just as he had faced most things in his life.

Head-on.

He had no family since his parents had died in a car wreck the year after he got back from Nam, and even though he was liked for his dry sense of humor at work, he didn't have any real friends to speak of, just a few old buddies from Nam. He was just too much of a loner to let anyone close. At least that's what his last girlfriend, Sandra, had told him.

He hadn't argued with her. She had been right. No one would really miss him, and there certainly wasn't anyone to take care of him in the next two months. Only the VA and he doubted they really wanted to see him at this point either, after the fuss he had made about getting a second and then a third opinion.

He had no real money except the little bit his parents had left him and his job driving a city bus could be filled in ten minutes.

The pistol would do everyone a favor.

He opened the door to his single-bedroom apartment and tossed the key onto the small kitchen table after kicking the door closed behind him, leaving it unlocked.

The place still smelled of the eggs and bacon he had made for himself for breakfast. It had been a good last meal for a condemned man.

The apartment had been a pretty good place to live, so no point in staining it all up with his blood. He'd leave the world in the bathroom, in the tub, with the curtain shut. He just hoped someone found him quickly so that the smell wouldn't ruin everything.

"Not having a good day, huh?" a voice said from the big chair in his living room to the left of the main door.

Holcomb spun around to face a man sitting in Holcomb's favorite chair in front of the television. The guy had long gray hair combed back, dark eyes, and tan skin. He looked Native American or Mexican descent. He had on standard Oregon casual, jeans and a tan button-down dress shirt with his sleeves rolled up.

The guy was clearly not the standard robber that Holcomb would expect going through these apartments. He'd been robbed twice in his four years living here, both times by hippie-types looking for drug money.

Two steps and Holcomb had the pistol out of the kitchen drawer and pointed at the guy.

The guy didn't even flinch. "Thought you were going to use that on yourself?"

Now the guy was just pissing Holcomb off. No one knew his plans. And no one but his doctors and a couple people at the VA knew about the cancer. He hadn't told anyone, not even his friends at work. So how could this stranger know what he had been thinking?

"Nice of you to do it in the shower," the guy said, nodding. "Saved a lot of clean-up and they found your body in ten minutes because your neighbor heard the shot, so no real smell issues. A young married couple moves in here next month. Nice folks. You would have liked them, but of course, you'll never get the chance to meet them, will you?"

Holcomb couldn't let the guy confuse him. He focused, got his mind clear like he used to do in the service before a mission.

"Who the hell are you and what are you doing here?"

"Just call me Kontar. I know, strange name, but my father was Egyptian on his father's side." The guy shrugged as if any of that meant something.

Holcomb waved the gun in frustration. The guy was really starting to make him angry. And a soon-to-be-dead man wasn't a good person to piss off.

"What I am doing here?" Kontar asked, smiling. "Actually, I'm here to recruit you to help in a fight for your country."

"Yeah, right," Holcomb said, leveling the gun at the man. "Ten seconds to tell me the truth or they end up cleaning this place after all because of two bodies. As you seem to know, it will make no difference to me."

"You won't believe the truth, but I'll tell you anyway," Kontar said. "I know you are about to kill yourself because of terminal cancer because I am from the future. Actually, looking back from my time, you killed yourself in that bathroom back there, curtains drawn, that gun in your mouth. Because you have no family or real friends, we figured you to be a perfect candidate to help us out with a mission to save your country.

"And which government agency do you work for?" Holcomb asked, shaking his head. "The nut-ball service?"

Kontar shook his head. "I don't work for your government. I work for the Inca Nation. But the survival of your country is wrapped up in the survival of mine, which is why I need your help."

"In the future?" Holcomb said, still not believing a word this nut case was saying.

"Actually, no," Kontar said. "I need your help in the past. Since you're going to die anyway today, or in a few months from cancer, I have a mission for you first."

"A suicide mission," Holcomb said, disgusted and about ready to shoot the guy. "Right?"

"Of course," Kontar said, smiling, showing perfect, very white teeth. "But considering what you were about to do in your bathtub, I figured you wouldn't have a problem with that."

Three

February 24, 1836
Alamo Mission, Bexar, Republic of Texas

WHEN THE SHOOTING from the other side of the long Alamo compound started, it woke up Holcomb. He had dozed off against the west wall, his gun across his legs.

DeWitt snorted and came awake beside him. They watched as the Texans on the south wall laid down covering fire for someone coming to the gate. A few moments later the large wooden gate was opened in the wall built between the south buildings of the mission and the church itself. Five men came through leading twenty horses loaded down with supplies.

"Looks like we're eating tonight," DeWitt said.

"Yeah," Holcomb said, taking in the scene in front of him. They had come in just after dark last night and he hadn't gotten much of a chance to look around, since they went right to the wall and cut down the cannon fire from the Aztec cannons.

The Alamo grounds were a lot larger than he had ever imagined

251

from the movies and stories he had been told. Between the buildings along the west wall and the barrack wall on the east, it was a good half a football field wide, and one and a half fields long.

A cannonade had been constructed right in the middle, large enough to let cannons turn in any direction and high enough to see over the walls in all four directions.

There were also four cannons along the west wall, two on the top of the building on the north wall, four along the south wall, and three in the back of the old church facing east. In the fort there were twenty-one artillery pieces of different caliber, an impressive fortification.

A guy by the name of Neill had managed to turn the old mission grounds into a pretty impressive fort in the months before they arrived.

From what Holcomb could tell, there had to be a good hundred and fifty men here already, mostly volunteers like he and DeWitt were posing as. Two names from the history books of Holcomb's time were in charge and he and DeWitt got to meet them both.

Travis led the Texas Regular troops while Bowie seemed to be in charge of all the volunteers. Both men seemed much smaller to Holcomb than their legends led him to believe.

And Travis was very, very young.

DeWitt and Holcomb were put under Bowie with the volunteers, but at the moment Bowie seemed to be sick and Travis was doing just about everything. Considering how young the kid was, Holcomb found him impressive. Even Congressmen Crockett nodded to Travis as the man in charge.

Supposedly, there were other teams from the future in the mix, but Holcomb hadn't really spotted any in the short time he and DeWitt had been inside, since everyone was dressed for the time period and didn't stand out. Supposedly, the Incas were also supplying much needed ammunition and food to the fighters inside the Alamo without anyone knowing about it, but both Holcomb and DeWitt had their own supplies in the form of small pills as food. Interestingly enough, the pills were filling. Not much fun to eat, but enough to keep them going.

They both also had their medicine to keep them going long enough to die for the cause. DeWitt had less time left to live than Holcomb, and at times coughed so hard he spit up blood.

Holcomb watched, his back against the west wall of the Alamo, as four men shut the gate at the other end of the compound and Travis welcomed the new volunteers and the supplies they brought.

Holcomb had to admit that there were some brave men here, fighting for a cause they felt was right. Many of them had families and children at home they would never see again. Even if they lived and became a prisoner of the Aztec, they would be sacrificed and their hearts eaten, as was Aztec custom with war prisoners of this time period.

Death was the only way out of this battle.

Holcomb watched the small celebration around the new arrivals and wondered if he would have had the courage to fight this fight if he wasn't dying anyway. He hoped so. Sometimes, your country, and a way of life you believed in, was worth fighting and dying for. He had thought that at first, when he joined the Army and was sent over to Vietnam.

When he got home, he hadn't been so sure anymore.

He just hoped this time the fight was the lives and the blood and the pain. Davy Crockett and all the other men here sure seemed to think so.

Four

Unknown Date, 23rd Century
Cuzco, Inca Nation

HOLCOMB FELT LIKE HIS BRAIN was about to explode. Kontar had been trying to explain time travel and different universes to him and a guy by the name of DeWitt for the last half hour and none of it seemed to make sense.

They were in what looked like a standard conference room, inside a huge building with no real character, inside the vast city of Cuzco, the capital city of the Incas.

Flying in on some strange plane with porthole-like windows, Holcomb had been stunned by the beauty of the 23rd century city spread out below. But as Kontar said, there wouldn't be time to look around. Holcomb, with his cancer, just didn't have that much time left. But he had no doubt at all that he was in a future city from what little he did get to see. No city on his earth in his time looked like Cuzco.

He had been shown a room to sleep for the night, a change of clothes and shower. After what felt like a short eight hours, he was given a breakfast that tasted a lot like cold Cream of Wheat cereal. He was assured it was good for him and would give him extra strength. Bacon and eggs would have tasted a hell of a lot better.

After breakfast, there had been yet another physical that once again confirmed what the doctors in his time had told him. He didn't have long to live.

Great, a fourth opinion confirmed yet again he was going to die, and not even the medicine in the 23rd century could save him.

After the physical, he had been introduced to another Vietnam vet from the east coast and put in a plain meeting room with tan walls to get their first briefing. If the first thirty minutes of this briefing were any indication, he and DeWitt might not live long enough to get through the lectures, let alone fight for their country.

"Okay, hold on a second," Holcomb said, holding up both his hands in a show of surrender. "Let me see if I got any of this right."

"Thank you," DeWitt whispered, shaking his head.

"DeWitt and I are from a timeline where the Spanish win over the Incas and the Aztecs and the Mayans. That forms what we know as Mexico and all the Central and South American countries. Right?"

"Correct," Kontar said, nodding.

"Good, got my own history correct then," Holcomb said.

DeWitt actually applauded him.

Holcomb went on. "You say we are sitting in a timeline where the Aztecs and the Incas both win against the Spanish and keep them out of Central America and South America. And you hate each other. Correct?"

"Yes," Kontar said.

"And in this world, the United States still exists in pretty much the same configuration as it does in our time line."

"It does," Kontar said, clicking something in his hand.

The wall behind him showed an image of North and South America. The Inca Nation was South America, the Aztecs held Central America and Mexico, and the United States looked normal, as did Canada.

"So why are we fighting at the Alamo again?"

"Because, if the Texans don't hold off the Aztecs at that time and win, this is what the world looks like by 1850, just a short time after the Alamo battle."

The map on the wall changed to one showing the United States cut off below Georgia with a line extending to the Mississippi and then up, with the rest showing the color of the Aztec nation.

"Without the Texans winning against the Aztecs, the Aztec/American war is never fought," Kontar said

"Like the Mexican/American war in our world," DeWitt said.

"Correct," Kontar said. "When the Aztecs discover gold in California, they wipe out all English and European settlers on the west coast and cut off all westward expansion with the help of the native tribes. They then buy the Louisiana Purchase from the United States and basically close off the area. In this timeline, the Aztec take over all of North America in the late 1920s while Europe was still fighting what you call World War One. With the vast resources of North America, the Aztec become very powerful and we fall to them in 2010."

Holcomb didn't much like the look of that map showing all of North and South America as bright red Aztec Nation. Not one bit.

"How many timelines does that happen in?" DeWitt asked.

"A great number," Kontar said. "See why the battle at the Alamo is so important?"

"Actually, no," Holcomb said. "In my timeline, the battle of the Alamo was lost, and it made no real difference at all, other than as a rallying cry. If I have my own history correct, that is."

"You do, but it does in these timelines," Kontar said, pointing to the ugly map showing all red of the Aztec empire covering everything. "If the Aztec win the battle of the Alamo easily, they simply sweep across Texas and don't stop. They defeat the Texas army easily under Sam Houston and take Louisiana and Florida easily as well. Only a truce with the United States stops them at that point, but that's too late."

"Santa Anna, in our timeline, had thousands of troops," Holcomb asked. "How many is the Aztec going to bring against the Alamo?"

"The War Chief will lead four to five thousand warriors," Kontar said with a straight face.

DeWitt just snorted.

Holcomb laughed. "You expect less than two hundred men to stop five thousand Aztec warriors?"

"No, I don't, actually. But with a few modern weapons to help out, you can slow them down and do some real damage, enough so that Houston and his men, with a little help as well, can stop them."

DeWitt shrugged and glanced at Holcomb. "We're both dead anyway in a few months, better to go out fighting for our country, even though this isn't really our country."

Holcomb nodded. DeWitt was right. It was much better than sitting in a hospice drooling on a bib waiting to die, or standing in a bathtub with a gun in his mouth.

Besides, he had always wanted to see the Alamo, ever since he was a kid. Looked like he was going to get a real close look at it.

Five

February 28, 1836
Alamo Compound, Bexar, Republic of Texas

THE COLD NIGHT had broken into a warm day, letting the dust and the dry wind swirl through the large compound. In the distance, the sounds of thousands of Aztec warriors chanting and moving equipment echoed over the rolling hills. Travis reported to everyone that the Aztec numbers were still under two thousand, but growing by the day.

And the great Aztec War Chief was still a few days from the Rio Grande. He would have thousands of warriors with him.

Kontar had told him and DeWitt the Aztec War Chief's name, but Holcomb had forgotten it at once, since it was long and had more consonants in it than vowels by a margin of five to one. He'd never been that good in school with the English language, so learning Aztec names in a few days time just didn't seem to be worth the effort in his final weeks alive.

He was just glad that the Spanish had gone into Florida and across into Texas and Southern California when defeated by the Aztec and Inca nations. Otherwise, the Alamo would have had some other strange name as well.

Holcomb was now very sure, after five days in the Alamo, that there were numbers of other teams from the future inside the Alamo. He and DeWitt had been given permission by Travis to fire when a target was clear, since more than enough ammunition and food had somehow managed to be brought to the fort, both from outside supplies coming in from Sam Houston and the Texas government, and also from missions outside the walls searching surrounding buildings now abandoned by the settlers of the area.

So all night and all day, the sporadic sounds of gunfire cut through the air.

The number of men inside the walls still numbered less than one hundred and sixty, but with enough food and firepower, spirits were high at the moment.

Holcomb and DeWitt had both kept any Aztec warrior from poking his head up within hundreds of yards of the Alamo west wall. The two Aztec cannon placements on the mounds in the town were nothing more than a killing field for the two men. Aztec warriors would rush up onto the platforms to try to load the cannons, or even move the cannons off the platforms, and DeWitt or Holcomb or both of them would make the warriors pay with their lives.

Other teams down the wall and on both end walls had been doing the same to the other Aztec cannon emplacements, so unlike the history that Holcomb had studied of the Alamo in his timeline, this time around the constant cannon bombardment of the walls of the Alamo wasn't happening. That allowed the men inside to be more rested and since they had better food and lots of water, they were going to put up one very nasty fight when the time came.

Also, the fort walls were not beaten down by the week of bombardment, meaning that it would be a lot harder for the Aztec warriors to get inside.

One day, while walking the west wall, Travis had noticed their accuracy and asked them about it. Holcomb had simply said, "Kentucky practice. I can knock the left eye out of a squirrel at two hundred paces."

DeWitt laughed. "And I can knock the right one out at the same time from three hundred."

Travis had just laughed and moved on. The kid was smart enough to not question his luck. Holcomb wished a few lieutenants back in Nam had been that smart. They and a lot of their men would still be alive.

Well, actually, they hadn't been born yet, since this was 1836, and in a different world where Aztecs were a powerful nation. Holcomb just shook his head at the thought. All of this was just confusing.

Twenty paces to their right, three men laughed and Holcomb

watched as they worked to raise a cannon a precise amount, using some sort of measuring device that didn't look like it belonged to this period of time.

After a moment, they looked pleased and called Travis to watch, having him focus on one of the cannon placements in Bexar that Holcomb and DeWitt had been guarding.

As one man signaled to fire, Holcomb covered his ears. The old cannons were amazingly loud. The explosion still rocked him and sent dust swirling in all directions.

DeWitt coughed a few times, hard, but then recovered. That cough wasn't sounding good.

Travis didn't seem to mind the sound of the explosion, and neither did Crockett on the other side of the cannon. Both just stood their ground and stared at the intended target.

Holcomb followed their gaze and a moment later one of the Aztec cannons just exploded, flipping over backwards and flying into a hundred pieces.

The three men manning the cannon cheered, as did all the men up and down the wall who had been watching.

"I didn't know those old things could be that accurate," DeWitt said, shaking his head in amazement.

"They can't," Holcomb said, laughing.

DeWitt stared at him for a moment, then laughed as well. "Nice to know old Kontar and his people are covering all the bases. Maybe we're going to have a fighting chance here."

"Well, we'll be fighting, that's for sure," Holcomb said. He had no illusion that they had any chance of surviving.

Six

Unknown Date, 2300
Cuzco, Inca Nation

HOLCOMB STOOD AT A TABLE in an indoor firing range and studied the fake antique gun in his hands. It looked old, right out of the eighteen hundreds, modeled after the type of long rifle you saw Davy Crockett carrying.

It was a Kentucky rifle with brass inlays on the long butt and along the wood under the barrel. It even had marks and wear, making it seem like it had been used a great deal and carried in a saddle holster.

But this rifle, under the disguise was far, far more.

Even though it looked like it fired the old style ammunition, it didn't. Hidden in the long stock was a clip that held fifty high-powered rounds. The used shells were stored in the long wood area under the barrel until removed. The rounds looked no bigger than a 22 caliber, but Kontar assured him that the small shells and tips had more length and velocity than a sniper rifle of Holcomb's time.

And even more amazing, when fired, the gun spit out the same smoke and smell that a Kentucky rifle did when fired.

The only problem would be carrying the amount of ammunition they would need, reloading the clips into the butts of the rifle, and hiding the spent shells. That would be hard, at times, but workable, Holcomb was sure.

In the service, both Holcomb and DeWitt had been top marksmen, but Holcomb just couldn't believe he would be able to hit the side of a large building from a hundred yards with the fake old gun, even though it felt a lot lighter than it looked and balanced perfectly in his hands.

"Try it," was all Kontar said, smiling at both DeWitt and Holcomb.

"Too stupid for words," DeWitt said. "We're all going to die, why worry about pretending to be from the time period."

"Because the Aztecs of this world have time travel as well," Kontar said.

That fact stunned Holcomb right to his core and made his stomach twist. It hadn't occurred to him that the two sides would be evenly matched.

"So we're not so worried about hiding your presence from the locals inside the fort," Kontar said, "but from the Aztecs outside the fort who are from our time period. If they can't tell who our plants are, if any in the timeline you are going to, and who are just locals, you'll live longer."

"Super," DeWitt said, shaking his head. "We're not only fighting five thousand Aztec warriors in 1836, but Aztec agents from the future? What's the point? Just shoot us now."

"The point is," Kontar said, looking first at DeWitt, then focusing on Holcomb as if he was going to understand more than DeWitt, "that we don't know which way this timeline will fall. We do know that much of the outcome will come down to this one battle, and we're hoping the

Aztec do not know that as firmly as we do, and once they discover that fact, we will already have won the day."

"So this is the first timeline your two people have fought over?"

"No," Kontar said, shaking his head. "We are fighting across many, many timelines at once, actually. We have turned the tide in other timelines by helping Sam Houston, by winning at the battle of New Orleans against the Aztec, by driving them back with surprise attacks out of Georgia, but never once have we tried to stop them at the Alamo before."

"How do you keep all this straight?" DeWitt asked a moment before Holcomb could ask the same question.

"It isn't easy," Kontar said. "But this timeline is the one I focus on, that I am in charge of."

Holcomb was shocked. "You're telling me that the fate of millions of people and your very culture's existence rests on your shoulders alone?"

"No, my culture is right here," Kontar said, indicating the building and the firing range around them. "I'm just trying to help other timelines follow this culture, to get the chance to develop to this point."

Holcomb could feel his head wanting to explode again. "So tell me, how many timelines that you know about developed to this point without outside help?"

"None," Holcomb said. "We had help in our past as well in the form of a very special gift from someone far, far into our future. But we're not allowed to talk about that."

Holcomb just shook his head and tried to focus again on the fake antique rifle in his hands. He knew guns. Guns he understood. Time travel just gave him a headache.

"Ahh, well," DeWitt said, picking up the rifle and taking a stance aiming down the range at a human-shaped target one hundred yards away. "I'm going to die soon anyway. This way might just be fun."

He pulled the trigger and the loud sound filled the range at the same moment as a perfectly shaped hole appeared where the middle of the nose of the target figure would be.

DeWitt turned and smiled. "I'll be go to hell, this thing actually works."

Kontar nodded. "Wait until you see what the pistols and the grenades shaped as rifle rounds will do."

Holcomb held the perfectly balanced gun in his hands. At least in this war, he was going in well armed. Outmanned, but with real fire power.

Seven

March 1, 1836
Alamo Compound, Bexar, Republic of Texas

HOLCOMB WATCHED from his normal spot on the west wall as over thirty troops arrived, riding through the covering fire and into the compound.

"Part of Gonzales' ranging company," DeWitt said. "If I remember my history correctly, those are the last reinforcements we're going to get."

"Unless Kontar changes the history," Holcomb said.

"Oh, yeah, forgot about that part. We can only hope."

At that moment the boom of an Aztec cannon filled the air.

Holcomb glanced up, waiting and watching for the flaming fireball coming at them. The Aztec had brought in more cannons and were now firing what Kontar, in a briefing, called "Flaming Arrows" from a greater distance and hidden from direct line of sight behind buildings.

It took exactly three shots for the cannon crew down the wall to narrow in on an exact location and destroy the cannon every time an Aztec cannon started firing, but in the meantime, when the Flaming Arrows landed, they seemed to catch anything near them on fire. Holcomb figured they were more annoying then damaging, since there wasn't that much besides staircases and window frames made of wood inside the big compound. All the rest was thick rock and mud walls.

This shot landed short of the wall and caused no damage at all in the hard surface.

Very few Aztec cannon shots had hit the thick walls, so the fort didn't look much worse for wear than when Holcomb had arrived.

He and DeWitt had just kept knocking down any warrior out there that moved within range. And the accurate range of the fake rifles they had in their hands was almost frightening. They seldom missed, and it seemed neither did the other few sharp-shooting crews from the future placed along the walls. That kept the Aztec warriors a great distance away.

The great War Chief couldn't be very happy about his troops not getting close to the fort. He and the main band of warriors still hadn't arrived yet, even though they had crossed the Rio Grande three days before. Holcomb and DeWitt had talked a lot about what they thought the War Chief would do when he arrived. The only conclusion they had was that he would send his men in a full assault against the walls, just as Santa Anna had done.

It would cost him hundreds and hundreds of lives, but it would get the job done fairly quickly, even against weapons from the future.

DeWitt nudged Holcomb and got him to turn away from staring out over the empty and silent town of Bexar that would be San Antonio in his timeline. "We got company."

A man with a long moustache and carrying a rifle and a large knapsack was coming up the wooden stairs toward them. He looked to be tall, maybe six foot and then some, with large arms and a slight limp on his right side. He had a cowboy hat pulled down low over his eyes to shade from the bright sun.

Both Holcomb and DeWitt started to stand, but the man signaled they stay in position behind the wall and then knelt in front of them, pushing his hat back.

"Stacy," the guy said, sticking out his hand.

"Sergeant Ben Stacy, from California?" DeWitt asked, taking the guy's hand and pumping it like it was old home week. "I'll be go-to-hell. What are you doing here?"

"Same damn thing you are, it seems," Stacy said, smiling. "Committing suicide by Aztec. I was hoping you were still alive when I got here. Kontar said you most likely would be.

"Fit as a fiddle," DeWitt said, lying.

Stacy laughed. "Yeah, me too." He glanced around. "So this is what the Alamo looks like. Bigger than I expected."

"Me too," DeWitt said, then broke into a coughing fit before he could say another word.

"He gets all choked up seeing old friends," Holcomb said, sticking out his hand. "I'm Holcomb. Snatched right out of 1981. Lung cancer, about a month left if I survive this."

Stacy smiled and took his hand. "1986. Prostate cancer, don't want to think about spending that much time left. Riding a damn horse was painful enough."

"Yeah, understand that," Holcomb said, trying not to laugh. "Welcome to the fight."

Stacy dropped the leather satchel and waited until DeWitt's coughing fit passed with a little help from an inhaler he kept hidden in his shirt pocket.

"This is from Kontar," Stacy said, indicating the leather pouch. "I told Travis down there it was personal stuff from your family. It's actually more clips, hidden in the shirts, and about fifty small grenades with six-second delays once you twist the caps."

"How is our old friend Kontar?" Holcomb asked. "He have any idea how things are shifting in the fight?"

"Haven't seen him since you have," Stacy said. "I was put in with those men down there three weeks ago so I could get in here and deliver this and help you two in the fight."

"Before he recruited me?" DeWitt asked, looking puzzled.

Holcomb just patted DeWitt's arm. "Time travel, remember? Don't worry about it."

"Gives me a headache just thinking about it," Stacy said.

"Me too," both Holcomb and DeWitt said at the same time.

All three men laughed and then Stacy took up a position on the wall beside them.

It felt good to have another fighter with them, another Nam vet. Holcomb had no doubt he was going to die in the coming fight. But he didn't mind so much and wasn't afraid of it at all. There were a lot worse ways to go.

Eight

May 20, 1981
Portland, Oregon, USA

KONTAR HAD SPENT THE AFTERNOON trying to explain everything, then left, giving Holcomb two days to decide and get his affairs in order if he decided to go.

After the strange man with the white teeth left, Holcomb had gone back to the park, sitting and thinking about how crazy it all seemed, yet how right it was as well. He had watched kids playing in the grass, a couple kissing on another bench, a boat going past with a woman sunning herself in a bikini on the bow.

In other words, a normal spring day in the park.

He had figured, just as his father had said, that this world was worth fighting for. That's why he signed up for Vietnam. But coming back, it had gotten so confusing. Nothing was as black and white as his father had explained it to be.

But now Kontar had given him straight black and white talk. He needed Holcomb's help in a fight to help the United States to even exist in a different timeline. Aztecs were a warrior race that still believed in human sacrifice, even into the 23rd century when Kontar was from. The United States and the Inca Nation were the beacons of freedom of human rights and freedoms in Kontar's time. And the survival of one depended on the survival of the other, it seemed.

Holcomb didn't pretend to understand, and Kontar promised to explain even more before the mission started.

Kontar had also promised that if Holcomb came along, Kontar's people could help someone or some member of Holcomb's family if he wanted. But Holcomb had no real family, so he had told Kontar that he would think about that.

Sitting on that park bench, in that park, two hours after Kontar had left, Holcomb had decided to go. He might not have his name in any history books, but if he helped at the Alamo and it made a difference, at least he would be part of a fight that an entire nation would remember.

He gave his notice at the bus garage, talked to a few friends there, and then went back to give notice on his apartment. What surprised him was how many people, both at work and in his building, seemed genuinely sad that he was leaving. He might not have that many good friends, but he clearly had people who liked him, and he liked them back, and some of them would even miss him.

One elderly woman down the hall even brought him a small plate of sugar cookies for a travel snack. He'd only seen her a few times in the hall, and couldn't remember her name, even though she knew his. She told him that he just made the place seem safer. She was going to miss that.

He had never noticed any of it. He just felt he had been walking through the world alone. It seemed he had been far from alone.

This time around, Kontar knocked on the apartment door and

Holcomb answered, a small bag on his shoulder that included his pistol and bathroom supplies and a few changes of clothes. Everything else he was leaving with a note on the kitchen table.

"Seems you have decided," Kontar said, smiling as he backed up and let Holcomb step out and pull the door closed.

"Just one favor to ask," Holcomb said as they headed down the wide hallway toward the staircase.

"Ask and I will do what I can do," Kontar said.

"If you can, I would love to have you use what little money I have left in the bank and add some to it and set up a small college scholarship fund for kids of city bus drivers. Put it in my name if you would, even though no one will remember who I am."

Kontar glanced at Holcomb as they went down the stairs to the lobby, clearly puzzled. "We can do that, no problem at all. That's very nice of you."

Holcomb shrugged. "Always thought about going back to school. Just never got around to it."

"What would you have studied?" Kontar asked.

Holcomb laughed. "History. I always loved history."

Kontar laughed. "With luck, for an entire culture in a different timeline, you're going to help make some history."

As they went out the door and into the bright light of the warm spring day, Holcomb said, "That's why I'm doing this."

Nine

March 5, 1836
Alamo Compound, Bexar, Republic of Texas

THE SUN WAS EASING BEHIND the low hills to the west. Holcomb, Stacy, and DeWitt had been firing consistently all day, picking off any warrior that moved in the direction of the Aztec camp, just as they had done for the past four days.

Travis had reported that the War Chief and the thousands of warriors with him had arrived earlier in the day. And as history in Holcomb's timeline had shown, no more men came to help those inside the Alamo. They were going into battle with thousands of Aztec warriors with around two hundred men.

But so far, the men inside the walls were in good spirits. No real damage had been done to the walls of the fort thanks to the sharp-shooters keeping the cannons at a distance. The fort had stayed a safe little island in a sea of death. Holcomb had no doubt that was about to change. If the Aztec War Chief followed Santa Anna's plan, he would attack tomorrow, on March 6th.

But many historians and many of Santa Anna's own officers had thought it stupid to attack directly at the fort. But that had been in another timeline, with another commander and a much weaker Mexican army. The Aztec War Chief was known for just taking what he wanted. There didn't seem to be any doubt in anyone's mind he was coming hard and soon. The key would be how much damage the men inside the walls could do to the Aztec force before they were killed.

DeWitt used an inhaler to stop a coughing fit and Stacy used the time to refill the clip in his rifle, tossing the empty shells over the wall wrapped in a small cloth bag. The bag had a special acid inside it that ate the shells and turned them into dust in a matter of days. The shells themselves were designed to deteriorate quickly anyway. No one in ten years would dig up any shells or signs of anything from the future at this sight.

"Incoming," a voice shouted and all three men went back to staring out over the wall.

Holcomb was shocked at what he saw.

Coming at full run, directly from the center of the city, were about fifty warriors, their war cries filling the air.

"All four sides," Travis shouted from a perch atop the center cannonade. "They're coming at us from four directions."

Firing started up at once, the sounds covering the cries of the warriors. One right after another the cannons of the fort fired, filling the air with smoke, the booming sounds echoing over the countryside.

Holcomb, Stacy, and DeWitt fired as well, Holcomb taking a warrior on the right and killing him, Stacy aimed at the left, and DeWitt the middle.

The cannons sent more warrior bodies into the air, and each of them fired five more times before the firing eased to a stop with no more warriors to kill.

The wave of warriors hadn't even made it to within a hundred yards of the fort on any side.

"That was just a test," Holcomb said, staring at the bodies strung along the field between the fort wall and Bexar buildings. "The War Chief wanted to know how strong we are."

"He sacrificed two hundred men to test us?" Stacy said, shaking his head.

"Sure seems that way," DeWitt said.

Suddenly Holcomb realized what he had said. With any test, someone had to be looking at the results.

"Watch for movement in the distance," Holcomb said, flipping his glasses to binocular vision and studying the roofs and walls of the city buildings. "Lower War Chiefs had to have been watching so that they could report back."

Beside him, Stacy fired and a brightly adorned warrior spun and fell about two hundred yards out.

Holcomb caught sight of another warrior staring at the scene from the top of a building and put a shot between his eyes.

A few of the other sharpshooters on the other walls were also firing, taking out anyone who might show their face.

DeWitt laughed. "The great War Chief ain't going to like any of this."

"We just pissed him off is all," Holcomb said.

"So, when do you three think he will attack us?"

Holcomb spun around away from the wall at the same time as DeWitt and Stacy to see Travis kneeling behind them.

Holcomb couldn't think of a thing to say to the leader of the fort. And clearly DeWitt and Stacy were just as shocked.

"Look," Travis said, "I know you three have military experience from some place I am not familiar with, as do a number of others who are volunteers here. And you are the best shots I have ever had the pleasure of watching. I'm just glad you are all here helping Texas in this fight."

"It's our honor, sir," Holcomb managed to say. Stacy nodded and DeWitt coughed as he nodded his agreement.

In the last week he had only said a passing hello to Travis. He figured he and DeWitt and Stacy were staying under the young officer's notice. Clearly they hadn't.

History always said that Travis was both smart and very brave. He had just proven history to be correct.

"What just happened was clearly a test," Travis said, "and you sharpshooters cut down the number of reports the War Chief will get about the results. Any theories about what's next? Will it be a full attack tonight or any chance he might just leave us and go around?"

"He won't attack at night," Holcomb said and again both his friends nodded. "From everything I know about the War Chief of the Aztec, fighting at night has little honor. They will prepare at night, and they have no problem in small skirmishes at night, but if they come in full attack, it will be at first light."

He had learned all that from Kontar in the distant future, but he wasn't about to tell Travis that.

"And he won't go around us either," Stacy said. "He can't show any weakness to those under him or they will challenge and kill him."

"Agreed," Holcomb said. "They're coming in full force at first light tomorrow."

Travis seemed to think about that for a moment, then nodded. "I agree."

He stood and saluted Holcomb and Stacy and DeWitt. "Thank you, gentlemen, for the honor of fighting and dying beside you."

With that he turned and went down the stairs and back toward the sick room where Bowie was being cared for.

"This is a long damn ways from Vietnam," DeWitt said after a long moment of silence.

Down the wall, Holcomb noticed that Davy Crockett had been watching the exchange. He gave Holcomb a thumbs-up and went back to watching out over the wall.

For the first time, Holcomb knew completely that what he did in this fight really mattered. Dying for this cause was the right thing to do. He knew now what his father had described about fighting in World War II.

"This doesn't even feel like the same world," DeWitt said, shaking his head.

"Actually," Stacy said, "it's not, remember?"

Holcomb glanced once again at Davy Crockett, one of his childhood heroes. "Tough to forget."

Ten

March 6, 1836
Alamo Compound, Bexar, Republic of Texas

THE MOMENT THE SUN tipped an edge over the hills in the east, the Aztec flaming arrow cannons filled the sky with streaks of fire, sending rolling thunder over the fort and the peaceful sunrise of a Texas morning.

The night had been long and quiet, with only an occasional shot cutting the stillness from a sharpshooter who picked off a warrior stupid enough to show himself.

"Here we go," DeWitt said as the cannons went off, bracing himself against the wall.

"It's been my honor," Holcomb said, glancing at the two men on either side of him that he now called friends, "to fight with you."

"I will remember these days for as long as I live," Stacy said, smiling.

"That's going to be at least another thirty minutes," DeWitt said. "If we're lucky."

"I'm hoping for more like an hour," Holcomb said, laughing.

A moment later, thousands of Aztec warriors seemed to appear out of nowhere among the buildings of the town and the gullies of the hills around the fort.

Waves and waves and waves of warriors.

"Make that thirty minutes after all," Holcomb said, starting to fire.

The sounds of the exploding cannons, and thousands of rifles being fired at once smashed into Holcomb as he fired off one round after another into the ranks, trying to pick off any warrior who looked to be dressed better than any other.

He went through his first clip in a matter of twenty seconds, reloaded, and went back to firing, cutting down warriors in the front lines so that others behind them might trip over the bodies.

It was like facing a sea of ants. The Aztecs swarmed everywhere, screaming and firing as they ran.

One bullet nicked the top of the wall near Holcomb and sent sand into his face, but luckily nothing got into his eyes behind his protective glasses given to him by Kontar.

Beside him, DeWitt was grazed by a shot across one arm. He just swore, wrapped the surface wound in a piece of cloth, and went back to firing, his inhaler stuck in his mouth like a bad cigar.

Holcomb just kept firing, through another clip and then another, his shots always dropping a warrior. And every warrior he killed was one less to fight against Sam Houston and the others defending Texas and the rest of the United States.

The cannons of the Alamo kept up a constant bombardment of the rushing warriors, smashing five and ten at a time into the air.

Suddenly, DeWitt tapped his arm and pointed out at the town's buildings. The main wave of the warriors were now only a hundred yards from the bottom of the west wall and closing fast, and on the buildings of the town, well decorated and brightly colored Aztec warriors had climbed up to watch the fight.

And one in the center looked to be the top War Chief himself, not more than nine hundred feet away.

The idiot was too arrogant to know he couldn't be killed.

Holcomb tapped Stacy and pointed to what DeWitt had shown him. Stacy glanced up, then smiled and nodded.

Holcomb used the old hand signals from Nam to indicate in the intense sound of the battle the way the three of them should fire. Stacy would take the ones on the right side, Holcomb would take the top War Chief in the middle, and DeWitt the chiefs on the left side.

Then on the count of three, they all fired, ignoring the wave of warriors approaching the wall below them.

Holcomb knocked down the War Chief with a shot directly between his well-painted eyes.

Before the others could react around him, Holcomb killed two more of the War Chief's top lieutenants, while DeWitt and Stacy cut down the others on either side.

If nothing else, they had cut the head off of the snake. It would grow a new one quickly enough, but with luck that might give Houston and his Texan army some time and a real fighting chance.

All three of them went back to firing at the rushing warriors below as the remaining brightly dressed war chiefs scattered back into hiding.

When the leading wave of the warriors reached the base of the wall and started trying to toss ropes with hooks over the top, Holcomb grabbed a few of the pen-sized grenades, twisted the caps, and dropped them as beside him Stacy cut a rope and then did the same.

Other warriors were bringing ladders at the walls. Others behind the leading waves were moving cannons into position.

There were just too many. But the Aztecs were paying a very, very high price for this attack.

Along the wall, other defenders followed suit, firing over and over and tossing explosive charges into the mass of warriors coming up at them from the base of the twenty-foot wall.

But nothing seemed to slow the warriors down, they just kept pouring at the wall.

Holcomb went back to picking off the warriors trying to set up cannons to fire directly at the wall from close range. Beside him, Stacy leaned forward to drop a few grenades. Suddenly he spun backwards, a gaping hole in the back of his head from a shot that blew his skull apart.

He went over backwards and then tumbled down the stairs.

Holcomb gave his friend a quick salute of honor and went back to fighting.

Farther down the wall, Crockett was shoving a ladder away from the wall and butting two warriors with the hard end of his rifle, sending them back into the mass of death below.

Holcomb tossed half-a-dozen grenades along the base of the wall in front of him and DeWitt and Crockett.

The smoke from the explosions and the gunshots drifted so thickly it felt like trying to fight on a thick foggy night along the ocean. Only this fog smelled of gunpowder and sweat and blood.

Lots of blood.

DeWitt jumped up and moved to his right along the wall, firing at a warrior trying to breach over the top of the wall. Then he dropped a grenade at the bottom of the ladder and fired downward into the mass.

Suddenly, he dropped over backwards, a bullet hole directly between his eyes.

They had all been wrong. It didn't look like they all were going to last fifteen minutes.

At a half dozen places along the wall the warriors were coming over the top.

Holcomb took his last ten grenades and twisted the caps on all of them, tossing them at different places along the wall at the bases of ladders.

A shot ripped through his left arm, spinning him around and sending waves of bright red pain across his eyes.

His vision cleared quickly and he dropped his rifle and grabbed his pistol, firing as he went.

Crockett moved toward him, firing and butting at warriors reaching the top of the wall.

"Retreat to the church!" he shouted.

"I'll cover you," Holcomb shouted back and Crockett nodded and scrambled down the staircase to the middle of the compound where dozens of Texans were retreating toward their last stand in the church.

Holcomb kept firing, protecting his childhood hero as much as he could, until a shot ripped through his left shoulder and he went over backwards, tumbling down the stairs to the hard dirt at the bottom.

Somehow, he managed to keep the gun in his hand.

A moment later, Crockett appeared in his vision and yanked him to his feet, pulling him toward the church.

Holcomb let the pain clear his mind and he focused one last time, firing at a warrior who was about to attack Crockett.

Then a shot cut through the Tennessee congressman, spinning him away from Holcomb. The shot had caught him in the chest, but he was still alive.

Now it was Holcomb's turn to pull his hero to his feet and stumble onward.

But it wasn't to be.

More fire from the right and more pain cut through Holcomb's legs and back and he and Crockett went down.

An Aztec warrior with a brightly painted face loomed over Holcomb as he struggled to turn over.

Crockett tried to get up to fight, but the warrior cut off his head with a quick swing of a sword.

All Holcomb could do was smile at the ugly painted face of the Aztec as the warrior raised his sword yet again.

Holcomb knew that they had accomplished what they needed to accomplish. He was sure of that. They had slowed the Aztec army and caused enough damage that Houston could defeat them.

This would be a good world he had helped create.

And maybe in Portland, Oregon, in this timeline, there would be a nice park on the river for people to enjoy. He hoped so. He loved that park, especially on warm spring days.

And as the warrior's sword came down to cut off his head, Holcomb just kept smiling.

It was going to be good to be remembered after all.

REMEMBER ME TO YOUR CHILDREN

A Seeders Universe Story

USA Today *bestselling writer returns to the world of his latest novel,* Dust and Kisses, *the first of many books that span time and space in his* Seeders' Universe.

In this heartfelt story, Tammy works with her best friend and love, Hal, to help in the formal discovery and burial of the dead lost in the Big Death. The survivors call the task The Respect Project.

On a Portland, Oregon, suburban street, Tammy discovers from the tragedy of a family that the future can be a hopeful place.

"TAMMY, CAN'T YOU JUST RELAX A LITTLE?"

Tammy glanced around at her best friend and lover, Hal Lemmon, as he tried to follow her up the center of the suburban street. The day was hot and Hal was sweating, staining his white tee shirt around the brown straps of the backpack he carried. His longish brown hair was damp where it stuck out from under his Yankee's baseball cap.

His handsome face was flushed and he looked tired, even though they had only gone four blocks in distance.

She was hot as well, which was why she had been walking fast, trying to get them to their starting target before they stopped or the heat got them. It normally wasn't this hot in Portland, Oregon, or at least that's what some long-time residents of the area had told her earlier.

She was wearing jeans with tennis shoes, a sleeveless tank-top with a sports bra under it, and she had her short blonde hair under a Dodgers baseball cap. Sweat was running off her neck and down her chest and she desperately needed a drink of water.

She had her Smith and Wesson pistol in a holster on her hip and Hall had a small twenty-two saddle rifle tied to the side of his back-pack. It had been years since they had gone anywhere without those guns, winter or summer. They both had admitted they would feel naked without them.

On both sides of the suburban street around them, the houses were like tombstones for the people who had been killed inside of them when the Big Death happened five years before. The once green grass lawns where children had played were brown and had long turned to tall, dry weeds. The house windows were dirty and almost every house had drapes pulled, at least on the lower floors.

Weeds and grass had started growing in patches of dirt along the street and up through cracks in the concrete. What had been perfect lines of lawns, driveways, sidewalks, and street were now blurred as Mother Nature slowly took back the neighborhood. Tammy had seen a projection on how in fifty years a neighborhood like this would be completely overgrown, in one hundred years it would be all plants and piles of rubble, and in five hundred years it would be almost impossible to tell what had been here.

Just as Mother Nature had killed most everyone on the planet one day with a burst of electromagnetic waves from space, she now was slowly reclaiming the planet.

The Big Death had hit at a little after eight in the morning here in Portland, so most people in this neighborhood were either at work or taking kids to school or some such thing. Tammy and Hal had been two of the million-plus lucky ones who had been either underground in subways, in vaults, or deep inside ships. She had been down in the vaults of her Boise newspaper, doing research through old papers not yet scanned, on a story that no longer mattered, other than being down there had saved her life.

Hal had been in a bank vault in downtown Boise getting something from his safe deposit box. She and Hal had stumbled upon each other on the second day of wandering around in the dead bodies. They hadn't known each before, but they stayed together and helped each other survive those first few years until they joined up with other survivors working to rebuild a civilization.

Over that first really hard year, they had fallen in love.

Now they lived together in the new city of Portland, Oregon, worked together both on the local newspaper, and searching for the dead, and she couldn't imagine being without Hal through any of it.

She looked around at all the empty houses. This neighborhood hadn't been cleared yet, which was the process they were sent to start.

They were to inventory the bodies in every home along the street and mark from the outside which homes had bodies so the removal crews could come and take them to the new cemeteries.

And in each home they were to look for information as to who lived there and double-check it with their database, even those without bodies in them.

The ultimate goal of the Respect Project was to give everyone who died in the Big Death a proper resting place and a record of their existence for the future, including where they had lived and what they had done for work.

It was almost an impossible task, but everyone in the five now-growing new cities around the country, which included Portland, and the new national government, were committed to the task.

"We can start anywhere, you know?" Hal said. "How about we start here, work back to the truck along both sides, then cool down and bring the truck to here and go the other direction?"

Tammy stopped and glanced at an address still visible on the side of one of the homes. From what she could tell, they were about halfway along the long subdivision street. Hal's idea was a good one. They had to get out of the sun. It was only ten in the morning and this day promised to be far too hot to stay out in the sun for very long.

She nodded. "Good plan."

"Thank you," Hal said, stopping and taking off his pack, letting it drop to the concert in the middle of the street.

They had been going out four mornings a week to catalog houses and bodies in the vast subdivisions that surrounded Portland. It had bothered her some at first, nosing into people's personal homes, but then she had grown numb to it. After all, the people they were investigating were all dead.

The thing she could never look at were the children's bodies, often in cribs. Every time they found a home with a child, Hal took that house on his own, even though they had clear orders to always stay together. Not that there was anything dangerous in these old subdivisions besides slowly rotting wood.

This subdivision had lots of signs that children lived in these homes, from swing sets visible in the back years, to small bikes and other toys left near the front doors.

She wanted a child someday, with Hal, but she felt the new world wasn't stable enough yet to commit to that, even though hundreds of healthy children were being born every month in the new Portland. Hal wanted children, he was clear on that, but he was willing to wait until she was ready as well.

At the moment, she just wasn't ready and when searching homes, she just couldn't make herself deal with the dead children.

She took a long drink of semi-cold water that tasted wonderful and then handed the bottle to Hal, who took a drink and sighed. Around them a slight breeze kicked up filling the air with faint noises of houses creaking and dry brush rustling. The sounds did nothing to break the death silence of the subdivision.

"Let's go get snoopy into people's lives," he said, handing her back the bottle of water.

"That one first," she said, pointing to a light blue house on her right. "Let's do two on that side, then two on the other side, as we work back to the truck."

"Sounds perfect," he said, smiling at her and picking up his pack.

She loved everything about him, his dark eyes, his solid build, and his strong arms. But mostly she just loved that smile.

Somehow, over all the years of living in the middle of death, that smile of his had kept her sane.

They headed up the front sidewalk of the two-story home that must have been very nice in its day. The drapes were pulled and more than likely the front door was locked. Both of them had been trained before they started this job to pick a lock. Hal was slightly faster at it than she was, but only by a second or so. They hadn't found a lock so far that had stopped them.

The people in charge of the Respect Project wanted all the homes to be respected as well, if possible, even though eventually they would all just rot away. Tammy was fine with that as well.

Hal left his pack on the front step and took out his rifle, slinging it over his shoulder before bending down and picking the front door locks. Thirty seconds later he stood and pushed the door open.

The smell of mold and dust and something with a slight tang greeted them and they both stepped back out of the smell and pulled out their cloth masks and tied them over their mouths and noses. That smell with a bite meant there was a body in the building.

They always wore masks when a body was in the building.

The masks also helped them with the dust and they went through about a dozen of the masks a day, maybe more on a hot day like today.

Even though there was some light filtering through the drapes and from a back window in the kitchen beyond the living room, they both clicked on flashlights. When they first started out doing this job, they had both tripped over various things in homes that they just hadn't seen in dim light. So they took no chances now.

Tammy panned her flashlight around the living room. More of a formal room that didn't look much used. A layer of gray dust dulled down all colors in the room.

Moving slowly to not kick up too much dust from five years of no one moving around in here, they headed for the kitchen and the family room beyond.

Tammy was relieved to see no sign of children's toys around the family room.

Hal slowly opened some drawers near the family dining area. Often families left personal information in drawers near a kitchen table.

While he was doing that, she turned and opened the back door leading into a two-car garage. There was one car there. And a spot for a second one. Tools were in their places on the walls.

Nothing else of interest.

"One car left," she said as she went past Hal and toward the rooms to the right of the big living room. One looked like a guest bedroom and was as sterile as the living room. Whoever lived in this house believed in keeping everything in its place. Even after sitting abandoned for five years and layers of gray dust making everything pale, that feeling of "in its place" was clear in this home.

It made her wonder what the residents of this home had been like. Clearly different than she and Hal. Their large apartment in a building in the downtown area was always awash with clutter of various types, mostly books. They were both just comfortable in that.

She would not have been comfortable in this place. It felt sterile and even more dead than most homes she had been in, as if this home had been dead before the Big Death hit.

"Anything?" she asked.

Hal shook his head. "Nothing. Drawers in perfect order, but no bills, no letters, nothing. More than likely all that is in a study someplace from the looks of all this."

With Hal leading, they headed upstairs.

The light was brighter upstairs as most of the back windows in the home had the blinds open. They all looked out over a lush backyard that had held a pool. Tammy had no doubt it had been beautiful in its day. And from the looks of the house, the lawn would have been mowed perfectly and the pool cleaned twice a week.

At the top of the stairs a hallway led the length of the house. It had a number of closed doors. Tammy had a hunch behind one of those doors would be the body they knew was in here from the faint musty smell. The smell had a slight tang to it after five years, but it wasn't a smell that was easy to miss.

And now that they were upstairs, the smell was thick.

And even though it was still fairly early, this upper area of the house was already heating up. Any body they did find would be well mummified in this kind of heat.

A mummified body was a lot better as far as Tammy was concerned than a body torn up from animals. Not all animals had survived the electromagnetic pulse. Dogs and rats and mice had been killed, but cats had survived. And with a cat trapped in a home with a dead human, they ate the dead human when they got hungry enough.

There were no signs this home had cats, so the body would be mummified and look moderately human even after five years.

The first two doors were to small bedrooms with no occupants. They had been furnished with small single beds and just left. One room was painted pink, one blue.

Clearly the rooms had been meant for future children that had not arrived yet.

And now never would.

The third door was to an empty bathroom and the next door was to a master bedroom and bath, also empty. The bed was made perfectly.

There was nothing out of place in this entire house. Tammy found that amazing and very closed up and creepy.

The next door on the other side of the hall was to a study with a big desk.

"Got it," Hal said, moving to the desk and file cabinet that would let them know who had lived here.

There was one more door at the end of the hall and that meant it had the body in it.

Tammy went to it and opened it slowly, making sure to not stir up any dust as she did so.

The blinds were open in the room and it was a fairly large family room that also did not look used in any way. This room had a large-screen television, a number of couches, a game table, and plush carpet.

It had been designed to be comfortable, but clearly not made comfortable.

Everything again was in perfect position. Nothing was used. It was as if the people living in this house had just existed in it and never really lived in it.

There was a door off the family room that was closed. More than likely that was where the body was. They had found many bodies, since they started this job, in various stages of bathroom routines.

Hal came in behind her. "This is the home of Ben and Cathy Freeman. He worked at a pharmacy downtown and she was an RN."

Hal held up his digital pad. "We already recovered his body when they cleaned the downtown area."

"This place sure looks like they were planning for kids," Tammy said. 'Clearly didn't get the chance."

Hal glanced around and nodded. Then he pointed to the door. "You want me to look and see who is in there?"

"We both will," she said.

Slowly she opened the bathroom door to keep the dust from swirling while both of them shined their flashlights into the small bathroom.

What she saw stunned her and took her a moment for her mind to wrap around.

What had been a fairly attractive, thin, brown-haired woman lay in the bathtub face up. She had mummified, but she still looked pretty good, with her long brown hair fanned out on the back of the tub over her.

And her face was calm in death. Very calm.

What had really surprised Tammy was that the tub water when it evaporated had left an ugly brown stain.

It took her a moment to see why. Both of the woman's wrists that were crossed over her chest had been slashed.

A razor blade lay on a napkin on the edge of the tub.

"Now that's a first," Hal said beside Tammy in the bathroom door. "More than likely she cut her wrists right before the Big Death hit."

On the counter was a note card standing up with the name "Ben" on it.

Tammy looked at it, then glanced at Hal. Clearly that was Cathy Freeman's suicide note.

Hal shrugged, meaning she could read it or not. Up to her.

Tammy wasn't sure if she wanted to read it, but at this point she felt she had no choice.

She picked up the note and opened it. Then read it aloud as Hal held his flashlight so she could see.

Dearest Ben,

I am so sorry for the mess I have left you. I have tried to keep this clean and simple and plan this in a bathroom we seldom use.

I am so sorry that I cannot bring the children into the world we so hoped to have. I could no longer look at the deadness in your eyes and the disappointment I felt every time we made love. My passing here will allow you to move on, to find a new wife, to be happy, and finally have and raise the children you so wanted.

Please don't be me mad at me, love. This is for the best. Remember me to your children when they are old enough to understand. Have a wonderful life.

Love Always,
Cath

Tammy carefully replaced the suicide note on the counter.

"Let's get out of here," Hal said, gently touching her elbow. "We got all we need from here."

Somehow Tammy nodded and turned and followed Hal out of the family room and down the hall past the future children's bedrooms, then down the stairs and out into the hot air of the dead subdivision.

Hal picked up his pack, stuck his rifle back in it, and led the way to the street.

She pulled off her mask and tucked it in her pocket, letting the warm air work to clear her mind.

They stopped in the middle of the street, both their backs to the house they had just been in.

After a moment, Hal gently touched her arm. "You all right?"

"Honestly," she said, turning to look into his worried dark eyes. "I think I'm done for the day."

"I agree," Hal said. "Too hot anyway. So what are you thinking?"

She looked into the eyes of the man she loved, the man that had helped her survive more death than she ever wanted to think about. "I am thinking about a long cold shower in our air-conditioned apartment."

"We are on the same track with that," Hal said, smiling.

"Then maybe a few hours in bed making love to you."

At that, his eyebrows went up and he looked at her puzzled.

"After all this death," she said, sweeping her arm around to indicate the dead neighborhood, "don't you think it's time we bring some new life into the world?"

He smiled bigger than she had remembered him smiling in a very long time. "I do. Very much."

She kissed him, then took his arm and together they headed up the hot street of the dead subdivision.

A hot breeze twisted through the dead houses around them, and maybe, just maybe, if they had listened, they would have imagined they heard the faint laughter of the children.

YOU FORGIVE THE NIGHT'S SCREAM

A Poker Boy story

USA Today *bestselling writer, Dean Wesley Smith, returns once again to his most popular series, Poker Boy.*

This time Poker Boy awakes to a blood-curdling scream that only he hears. Some of his team think the scream a sign he faces death.

But Poker Boy plays professional poker. He faced worse over a no-limit poker game numbers of times.

A funny and touching story of redemption and cold feet.

One

I WOKE WITH THE SOUND of a woman's scream echoing in my head.

High-pitched.

Full of terror.

I sat bolt upright in bed.

My heart pounded like it wanted to get out of my chest and run for the closet and every Poker Boy superpower sense I had was amped up to full power.

Beside me, my girlfriend and sidekick, Patty Ledgerwood, aka Front Desk Girl, lay sleeping soundly, her wonderful long brown hair like a shadow over her pillow in the dim light coming from cracks around the side of the drapes.

Outside, the city of Las Vegas never slept and certainly never turned off its lights. The strip was only a few blocks from Patty's apartment building and my invisible office floated just to the west of her apartment and directly over the MGM Grand Hotel and Casino complex.

I held my breath, waiting for another scream, trying to listen over the pounding of my heart.

Nothing.

A little noise from a truck on the street below Patty's apartment. Then a couple quick beeps as it backed up.

Nothing else.

Yet every danger Poker Boy sense I had was shouting, making me want to get out of there.

That scream had been close, as if it was inside this very apartment. Yet Patty was still sound asleep.

Something was very wrong.

Very wrong.

I've had bad dreams before, but when that scream let go, I have no memory of actually being in a dream.

The scream was real. Outside of my possible dream.

At least real in one fashion or another.

I gently touched Patty's shoulder.

She stirred and rolled to look up at me. "What—"

I put my finger to my lips and shook my head. Then I eased out of bed. I was wearing sweat pants and nothing else. I slipped on my thin brown slippers.

Patty came awake at once, saying nothing and moving silently out of the other side of the bed, slipping on her white bathrobe over her nightgown and her slippers as well.

I stood hear the door to the bedroom that led out into the living room, listening for any noise coming from either the living room or kitchen area.

Silently, Patty came over and touched my arm, using her powers to calm me down some. The pounding of my racing heart subsided and I mouthed the word, "Thanks." One of her superpowers was the ability to keep people calm and focused. I loved it in stressful situations when we worked together. We had discovered that as a team we were far stronger together than apart.

Plus I was head-over-my-slippers in love with her.

She pointed to her ear and shook her head, meaning she was hearing nothing.

I wasn't either, so silently I went out into the living room.

And as I walked ten steps, the temperature of the room dropped a good thirty degrees until suddenly I could see my breath in the dim light.

Patty grabbed my arm and pulled me back into the bedroom, a panicked look on her face.

I'm glad she did. I would need a lot more clothes to go back into that living room.

"Out of time," she whispered and I did, slipping us between instants of time. It felt like I stopped time when I did that, but in reality, time never stopped. I just moved me and Patty inside an instant of time.

Normally, in a busy casino or outside, I could tell instantly when I did that, but in the silent and dark apartment, nothing seemed to change.

"You know what caused that chill?" I asked, shivering as I tried to warm up a little. All my senses were still screaming that there was danger close by and the memory of that scream seemed to echo in my mind.

I moved over and grabbed a sweatshirt that said "The Golden Nugget Poker Room" and pulled it over my head, easing the chill some.

"Did you hear something?" Patty asked.

I nodded. "A woman's scream. That's what woke me up."

"Oh, no," she said.

Even in the dim light I could tell her face went white.

I glanced up at the ceiling. "Stan. Help!"

Patty nodded and a moment later Stan appeared.

The God of Poker had on what he always seemed to have on. Tan slacks, button down sweater, and loafers. In all the years I had worked for him, I had seldom caught him out of that outfit, day or night.

"Wow," he said, instantly spinning around, looking for the danger. I could feel him strengthen the time bubble and put a shield around us, which helped my screaming warning senses some.

"What is causing that?" he asked.

I shrugged, since I honestly had no idea.

"He heard a scream," Patty said. "In his sleep."

"Oh, shit!" Stan said and instantly vanished, leaving the screen and the stronger time bubble.

I looked at Patty who clearly wasn't in the mood for any of my one-line jokes, so I wisely said nothing. Not a skill I often had, but at the moment with every warning sense I had still going off, it seemed prudent.

Besides, the way they were acting was starting to scare me to death.

The longest five seconds later, Laverne, Lady Luck herself, appeared in our bedroom with Stan and Ben beside her.

Lady Luck didn't have on her normal power business suit, but instead wore a pair of jeans and an old sweatshirt. She looked down-right normal for one of the most powerful beings in all the universe.

Ben was a god in the book world that was a member of our team. He looked like a little old librarian and had a perfect memory of every-thing he had ever read and the history of all the gods.

Lady Luck instantly strengthened the shields around them even more and the sense of warning and fear again decreased but didn't vanish by any means.

"Who heard the scream?" Lady Luck asked.

I sort of half raised my hand.

"Damn it," she said.

Now when Lady Luck swears, you know things can't be good. And I wasn't sure if I wanted to know just how bad things actually were, since all the bad seemed to be focused at me.

Two

PATTY HELD ONTO MY ARM, keeping me as calm as her super-power could manage. But I was feeling anything but calm.

"So what's out there in that cold?" I asked.

"A banshee," Lady Luck said.

Ben nodded, confirming what Lady Luck said but not adding to it.

I almost said that I thought those were myths, but then realized who I was and who was standing around me. I just hadn't been in this superhero business long enough to know what was a myth and what actually had some reality attached to it.

"So tell me exactly what you are worried about," I said.

"The banshee is a fairy that is known to mourn the coming loss of a life," Ben said.

"By screaming?" I asked. "More like it would scare a person to death."

"By screaming," Stan said, nodding. "And the person who hears them is supposed to be the one who will die very shortly. It's both a warning and a sad cry that the person is dying."

Well, I had to admit, I didn't much like the sound of that.

I took a deep breath and could feel Patty's calming influence flow through me. Honestly, over the last few years, I had faced death and the end of the world a few times. And a lot of really tough players in no-limit poker games. So if some being was giving me a warning, I needed to thank her and just flat ask her what was going to happen.

And when.

Never hurt to know when a fella was going to die, I figured.

Seemed so simple. I'm sure there were a dozen reasons it was a stupid idea, but my friends around me just seemed determined to stand next to me when I died and do nothing, so I needed to do something.

And my terrified mind couldn't come up with one other idea. I knew death could follow me anywhere, since I had met two gods of death so far, and sort of liked them both, honestly. So running was out of the question.

I moved over to the closet and pulled out my heaviest Oregon coat. Since I was originally from Oregon and my home casino was in the mountains of Oregon, I at least had a few heavy coats, one of which I had brought to Vegas and stashed in Patty's apartment because at times I had been damned cold here as well.

"What are you doing?" Patty asked, again taking my arm as I came back to her zipping up my parka.

"Going out to talk with the banshee," I said, giving her a quick kiss and heading for the door into the dark living room.

"Not a great idea," Lady Luck said.

I stopped and looked at her. "Has a banshee killed anyone?"

"No, she just warns people," Lady Luck said, her voice sounding sad and tired.

"Then it seems I'll be fine. When was the last time anyone just talked with the banshee?"

Ben shook his head. "There are no records of anyone doing such a thing."

"Five hundred years," Lady Luck said softly.

Ben glanced at her and said nothing. He knew something he wasn't saying.

"Well, if this kills me," I said, doing my best to screw up every ounce of courage I had, "someone tell the next person to not try it."

"I'm coming with you," Patty said.

"No, I heard the scream, I'm the one the banshee is trying to warn."

I glanced at Lady Luck and nodded. I almost said, "Wish me luck" and then stopped as I realized how stupid that really would have sounded to Lady Luck.

Her expression didn't change from extreme seriousness combined with sadness, something I had never seen on her face.

"While I'm gone," I said, standing near the door of the living room, "someone might want to check with Death, see if I really am on a list at the moment. We did save his ass and help his daughter."

Lady Luck nodded. "I'll do it," she said, and vanished.

I took a deep breath and turned and went into the living room.

The intense cold slapped me and I staggered, but managed to move forward.

"My name is Poker Boy," I said to the cold air, my breath freezing in front of my face. "I heard your scream and came to see if I could help."

Being brash seemed to be the most logical thing I could do.

And that's what people who rescue other people do, after all, go toward the sound of a scream.

"Thank you," a soft female voice said from the other side of the couch.

"Can you stand a little light?" I asked.

"It is not a problem," the voice said.

An instant later the table light beside the couch clicked on. A beautiful and mostly nude small woman sat on the couch under the light. Her skin was a light blue and she had two fragile-looking silver wings tucked behind her.

Her beautiful, long, silver hair cascaded around her and covered most of the important parts.

But there was no two ways about it, she was stunning.

I moved over to a large chair facing her across a frost-covered coffee table and sat down, my hands in my pockets of the heavy ski parka. Somewhere between the door and the chair I had lost touch with my feet, since they were only in thin slippers and I was sure they were already frozen.

"So I assume you were calling me for help?" I asked, doing my best to not push any power toward her for fear she might think I was trying to meddle.

"I was," she said, nodding, moving her silver hair around in such a fashion that any good strip club would hire her in a moment.

"Not warning me like you normally do."

"No, calling you for help," she said.

Relief flooded through me but did nothing to warm me up. You would think it would have.

"I have been stuck in this frigid-state for almost five hundred years now," she said, her voice taking on a little more power. "I have done my job as instructed for five hundred years."

I nodded, a little worried about what was coming next.

"I would like you to help me become free of this punishment."

Oh, great, she's asking the newest member of all the superheroes in God's world for help with something that happened five hundred years ago, as if I should know what that was.

"Why do you think I can help with this?" I asked.

"I have watched you and your team save many, many lives," she said. "I hope you can now save mine."

I nodded. "We can try. But can I bring a few members of my team in here to help me?"

"You can," she said, nodding.

Being afraid to stand on my frozen feet, I shouted to the door. "Patty, Stan, Ben, could you join us?"

She nodded, making her hair dance around the important parts of her body. "I am honored you are willing to try to help me."

Stan had bundled all three of them up in parkas and gloves and they came in slowly like an expedition to the South Pole lost in Patty's apartment. No dog sleds, luckily.

Patty came over and sat on the arm of the chair beside me, calming me some with a touch. Stan and Ben both nodded to the banshee and remained standing.

She nodded back.

I turned back to the banshee and said, "We are ready. Could you tell us what caused this punishment five hundred years ago?"

"It is not punishment for a crime," she said. "It is punishment for love. I loved the wrong woman."

Well, I was as liberal as the next person, but honestly, that answer surprised me, right down to my frozen feet.

Three

I NEEDED TO GET THIS GOING before I froze completely to the chair. "May I ask first who put this punishment on you?"

I glanced over at Ben who was shaking his head from side-to-side. "You don't want to know," he said softly.

"I did," Lady Luck said, entering the room right after Ben said that.

She did not have a ski parka on and seemed oblivious to the intense cold.

If I got many more surprises like that, the blood actually might reach my feet again.

Patty squeezed my arm to keep me calm.

"How are you, Laverne?" the banshee asked, smiling.

"I am well," Lady Luck said, moving to the end of the couch and sitting down and facing the banshee. "You are as beautiful as ever."

The banshee nodded her head thank you, again doing wonderful and alluring things with her hair over her perfect blue body.

Who knew a blue body could be perfect?

Then the banshee said something that got me even more confused, which in this frozen state, was going some.

"Thank you for saving my life."

Laverne smiled and nodded. "I am sorry that it had to be in this fashion. It was what your husband would accept as a punishment short of death."

"I have survived," the banshee said. "Loving you was worth it. Is my husband still angry at me?"

"He is not," Lady Luck said. "He is retired, his daughter has taken over his month of duties as Death just last year, and he spends most of his time surfing in Hawaii with his new wife."

I just about choked. This banshee had been married to Death himself. And she had been in love with Lady Luck. Wow, I really needed to spend time with Ben and learn about some of the history of the Gods.

"Then is it possible to return me to the normal world?" the banshee asked.

"I just spoke with your ex-husband," Lady Luck said. "Poker Boy and his team helped his daughter make the transition last year, and I told him that Poker Boy was trying to help you now after five hundred years of punishment."

"Thank you," the banshee said. "He never knew you were the one?"

"He knew," Laverne said. "Right from the start. And he knew it broke my heart, as wells as yours to do what I did. That's why he allowed the punishment."

"I have been wailing over death and broken hearts now for five hundred years," the banshee said. "And with every one I mourned the loss of your love."

"You never lost it," Laverne said.

Once again my toes felt warmer from the shock of that statement.

"You are married, have four grown daughters?" the banshee asked, staring at Laverne in clear surprise.

"My husband and I have," Laverne said, smiling, "shall we say, an open arrangement."

I just about said, "More information than I needed." But my teeth were chattering too much luckily to get that stupid joke out.

Laverne stood and with a "thank you" into the air, more than likely to the banshee's former husband, she waved her hand.

Intense heat filled the room and the banshee sat there, smiling, soaking it all in.

And then finally, after a few seconds, it was over.

I did feel warmer, but not much.

Water was dripping all around Patty's apartment from the melting frost and I could feel the temperature on my face returning to normal, although it would not surprise me to have frostbite on my nose.

The banshee now was no longer blue, but a tanned golden brown all over. And I do mean all over. And her hair was now just as long but a rich brown. And her wings shimmered in a rainbow of colors.

Laverne reached out her hand to the banshee and then said, "Jayne, welcome back."

Jayne took her hand and stood, smiling, her long hair doing little to cover some pretty amazing assets.

"It's a pleasure to be back."

Then Jayne turned to me and said, "Thank you, Poker Boy, and your entire team, for being willing to take a chance on talking to me."

I just nodded, not trusting myself to say anything sane.

"We have some catching up to do," Laverne said, smiling.

"Now that's something I've been looking forward to for five hundred years."

Then, like two teenage girls, they both giggled, and vanished.

Lady Luck giggling was unsettling, to say the least.

Stan shook his head and said, "See you tomorrow."

Then he and Ben vanished.

Patty stood and shivered, water dripping off her coat from the melting frost.

"Would you do me a favor," I asked as she offered to help me out of my chair.

"Anything, my frozen love."

"Would you start a warm shower running. I'm just going to teleport out of these clothes and into the shower from here. I don't think my feet will carry me."

She laughed. "I'll be there, naked, standing under the hot water, ready to catch you."

And she did.

And I got real warm, real quick. I'll leave it at that.

A BUBBLE FOR A MINUTE

Mike Resnick asked me one fine day to write an alternate history story for an anthology about Wallis Simpson. I asked, "Who's he?"

Mike laughed, said I had some research to do, and hung up.

Since at that point in time I had been playing with how music and time travel sort of go hand-in-hand, I did my research and wrote this story for him. I was very proud of it and Mike liked it as well. (He seemed surprised I could learn so much about Wallis Simpson so quickly.)

The anthology called By Any Other Fame *edited by Mike Resnick and Martin H. Greenberg appeared and vanished, almost without a trace in 1994. I liked the story a great deal and was bummed, but that was the nature of traditional publishing in those days.*

So in a continuing effort to bring some of my favorite stories back to a wider audience at times in this magazine and then later in book form and in collections, here is the story again. Even after twenty years, it's still one of my favorites.

I hope you enjoy it as well.

One

THE LAST NOTES of the old song, Paper Moon, faded into the thick antiseptic smell of the small nursing home room and the needle on the record made an impatient clicking, demanding that someone stop it.

In the wheelchair beside the bed, the old woman named Wallis Simpson nodded, almost in time to the clicking needle. She had a faint smile and distant haze in her eyes that gave her ninety-eight year old face a peaceful look. Seventeen-year-old Gary Sullivan studied that face for a moment, shaking his head at the incredible story she had just told him. A story of her youth and her marriages. A story identical to the stories she had told him every day for the last week. Identical, that is, right up until the story reached 1932. Right up until she stopped and asked him to put on the long-playing record of Paper Moon.

Gary pulled back the sleeve on his sweatshirt and leaned forward in his chair over the old-fashioned phonograph. Carefully he picked up the arm and put it back on its holder. It was amazing something this old still worked and even more amazing that the old record hadn't been worn into dust since she listened to it so much.

He clicked off the machine and the small tape recorder on the nightstand beside it, then faced Mrs. Simpson. "Would you mind if I came back again tomorrow?" It was the same thing he had asked for the past two weeks.

She took a moment to come back from whatever time she had been inside her own head, then smiled at him. "Of course not." Her voice was soft and almost hoarse after the workout she had given it telling him her story today. But her voice still had a tremendous power and aliveness that he had admired since the first day he had interviewed her.

"Besides," she said. A light smile slowly filled her face and smoothed out some of the wrinkles. "Who else would I have to talk to? Who else would believe in me?"

"Great," he said, with as much enthusiasm as he could muster, even though he had no idea what she meant by believing in her. It was just part of that song she loved so much.

He stood and, for the first time in the last half hour, noticed just how hot and closed-in this modern little room was. It felt like a prison and suddenly all he wanted to do was run for the door, escape, see what had changed.

What had changed seemed to be his constant question. Today, her story had ended with her marrying a business man by the name of Harvey. With him she had two children. Gary had no idea what that would do to the world outside. But he doubted it would be enough to help his dad. So far, in two weeks of trying, none of her stories had been enough. But somehow he knew that if she just kept telling stories, in one his dad would still be with him and his mother.

Mrs. Simpson turned her wheelchair slightly to face where Gary stood. "You know," she said. "This little experiment of yours has made me the envy of the wing. No one ever comes to talk to most of these folks, except on holidays and the like."

He took a deep breath of the hot air and forced himself to smile. He didn't have the heart to tell her that his little experiment, as she called it, had started out as nothing more than a history paper for a senior high class. A simple assignment that had been done and turned in two weeks before. But he had kept coming back because at first he didn't understand why she kept changing the last part of her stories.

And then, after a few days, he needed her to keep changing the stories until she came to the right story. The exact right story that would bring his dad back home.

"Well," Gary said, "how about same time tomorrow afternoon? You know how important reputation is to high school students."

She laughed. "Thanks for believing in me," she said again. She said that at least once every day and it was starting to give him the creeps. He just nodded and turned into the hall. The name beside her door now said Mrs. Harvey. It had been the twelfth time her name had changed, yet he still thought of her as Wallis Simpson, the name she had been the first time he asked her to tell a story.

Gary forced himself to walk slowly and carefully to the front door, smiling at the nurses at the nurses' station and taking slow, deep breaths of the thick antiseptic and death-filled air. The front door was only a few yards ahead.

He wondered what world he would find beyond it this time.

Two

THE ASSIGNMENT had been given by Coach Kinser, the heavy-set ex-jock who taught Gary's third period. He was also Gary's football coach, which made getting a good grade even more important. "Go to a nursing home," Coach Kinser said, "ask permission to talk to a resident, and interview that resident about his or her past."

The entire class had groaned and the Coach had just smiled. "History is an oral tradition," he had said. "You will enjoy it."

Gary, of course, had waited until a few days before it was due and then found Mrs. Simpson. "Wallis," as she said she liked to be called. Her room was the standard modern nursing home room, just like the one Gary's grandmother had died in. There was a bed with metal rails, a small desk, a small nightstand, and a television across from a rocking chair. Nothing else decorated her room and the place instantly made him feel like he was being smothered.

His first thought was to make the interview fast and get it over with. But Wallis Simpson was a good storyteller and, as Mr. Kinser had said, Gary enjoyed listening to her.

It took over an hour the first day and filled a tape.

That first day she told him about her early years. She was from Baltimore and had been married twice. Her first marriage was to a naval officer by the name of Earl Spencer, whom she divorced in 1927. Her second marriage was to a Washington D.C. businessman named Ernest Simpson.

From the way she talked it was clear that she loved Ernest and everything he gave to her. She talked about how much they traveled and how she met kings and presidents while at his side.

On a business trip to England she and Ernest had become fast friends with the Prince of Wales, who later became King Edward. She said she had many wonderful stories about trips with the Prince and parties at his castle.

But when her story reached the summer of 1932 and the party she and Ernest attended at the White House, everything suddenly changed.

The Prince of Wales had gotten them an invitation to the party to meet the new American President. It was at the mention of the party that she asked Gary to put the long- playing record of Paper Moon on her old phonograph.

He did as she asked and while that record played, she told him about the party and meeting President Roosevelt and the First Lady and then about how Ernest was killed in London and how she returned to the states and never remarried. Her story ended with the record and Gary thanked her and went home, thinking he had more than enough information for his paper.

But it turned out he didn't.

He actually wanted more about the White House party and the young President Roosevelt, figuring that would make the most interesting paper for the Coach, since the Coach had a thing for the Roosevelts.

So the next afternoon Gary stopped by the nursing home again to see Mrs. Simpson. She seemed happy to see him and again she went over the same story of her life, right up until the party at the White House.

And again, when she mentioned that White House summer party, she asked him to put on the record.

This time she told him much more about the party and about how she and Ernest had taken a limousine from the hotel. Then she went on to tell him about how she had fallen for the limousine driver. Two years after the party she went back to Washington, leaving Ernest in London, and got a divorce. She married the limousine driver, a man by the name of Barkley. He died five years ago and she was now all alone.

At first Gary had wanted to ask her about her change in her story, but then just shrugged it off to senility. And he was so startled by the change in story that he forgot to ask her more about President Roosevelt.

She thanked him for believing in her and, as he left the room, he noticed the nametag on the door. It now read Mrs. Barkley, where the day before he was sure it had read Simpson.

As a lark, and with the same excuse that he needed more information about President Roosevelt, he went back the next day. In that day's story she met a businessman at the White House party and married him three years later. Not only had her name again changed on her door, but on the way home that afternoon his mom's favorite grocery store, DANNY'S, was gone, replaced by a small shopping mall.

He asked his mom about the store, but she just gave him a blank look and shook her head. And there was no store by that name listed anywhere in the phone book.

The next day DANNY'S Grocery was back after Mrs. Simpson told him a story about how she and Ernest traveled to Africa, where he died in a hunting accident.

By this point Gary had figured out what seemed to be impossible: that her stories were somehow changing the world.

And he had also figured out that maybe, if he got to the right story, his dad would come back. His dad who had left him and his mother when he was five. A dad who his mother would never talk about and who he had dreamed about for as long as he could remember.

So he kept going back every day, listening to Mrs. Simpson, or whatever her name was that day, tell the same story right up to the hot summer of 1932, right up to the White House party.

Then he would listen to her change the world around them.

Three

ON GARY'S seventeenth visit to Mrs. Simpson he finally got his wish. His dad came back.

Her story the day before had left her with two children and today, for some reason, there was a vase of fresh flowers on her nightstand. She looked happier and healthier than he had seen her and he commented about it.

She thanked him and they started into the same routine. She told him about her early life, her uncle and her grandmother, both of her marriages, and all the traveling she did. Gary had this part memorized and it never varied. And as always, when she reached the summer party at the White House, she asked him to put on the record of Paper Moon.

"Why Paper Moon?" he asked her as he placed the record in place.

She smiled, her mind obviously a long way back in time, remembering. "It was the song the big band at the White House played three times. I danced and danced that night, feeling like a princess gone to the ball. I remember wanting the song and the night to last forever."

She smiled at him. "So I bought the record. And besides, didn't you know that music has magic in it? With music, the world can be more than just make-believe."

Gary just nodded as the shivers ran up and down his back. With his hand shaking he carefully started the record.

"He was so handsome," she said, her eyes glazed as she looked off into the past, "standing there beside Eleanor, greeting his guests." She paused and looked at me. "You know he couldn't walk, don't you?"

"President Roosevelt?"

She nodded. "They had his braces locked in place so he could stand and greet his guests. He told me later that hurt him, which was why he didn't give many parties."

Gary had a sinking feeling that he didn't want to know where this was heading, but he just nodded and she went on.

297

"After dancing a few times, I got this message that the President would like to talk to me. He told me I danced beautifully and wished he could join me." She smiled, remembering an obviously joyful event.

"He was sitting in a large overstuffed chair and when he said that, he reached down and knocked on his braces through his pants. 'Not much chance of that,' he said and then laughed as if it were funny. I laughed with him."

She swayed back and forth in time with the music as she talked. "I remember I was hot from the dancing and the humid evening, so I sat on the footstool in front of him and we talked for the next hour between interruptions of other guests and business from his advisors."

She looked up at Gary as the song continued. "You know it was that hour that I think I fell in love with him. I know that seems hard to believe, but it only took an hour. After that evening Ernest and I went back to England, but Franklin and I kept in touch and I saw him three or four times a year for the next few years.

In 1936 I went back to Washington and divorced Ernest. Franklin and I saw each other much more during his second term, usually meeting in the home I owned in Maryland. Even though the people wanted him to, he decided to not run for a third term in 1940. He divorced Eleanor in 1941 and we were married the next year."

Suddenly she seemed to age and her face turned pale. "I'm sure you know he was executed right after the invasion of fifty-two. I've been alone ever since."

The last note of the song ended and faded into the dingy-looking room. Gary took a few deep breaths trying to calm the panic filling his stomach. Oh-God-oh-God-oh-God. What had he done? He picked up the arm of the record player and stopped the clicking.

Invasion of '52?

What was that?

What had happened?

Slowly, he looked around the room. The flowers were gone and the bed had become a wooden frame with nothing more than a stained mattress and a rumpled sheet on it. This was the first time that the changes in her story had actually come into her room. He had no memory of when they had happened, even though he had been sitting here the entire time. In her other stories he had always remembered what had changed, but had never been near anything when the change took place.

Mrs. Simpson, or he would assume now, Mrs. Roosevelt, looked to be almost in a coma.

Her eyes were glassy and she seemed about to collapse. Only the belt strapping her to the wheelchair held her upright.

He patted her hand and thanked her, but she paid no attention. He stood and turned for the door. His legs felt weak and his stomach twisted as if he had just been caught with his pants down in front of the entire school.

"Tomorrow?" he asked as he reached her door, not really wanting to go beyond it. But again she didn't notice his question.

Even though it was still mid-afternoon, the hall was almost dark, with only a few bare bulbs in the ceiling fixtures. The smell was of a musty attic, and the floor was stained and unwashed. Very, very different from the modern nursing home he had entered less than an hour before.

This felt more like a jail for the elderly.

At the end of the hall, near the entrance hung a huge sign in a foreign language Gary didn't recognize. All he had taken in school was French and he hadn't really paid much attention to that. Behind an old wood desk where the nurses station had been when he came in was an old guard wearing a black uniform and reading a tattered paperback novel.

As Gary took a deep breath and started toward the front door he remembered.

He remembered what life had been like before she told her story and what life was now like for him in this world. Memories like clear plastic, one over the other, flooded into his mind.

This time he remembered his dad. In this world he had a father who had not disappeared when he was five. In this world Germany had joined with Russia and won World War Two. Japan controlled the West coast of what had been the United States and Maryland was now nothing more than a German satellite state.

And in this world his dad was a drunk who beat him and his mother. His dad never worked and blamed his mother for almost everything that was wrong in the world. He was an ugly, sadistic man who hated everything and everyone around him. Nothing like the dream father Gary had imagined him to be.

Gary staggered against the wall out of sight of the guard and forced himself to take deep breaths like the Coach had taught him to do in pressure games. How did Roosevelt not running for President in 1940 cause America to lose the war?

How could one woman change the world so much?

It wasn't possible, yet Gary knew it was.

And how could his father hit him?

Gary looked down at his arm where the angry red bruise had appeared.

He looked quickly in both directions down the hall. His memory of the clean, modern nursing home overlaid the prison-like feel of this old building.

But his memories of the world before were quickly fading. He would have to get Mrs. Simpson to switch it all back, to tell a new story. But what if her new story was worse than even this? What would happen if in the next world he hadn't even been born?

Then what would happen?

He wanted to pound his fists against the wall and scream. Why hadn't he thought of that before now? How could he have been so stupid, hoping that he could find a world where he would know his dad? Well, it had worked and he had real vivid memories of his father now. Real vivid memories bruises and beatings and of wishing his father were dead, night after night, over and over again.

He eased back into Mrs. Simpson's room. She still sat beside the old phonograph, her eyes glazed.

"Mrs. Simpson, I mean Mrs. Roosevelt?" Gary said, sitting down across from her and keeping his voice low. "Would you mind telling me a story about your life?"

Nothing. She didn't move and Gary passed a hand in front of her unseeing eyes. No blink.

Nothing.

As far as he knew she might have been like this for years in this world. Maybe there was no going back. He took a few more deep breaths to fight off the panic, but this time it didn't seem to help. "Mrs. Roosevelt. Can you hear me? Please talk to me."

He shook her shoulders, slowly at first, and then harder, but her blank stare went right through him.

He stood and paced back and forth in front of the door. He had enough memories of this new world to know that if he was caught in here, he would be in trouble.

Big trouble.

Carefully he poked his head out and looked toward the guard. The old guy was still reading and except for a low moaning coming from a room down the hall, everything was the same. No movement.

Nothing.

Gary went back and shook Mrs. Roosevelt one more time without luck. She was dead to this world. And now he was stuck here.

Footsteps came from down the hall and Gary quickly darted in behind the open door. The guard passed by, walked to the end of the hall, and went into a room there, letting the door bang closed behind him. The banging echoed down the hall and Gary turned to see if Mrs. Roosevelt had noticed.

She still sat there blankly staring over the old record player. And for a minute Gary stared at it, too, remembering what she had said and remembering the words of the song she loved so much.

That just might do the trick.

Gary quickly stuck his head out the door to check on where the guard had gone, then went over to the old machine. It was still on and still had the record of Paper Moon in place. Maybe that would take her back to the party and both of them out of this nightmare.

He listened for a moment to make sure the guard had not come back out of the room, then put the needle in place and started the record. As the first few notes filled the room he wanted to stop it. It sounded so loud, far loud enough to bring the guard.

He went to the door quickly and checked the hall. The opening of the song seemed to be amplified in the stark hallway. It could be heard all over the building, he was sure.

He went back over to Mrs. Roosevelt and again shook her shoulders. "Wake up! Please? "I'm playing your song for you."

Slowly, he felt some life come back into her shoulders where he held her.

He let go and sat down. After a few bars Mrs. Roosevelt's eyes flickered and she smiled faintly.

"Tell me about the party," Gray said, trying to keep his voice under control and not panic filled. "Tell me who you met there at the White House. Please?" He glanced at the door and then back to her.

"Why," she said, her voice gaining strength and power with each word. "I met the President and the First Lady and lots of others. It was a wonderful party and I danced and danced all night. You know, after Edward and I were married I thanked him for getting me invited to that party by taking him on a tour of Washington D.C. It was such a sweet thing for him to do, don't you think?"

"Edward?" Gary asked. "Who was Edward?"

Mrs. Roosevelt laughed, a strong, hearty laugh. "You are teasing me, aren't you? Why, he was the Prince of Wales and then the King of England. After his abdication we were married. I am the Duchess of Windsor."

She reached over and patted Gary's hand. "A young man like you should study his history more."

Gary only nodded in agreement and glanced around at the room. The air shimmered like a heat wave had hit it and the layers of the dark prison-like room faded away, replaced with a modern nursing home room.

And the old record player was also shimmering and fading, as was Mrs. Simpson. In her place sat an elderly gentleman named Harrison and he was finishing a story about how he fought in the Pacific and how the kids of today just didn't understand how important history was and how smart it was for Gary's history teacher to have them do this assignment.

Gary agreed, quickly thanked the man, and headed for the front door.

The relief washed over Gary as he went down the hall.

He felt light, almost like dancing. He could still remember his dad from the other world, but it was fading into the background like remembering a bad nightmare, pushed into the corners by the warm sun and the smiles of the nurses. He doubted if he would ever again wish for a father he didn't have.

And for one final time, faintly from down the hall, he thought he heard Wallis Simpson say, "Thanks for believing in me."

A DESERT SHOT

A Poker Boy Story

Poker Boy and his boss, Stan the God of Poker, find themselves, without warning, in the desert staring at a very dead golfer. Only problem: No golf course within miles.

If not strange enough, the self-proclaimed "Worlds Greatest Detective" joins them to ask for help solving the crime.

As far as Poker Boy feels, how golfers dress constitutes the only crime. But the body smells and the detective could annoy a cactus, so something needs to be done.

One

STRANGELY ENOUGH, as a superhero, I seldom see a body. It happens, sure, but rarely. If someone gets to the body state, I figured I failed in my Poker Boy superhero duties.

The body on the hard desert dirt in front of me hadn't been anyone I had known. The body had been out in the hot sun long enough that it had started to get ripe-smelling. I had a hunch the ripe odor would turn real sour real quick if this guy didn't get moved out of the sun sooner rather than later.

The body had on a light tan golf shirt, golf shoes, matching tan golf slacks, and a tan golf glove. The tan sort of washed out his already really white skin. Not a good choice of color for his last day on the planet.

Of course, I had on my black leather jacket and black fedora-like hat standing in the hot desert sun, so I wasn't one to give fashion advice.

From what I could figure, the dead guy had been about forty with a slight gut and about forty extra pounds. No telling what killed him. No blood stained the bland clothing in any place I could see.

And I sure wasn't touching the body to move it. That would be up to the police.

However, I did find it odd that there wasn't a golf course within ten miles of this spot to the north of Las Vegas. In fact, there wasn't much of anything near this spot but sagebrush and rocks and more than likely a large herd of rattlesnakes. Or bunch of rattlesnakes, or group, or whatever a mass of nasty, mean, and deadly snakes are called.

About a mile to the east, I could hear faint freeway noise of trucks and cars with no mufflers, but otherwise the desert blanketed the dead guy with silence and a lot of heat.

Way too much heat for a leather jacket.

Stan, the God of Poker, had brought me to this spot next to this dead guy with the balding head and blank, dead stare in dark eyes. So I turned to Stan who stood there in his dark slacks, tan button-down sweater, and loafers and asked the most logical question I could think to ask after being surprised by teleporting from a comfortable diner booth in my office to a spot next to a body.

"Think maybe we should call the police?"

Stan took us out of time, which had the effect of cutting off the freeway sounds and wind that was keeping the guy's ripening smell away. He motioned that I should follow him and we moved about fifty steps away from the bland dead guy, staying inside the time bubble the entire time.

"Thank you," I said. "So what are we doing here? And who's the dead guy?"

"Not a clue," Stan said. "And I honestly don't know why we're here."

Now that made me turn my attention from the now distant dead body and look directly at my boss, the God of Poker.

He shrugged, actually looking puzzled.

"So you didn't pluck me from that hamburger and vanilla shake in my office?"

"I did not," he said, shaking his head.

"Now I'm worried," I said.

"Yeah," my boss said, agreeing.

"Stop fretting," a voice said from behind us. "I brought you here."

Stan and I both spun around to look down at a short man in dark brown golf slacks, a white golf shirt, a golf hat with a Dunes logo on it, and a brown golf glove. His face was almost round and clearly he had spent far, far too much time in the sun without enough sunscreen. I could barely see his green eyes through the bright red folds of skin on his cheeks that threatened to crawl up and cover his bushy eyebrows at any moment.

I glanced at Stan who had dropped all pretenses of a poker face and was looking as puzzled as I felt. The guy clearly had a lot of magic since he had walked right into the time bubble Stan had around us.

"Laverne," Stan said. "A little help?"

Lady Luck herself appeared next to Stan facing the little golfer.

She frowned.

I can say clearly as a poker player that when Lady Luck frowns, bad things happen.

She glanced over at the body lying on the hard ground of the desert, then back at Stan and me.

The little golfer bowed slightly to her, the smile on his face making the sunburn seem brighter. With the smile, his eyes sunk farther into the rolls of red flesh.

"Work with him," she said to Stan, shaking her head. "He obviously needs your help. You too, Poker Boy. Shouldn't take too long."

She looked at me and I nodded, damn near the only thing a sane person could do when commanded to do something by Lady Luck herself.

Then she vanished.

"I love her," the little golfer said, smiling at me. "Don't you just love her? A little brisk at times, but still a real charmer. Don't you think?"

I said nothing. There wasn't enough money on the planet to get me to say a word about Lady Luck.

"So who are you and what do you want?" Stan asked, his voice cold and low.

The little golfer smiled and bowed slightly, tipping his golf hat just a slight touch. "I'm Benny Douglas, the world's greatest detective, at your service."

I had no idea who he was. Not clue one. Or what area he was a god in.

But Stan seemed to know him and he sighed and nodded. "Your reputation precedes you."

"I hope like the sweet smell of a dozen roses for a beautiful woman on a first date," Benny said.

"Whatever," Stan said.

Oh, wow, Stan didn't much like this guy and was not bothering to hide the fact.

"So what do you need us for?" I asked.

"To help me solve poor Dan's murder, of course," Benny said, indicating the body that wasn't decaying or smelling at the moment because Stan was holding us in a time bubble outside of the flow of time.

I decided right then that I didn't much like this short little golfer who called himself a detective. So I figured a really, really stupid question might just get under his skin a little.

"So who killed Dan?" I asked, expecting him to give me nothing more than a dirty look.

Benny actually sighed at my seemingly stupid question. "Sadly, I think I might have. But I need you both to help me prove that I didn't. And find out what really killed him."

I stared at the short detective. That was not at all the answer I had expected.

Two

"TIME TO CALL THE POLICE," I said, turning to my boss. "Let them figure it out."

"Almost starting to agree with you," Stan said, staring at Benny.

Around us the silence in the time bubble seemed to almost match the look of the empty desert.

Benny held up his hands for us to stop. "Look, let me explain what happened and we can go from there, all right? I trust you two, heard you've helped a lot of people, figured you could help me some on this.

And remember Laverne told you to help me and don't you both work for that fine lady?"

I stood there, saying nothing. I wanted to say, "Asking for help would have been nice." But I said nothing instead.

Stan did the same.

After a moment Benny caught the clue and started talking even faster than before, which I was surprised was possible.

"Me and Dan there were on the third hole and we were partnered up in a match against Goldenburg and his assistant Tammy. She's a sweet one, that Tammy, fills out those golf shorts real nice if you get my drift, and can hit a driver farther than the rest of us without even messing up her long brown hair."

"Are you talking about Goldenburg, the God of Magic and Illusion?" Stan asked.

Benny nodded like his chin was on a spring on his chest and some kid had ahold of the string and was pulling it. "Sure, who else?"

Stan just stared at Benny.

I decided to just keep quiet and ask who Goldenburg was when I really needed to know.

"So which team was winning?" Stan asked.

"We were," Benny said. "Two up and about to take the third hole as well. Goldenburg can't hit an iron to save his life, and Tammy, bless those tight shorts, can't putt, but it sure is fun to watch her try, if you get my drift."

"The bet?" Stan asked.

"We win," Benny said, "Tammy works for me for a month trying to get a hundred years of paperwork in my office filed," Benny said. "You know how it goes, a fella gets behind and then there's never enough time to get all the basic stuff done and besides, watching Tammy around the office for a month sure couldn't hurt a guy, if you get my drift."

I bit my lip to not say anything. I bit it hard. Patty Ledgerwood, my girlfriend and sidekick says I look cute when I do that. But cute or not, at least it kept me from spouting out something that would derail Stan's questions.

"If you lose?" Stan asked.

"I wash dishes in Dan's restaurant down off The Strip for a month to help pay for a month's worth of dinners Goldenburg and Tammy were going to eat there."

Benny shook his head and looked over at Dan's body. "We weren't going to lose, no way. Until this."

"So how did you kill your own golfing partner?" I asked.

Benny just shook his head. "He missed his second shot on the third hole and I might have made some comment about him being a dead weight or something like that and when I got done putting my club back in my bag he was gone."

"And then what happened?" Stan asked

Benny shrugged. "We looked for him all over, but after five minutes Goldenburg said we had looked long enough and the rules of golf said we had to move on."

"Pretty sure that rule applies to lost golf balls, not partners," Stan said.

I again kept my mouth shut since I knew nothing at all about golf. It wouldn't have surprised me, though, to know that there was a rule that you could only look for a lost partner for five minutes before moving on. Golf seemed that odd to me.

"I told them to keep going and I would search for Dan," Benny said. "I traced him here and that's when I got you two because, honestly, I didn't know what to think and all this seems just odd to me, being a detective and all, but I sure can't trust my own gut on this one."

"So what's your gut telling you?" I asked Benny.

"That this is some sort of Goldenburg trick on me to get free dinners for a month at Dan's place and I wouldn't be surprised that even with Dan dead, Goldenburg will still collect after he wins."

Suddenly something that had been dinging in the back of my mind sort of dinged again, only slightly louder, like a timer on a microwave going off.

"What did Dan get if you two won?"

Benny looked at me and opened his mouth and then shut it. The little golfer detective was speechless for the first time since he pulled us to this body.

Stan laughed. "Seems like Dan only won with you washing dishes for a month."

"So you saying him dying is a trick to get me to wash dishes at his place? I mean, not a very logical plan for a long-term business model."

"Is he really dead?" I asked Benny. I hadn't been able to get much of a read on Benny up until that question. I seldom did on the more powerful gods, but suddenly I could feel Benny being very uncertain and confused.

"Smelled dead," Benny said.

"How about you go check him out to be sure," Stan said, releasing the time bubble.

The wind snapped against my skin once again and the distant sounds of trucks on the freeway echoed over the sagebrush.

Benny shook his head slowly back and forth. "Never touched a dead body before and you know, maybe you're right, maybe we should be calling the police and all that."

"Go roll him over, see if he really is dead," Stan said, his boss voice in full command.

I had a hunch that Dan was far from dead.

Benny took a deep breath and then in his brown golf shoes headed across the hard desert ground toward the body.

If nothing else, this was going to be entertaining watching him sneak up on his dead golfing partner.

Three

BENNY FINALLY reached the body and I could tell he had been holding his breath the entire time since he swayed slightly like he was about to pass out.

He gently reached down to roll Dan over and the body vanished, leaving only the carcass of a very dead coyote that clearly had been picked over by birds and other desert animals and was the source of the ripe smell.

Dan's body had been only an illusion, made very real by the smell.

Nice trick.

A good illusion is always in the details and smell was the detail that made this one.

Benny jumped back and instantly teleported to a spot back in front of us. His face was bright red, his green eyes intense and clearly angry.

"Where the hell did Dan's body go? Did you two do that? Did Laverne? Who would take Dan's body? We need to go to the police. Body theft is a serious crime."

"As if murder isn't," I said, shaking my head.

"There was no body," Stan said.

I was having trouble understanding that Stan needed to even explain that to Benny.

"No body, no murder?" Benny asked, clearly puzzled.

The little golfer who claimed to be the world's best detective wasn't really carrying a full bag of clubs when it came to deductive reasoning.

"An illusion," I said. "You said Goldenburg was the God of Magic, right?"

Benny nodded, slowly starting to understand.

I turned to Stan. "To project an illusion like that, wouldn't Dan have to be involved?"

"More than likely," Stan said. "At least at some point. Don't blame Dan, though, since he only got something if they lost."

"So, Benny," I asked our little golfing detective, "what hole are they on and is Dan with them?"

Benny seemed to stare off into the distance for a moment, then grow even redder in his face, something I didn't think was possible.

"They are on the sixth hole and Dan's as healthy as he gets, which isn't going very far since last year he had two bypass surgeries and has a blood sugar level that would kill a honey bee."

Benny kept staring off into the distance. "I bet we're now two holes down because I was gone and Dan can't play a lick of golf and more than likely has fallen down a few times staring at Tammy's shorts, not that I blame him for that, if you get my drift."

Benny glanced up at me and then at Stan. "So you two are telling me that I didn't accidently kill Dan, that's really him playing golf with Goldenburg?"

Stan and I both nodded.

"And that Dan was helping Goldenburg trick me so that they could win the match and I would end up doing dishes for a month in his place?"

Stan and I again both nodded.

"Wow, you guys are as good as everyone says you are," Benny said. "I never would have figured that out on my own."

I almost said that I had guessed that, but again did the cute thing and bit my lip.

"What are you going to do when you rejoin them?" Stan asked.

"Nothing," Benny said. "Just going on as if nothing had happened and win the match and get Tammy and those great shorts of hers to help me get my office straightened out. I really should have hired someone fifty years ago, but you know how it goes when a fella gets busy."

Stan and I both stood there in the wind of the desert and said nothing. Lady Luck had been right. This hadn't taken very long at all.

"I owe you two," Benny said, smiling, his green eyes lost in the rolls of red flesh on his cheeks. "You solved the murder and saved my life."

"There was no murder, Benny," Stan said.

"Yeah, whatever," Benny said and tipped his golf hat and vanished.

I turned to Stan. "How about I buy you lunch and you tell me who that guy really is."

"The world's greatest detective," Stan said, keeping a perfect poker face. "He told you."

"If he's the world's greatest detective, then I'm Sherlock Holmes."

"You can't be," Stan said.

"And why not?"

"Because Sherlock Holmes is a fictional character."

"And Benny isn't fictional, at least in his own mind?"

"No, he's the world's greatest detective as he said."

"It's going to be one of those lunchtime conversations, isn't it?" I asked.

Stan just smiled and jumped us away from the dead coyote and hot sun and sagebrush and back to my office.

I never did find out if Benny ended up winning the services of Tammy for a month. And the first time I used the phrase "…if you get my drift" around Patty, she made me swear to never use it again.

It seemed she also had met Benny at some point in the past.

GODS AREN'T FUNNY

A Poker Boy Story

In the Poker Boy novel in this issue (which is the origin story for Poker Boy and his team), Poker Boy's boss mentions something that happened earlier, before the novel.

This story details that event, written as the third Poker Boy story I ever wrote and never published anywhere but in a fun little chapbook that Nina Kiriki Hoffman and I did and gave to about twenty friends.

I figured since Stan, the God of Poker, mentions this event a few times in the novel, I had better let everyone read the story first.

Poker Boy, still a freshly-minted superhero just learning the ropes at the time of this story, runs smack into the charms of someone who knows his secret name, knows who he is. And won't let him use his superpowers.

As a red-blooded young man with needs and hormones, Poker Boy must face those challenges in an epic battle of perfect skin, stunning looks, and a hormone-clouded mind.

I WAS STARTING to really dread Christmas Eve.

I mean, do you blame me? Two Christmas Eves ago my old girl-friend, Julie Downer, came to me for help. Then she didn't like my suggestions about what to do, even though I offered to pay for her new boob job.

Eventually she ended up getting her breasts sucked out through her ass by the Silicon Suckers, which needless to say, killed her.

Makes me shudder just to think about it.

And then last year short Bob showed up in the poker room, knowing he was going to die in the morning, and wanting to leave with ten thousand so that he could go out of the world exactly as he had come in: Dead Even.

As a poker player, I understood his desire, but his poker playing ability sucked, right along with his bad temper. I ended up just giving him the ten big ones on a sham bet. He died right when he said he would.

So do you blame me for being a little spooked about this third Christmas Eve? Two years in a row someone who had come to me for help on Christmas Eve had died. And neither of them I could have done anything about, even though during the last year I had wondered if I could have.

Guilt trips are often my strong suit, which I understand from other superheroes, is one of our professional hazards. We help fifty people, but it's the one we can't help that haunts us. I had two on two successive Christmas Eves that I couldn't save. I was in guilt trip heaven.

Now, it was Christmas Eve morning again. So far no one had shown up, and I was determined to forget Bob and Julie and just have my normal Christmas Eve.

The day dawned bright, the air crisp, the light snow not bothering anyone getting to Spirit Winds Casino.

My plan for this Christmas Eve was the same as I had done for the last dozen or so holidays, at least the ones people didn't die around me.

I would go over to the Casino in the early evening, and get into a poker game with the rest of the non-family poker players. Many poker players don't have family, and many of us like it that way, so I had little worries that there wouldn't be a game.

I would play until some time in the morning, go home and get some sleep, and be back in the poker room after a turkey dinner in the buffet. If I timed it right, I would be there for the really good games that always started later Christmas Day.

An aside. A really good game to a professional poker player like myself is when there are a bunch of people with a lot of money and very little skill. Those kinds of players were there to have fun, and I bless them for their goals. I did everything in my power to have fun right along with them as I took their money.

Late Christmas Day seemed to have an extra number of these types showing up, done with their family obligations and ready to have some fun.

I loved my holiday schedule, I loved the sameness of it year after year, I loved not having to put up a tree or buy anyone presents or hang stupid lights on my gutters. I just did my thing and enjoyed it. So even though I was a superhero, sworn to help those I could help, I didn't want anyone to come asking for help this Christmas Eve. My track record just wasn't good on this day.

I'd even lost a dog the first year, and that was the only time in my memory of being Poker Boy, superhero who helps people and saves dogs, that I had ever lost a dog. Other people had died when they didn't take my advice, which wasn't my fault. And there really hadn't been anything I could have done to stop Bob's massive heart attack last year. I could sort of live with that, but I hated not being able to save dogs.

I had almost made it to the poker room when I saw her.

She was sitting on a bench near the front door of the casino, her back to the window, her posture straight, her eyes focused on the people who went past, watching every move, clearly searching for something or someone.

She had longish blonde hair, a body that looked tanned and in good shape, and she definitely had her proportions in order. She was also at least fifteen years younger than me.

So sue me, I'm human underneath all the superhero stuff. I can look at a good-looking woman, even though a woman like the one sitting there never looked back.

Then she looked up at me, directly at me, actually seeing me, and I was struck by her deep, blue eyes.

She smiled and I was pulled by her wonderful, friendly smile.

She patted the bench beside her and I knew at once I was hooked, not by the woman's charms, or good looks, or great, perfectly proportioned body, but by some power even greater than my Poker Boy casino-fed powers.

I moved over, walking like a stiff-legged zombie in a bad movie, and sat beside her as if I didn't have an ounce of control over my body. And when a superhero loses control of his body, that's a very bad sign.

An aside. I have been with my share of beautiful women over the years who have made me lose control of all, or part, of my body, and that is not what had just happened. This was no little head controlling the big head. This was magic or superpower or something besides womanly charms, although I must admit, womanly charms often act like a superpower on me.

Just not this time.

When I was seated, I felt the control over whatever had made me do the monster walk loosen, and then vanish, like heat coming from an oven when you open the door and try to look in too fast.

My eyes fogged for an instant, I felt flush, and then it was gone.

"Wow, that was pretty good," I said. "You use that power for helping others, or just making people walk funny?"

She laughed, the sound high and just a trifle shrill, but she was so good-looking, and had such perfect skin on her perfectly proportioned body, I didn't much care about a slightly-off laugh.

"No," she said, "I'm no superhero like you, Poker Boy."

My instant reaction was *Shit! She knew my name!*

But she went on talking before those words came out of my mouth.

"Dave gave me that power," she said, "to make sure I got your attention when I found you. I could only use it the one time."

"Dave?" I asked, actually getting the word out of my suddenly dry mouth. My stomach was twisting like I had just had two big polish dogs and forgot to take an antacid. There was only one Dave I knew who could give superpowers away like they were quarters.

"Dave," she said, nodding. "I was sitting in his office just yesterday."

For a moment the word "Dave" echoed a little around the lobby of the casino like she had shouted it into a deep canyon.

An aside. In my world there are a number of what are called Gambling Gods. My superpower as Poker Boy, I am sure, comes directly from the Gambling Gods. Now these gods are more like what I would have imagined the old Greek gods were like.

And there is a very clear hierarchy in the Gambling Gods' world.

The hierarchy is set up just like a casino management. In fact, there's a major discussion about whether the gods just recently patterned their world on how super casinos were run, or if casinos patterned their management after how the gods have always been.

I actually think the Gambling Gods have always had the same

management system, and modern super casinos just followed along naturally. Or not so naturally, but that's only my opinion, and I really don't know for sure.

Near the top of this system is the General Manager, one of the many Gods working right under Lady Luck herself. The General Manager is one of the most powerful, can stomp on other gods like they were ants, and pretty much controls the nature of the world behind the normal world that most people see in the gaming and hotel worlds.

Below the General Manager comes the Head of Casino Operations, then the Head of Hotel Operations. Below them are all the directors, such as Director of Security, Director of Food and Beverage, Director of Entertainment, and so on. And below that group are the regular gods, such as the Keno God and the God of Poker.

The gods below those, if there were that many, didn't much count, and I figured I had as much power as Poker Boy as many of the lower level gods, like Pit Bosses and Shift Supervisors. But they are still considered gods in the realm of things, and I am only a superhero, so what do I know. I certainly have no plan on putting my powers up against any of them.

Now this woman had just finished telling me she had talked to Dave, had been in Dave's office, and had gotten the power trick to get me to sit down from Dave.

To say I was stunned would be an understatement. Dave was the General Manager.

You didn't bow to Dave, or worship him, but you certainly didn't mess with Dave, or make him angry. I honestly hoped I would never even meet Dave. I figured it was just safer that way.

And no way in hell did I ever want to meet Lady Luck.

Now Dave had sent this good-looking woman to me.

Up until this moment, I wasn't even sure if the General Manager of everything even knew I existed.

I desperately wanted to ask her what Dave's office looked like, what Dave looked like for that matter, but somehow I refrained from being a god geek and asked the most intelligent question I could think of.

"Dave sent you to me, huh? It must be really important."

Duh. Dumb-ass question. This was not getting off to a good start.

"I think it is," she said. "My name is Audrey Koch. Can I buy you a drink and tell you about it?"

Here was a beautiful woman asking to buy me a drink on Christmas Eve, and I was scared more than I have been in years.

"Buy me a Diet Coke" I said, keeping my voice level and my poker face on. Thank god I was a poker player and I could do that under stressful situations. "I'll be glad to listen."

"Great," she said, standing up quickly like the bench had an ejection button.

I got up a little more slowly, making sure that all the *Come-and-sit-beside-me* spell was gone. It was, and two minutes later we were in the bar.

The place had twenty tables and a big screen t.v. Only one other couple sat against the far wall, so we took a table in front of the window looking out at the people headed from the hotel to the casino.

Audrey ordered an eggnog drink that sounded like it could cause diabetes all by itself, and I stuck with my original plan. I didn't want any alcohol because I still held out hope of getting to the poker table tonight. But with Dave sticking his all-powerful nose into my Christmas Eve, that hope was fading quickly.

"Here's my problem," Audrey said, getting right to the point. She looked me right in the eye and with the most serious of expressions on her face said, "I need to get laid. And it has to happen in the next four hours and ten minutes."

She actually looked at her watch as she said that second sentence.

I glanced at my watch as well. Seven-fifty. Four hours and ten minutes until Christmas.

She wanted to get laid on Christmas Eve. Why?

I must have heard her wrong. That couldn't be the big problem. The General Manager of the Big Casino couldn't be pimping me to some woman. It wasn't possible.

Besides, this woman could get just about any man she blinked at.

"Would you repeat that?" I asked.

She laughed, the sound echoing through the almost empty bar. Again the laugh was just a little off, but the wonderful blue eyes and the perfect smile made me not care at all.

"I need to have sex before midnight with a superhero. And Dave thought you would be the best choice for me."

"Oh, Dave thought I would, huh?"

She nodded, smiling. "And I agree. You're older than I usually like in men, but you're cute."

Okay, I'm a poker player, a guy who is usually in complete control of his emotions, yet right at that moment I didn't have a clue if I should feel angry, excited, flattered, or insulted. I was being pimped by the big guy in the Executive Suite to a young, very attractive woman. There had to be something I was missing, and I needed to resort to my superpowers to find out.

I turned on my Tell-Me-No-Lies Superpower and stared directly at her.

An aside. I used to call this power my Empathy Superpower, but that never seemed to fit, so this year I finally renamed it.

"Why do you need to sleep with a superhero before Christmas Day?" I asked, directing all my power at her.

No person could resist me.

She resisted.

But no person could resist me.

She still resisted, bouncing my superpower away like it was water on a freshly waxed car.

Then she blushed.

"Dave said you might try to get the truth out of me," she said. "He's blocked all your powers from working on me."

Then she shrugged and smiled. "Sorry."

I stopped focusing my useless power and sat back. What good was a superhero with his superpowers not working? I pushed that thought away, and all thoughts of feeling sorry for myself, and directed my attention to her.

"You're not going to tell me why you want to sleep with me inside this time frame, are you?"

"I can't," she said, the look on her face deadly serious.

I sat there thinking while the waitress served our drinks and took Audrey's money. I could only come up with a couple of reasons for this strange request.

First, the General Manager was rewarding me for all my good deeds over the years. But that didn't seem to be Dave's style. And this kind of reward certainly wasn't mine either.

Second, this was a bet. Bets in the Gambling God's world were everyday things. Someone might have bet I would sleep with this woman before Christmas Day, giving up my evening of poker for sex. And Dave was in on the bet in some fashion.

I could think of no other reason this woman needed to sleep with a superhero this evening, before midnight.

None.

And if there was a reason, she should be able to tell me. Only things like bets made silly rules like not telling.

So it had to be a bet.

And I was just a pawn in the bet. Nothing more. But did I want to play poker tonight and let one side win the bet, or sleep with a beautiful, young woman, and let the other side win?

Actually, that was a tough choice for a professional poker player at my age. At twenty-nine, there would be no thought. The little head would have controlled the decision and thirty minutes later I'd be looking at this young woman's nude body.

But at my slightly older age, sleeping with a woman always brought many side effects. I don't mean this to sound like I don't have relationships. I do. Just not ones that started in Dave's office and brought me into the picture doing a zombie walk. Thinking back, not one of my long-term relationships with women has started that way, and I doubted this would either.

My little voice told me there was still something I was missing.

An aside. My little voice isn't a superpower, but it saves me more often than my powers do.

"Okay," I said, facing her as she sipped on her sugar-drink. "You want to sleep with a superhero before midnight, but you're not going to tell me why. Am I right?"

She nodded, her beautiful eyes staring at me.

"And I'm the superhero that Dave sort of picked out of a hat for you, right?"

This time she nodded a little slower. From what I could tell, that wasn't the complete truth, but I was getting close.

"You didn't even know I existed before Dave mentioned my name, did you?"

She shook her head this time, still saying nothing.

So I was just a convenient superhero, doing nothing on Christmas Eve but playing poker. This was making me a little angry, I had to admit.

"And I assume this is what you really look like, that you don't have AIDs, and you don't want to get pregnant."

"This is what I really look like," she said, spreading her arms, which

319

gave me a clear view of her assets just above the table, "No magic, no nothing. I don't have any diseases, and I will never have kids."

"Yet right now you want to check into a hotel room and have sex with me?"

"I already have a room," she said, smiling at me.

Damn, if this woman was just a half-an-ounce less beautiful, had a fraction less fantastic smile, and didn't have such perfect skin, I wouldn't be having any problem. I'd be telling her it was nice meeting her and move on to the poker room.

But it was hard for any mortal man, superhero or not, to turn down an offer of sex from a goddess-like woman.

Then I realized what word had gone through my head.

Goddess.

No wonder she had access to Dave. This woman was one of the Gambling Gods.

Oh, shit! Now what should I do?

Sleeping with a Gambling God can only cause trouble. I've heard that a dozen times over the years.

But not sleeping with a Gambling God in this situation could cause even more troubles. Again I needed more information.

And I had always felt the best way to get information was directly.

"Can you tell me more about yourself?" I asked, sipping on my diet coke. "For example, I know you're one of the gods. Which position do you hold?"

Her face turned white and she tried to cover it quickly by bending forward and taking another sip of her drink. I'm a poker player. I can read expressions like other people read books. I knew for a fact I had hit the right answer with my little fishing question.

Finally she looked up at me. "How did you know? And without your superpowers?"

"You're dealing with a poker player. How would I not know?"

She nodded, taking that in. Finally she said, "I guess I can tell you. I'm the Keno Manager."

"So Audrey isn't your real name," I said. "You're Betty."

I had made it a habit of following all the main and lower gods, and who left, who got moved, who moved up or down, and so on. I was a poker player and a superhero. It was just part of my superhero job.

I reached across the table, hand extended. She took my hand and I shook hers, saying, "Nice meeting you, Betty."

"Nice to meet you as well, Poker Boy," she said, smiling, those teeth perfect in the bar light.

So now that I knew who she really was, there were only two options available as to why she was doing what she was doing. First, it was a bet as I had figured before.

But the second reason felt to be the more likely prospect. Betty wanted to move either up, or sideways, in her job status in the Gambling God Big Casino.

Suddenly I knew the answer. Dave was involved, therefore this wasn't a bet. This was an audition.

Betty was trying to move over to Poker Room manager and take Stan's job.

And Dave must have figured that if she understood a major poker player enough to get him to sleep with her instead of playing poker, she might get the job.

Now twice over the last few years since he hired me and told me I was a superhero, I had talked with Stan, both times in the middle of adventures. Usually the Gambling Gods didn't get involved in my adventures, and I doubted they even paid much attention most of the time.

But I liked Stan. He treated me fairly. I wasn't so sure yet that I liked Betty. Granted, any normal, heterosexual man would want to sleep with her, but that aside, I didn't have a good feeling about her.

And she had clearly let me surprise her as well. No one surprised Stan. And he seemed to understand poker players.

Betty clearly understood sex. And since Keno had the worst odds of any game in a casino except the Big Wheel, she understood suckers. And she was playing me as one during this entire exchange.

Poker players hated being played as suckers, even though the payout was sex with a goddess. It still wasn't worth it.

I took a sip out of my drink and leaned forward over the table. "Betty, you are a stunningly beautiful goddess."

"Well, thank you," she said, beaming that beaming smile at me.

"And I think you will make great middle management in the Big Casino."

"I hear a but coming," she said, her smile now gone.

"But I don't think you'd make a good Poker Room Manager. You're going to have to find another way to move up."

She sat there staring at me for a moment, her mouth slightly open.

Clearly I had hit the nail right on the head. I had read her reasons and motives like I read a mid-level poker player.

"Dave told me I wouldn't be able to fool you," she said. "But I don't understand how you knew without your superpowers. Did Stan tell you?"

"No one told me," I said. "I'm a poker player. Knowing people and understanding why they do what they do is my job, and how I make my living. And I'm very good at my job."

She nodded. "Dave told me that if I didn't understand poker players, I could never have the job. Clearly I don't. At least not yet. You want to give me a private lesson?"

She smiled such a seductive smile, I thought the glass in my hand might melt. Yet somehow I managed to hold on.

"Sorry," I said. "I hope you don't hold this against me." Actually, I hoped that a lot, but I figured that since I helped Stan keep his job, Stan was going to help me as well if I needed protection from Betty.

"No hard feelings," she said, still smiling, only with the seductive part dropped. "But tell me, how would I have gotten you into bed if I had known poker players."

"Just play good cards," I said, giving her the same advice I gave any beginning poker player. "And never get in the way of a big game."

She nodded. "And tonight's a big game for you?"

"It is," I said. I had really been looking forward to my Christmas poker ritual, especially after the last two years.

She laughed softly, and stood, extending her beautiful, perfect-skinned hand. "Well, Poker Boy, it certainly has been an education meeting you. I'm sorry we're not going to have that roll in the sheets."

"Not half as sorry as I am," I said, taking her hand and holding it.

Her off-kilter laugh echoed through the mostly empty restaurant as she faded away, leaving me with my hand extended into mid-air.

I turned and headed for the poker room.

No one had died on me yet on this Christmas Eve. And I kept Stan's job for him, which had to be worth a little.

So far, so good.

And I hadn't even played a hand of cards yet.

WAITING FOR THE COIN TO DROP

USA Today *bestselling writer Dean Wesley Smith has two major ways to approach time travel. First is the alternate timeline approach, where any change in history starts a new timeline. His entire series of Jukebox stories and Thunder Mountain series of stories works that way.*

Then he has the theory that time is tied to mass and energy, with anything physical having a complete tie to an instant of time and energy. And if something is changed in the past, it resets the next instant.

He developed a series of stories that are space opera starring Captain Brian Saber around this second approach to time and mass. This story approaches another side of time being tied to mass and energy.

A slightly ugly side.

This story first appeared in Fiction River: Timestreams *in the summer of 2013.*

NICK STARED AT THE SIGN on the antique gumball machine near the door in Donna Hayman's living room and sighed.

Wait for the Coin to Drop.

If he waited for a coin to drop in that machine, he would never live long enough. Sometimes he really wished mechanical things would work here. Anything. But nothing mechanical did work, nothing electrical, nothing that required a moving part, even down to simple door hinges.

Just to get into Donna's apartment, he had had to use a sledge-hammer and smash open the door. It took a crowbar to open a refriger-ator, and that was after removing the screws on the hinges.

Now, after almost a year of living in this apartment building, he had almost every apartment open so he could come and go with ease. Counting Donna's, there were only six more apartments on the top floor left to open, six more hidden lives to explore, six more adventures to take before his research was finally finished and he could go home.

He stopped inside the door and glanced around at Donna's apart-ment. He could almost smell the uncut Canadian bacon and pepperoni pizza on the coffee table. He knew that wasn't possible, since he needed special implants and a breathing device to even breathe or walk or see light through the air of this time period. Air molecules that didn't move were as hard as steel. And since nothing moved, no smell could move to his nose either. Without the special implants, he would have died instantly on arriving in this moment in time.

Outside the clean window, the city of New York spread out, the deep canyons of the buildings tightening down in the distance. No sound came from the city, since it too was frozen in this moment, this instant of time, as was everything else around him.

He shook his head. It still smelled like pepperoni pizza in this apart-ment. He hadn't had a bite of pizza for almost a year. It hadn't occurred to him to bring any with him, or program it into his food replicator. No wonder he was imagining the smell. But he did remember to bring along his fine cigars and best whiskey. And after each day he allowed himself a few sips and a cigar, so life without pizza hadn't been all bad.

He had no idea if Donna Hayman was home at this very instant in time, but it sure looked like she was. He hoped she was. If nothing more than to give himself another beautiful woman to look at for his last few weeks in the building and in this time period. He knew, from his files that he had brought with him from the future, that Donna had been good looking at one point in her life.

He doubted she would be as good as Betty in apartment 310, or Sandra in 241, or Kitty in 608, whom he had found in the shower, her head thrown back, her naked body frozen in a moment of showering, her almost perfect body covered in a silvered sheen of water.

He had to admit, he had spent far, far too much time in that bathroom, staring at her, a woman long dead as far as he was concerned. Kitty would never realize that for a fraction of a fraction of an instant in time, she had had a visitor from the future staring at her in a very private moment.

At first it made him feel a little perverted. But his job here was to study the people and he had decided there was nothing at all wrong with admiring a perfect human form.

After a time, he thought he had actually fallen in love with her. An impossible romance, since the only way a person from his time could travel back to another time was inside an instant, a fraction of a second too small to even measure, where nothing moved, and the laws of conservation of mass and energy wouldn't allow anything to be changed from one instant to another.

That fact, that reality, solved all time paradoxes.

And that allowed for middle-aged writers like him, with far too much time on their hands, to go back in time for a year to study the people who lived in a crowded apartment building in New York and write a book about their long-dead lives of 2015.

Granted, studying people in the past was nothing really new or original. But that wasn't his focus. He had decided that for his book, he would put a special spin on the idea of ordinary people's lives.

He would study their secrets. He would learn their hidden desires, their fetishes, their affairs, and their faults.

Every person, either in 2015 or 2259 had secrets. And a lot of people loved reading about other people's secrets. His challenge to research his book called "The Secrets of Lexington Avenue" was to look into everyone's lives in this building, and then through historical documents, if possible, learn how ten of these people fared with their secrets.

So, for almost one year now, he had lived in a special time bubble set up in the lobby area. And every day he left that time bubble and broke open people's doors and cabinets and everything else they kept secret and closed off and hidden from their neighbors.

Of course, in the next fraction of an instant of real time for this building and these people, the universe would reset everything as if he had never been here, broken down a door, or even existed in this moment.

It was impossible for him to do any real harm in this time.

And to him, all these people were long dead, including Kitty in 608. And to Kitty and everyone else in this building, he was below notice.

He had been surprised that living alone in a city of frozen, uncaring people had bothered him for the first few months. But eventually he got used to it.

And now, after almost a year, he had come to like the people of this building, for the most part. He hadn't expected that. He had expected them to just be statistics in his research. But by looking for their secrets, looking through their hidden lives, they had become more than frozen flesh and data. They had become human to him.

And he had no doubt that was going to make his book a much stronger book.

Of course, there were a half-dozen he had also come to hate when he discovered who they actually were. So far he had found two child molesters living in the building. Even though they would never notice, he had cut off their hands. It made him feel better, even though in the next instant of time, everything would reset and the monsters would continue on in their own time.

But screw it, it made him feel better doing that.

Even more surprising to him was that over a quarter of the people in the building had very few, if any, secrets. They simply lived their lives, many of them very sad and dull lives.

Just as life treated them, he was sure he would go home and just forget them. They would live on as nothing more than a few notes in his research. He had come to realize that in many cases a person without secrets, without desires, without courage, was not worth studying.

Or remembering, for that matter.

However, a large number of people in the building lived interesting lives, had fascinating secrets, and often varied sex lives. He knew his readers would be interested in that, so for each person he tried to determine what their sexual desires and secrets were.

There were twelve gay couples in the building and at least sixteen men and a dozen women who liked to look at pornography on their computers. Eight others were heavily into different aspects of bondage. Some had pornographic pictures in hidden boxes or in the back of drawers, often of themselves with some unknown partner.

Fifty people in the building played musical instruments and another dozen were travel freaks, people who seemed to live to do nothing but leave town and see the world beyond the confines of New York City.

Six were working on novels and from what he could tell, none of them were any good. And three were working on plays, none of which were ever produced that he could discover.

Almost half of the people in the building were having money trouble of one sort or another.

He had no doubt he would have trouble focusing on just ten people in this building for his book.

Maybe Donna would end up being one of those top ten most interesting. He could call her the "pizza woman" since that pizza really seemed to have invaded his imagination.

Nothing could smell or feel hot or cold in this instant of time. And if not for his specially contained living bubble that sucked energy from his own time period and allowed him to live in his real time, he wouldn't even be able to shower or eat.

He had once tried a bite of a steak in one of the first apartments he had broken into. It had tasted like sawdust and his special implants had warned him away from such action by instantly causing him to throw it all back up all over the plate of the apartment occupant.

Nick ignored the imagined smell of the pizza and forced himself to really look at the apartment around him. He needed to find out just how human Donna Hayman of apartment 719 really was, and what her secrets were.

Just as he was doing now, living in the past, Donna clearly also had lived in the past in her life. Every detail screamed out another era long before 2015. From the old gumball machine with its strange sign telling someone to wait for the coin to drop to a huge mural on one wall with the pictures of *Gone with the Wind* stars taken at the opening of the famous picture in Atlanta.

The furniture was of the 1940s, overstuffed and comfortable-looking. A Shirley Temple doll sat on one chair and a game of Monopoly with metal pieces and wood houses covered an end table, looking like it was half-played.

The room looked lived in, with the pizza on the coffee table and Coke in an old bottle beside it. His stomach rumbled as he got nearer the pizza. He was going to have to call the day early and head back to his time bubble to get some dinner.

"You want a piece?" a woman asked from behind him.

He spun, his heart threatening to explode out of his chest. It had been almost a year since he had heard another person's voice, even though he had talked to the frozen residents all the time.

Facing him was a woman with a very nasty-looking knife held casually in her hand like she was used to using one in all different ways, including cutting pizza.

Not possible.

She was moving and breathing and blinking and doing everything a live person would do.

Not possible. He was inside an instant of time, a random instant. No one else could be here at this moment.

His mind just wouldn't believe what he was seeing. Then finally he caught his breath and realized that the live person he was staring at wasn't Donna Hayman, the resident of this apartment.

"How?" he asked, which was just about all he could manage to get out.

He lowered his hand slowly and let it hover over his emergency recall button covered with a protective cap on his belt. He had thought about hitting that button that would send him back to his normal time a great deal during those first lonely days, but after three months, he had sworn to himself he wouldn't give up on this idea or this book.

The woman smiled at him and her face seemed even more attractive in a classical model way, except for the fact that the smile didn't reach her green eyes. She had on a knit yellow sweater and shorts that allowed her beautiful, thin legs to stand out. She was barefoot and her long, blonde hair was pulled back into a ponytail.

Damn, she was the best-looking woman in the building.

He was dreaming. This wasn't real. It simply couldn't be real.

"Don't bother to hit your recall button," she said, her voice low and husky. "You're inside my bubble now and it won't work."

He shook his head. His mind was reeling. This could not be happening. It was against all the laws of physics that he understood, and he had spent some time studying them before he was allowed to take this research trip. And this was really, really against the laws of time travel.

"You sort of stunned me," she said, again smiling at him, "when you started banging on my door with that ax."

He watched as she twisted the knife in her hands. Crap, he had left the ax out in the hallway.

She went on. "Clearly, you're from some point in the future. What year is it where you came from?"

"2259." His voice sounded high and he swallowed the dryness.

"What month and day is it for you now?"

He had to think for a moment and do a little calculation, since he hadn't thought of what day it was back in the future, in his real time, for a while. "August twenty-first."

That time he managed to keep his voice normal and level, even though he was having an impossible conversation with a woman twisting a knife in her hands.

She nodded. "Two more years and twelve days. That's what I figured."

"Until what?"

"Until I get out of this jail," she said, waving the knife around at the apartment. "I've been here for six years, 353 days. Nine-year sentence in this instant in time, living in this stupid apartment that a woman by the name of Donna created."

Suddenly Nick understood exactly what had happened. He had broken into a prison cell.

After time travel had been discovered and the realization that nothing could be affected in the past, society had started dumping criminals into the past, letting them live in contained time bubbles in an instant in time, isolated, unable to hurt anything or anyone until their sentence was up.

It was fantastically cheaper than prisons. He had read studies on it. No guards, self-replicating food, and no need to even bother with keeping track of the prisoners. Their locations and instants of times in the past were always kept a secret, thus they would be impossible to find.

This woman was a criminal and this was her cell.

Somehow, when he had traveled back in time, he had ended up in the same instant of time she was in. Against all odds, but more than likely the time travel machines used a bunch of the same settings and that's how they had both ended up in this same instant in the same area.

The thinking went that there was so much room in the past, there was no real reason to spread out the criminals over too wide a number of time moments.

The woman stared at him for a moment, clearly shocked at his stunned reaction. "You weren't looking for me, were you? You stumbled in here by accident, didn't you?"

He nodded.

She shook her head, clearly sad about something. Then she brightened. "Well, this is one for the record books."

Again, all he could do was nod. More than likely this little accident would help the sales of his book, but at the moment that was the least of his worries. The knife in her hand bothered him a lot more.

"So, you want some pizza or not?" she asked, moving with the knife toward the couch. "I think it's still warm."

"So, what did you do?" he asked, trying his best to make his voice stay level and his tone conversational, like he was asking her the time of day.

"Stabbed a man," she said, smiling as she held up the knife.

This time the smile got to her eyes and he knew she was kidding.

She laughed and then said, "Drugs. Smuggling the most recent designer drug from a modeling assignment into the wrong country. Stupid."

The realization hit him as to who he was looking at. Her name was Nancy. Nancy Robinson, a supermodel convicted and sentenced back when he was still working on his third novel. Her face had been all over the world net, and they had even filmed her disappearing back into time to serve her sentence.

Now, after the six years, she had aged slightly, but was still a stunning beauty.

"So, who are you and what the hell are you doing here?" she asked, picking up a piece of pizza.

She bit into the pizza, watching him with her intense, green eyes.

"My name's Nick," he said. "I'm a writer here researching a new book on the secrets of people living in this building. Including Donna Hayman, the woman who was supposed to be living in this apartment at this point in time."

"Welcome to her apartment," Nancy said, looking disgusted. "Trust me, she's not home and she has no real secrets, unless you call dying her hair and being behind on her credit cards a secret."

Then she laughed, the sound husky and odd in a weird way. She indicated that he should sit down and have some pizza. "Might as well get comfortable. It does look like you stumbled on a really big secret in this apartment."

He smiled and let himself relax a little. "It does, doesn't it?"

He took the offered piece of rich-smelling pizza and carefully bit into it. It tasted even better than it smelled, if that was possible.

For the next thirty minutes, while they finished off the pizza, they talked and laughed about all sorts of things, and he got the short version of the events that put her in this jail cell.

All he kept thinking was how fantastically beautiful she was, how lucky he was to have found her, and how much more enjoyable the last few weeks of his research trip was going to be. He should have started at the top floor instead of the bottom floor. He would have found her ten months ago.

After he told her about a few of the other residents in the building, she smiled and sighed. "I like you, Nick. It's going to be good to have company for the last two years of my sentence."

"I only wish," he said, laughing. "I've only got two weeks left on my research time, although I might be able to extend a month or two before hitting my recall button."

The emergency recall button, and the main one in his time bubble in the lobby, were the only way anyone from his present could track him to this moment and bring him back. He had been warned that if something happened to those two buttons, there would be no finding him.

She looked at him, a puzzled frown wrinkling her wonderful face. Then sadly she shook her head. "You don't understand, do you?"

She pointed to the door. "Your recall button is blocked in here. Go ahead, try to leave."

He stared at her, again trying to absorb her words. He then glanced back at the shattered wooden door that he had stepped through and the hallway beyond. There were two other shattered doors he had gone into earlier in the week.

"This is a prison, remember," she said, softly. "No one leaves here until they call me back when my time is up. It is why I never crashed through that door and explored the city."

"You don't have the special implants to do so," he said, pushing the panic he was feeling down. Suddenly the pizza wasn't settling so well in his stomach. "You would not have been able to move through the air out there."

"Of course I have them," she said, sadness filling her eyes. "Every prisoner has them just in case something goes wrong with the bubble.

331

We also have special recall buttons that will only go through the bubble when our time is served."

He shook his head and stood and headed for the shattered front door to the apartment. She couldn't be right. She was just pulling some sort of sick joke on him.

As he reached the door, he started to step through the opening and his leg banged into what felt like a very hard surface. Pain shot up his leg and he grabbed his knee for a moment. There didn't seem to be anything in his way, yet there was something there.

"Force field around the bubble," she said from behind him, her voice soft. "A prison far more effective than any cell invented. And it will remain in place for just over two more years."

"Sorry, got to go," he said, his voice again high and showing the panic he felt. He pushed his emergency recall button and waited for the tingling feeling of the time travel kicking in.

Nothing.

He just stood there, with a former supermodel staring sadly at him. He clearly wasn't going anywhere, at least for two years and twelve days.

But at least he had a beautiful supermodel to keep him company.

———

Six months later, he was still sleeping on the couch.

Day after day of those six months he had stared at that stupid sign on the gumball machine.

Wait for the Coin to Drop.

He had come to find the secrets of the residents of an apartment building. And he had done just that.

It seemed the resident he had ended up trapped with had enough secrets to fill a dozen books. To start off with, she was bulimic, with no desire at all to help herself do anything else. In the small three-room apartment, the sounds of her forcing herself to throw up after every meal soon went from worrisome to completely revolting.

She had told him, on the second night, when he made a pass at her, that she had once been a man, had had the operation, and now hated everything to do with men. In fact, during the second month of his time with her, she had told him that he disgusted her.

It seemed that everything about her was fake. She took off her small breasts every night and hung them with her blonde wig on the wall beside her bed.

Worst of all, she was the most shallow human being he could have ever imagined in even a horror novel. The only topic of conversation that was allowed was her looks and her career and if she could save her career when she returned. She wondered if the world will have forgiven her "little mistake" as she called it.

She had quit school in the tenth grade and seemed proud of that fact. She had brought nothing to read and claimed that she had never read a book, ever, in her entire adult life. And there wasn't a thing he could use to write on in the entire prison cell. What little bit of writing he managed to do was to fill the last of his notes in the pad he kept with him each day before it ran out of power.

Every day Nancy spent hours and hours and hours in the bathroom, staring at herself in the mirror.

Three small rooms filled with secrets. They had become impossibly small within the first week and downright tiny by the end of the first month. Plus he had no clothes to wear besides what he had been wearing, so his main chore was to cook himself something to eat twice a day and do laundry every third day.

The rest of the time he just lay on the couch and stared at the sign on the gumball machine sitting beside the open door that promised his freedom, yet never brought it.

The gumball machine became the symbol of his life.

Wait for the Coin to Drop.

He was trapped in a moment in time with the secrets he had uncovered, the same type of moment that existed when a child waited for the coin to drop in the gumball machine to deliver the promised reward.

A PINCH OF HOW ROSIE LIVED

USA Today *bestselling writer, Dean Wesley Smith, dives back into one of his favorite topics with this touching tale of being trapped and finding out how to escape.*

Rosie lived to bake in her own kitchen, even when he old body wouldn't allow her to do so. But Dot wasn't living for anything.

She learned that from Rosie.

A heart-warming story of the dreams in all of us.

One

THEY SAY THAT when you get old, you lose your sense of smell. For me, I sometimes wish that had been the case. But I suppose if it had, I would have never met Rosie.

Actually, the day my son dumped me into the Shady View Rest Home was the day I most wished someone would have plugged up my old nose. The odor of disinfectant seemed to cling to everything, as if that was the rule of the place and nothing could come in unless it smelled like it came out of a blue bottle.

But there were other smells. The old nurse who tried to smile as she filled out my forms, but didn't really care, smelled of garlic and hand lotion.

The young orderly who wheeled me, with my son walking along beside me, down the wide hall toward my new room smelled of sweat and dried vomit.

And my new room smelled what I imagined death smelled like. I didn't have to be told that the person who had the bed before me had died. It was the way of these places.

Someone would move in the day after I died, too.

But for the moment I sat in the little room and just hated the smell, almost more than I hated my son for forcing me into this place.

"I've got to be going, mom," he said, a fake smile on his face. But I knew the skinny little bastard I had to call a son didn't have anywhere important to go. He didn't want to be here any more than I did. He wanted to be home with that new wife, sitting in his favorite chair, watching his favorite programs, pretending he had done his duty as a son.

I also wanted to be home, in the house I had lived in for almost fifty years. But I'd gotten sick a few months back, a bad case of my stomach fighting with the lower part of my body. And by the time I was out of the hospital, my son had exercised his power of attorney and sold my house. Then, thinking I was going to die at any minute, arranged that I move into this rest home for my final few days.

Well dying wasn't in my immediate plans. He said, after I stopped yelling at him, that it would be easier and better for me to go ahead and stay at Shady Hills Home.

Easier for him was more like it. This way he didn't have to bother with his old mother. Bother with me was the last thing he wanted to do. And at the moment it was the last thing I wanted him to do. He'd bothered with me right out of my home and I was never going to forgive him for that.

"I'll be fine," I said, letting him hear what he wanted to hear because it would be the easiest and quickest way to get rid of him. "You go along now, and let me get settled."

The little shit patted my hand and said "I'll talk to you soon." Then he almost ran from the room.

Even the young orderly who had wheeled me down the hall gave me a puzzled, eyebrow-up look.

I waved my hand and climbed out of the wheelchair, moving over to check out the television on the nightstand. "Don't mind him," I said. "Some parents dump their children. Some children dump their parents. I just wasn't smart enough to do it first, when I had the chance."

The orderly laughed. "I hear you there, lady. You want me to come back and get you for dinner?"

I turned and stared at the nice young man who stood, half smiling, still holding onto the back of the wheelchair. He had stringy black hair that hung down next to his right eye, a nice, friendly smile, and some light in his eyes. I knew right off I'd enjoy being around him.

"No, thanks," I said. "I can still put some miles on these old legs. Just point me in the right direction and tell me the time."

He glanced at his watch. "Dinner starts at five, in about two hours. Just go to the right down the hall and when you see the big double doors on the left, you're there."

"Service, or do I have to cook my own."

This time he really laughed and his laugh lightened my mood a little. "Full service. But no candles or wine."

"So I don't have to make a reservation, huh?"

"Already got yours in," he said. He turned and headed out the door. "Call me if you need anything. Your bags are in the closet."

"Thanks," I managed to say before he disappeared to the right down the hall.

I moved over and sat down on the bed and glanced around the tiny little room, with its hospital bed, dresser, nightstand, television, and single chair. "So this is where I get to die. Just wonderful."

Two

THE NEW SMELL overwhelmed me in the hall just inside the back door. Dinner had turned out to be overcooked green beans, mashed potatoes, and something that appeared to be chicken, but tasted more like the potatoes. With the express purpose of walking off the food I had managed to choke down, I decided to explore.

The Home, as one blonde nurse's aide so lovingly called it, was a large rectangle. Each side of the rectangle was called a wing. Two nurse's stations anchored opposite corners of the rectangle so that no square foot of the home's halls would be left unobserved from at least two directions. Guess they figured that way none of us inmates could escape.

The back door was a set of air-lock double doors leading out to a small parking lot near the lunchroom. Obviously that parking lot was used only for staff parking and loading supplies.

I had been standing near the back door, staring out at the lot, when the smell hit me. Not the smell of death, or of antiseptic. This smell was of apple cinnamon, mixed with a little spice. And as it drifted over me, I actually felt warm, as if I were in a wonderful kitchen somewhere and apple pies were just coming out of the oven.

I turned around, but there was no one beyond the few residents sitting outside their rooms in their wheelchairs. It seemed that a home policy was to wheel the residents who couldn't walk back to their door after eating, but not inside. Then a while later someone else would come along and put them away.

I suppose the theory being that at least the view in the hall would help break the boredom for the residents. From the looks of most of the residents sitting outside their doors, boredom was the least of their problems.

The wonderful fresh smell of warm cinnamon stayed with me.

With my nose in the air sniffing like a tracking dog, I moved a few steps back into the hall, trying to trace where that wonderful scent was coming from.

When I turned to the right the smell almost vanished, so I quickly moved back and into the left hall. The smell seemed to get stronger and stronger as I moved until finally it surrounded me and a little, shriveled woman sitting in a wheelchair outside her room's door. The sign next to the door on the wall said Rosie Manning,

I walked a few steps past her, but the smell started to fade so I moved back and stood in front of her. She was the source of the smell. Of that there was no doubt, but I couldn't really believe it.

Rosie Manning was a woman of maybe seventy pounds, her back bent over so much that her chin barely stayed above her lap. She seemed to be shaking slightly as she slowly took shallow breaths.

I bent down in front of her and was even more startled. The remains of her dinner covered the bib in her lap and she seemed to be drooling.

And her eyes were blank.

Totally blank.

It was clear that whoever Rosie Manning had been was now long since gone. Only her body was hanging around until something in it decided to stop.

I stood as the nice young orderly who had wheeled me to my room approached.

"I see you've met Rosie," he said, moving around behind her chair. "Afraid she's not real talkative, though. In fact, in the ten years she's been here she's never said a word.

Ten years? I was shocked. "It was her smell," I said, "that made me stop." The thick odor of apples and cinnamon still filled the air like a grandmother's kitchen in the fall.

The young guy wrinkled his nose and took a deep sniff. "I don't smell anything different." He bent over Rosie. "Rosie, did you have an accident in your diaper?"

He shrugged to me as he stood and pushed her into her room. "Guess the nurse's aide will have to check."

I stared after him for a moment, wondering if he had just been pulling my leg. After a few moments the smell started to fade, so reluctantly I headed back for my room, my new home, for my first night's sleep in my new and final bed.

Three

THE SMELL CAME back to me in my dream, seemingly stronger than it had been earlier.

I found myself, in my dream, walking back down the hall of the home, again following the smell. And it led me right back to Rosie's room.

Only this time, her room wasn't the normal nursing home room like mine, but instead was a huge old kitchen full of hanging pans, large pots on the stove, and green trees outside the window over the double sink.

Apples filled a bushel basket on the wooden table and two large pies were cooling on the counter. A small, straight-backed woman worked at the stove, her back to the door as I stared in.

After a moment she turned and smiled. "Come in, my dear," she said. "The pie will be cool enough to eat in a few minutes."

Even knowing it was a dream, I felt hesitant. But the smell was so wonderful that I couldn't stay out in the stark hallway one moment longer. I stepped through the door and was instantly surrounded by warmth and the wonderful smells of cooking. I had never felt so safe and comfortable before.

The woman smiled, wiping her hands on her apron. "I'm Rosie," she said. "Rosie Manning."

She extended her hand and I took it, feeling the firm warm skin in my palm.

"Dorothy," I said, as I shook her hand. "Dorothy McDonald. Dot to my friends."

Rosie smiled. "Rest your feet, Dot." She pointed to an open kitchen chair and I moved to it while she checked on the pies. The door into the kitchen still led back into the hallway of the nursing home and down the hall I could see one of the night nurses working near a cart. But I couldn't hear the nurse.

I would have never recognized that the woman who stood in front of me now in my dream was the same woman who had been a dead hulk in a wheelchair earlier.

"This is a wonderful dream," I said, feeling the top of the wooden table. This kitchen reminded me so much of my own kitchen in my own house. The house my son had sold out from under me.

"Isn't it?" Rosie said as she slid one of the fresh pies onto the table in front of me.

She retreated to the counter and pulled out two plates, a knife, a pie server, and two napkins

"You know this is a dream?" I asked.

"Of course, my dear," she said as she returned and sat down across from me, moving the basket of apples away from her slightly.

I laughed. "I suppose that makes sense. It's my dream, so someone in my dream would know it's a dream."

Rosie laughed too. "You may be right." She expertly sliced the fresh apple pie, sending a warm, wonderful odor filling the air. "But it's my dream too."

I sat back staring at her as she dished up the pie and slid a piece in front of me. I knew this was a dream, yet it felt somehow different. Different in a way that made me want to wake up. Yet the smell of the pie in front of me kept me from pushing myself back to the reality of my small room.

I picked up the fork and took a golden bite of pie.

The taste was even more heavenly than the smell and I felt myself relax into the dream. What could it hurt? It was certainly a better place to be than the small nursing home room that smelled of death.

Four

THE NEXT MORNING my memory told me that in my dream Rosie and I had sat around and talked for hours about all sorts of things we'd done. It seems that up until a stroke knocked her down ten years ago, Rosie had lived a full life as mother and then grandmother. Her husband had been on the city council at times and had died of a heart attack on their third trip to Hawaii.

She had continued to travel until the stroke forced her children to put her in the Home. And the memory of all this conversation in my dream felt real, as if I had actually spent the hours talking to her.

And what really bothered me was that normally I never remembered my dreams.

After breakfast, I went back to my room and to my newly installed phone. It had been the one thing I had insisted my son add into my room. At least this way I could still have a small touch with the outside world. I hadn't expected to want to use it this soon.

One phone call to Emmie, the daughter of my old neighbor, told me what I wanted to know. Emmie worked in records at the county and her mother always told me that Emmie and her computer could find out more about a person than another person had the right to know.

It only took Emmie a minute to tell me that Rosie Manning had indeed been married to Harold Manning, who at one time had served on the city council and later on the planning and zoning commission. He had died fourteen years ago while in Hawaii.

I hung up the phone shocked.

And very much in denial.

Somehow, some way, I must have known Rosie from before her stroke, maybe I had even been in a kitchen like the one in my dream. There was no other explanation.

I made myself focus on the game shows on television until lunch and took a nap until dinner. It felt like a routine I was going to be doing for a very long time to come.

But after dinner, I again found myself walking past Rosie's room.

And again I could smell the wonderful odor of cooking around where she sat, her almost dead body hunched over in her chair, the stains of her dinner on her bib.

I stood over her for a moment, my hand resting on the back of her chair. Her thinning white hair barely covered the red, flaky surface of her scalp.

I was almost afraid to go back to my room.

Afraid to lie down and sleep.

Afraid of the pleasant dream I might have. Afraid because I didn't understand what was happening.

Five

THE SECOND DREAM started the same as the first.

I walked down the hall and stood in front of Rosie's door, watching her work at her counter inside a kitchen five times larger than her nursing home room.

This time the smell that filled the air around me was rich with chocolate and vanilla. From where I stood I could see she was mixing up an icing while two halves of a chocolate-layered cake cooled on racks.

She turned and saw me and motioned me to come in. Then she went back to working in the bowl with a small electric hand mixer.

Hesitantly, I moved inside and stood near the wooden table, enjoying the smell and the warmth and watching until she'd finished.

Finally she turned off the mixer, pulled out the beaters, turned and held one up for me. "Just in time to lick off the icing."

I took the one offered and watched as she licked the other, obviously enjoying the task like a kid would have done.

I followed her example and a few moments later found myself working at getting every lick of the sweet-tasting frosting.

I finished and handed her back the beater. She smiled at me, a fleck of white frosting on her chin. "Glad you came," she said. "I wasn't sure that you would."

"It's just a dream," I said, my voice sounding in my ears a little more insistent than I wanted it to sound. "I didn't have a choice."

She laughed and moved back to put the beaters in the sink. "Of course you do," she said.

I shook my head slowly from side to side as she moved to the cake on the racks. What she had said made no sense to me. "How can you control your dreams?"

She shrugged while testing to see if the cakes were still too hot to frost. They obviously were, so she turned back to me. "I don't know how, but I know I do, ever since I had my stroke." She laughed. "Actually, I did before the stroke, too. Much of my life was like a wonderful dream."

She turned and indicated the full kitchen. "I live in here, now. I really never go out there much at all." She pointed to the door that led into the hall of the nursing home.

I glanced at the darkened hall and then back at her. She was smiling. "Tea?" she asked.

I nodded and she went to work getting out a kettle and filling it with water, then placing it on the stove.

The next morning I remembered when I woke up that we had spent three wonderful hours talking about our lives, our dead husbands, and our children. I remembered I told her what my son had done to me and she shook her head in sadness. "You deserve so much better," she had said.

In the morning I agreed with her even more than I had in the dream. I did deserve better. And so did she.

At breakfast, lunch and dinner I sat with her while the aide fed her a sloppy mush that served as her food. More of it ended up on her bib than in her mouth.

Six

THE THIRD DREAM, she had just finished a steaming hot bowl of popcorn and the smell was so wonderful I almost walked into her kitchen before she invited me in. But luckily she saw me standing there and waved me to the table before I had barged rudely in.

"I already have the water on for tea," she said as I sat down and took a handful of popcorn. In the real world, outside this dream, I would have been hesitant to eat popcorn due to my dentures. But this was a dream and I knew it. And if a person couldn't eat popcorn in a dream, what was the point of dreaming?

She sat down across from me and took a handful of popcorn. Then between bites she said, "I'm going to be moving on tomorrow."

"What?"

"My old body will finally give up tomorrow and I will move on." She shrugged. "Not much I can do about it."

"How do you know?" I managed to ask. For some reason the thought of her not being here in my dreams scared me in a very selfish way.

She shrugged. "I just know. And when your time comes, you'll know, too."

"Since this is my dream, can't I change it?"

She smiled a sad smile at me. "I want to move on. If you were stuck with a body like mine, you would too. Now, let's talk about more pleasant subjects."

At that point, the kettle started to boil and she stood to retrieve it.

For the next three hours we talked and laughed and I forced myself to not talk about what she had told me. And a huge part of me didn't believe her.

The next morning at breakfast I looked for her, but she wasn't there. The head nurse told me that she had died before breakfast.

That night, for the first time since moving into the Home, I didn't dream.

And the next day the smell of death and antiseptic closed in around me like a heavy, smothering blanket.

Seven

IT TOOK ME two days of feeling trapped and smothered before Rosie's words finally sunk all the way in. I did deserve better and unlike her, I might still be able to get it.

With one phone call I reached John, an old friend of my husband.

An old attorney friend.

It took me a good half hour, with him asking pointed questions about my affairs, before I had fully explained everything my son had done and what I hoped John could do for me.

That night I dreamed of a different kitchen. The walls were blank and the counters empty. And there were no smells, but it was a start, because somehow I knew it was my kitchen.

And the wonderful smells would come.

John called me back the next morning and told me he could, with very little work, get my money from the sale of my house out from under my son's name, as well as the rest of my savings. He also told me he'd found a wonderful little cottage with a great kitchen he thought I should see.

That afternoon a real estate agent named Sherry came by and took me to see the house. I should have known it would have the kitchen from my dream, but it still surprised me that it was.

The next day John came by and had me sign papers, including the papers for buying my little house.

By the time my son learned of what I had done, it was finished and he had nothing to say about it. I had a new home.

That night, my last night in the Home, I dreamed of Rosie again. I dreamed I was standing in her kitchen door and she was smiling at me. Her kitchen smelled of butterscotch pudding and felt warm and welcoming as always. But this time I didn't go in and she didn't invite me. We both knew it wasn't yet my time.

"Come visit me any time," I said to her through the door.

"I just might," she said.

Without me telling her she knew I now had my own home and kitchen, again. And my own life again, something Rosie could never get back for herself after her stroke.

So instead she had built a world and a wonderful kitchen inside her head and lived there.

"You have a wonderful dream," she said, smiling.

I laughed, remembering my own words from days before. "So do you," I said. "Thanks for inviting me in."

She shrugged, the smile never leaving her face. "No need to thank me. It was your dream, too."

I laughed, waved good-bye to her and turned away.

In my dream I walked back to my room, letting the smell of warm butterscotch fade slowly behind me down the dark hall of Shady Hills Nursing Home.

IN CASE OF EMERGENCY

USA Today *bestselling author, Dean Wesley Smith, delves into one of his favorite topics: Music. People always say that music can fix just about anything. Maybe it can.*

Titantic Dougherty, one of the biggest and strangest characters to ever walk into a bar clearly believes it can.

Sage, the bartender, isn't so sure.

But in one neighborhood bar, with just regular people, unexplained things can happen when Titanic Dougherty ducks in through the door.

One

MARY JUDE WAS runnin' the drinks and I was makin' them that first night Titanic Dougherty ducked through the door and slid his black leather briefcase up on the bar.

It was a normal early November night at Sandy's, with about twelve regulars scattered around the six wooden tables in the middle and eight booths with lit beer signs over them that ringed the place. The Coors sign over the second booth on the right flickered, so none of the regulars ever sat in that booth.

The evening was still young and even a few of the day-crowd regulars were at the long polished wooden bar.

The place now smelled more of wood polish and spilled beer than it did of smoke, but if you really paid attention, the decades of smoke that clouded in the place still left a faint background hint. I kind of liked it. Reminded me of simpler times.

Sandy's was tucked off to the side of Portland, Oregon, near the river and the shipping docks. From the outside, it was hard to spot because of the big pine trees on both sides and the gravel parking lot that made the cinderblock building tucked back in the trees seem like a long ways from the road.

Plus Jacob hadn't bothered to fix the sign since it got knocked sideways in a windstorm two winters ago, so other than some spotlights on the front of the building, the place was a dark building. At night, no one with a sane mind would come in that front door, yet we seemed to keep a steady stream of customers up, mostly regulars from around the older neighborhood and dock workers.

The sight of Titanic, someone brand new to the bar, stopped everyone in the bar cold, and I figured the shock of seeing someone that big might've even stopped the old juke if Benny, a drunk regular from the day shift, hadn't just plugged it and punched up *She Ain't Pretty But She Don't Snore*, the most obnoxious song to ever blare out a speaker.

My name's George Armstrong Sage. Everyone calls me Sage. I've been the bartender here at Sandy's Lounge since Jacob, the owner, got shot by a wild-eyed kid trying to get enough money for his next fix.

Jacob survived, but hasn't done much bartending since. That was three years ago and I've seen some strange happenings in all those nights, but nothing comes close to Titanic Dougherty and that black briefcase of his.

Describing Titanic ain't no easy chore. Let me put it this way, I'm no short drift at six-four, and most don't give me shit since I weigh in at over two-eighty.

I got a face that spent its time being hit by football players and baseball players and shoulders that hint at my days of playing ball. But standing next to Titanic, I'd look like that damn doughboy they show bouncing around on those commercials.

Titanic was one big son of a bitch.

That first time Titanic ducked through the front door, he was decked out completely in black, right up to one of the only black baseball caps I've ever seen. The black, tent-sized sweatshirt he wore had the number two on both shoulders and the huge muscles in his legs stretched his jeans.

I figured he might have played for a team somewhere, but I didn't recognize him. That didn't mean much since I spent my time at first base for a few years for a few teams and no one recognizes me.

"Double scotch," he said, carefully pushing the business-looking briefcase to one side. "Rocks, splash soda."

His deep-voiced request finally jolted me enough to get me to close my mouth and quit staring.

He swiveled around on his stool and glared at the other dozen or so who were silently gaping at him.

I don't know who would have won that stand-off, him or the regular customers, if the words of the song hadn't broke the tension.

...with sharp-edged curlers and flannel to the floor,
thank God, Mother, at least she don't snore.

Slowly, Titanic turned, looked at the jukebox, and then smiled.

The smile grew until he started to laugh a deep, glass-shaking laugh. That got everyone else laughing and talking.

I scrambled to the well and fixed him a solid double scotch, like he ordered, and slid it in front of him as he turned back to face the bar.

He pulled out his black leather wallet, fumbled in it with huge fingers and then pulled out a twenty and shoved it toward me. "Thanks," he said. "Hold on to that and let me know when you need more."

By the time I had rang up his drink and fixed a few for Mary Jude to take out to the lovebirds in the back booth, Mary Jude was looking at Titanic sort of glassy-eyed.

And Titanic was ready for another.

I slid the second one up beside the first. "This one's on me," I said and stuck out my hand. "Sage is what they call me."

"Thanks, Mr. Sage," he said, gripping my hand with a solid grasp that made me feel like a child shaking hands with an adult. No one had ever really done that to me before.

"They call me Titanic. Titanic Dougherty."

Much to my relief, he let go of my hand and picked up his drink.

347

The glass looked like a child's cup in his hand. "Nice place you got here," he said. "Yours?"

"Nope. I'm just the regular hired help."

He nodded kind of slow and sipped on his drink. "You pick the songs?" He motioned toward the jukebox.

I laughed. "Are you kidding? Some curly headed kid from Bently's Music services the thing. He comes in during the afternoons about once every two weeks. Worst songs I've ever heard."

Titanic laughed his rumbling laugh. "I'll agree with you on that. Maybe, just maybe, I might be able to fix that."

He patted the briefcase and then downed the rest of his drink and slid it toward me for a refill.

At that point I figured he was some sort of music salesman.

Mary Jude come up right about then with a long list of drinks. Seems Titanic had made a few people nervous to down their drinks.

I didn't have time to ask him what he actually did after I refilled his drink.

When I finally did have the time, he started asking me questions instead and I found myself telling him all about my ex-wife, Rita, and how she, without meaning to, had pushed me to try to become rich to the point where I no longer could stand the pressure.

I told him about how I once had played pro baseball and loved it more than anything.

I even ended up telling him why I was bartending instead of working as an electrical engineer like I had trained for in college.

He also asked Mary Jude a bunch about herself and I found myself listening and learning more about her than I had known after six months of working with her.

Hell, I didn't even realize that she had been married and had two kids living with her ex-husband and his new wife in Alaska. She said she hadn't seen them in half a year and probably wouldn't until summer.

She told Titanic all about how lonely she was and about her studio apartment and about how she never dated because the only time she ever met anyone was at work.

Boy, I understood that about this place. Once you knew the regulars, there was no one here to interest her or me, for that matter.

After a half hour, I found myself looking at her and not seeing Mary Jude, the cocktail waitress, but Mary Jude, the person.

348

An amazing transformation.

It was funny how that big guy could draw information out of people.

He left that night after drinking seventeen dollars of the twenty and leaving me the rest. I realized later that I knew nothing more about him than I had the moment he came in.

Two

HE DUCKED BACK in the front door two nights later at nine o'clock. Like the first time, everyone stared, but after a second, a few waved hello. He had on a white sweatshirt this time, Levis, and a red baseball cap with the word "Davis" across the top.

Again, he carried the black leather briefcase.

He slid the briefcase up on the bar and took the stool next to old Richard Butler. Richard was one of the regulars who worked down at the docs and drank his supper every night.

Usually Richard was gone by nine with six or seven bourbon-waters under his belt.

For some reason, tonight he had stayed late and was still in his normal spot at the bar.

"A little better music this time," Titanic said as I slid the bar napkin in front of him and he flipped a twenty at me. Someone had punched up a country song, but not a person in the bar was paying attention to it. I wouldn't have noticed if Titanic hadn't said something. I guess I only heard the bad ones.

"You like music, huh?" old Richard said, looking up from the bottom of his last drink.

"Same?" I asked Titanic, picking up the twenty.

Titanic nodded, then turned to Richard. "Don't you?"

Old Richard shook his head side to side in a drunken exaggerated motion. "Naw. My son liked the stuff and it drove me to drink." He picked up his empty glass and tried to get something more out of it while chuckling to himself.

I headed down the bar toward the well to make Titanic's drink and by the time I got back, Titanic had old Richard telling him all about his son and about how he was killed on a music field trip while still in high school. Hell, I'd been serving Richard for three years and not once had he mentioned he'd had a son.

Or that the son had died.

For the rest of that evening, I watched Titanic get people who got near him at the bar to talk about themselves and about their lives and their loves without once mentioning one thing about himself.

I think he knew I was watching him, because every so often he would look up at me and point over at the jukebox and say, "Interesting song. Listen to the words."

Then he'd go back to whatever conversation he was having at the time.

That instruction from him always brought the song out loud and clear as if it hadn't been playing the moment before. Usually the words would mean something to me, or get me remembering a part of my life with Rita, or something about my work or my ball-playing days.

Again Titanic stayed for seventeen dollars of his twenty and like he had the first time, left without a word about himself ever being said.

Three

AFTER THAT HE started coming in twice a week.

Mondays and Thursdays. He always dressed comfortably and always had the black leather briefcase with him. He became another of the regulars, accepted by most of the old-timers as if he'd been around for years instead of weeks.

I loved that about bars like Sandy's. Once you were in, you were accepted, no matter how strange you looked or what you did or didn't do outside of Sandy's.

It was the Thursday night during his third week that I finally got up enough courage to ask him what he did with the briefcase. I did it real casual-like as I slid a drink in front of him and I think I almost caught him off guard.

Almost.

He paused for a long second, looking at me, then he smiled and patted the case lightly with one big hand. "I use it for emergencies."

"How's that?"

He pointed a finger up in the air. "Notice the song? Good message in this one."

The old Kenny Rodgers' song blared over my consciousness like someone had turned up the volume. Without thinking I found myself following the words as I walked back toward the well.

When I turned around, Titanic had picked up his drink and joined a group over in the corner, leaving his briefcase and his money sitting in their normal spot on the bar.

About a month after Titanic started coming into Sandy's, Mary Jude started having troubles.

The only reason I noticed it was because Titanic started talking to her a bunch more and I overheard some of her problems. It seemed the loneliness was getting to her and her ex-husband was being a real bastard about letting her see the kids. She just couldn't afford to fly up to Alaska or help fly them down.

It looked as if she might not even get to see them this summer and that had her awful depressed.

I noticed one Tuesday she came in for work with her eyes red.

I asked her if there was anything I could do, but she just shook her head. That night Titanic came in and talked to her and she seemed to be a lot better by the end of the night.

But she was back depressed again the next night.

The following Monday she didn't show for work.

Titanic came in at nine and he didn't look happy. He sat his black briefcase down on the bar and looked over at me. "Mary Jude?"

"Didn't come in," I said. "I tried to call her, but didn't get an answer."

He nodded. "She is one very sick woman and there doesn't seem to be much more I can do to help her." He stood with both huge hands on the case and stared down at it as if it might explode at any moment.

"Help her?" I asked. "You a doctor?"

He looked up at me and smiled that same smile adults give kids when they ask a reasonable question that seems to have an obvious other answer. "No, I'm not," he said. "I am a musician. And I think it may be time I play my latest song."

He clicked open the latches on the briefcase and opened the case. The sound of those latches clicking shocked the bar into silence.

Inside, the case was lined in a black velvet and completely empty except for one forty-five record in a paper slip.

He carefully picked up the forty-five and closed the case.

"May I play this on your jukebox?"

I stared at the record for a moment, then looked up at him. "I don't have a key."

"I can open it."

"Then be my guest," I said.

I didn't know what to think. One moment we were talking about Mary Jude and how sick she was and the next he tells me the first bit of information I've heard about him, then opens up a case he's brought with him every night and pulls out a stupid record.

He moved over to the jukebox and with a movement of his hand that I couldn't follow, had the top up. He studied the insides for a moment, then inserted his record carefully. At this point, not only was I watching him, but so was everyone in the place.

He closed the top of the jukebox and turned back to face me.

"I'm sorry for what this will do to you. And to all of you."

He swept his arm around to include everyone in the bar. At that moment there were about twenty of the regulars scattered around, most of them he had talked to at one point or another.

"It is better people learn their lessons without help," he said, his big rumbling voice filling the silence of Sandy's. "But I feel Mary Jude may be in danger and I must try to help her."

He patted the jukebox. "And this is the only way I know how."

"Just exactly what are you planning on doing?" I asked.

"I'm just going to play my latest song," he said. "Nothing more."

With that, he turned to the jukebox and punched two buttons. Right at that point you could hear the traffic outside on the distant street that ran in front of the bar.

No one said a word.

The song started low, almost as if it really didn't have one starting point but had always been there below the level of hearing. I think the instrument was a flute, but someone later said they'd heard a guitar.

All I know is that when it started, I suddenly felt light-headed.

And when the words started with the sound of Titanic's voice, deep and full and rich, I felt the room spin.

Titanic slowly faded away, as if his massive frame had never been standing there.

Everyone agreed later that he had disappeared.

Or at least everyone thought they saw him disappear.

And everyone agreed that after a few seconds, he was back, dancing with Mary Jude.

I remember half watching them dance, his huge frame agile and light as he led her in and out of the tables. She was smiling and radiant, staring up at his face.

But the other half of me was years away from Sandy's Bar, drifting over my past decisions and events of my life as smoothly as Titanic and Mary Jude drifted past the tables in Sandy's Lounge.

I saw clearly what I had done right and where I had been wrong.

I understood for the first time why Rita had pushed me so hard.

By the end of the song, I finally understood what I needed to do to be happy with myself.

How I had been only hiding in Sandy's.

Everything.

As the last notes of the music died into the walls and the wooden tables and the beer signs, Mary Jude and Titanic faded away as if someone had turned a fan on a cloud of smoke.

And the silence that followed lasted one damn long time.

Four

JACOB LOST MORE than half of his regular customers that night, as Titanic's song changed their lives as it changed mine.

But not a one of us could remember the words to his song.

Or the tune.

We just remember listening to it. And what that listening did to each of us.

Jacob told me that Mary Jude had called him and quit. She had said she was going back to Alaska to fight for her kids like she should have done the first time.

No one ever saw Titanic again, and we couldn't find his record anywhere in the jukebox.

Two weeks later I quit tending bar at Sandy's to take a job as a scout for the local semi-pro baseball team. It was a start back, a start to a new life of not hiding.

Titanic's black briefcase was still sitting behind the bar the day I left, as empty as I had been before he had played his most recent song. I patted it on the way out and said, "Thanks."

THE 13TH FLOOR PROBLEM

A Poker Boy Story

USA Today *bestselling writer once more returns to his favorite character, Poker Boy.*

Poker Boy and his team must figure out why the 13th floors of every major building in Las Vegas were about to disappear. Was it magic? Was it an evil plan to destroy Las Vegas? And who had the power to do such a thing?

One of the more puzzling mysteries that Poker Boy must solve. And he does it in his normal strange and funny way: He asks stupid questions.

This story originally appeared in Fiction River: Hex in the City and is part of my monthly focus to let readers of this magazine read some of my stories from WMG Publishing's other main publication.

One

AS A PROFESSIONAL poker player, I don't have any superstitions. Not a one. I don't believe that if I won a tournament with one sock inside out, that I needed to always wear one sock inside out for good luck. I know for a fact that Lady Luck, actually named Laverne, paid no attention at all to how my socks were worn, or if I threw salt over my shoulder, or if I walked under a ladder.

She was just too busy. Now don't take me wrong, I wouldn't want to cross her, but she just wasn't the type to pay attention to the small stuff.

In life and in poker, I have had my fair share of good luck and bad luck, even though as Poker Boy, I know Lady Luck likes me, and my team. In fact, one of her four daughters, Terri, the Queen of Clubs, has just joined my team of superheroes.

My team works to save the world when it needs saving and it is often Lady Luck who gives us the assignments.

As it happened, just luck or coincidence or whatever, most of my team was having lunch in my office when we learned about what we came to call "The 13th Floor Problem."

My office, actually it's my team's office, but everyone calls it my office, floats about five hundred feet above the top floor of MGM Grand Hotel and Casino. It has windows on all four sides, floor-to-ceiling, with a view that was worth more than I wanted to ever imagine.

How it stayed in position was beyond me, even though Stan said I was the one who put it there and kept it there. As far as I was concerned, it stayed in place by some sort of magic I didn't understand. There were a lot of things in the world of gods and superheroes that I didn't understand and how my office worked was one of those things.

The office was, of course, invisible, and, as Stan said, out of phase with the real world so that if a plane hit it, the plane would pass right through. I'm sure if that happened, it would give everyone in the office a heart attack. The last thing I wanted was a plane passing through me.

But the office did have a wonderful view of the Strip and the airport and the entire city around it. Patty Ledgerwood (aka Front Desk Girl and my girlfriend and sidekick) and I often came up here at night and sat together and watched the stars and the planes landing and the cars on the Strip and all the bright lights spread out below us. As I said, a view worth more than I can imagine.

I had decorated the office so it looked like an exact replica of the 1960's diner booth the team used to meet in. The Diner, as the place is called, is in the downtown Vegas area on a side street a block from the Horseshoe Casino and Hotel.

Just as in the Diner downtown, this booth had slick, red seats on three sides. I had added wooden chairs that could be pulled up to the end of the booth and a couple tall, tree-like plants behind the booth to give the place a little less cold feel.

The booth filled most of the room and could seat eight in a pinch.

There were only three ways to get up to the office. I had put a door leading to Patti's apartment and another door leading to the Diner in downtown Vegas. You step through and you were instantly in the other place. Otherwise you had to teleport.

I could teleport, but besides Stan, the God of Poker and my boss, I was the only one on the team who could. Everyone else either hitched a ride here with me or Stan or used the door from the Diner.

I was told it was rare that a lowly superhero like me could teleport. Or step between instants of time. But I had learned how to do both. I figured if I could learn it, so could other superheroes, like my girlfriend, Patty. She was a superhero working in hotel hospitality area of the Gods.

She was willing to learn, so we had worked on it a few times, so far without luck. But we had time and one of Patty's superhero traits was extreme patience. She had to have that to put up with me at times. I was a professional poker player, after all.

It had become a habit for the team to have lunch together in my office around the big booth at one in the afternoon. We all liked the view and the companionship. Sometimes being a superhero could get lonely, at least that's what others told me. As a poker player, I always had people around me. It was part of the job.

And I was lucky enough to be tangled up with Patty.

Screamer and his wife, Terri, were sitting at the table working on burgers and vanilla shakes that Madge from the Diner had brought up. Having the great food and milkshakes from the Diner in downtown Vegas just a step through a door away was a great benefit.

Screamer had been a member of the team since we started. He was a superhero working with the police and could, with a touch, connect minds and be inside another person's mind. He got his nickname Screamer from making hardened criminals scream in fear from the images he put in their heads.

Terri was Lady Luck's daughter and a superhero in the beverage side of things. She and Screamer had been separated for a number of years while he got his newly acquired brain-reading powers under control. Now that they had worked out a way to be together, they never seemed to be apart.

Patty worked at the MGM Grand front desk and was on lunch break, so she still had on her front desk outfit and her long, brown hair pulled back tight. She nibbled at a salad while I worked at a cheeseburger with a huge basket of fries. I had switched away from my standard vanilla milkshake today for a cherry Diet Coke. Patty was mixing my fries with her salad, taking a bite of lettuce, then a fry.

Stan, the God of Poker, and my boss, also had a cheeseburger. He had on his standard tan slacks, tan shirt, and tan vest. He was the most nondescript man I had ever met. You could almost look right at him and not notice him. That made him downright scary on a poker table.

I had just taken a huge bite of my cheeseburger when Laverne, Lady Luck herself, appeared, pulled up a chair, sat at the booth, and grabbed one of my fries. Between her and Patty, I was going to be lucky to get any of them.

Laverne wore her normal gray silk business pants suit and had her hair pulled back tight, giving her face a stark beauty and sternness. She just radiated power and toughness.

And not once being around her did I fail to get nervous. Having Lady Luck herself just come to have lunch with you was a stunning thing I would never get over.

"Hey, Mom," Terri said, working at her hamburger and leaning against Screamer.

I managed to get most of the ketchup off my chin and nodded to her. Stan just kept working on his cheeseburger.

Madge appeared out of the door from the diner and smiled at Laverne. "Anything I can get for you?"

Madge was the waitress and the owner of the Diner downtown. She was also a superhero in the food and beverage industry and seemed to have been around the world of the gods for a very long time. She was fairly short and clearly overweight and she always wore a dress far, far too tight and too short for someone her size. She had a gruff way about her, but was always willing to help out the team where she could. She knew everyone, which had helped a few times on different assignments we had tackled.

Laverne shook her head. "Thanks, Madge, but we have a problem we need to get started on."

I swallowed the last of the bite of my cheeseburger I had been chewing on and pushed the rest away. When Laverne came looking for us like this, it meant eating was going to take a back seat very quickly.

Besides, my stomach was already twisting from my sense of

looming danger, so putting more food down there wasn't a good idea at the moment.

"What's happening?" Stan asked, then took another bite of his cheeseburger.

"All the thirteenth floors are vanishing," Laverne said, as if she said a statement like that every day.

Then she took another fry.

"No building or hotel in this city has a thirteenth floor," Terri said, looking puzzled.

"Floor Twelve B or the Fourteenth Floor, whatever they are called," Laverne said, shrugging. "They are all vanishing. They will still be there, so no building is going to fall down, but the floors will become totally invisible by midnight."

"The Magician is back," Madge said, shaking her head and sighing in a way I had never heard before.

"Maybe," Laverne said, taking one more fry. She gave me that serious stare that scared me down to my very toes. "And if The Magician is behind this in any way, we need to stop him. And quickly."

At that, she vanished with one of my French fries in her hand.

The stunned silence around the office matched how I felt.

I just wish I had a clue what was happening.

And how she seemed to know something that was going to happen in two days.

And who the hell The Magician was.

Two

EVERYONE HAD STOPPED EATING.

Terri was just shaking her head, her long black hair going back and forth around her face.

Madge was frowning, never a good sign when a waitress used to attempting to smile was frowning.

Stan looked angry and Patty looked confused, just as I was feeling.

"Time for milkshakes," Madge said.

At that moment every bit of food on the table vanished and Madge turned and stepped through the door back to the Diner.

The group had a habit of ordering milkshakes when we were

working on a problem. Usually only big problems. So Madge thought this problem big enough for milkshakes and had cleared the table.

Again not a good sign.

I stared at the place on the booth where my French fries had been and kind of wished I had the power to bring them back. And then I wondered where they had gone, and then finally decided I didn't want to know any of those details. Not at the moment, anyway.

I glanced around at my team, then decided that none of them were going to speak, so it was up to me to be my normal clueless self and ask dumb questions. Sometimes my dumb questions got to the heart of the problem facing us, sometimes they just made me look silly for asking.

I wanted to start with how someone knew what was going to happen two days in the future, but decided on something more basic. "So someone want to give me the background on The Magician?"

"Right now he goes by Nick Scipio," Stan said without looking up. "He's been around for longer than anyone knows for certain. The protector and father, basically, of modern magic. Over the centuries he's taken many names when free, from Dedi in Egypt to Robert-Houdin."

"Is he a god?" Patty asked.

"He's an elf," Stan said.

I moaned. We had dealt a number of times with the elves and trolls and their fights. Because I had caught the one person causing elves and trolls to always battle, I was honored in their hidden casino here in Vegas, but I seldom went there. Just often enough to not insult them by never going there.

"You said something about him being free?" Screamer asked, and Terri nodded beside him, her black hair moving around her face.

"He is sort of locked up in a time cell," Stan said, "between moments of time, that should make it impossible for him to escape. But he often does. It's been a good fifty years since his last escape, at least that I heard about."

"So why make all the 13th floors disappear?" I asked.

"You could ask him yourself," Madge said, appearing from the doorway of the Diner carrying six milkshakes.

Behind her strolled a tall, thin man with black hair covering the tips of his pointed ears. He wore a white frilly shirt like he was on the way to a wedding and a long, black cape. In one hand he carried a cane, but clearly didn't need it.

"I figured Madge would know where you all met," he said, his voice low and soothing in an odd way.

He looked around at the view, clearly impressed, then he stopped in front of the booth and bowed slightly. "The Magician at your service. And I want to be very clear that I will have nothing to do with the building floors disappearing in just under two days. But I must admit, it's a nice bit. I kind of wish I had thought of it."

He pulled up a chair and sat on it, facing all of us.

"Vanilla as always," Madge asked, placing the milkshake in front of him and then continuing on with the rest of ours.

"A wonderful memory," The Magician said. "Now a glass of fine whiskey and a cigar and I would be as happy as can be."

"Drink your milkshake, Nick," Madge said, shaking her head and moving off to one side behind the booth. She never sat with us, but often took part in the meetings and it was clear she had no desire to miss this one.

"Good seeing you again, Stan," The Magician said, as he stirred his milkshake and sipped it.

I stared at Stan, then back at Nick Scipio, The Magician. Clearly they had history. And I was just about to ask what that history was when Lady Luck appeared and scooted into the booth beside her daughter.

"Nick," she said, nodding.

The Magician bowed slightly. "I am honored, as always."

"Cut the crap," Laverne said, "and explain to me what's happening and how you know about it."

When Lady Luck gets blunt, things really have to be going wrong. This just looked worse and worse by the moment.

Three

THE MAGICIAN DIDN'T let Lady Luck's brashness even seem to phase him. He took a sip of his milkshake, nodded a thank-you in Madge's direction, and then turned to face Lady Luck. From my position beside Patty across from Teri and her mother, I could see Nick's dark eyes. And I watched them closely as he spoke, seeing if I could get a read on him and if he was lying.

"In my little confines," The Magician said, "which are very

comfortable, I might add, I have sometimes been able to see out ahead in time. Not far, and often not that accurately, since the future is always in flux by events of the present. But I did see that in two days all the 13th floors of every building in Las Vegas will become invisible. For some reason, all authorities will, at the time, know this will happen and will have all the floors from twelve-up completely evacuated. It will cause a very large event that will be difficult at best to explain away, except as a magician's illusion gone horribly wrong."

"I know all that," Laverne said, waving her hand in dismissal. "So who could actually pull off this kind of illusion?"

"Besides me?" The Magician asked. "No one. Which is why I don't think this is an illusion."

"Magic?" Stan asked as Lady Luck frowned.

Silence fell over the booth. And I had no idea why so many of them were upset. We were sitting in a booth in an invisible office five hundred feet above the MGM Grand Hotel and Casino. If that wasn't magic, what were we talking about?

"So who could pull off this level of magic?" Lady Luck finally asked. "And why would anyone break the ban?"

I wanted to scream WHAT BAN? But instead I just sat watching The Magician. From what I could tell, he had been telling the truth and seemed as worried as the rest of the people around the table.

I'm sure I looked worried as well, but not for the same reason. I was worried because I had no idea what they were talking about.

"I don't know the answer to that," The Magician said. "But I will be glad to help find out. If this actually happens, it will give all magicians a bad name and magicians in general will take the blame since it will be the only way to explain away such an event."

"Thanks," Lady Luck said, nodding. "You up for talking to your people?"

He took another long sip of the vanilla milkshake, then nodded. "Let's go."

"The rest of you keep working on this," Laverne said.

And she and The Magician vanished.

I sat there in the silence they left behind, so confused I didn't even have a question to ask. So Patty got the ball rolling.

"What did he do?"

Stan shook his head. "Not much, actually. Just pissed off the wrong god at the wrong time with a stupid trick. He and Laverne actually like each other, so she put him in a comfortable cell to keep him out of the way for a few centuries. He comes out, or as he likes to call it, "escapes" when he wants or needs to."

"So," I said, taking a deep breath, "someone want to explain to me the difference in magic and what is holding this office in the air?"

Screamer and Teri both laughed and Stan just shook his head. Patty just patted my leg, which meant my question was really stupid.

"Real magic," Teri said, "not the illusions that magicians do, is powered from the dark side. It does not come from any one person or skill, but by tapping into the pool of dark energy that rests just under the surface of everything."

Stan nodded and looked at me. "Your power to teleport, step between moments of time, and keep this place in the air comes from you, the depth of your ability to help others. It is a power of your mind and who you are. Just as studying another person and knowing how they are going to act in a hand of cards is a trained skill."

"Okay," was all I could manage to say. I sure didn't feel like I had a powerful mind. Far from it at the moment, in fact.

"That's why some of us can see slightly into the future as well," Stan said. "Like you watch a person and can predict a play or know his cards, others can watch life and know what might be possible in the future. A skill."

Well, that sort of explained that question at least, so I nodded.

He looked squarely at me and then went on, his tone and voice very, very clear. "All our powers are powers of light and come out of who we are and our own skills and talents. Nothing we do is actually magic."

I decided to just keep pushing my ignorance out there for everyone to see. "So this stunt of making entire floors invisible comes from a magic that is banned?"

Stan and Terri both nodded.

Stan said, "Actual magic has been banned for centuries, but some people try it anyway at times."

"And what happens to them?" Patty asked.

"The dark magic consumes them," Screamer said, his voice sounding disgusted. "And they became part of the dark pool of power. Not something I would ever want to experience. Think of the worst images of hell and multiply that by one hundred."

With that the silence just settled over the room again. Outside the windows, the sun was shining, planes were landing at the airport, and the world kept going, unaware that entire slices of buildings were about to vanish.

I took a sip of my milkshake and let the coolness calm me a little. I just couldn't get one word out of my head and I finally just blurted it out. "Why?"

"Why do they get consumed?" Screamer asked, looking at me as if I had lost my mind completely.

"No," I said, shaking my head. "Why make floors invisible? If this really is someone using magic and risking his or her life to do so, why do this stunt? It seems very petty, has no obvious return for the stunt, and flat makes no sense."

And yet again the silence filled my office around the booth.

I was right.

I knew it. And their lack of an answer confirmed that for me.

No one who knew how to do dark magic and the repercussions from the use of dark magic would ever do something this stupid and out in the open.

And for no gain that I could see.

Suddenly I had yet another idea.

"What happens if this isn't real dark magic? What happens if it is a superhero having some issues with power control?"

Stan looked at me with a look that I couldn't read, but that wasn't unusual for me with Stan. He was the God of Poker, after all.

"Are you suggesting," Screamer asked, leaning forward, "that what is about to happen to all the 13th floors might be nothing more than an accident about to happen?"

"Possible," I said. "So what kind of superhero needs to learn to make things vanish in their training?"

Teri started to say something, then shut her mouth and shook her head.

Screamer just shook his head.

Stan and Patty both said nothing.

Finally, from behind the booth Madge said, "Cleaners. And some food superheroes as well."

"Like you made our lunch remains vanish," I said, glancing back at her.

She nodded.

"Are there Gods of Cleaners and Superheroes of cleaning?" I

asked, then knew the answer. Of course there were. I had watched a person come into a room and it seemed to just get clean, as if by some sort of magic, which was more-than-likely a special power. I always admired people who could do that type of cleaning, since every time I tried to clean something, it looked worse instead of better.

"Damn," Stan said softly. Then he said, "Everyone's with me."

"Except me," Madge said. "I'll have milkshakes ready for you when you get back."

Stan nodded and then a moment later all five of us were standing in a huge warehouse that smelled of ammonia and other cleaning solutions.

Four

THE BUILDING AROUND us was so large I couldn't see any wall in any direction. Nothing but aisles between huge stacks of cases of what looked like varied cleaning solutions and supplies.

The roof had to be ten stories overhead, the lights dim, the floor smooth concrete, and the temperature worse than air conditioning set too low. The stack closest to me had to go up four or five stories into the air, pallet on top of pallet. How they stayed stacked like that was anyone's guess, or how anyone did the stacking was another skill I really didn't want to watch anytime soon.

A moment after we arrived, the Magician and Lady Luck arrived as well.

She turned to me. "You think this might be a new superhero having issues with powers?"

I nodded. "An idea that makes sense. Other than to do as an illusion, this future event makes no sense otherwise."

The Magician nodded. "Now I see why these people hang around with you."

"Thanks," I said, "but why are we standing here in this warehouse?"

"What, you don't like my office or something?" a voice blurted behind me.

I spun around to face a short, stout, matronly woman wearing a light blue cleaning uniform. On the cloth sewn-on name badge it read "Hygieia" and under that it said in small letters "Call me Jean."

Laverne stepped up in front of me to face the new woman before I could say anything about her "office."

"Jean, thanks for meeting with us," Laverne said, her voice very stern, so much so that I shuddered slightly. "Every 13th floor of every building in Las Vegas is going to vanish in just under two days."

"Good," Jean said, shrugging. "We won't have to clean them."

"We think it's one of your people who is going to cause the problem," Laverne said.

She frowned at Laverne, started to say something, then stopped and really looked around at all of us. "Stan, Poker Boy, Patty Ledgerwood, Screamer, your daughter, and The Magician. You have the A-Team on this, so it must be serious."

"It is," Laverne said. "Very serious. We can't let this happen. Are you training someone in the Las Vegas area?"

"Always training someone it seems," Jean said.

Beside her a very, very short man appeared wearing a hood over his head and only allowing just part of his face to show. I had no idea who he was or what his job was.

"You are training one called Dee, my sister," the short man said, his voice very deep.

"Oh, yeah, her," Jean said, nodding. "She's a strange talent, very powerful, only been on the job a few months, but seems to learn quickly."

"She has many fears," the short man said. Then he vanished.

At that point I had about fifty questions I wanted to ask, but as I had learned years before, when dealing with Gods, it was better to just keep silent and let them go on and then have someone explain later what happened.

"I'm not sure how Dee having fears could cause this," Jean said, looking puzzled.

"Maybe she's afraid of the number thirteen," I said, instantly breaking my rule about keeping my mouth shut.

Silence.

And in a huge warehouse with the ceiling towering four stories over my head, that silence seemed awful loud as everyone stared at me.

Finally Jean said, "I will bring Dee."

I instantly felt sorry for the poor girl. If I had been brought into a group like this, I would have more than likely fainted during my first years of being a superhero.

"Hold on," I said before the God of Cleaning could jump away. "I'm afraid, as a new superhero, she won't be able to answer any questions with a crowd like this. This group still intimidates me at times and I've been at this for a decade or so."

Jean nodded. "What would you suggest, Poker Boy?"

"Patty and I could go talk with her alone and the rest of you can keep track of how the conversation goes."

Jean glanced at Laverne who nodded.

"She is working on the third floor of the Golden Nugget. Tall, skinny, very young and very smart."

"Blind camera spot end of the hall," Stan said, "against the wall across from the elevators."

I nodded and jumped with Patty to that spot.

Five

FAINT MUSIC PLAYED in the hallway and it smelled like the carpets had just been vacuumed. Down the plush hallway to our right was a maid's cart, so we headed in that direction.

As we neared the cart a tall woman with red hair appeared wearing a maid's uniform and carrying an armload of towels. She smiled at us, then dropped the towels into her cart. She was very young and hadn't yet seemed to grow into her body or her face.

It was clearly Dee. Under the sleeves of her shirt I could see signs of tattoos and another tattoo peaked out of her high collar.

As she started to turn back to go into the room I said, "Dee, we need to talk with you."

She stopped, suddenly looking puzzled. Her bright green eyes got very round.

"I am Poker Boy, this is Patty Ledgerwood."

Patty extended her hand. "Great to meet you," Patty said, giving the young superhero her best calming power.

Dee shook Patty's hand and seemed to relax a little. I didn't add in my calming power just yet, but I had a hunch I was going to need it.

"Your boss, Jean, says great things about you," I said.

Suddenly Dee looked panicked again. I remember early on in my superhero starting months, I thought no one knew I was secretly a superhero, so I was always shocked when another person knew that.

Like me, she was going to be surprised as she learned just how many superheroes and gods there really were.

At the end of the hallway, the elevator dinged and the door started to open. So I slipped us out of time and into an instant between moments of time so that we wouldn't be disturbed. Since we were in a hallway and couldn't hear any traffic noise outside, nothing seemed to change, so Dee didn't notice.

"How do you know Jean?" Dee asked, looking first at Patty, who was still smiling and then back at me.

"We know many of the different gods," Patty said. "I work in the hospitality area and Poker Boy here works in the poker area, just as you work in the cleaning area. We are all at the same level, just under different departments."

Dee nodded and relaxed again. This girl really, really was the nervous type, of that there was no doubt.

I decided since Jean and Laverne and Stan were watching, to just jump to the problem. "Dee, are you scheduled in two days to clean Floor 14 here?"

Panic flipped across Dee's face and I sent calming waves at her, just as Patty was doing, trying to help her stay under control. I could feel my calming and trust-me power boosted a little as well, more than likely from Stan.

Dee calmed down and then nodded. "It's the 13th floor and I'm deathly afraid of it. I don't know what to do."

"We can help," Patty said, smiling as both of us kept aiming our combined calming powers at the young superhero. We were hitting Dee with so much calming juice, we could have put a horse to sleep smiling.

"But it's part of my job to clean that floor," Dee said, looking like she was about to burst into tears.

Suddenly I had another idea.

"We can help with that if you let us," I said. "We can help you never fear anything with the number 13 again."

"You could do that?" Dee asked. "And Jean wouldn't mind?"

"If it's going to help you do your job," Patty said, "I'm sure she wouldn't mind at all."

Dee stared at me, then at Patty for a moment. I could feel Stan boosting my "trust me" power I was pouring at Dee.

Finally Dee nodded.

"Stan, bring Screamer," I said into the air.

A moment later Stan and Screamer appeared.

Dee jumped. "Are you gods?"

"He is," Screamer said, smiling at Dee as he pointed at Stan. "Great to meet you, Dee."

Screamer extended his hand and the moment he touched Dee, she froze.

Patty and I kept our calming powers aimed at Dee and turned up to full power.

"Need help to clean this out, Stan," Screamer said.

Stan nodded and touched Screamer's shoulder. I knew at that moment in time they were both inside Dee's mind, working to clear out her fears of the number thirteen without really hurting her or changing her in any way and leaving no trace they had been in there.

After a moment Stan nodded and dropped his hand from Screamer's shoulder. Then Screamer let go of Dee's hand.

"So what can you do to help me?" Dee asked, staring at Screamer and then at Stan.

"Do you still fear the number thirteen?" I asked.

She frowned for a moment, then shook her head. "No, I don't. Wow, you guys are good."

"We'll let you get back to work now," Patty said, touching Dee's arm one more time to really leave a calming and pleasant feel with the young superhero.

"Thanks," Dee said, smiling. "I hope to see you again."

As I dropped the time shield and jumped all of us back to my office in the air over the MGM Grand Hotel, all I kept thinking about was that I had no doubt we were going to see more of that young superhero in the future. I had a hunch she might just be helping the team down the road at times.

I guess that was my way of seeing into the future a little.

Madge was waiting for us with freshly made milkshakes. Laverne and The Magician and Terri appeared a moment after we did.

"Jean thanks you all," Laverne said. "As do I."

"I thank you as well," The Magician said, bowing slightly. "Your quick thinking and action has saved illusionists everywhere from a very difficult black eye."

Smiling, I slid into the booth and Patty slid in beside me as Terri gave Screamer a big kiss and then joined us.

It had seemed like hours ago that my French fries had disappeared from the table, but actually, this time, we had saved the city in just under a half hour.

"Madge," I asked, smiling at her as she placed the last milkshake on the table, "is there any chance you could make those French fries reappear?"

"Make that two orders," Lady Luck said, sliding into the booth beside her daughter.

"Three, if you don't mind," The Magician said, pulling up a chair.

Madge laughed and turned for the door to the Diner. "I had a hunch you would want some after lunch got shortened, so four orders of fries are cooking right now."

"Seeing the future again, Miss Madge?" The Magician asked, winking.

She smiled at him and winked back. "Depends if you have enough magic up that sleeve of yours to handle a future me."

"Have I ever failed you, Miss Madge?"

Madge laughed like a young girl and disappeared through the door.

All Patty and I and Screamer and Terri could do was just stare open-mouthed at The Magician as he sipped on his milkshake, smiling.

Lady Luck just shook her head as I tried desperately to clear the image out of my mind of a tall, skinny elf and an overweight waitress together.

I have a hunch it's burned there forever.

THE MOUTH THAT WALKED

Cats seem to not care much about anything around them. Anyone who knows cats knows this to be not true. And watching a cat stalk and kill a mouse or bird shows yet another side of the creatures we let live with us.

This story, originally published in Amazing Stories *back in the late 1980s warns those who don't know cats what they can do when pushed. A cautionary tale.*

At times, because of the nature of older stories appearing and vanishing in moments, I will use this magazine to spotlight a favorite story of mine from the past. For this story, Amazing Stories was on the verge of folding in that incarnation when I sold it to them, so very few people saw the story at publication, and no one under forty would have had a chance to ever read it. So I'm jumping the story forward in time. Enjoy.

One

CRAIG LIEBERMAN SUCKED at the two inch long scratch on the back of his hand and developed his new rule: Never pet a cat.

Never.

Not on the street.

Not on the steps to his building.

Not even if one brushed up against his leg outside his apartment door. He would never again stop to pet a cat.

Damn things were obnoxious, anyhow. Half the time they smelled of wet fur or rotted fish. They never came when a person called and the only half-good thing they did was kill rats.

He sucked on the scratch even harder, pulling the faint taste of blood into his mouth. The scratch would probably get infected. There was no telling where that cat's claw had been.

He looked back down the street at the yellow tom and resisted an impulse to pick up a rock. Damn thing. It had ruined any chance of friendship with any other cat. Craig Lieberman never forgot and he wouldn't forget his new rule.

At the next corner, he turned toward his apartment instead of going toward the library. He'd better get home and get some disinfectant on the scratch before it ended up costing him a trip to the doctor. His usual reading of the daily paper could wait.

Important things first.

In the next two blocks he saw seven cats.

The first three he avoided, the next two he kicked at and missed, and the other two he threw rocks at.

The last marble-sized rock hit a small black and white cat just above the right front leg and sent it running up an alley. The direct hit gave Craig a small thrill deep in his stomach. That would show those damn cats that they couldn't get away with scratching just anyone who showed a little kindness.

Stupid animals, anyhow.

Half a block later, he rounded the corner onto his street and stopped cold. The front steps of his apartment building were covered with cats. There had to be a hundred of them, their fur a rainbow of colors.

Craig hadn't seen that many cats in one place since he had visited an animal shelter when he was a child.

Craig started to move toward them.

In unison, they turned and looked at him.

The light film of warm sweat that covered his face turned ice cold, as if someone had slammed him straight from the warm summer day into a deep freeze.

He could feel their stares like needles jabbing his skin. The weight of their aloofness held him tight. He suddenly knew, without a doubt, exactly how little he mattered to them.

He was nothing.

It was below them to even acknowledge that he existed.

But they did, in unison, and then, as if on signal, they all looked away.

The sudden fear and crystal clear awareness that he had felt melted like a sliver of ice dropped on hot pavement. His first impulse was to turn and run for the police station, but the little voice in his head told him he was just being stupid. Besides, it would do no good. The cats would simply be gone by the time he got back and then the police would laugh.

He laughed at himself instead. What harm could cats do him?

None. They were just cats.

The heat of the day must have gotten to him. That's what had happened.

He was just about to pull out his handkerchief and dry his forehead when he noticed a man in a gray suit sitting in the middle of the cats. Craig would have sworn the man hadn't been there a few moments before. He hadn't been.

Craig was sure.

The steps had been covered only with cats. The man had somehow come up out of the middle of them. Craig shook his head at that thought.

Sunstroke.

He'd better get inside quick.

The man motioned for Craig to come closer.

Craig studied the cats and the man, then took a deep breath and moved forward. His own hallucination couldn't bother him. He'd get inside, call the doctor, and then lie down. He'd be fine in an hour or two.

Not one of the cats looked at him.

Craig hesitated, then stopped just short of the bottom step. The cats weren't going away.

"We need to talk," the man in gray said.

The man's voice was deep, his words clear, yet somehow flowing together. Craig studied the deep lines in the man's face. The man was both old, yet somehow very young. And his eyes bothered Craig. Cat eyes: Large and green, with bright yellow flakes of color, like gold scattered through solid rock.

"These your cats?" Craig asked after a moment, avoiding the man's gaze and making a sweeping motion with his arm at the steps. "You really can't have them here. I could call the Super and—"

The man laughed softly and the cats around him stirred without looking up at Craig. "No one truly owns a cat. All good people know that. We came to talk to you."

"Look, I'd like to get into my building. I don't think I'm feeling well. So, if you don't mind, could you have a few of your friends move aside and…"

"We need to talk," the man said softly, but firmly.

Craig realized he wasn't going to get anywhere by pushing. And no way was he going to go wading up into those cats. They'd rip the cuffs of his pants to shreds and he'd only had this pair for a few years. Besides, he'd already been hurt today.

"So go ahead and talk," Craig said.

"We would first like to apologize for the cut on your hand. As with most scratches, it was an accident."

Craig looked quickly down at the red scratch on the back of his hand. "How'd you know about that? And just who are you apologizing for?"

"I talk for myself and for those you call cats," he said softly. "It is my curse. I am known as The Mouth That Walks. It is my plight to deal with humans on their own level. Would you accept our apology for the scratch?"

Craig scanned the cats. They didn't look at him. None of the other passersby on the street seemed to even notice anything was strange. This was just too much. How could all the people on the street not notice a hundred cats on one building's front steps?

"Sure," Craig said, after he had looked around enough to realize he would have no immediate help in clearing the steps. "Why not?"

"Good," Mouth said. "Now, would you please apologize for striking my friend with the rock and we can have this unsightly mess settled."

"And just why should I do that?"

Craig was getting mad. Who ever heard of apologizing to a cat? This guy was totally crazy.

"Because you had no reason to strike my friend. She had done nothing to you."

"It was just a damned stray cat," Craig said. "Why are you picking on me? And besides, I can throw a rock at it if I damn well please. If I were you, I'd have these steps clear by the time I get back."

Craig spun and headed off down the street, not looking back. He'd read the paper first after all. The scratch really wasn't that bad.

All the way to the library he had the feeling he was being watched. Along the way there were a lot of cats. Many more than he had ever noticed before. But not one got close enough for him to try hitting with a rock.

Two dozen cats guarded the library steps. As Craig approached, more jumped up from the bushes.

A young couple came out of the front doors and started down the steps, seeming not to notice the unusual number of animals. The cats moved out of the couple's way and then, like water filling in behind a boat, returned to their places.

Craig stopped twenty feet in front of the steps as more and more cats joined the mass of colored fur. Then again, just as suddenly as before, the man dressed in gray appeared in place of a gray tom.

It was everything Craig could do to not run.

His stomach felt as if he'd had peppers for breakfast. He made himself take a deep breath. He could feel his heart pounding. "Just a trick. Just a trick," he repeated over and over to himself. Nothing more. Any half-baked magician could do the same stunt.

He really hadn't seen that man just grow out of that old tomcat.

"Just a trick. Just a trick."

"That was interesting," Craig finally said louder, looking up at the man in gray while trying to keep his voice as calm as he could. "How'd you do it?"

"Do what?" the man said.

"You know what I mean. How'd you just appear like that? You good at magic or something?"

The man in gray laughed a soft, slurring laugh. "You might say that."

"How'd you know where I was going? And how'd you beat me here?"

Again the man laughed. "We know all the secret ways and we always know what humans are thinking. If you had spent any time around us, you would have known that without asking."

"Sure you do," Craig said. "And I'm the Pope."

He started for the library steps. A bunch of damn cats and a crazy man weren't going to stop him.

The cats closed ranks and then, as a unit, looked up at Craig.

A wall of clear, hard ice dropped between Craig and those steps.

The coldness in the cats' eyes stopped him and then drove him staggering back, until finally, they looked away. Craig again found himself sweating in the warm summer air.

"Would you please apologize?" the man said, "So that we may all move along."

"And just what will happen if I don't?"

The man shook his head. "It would not be pleasant. Have you ever watched one of us catch a rat?"

Craig nodded. He'd watched a cat on his uncle's farm keep a field mouse running in circles for most of one afternoon.

The man in gray smiled. "Good, for it is our greatest sport. My brother, Claws That Dig, actually kept a rat trapped, but alive, for two full days before the rat died of heart failure. My brother is much honored."

"You're crazy," Craig said and spun away before any of the cats could look up at him. He headed back toward his apartment at a brisk walk, restraining himself from breaking into a run.

Along the way cats paced ahead and behind him, just out of his throwing range.

Cats covered Craig's apartment building's steps as he got in sight.

A large gray tom sat in the middle of them, calmly gazing up the street away from Craig, as if all the sights in the world were in that direction.

Craig had decided he was just going to plow right into the middle of them without stopping. He might get a cut or two, but he would show them who was the strongest. They would just scatter and run and he'd be done with them.

By the time he was twenty steps away, a hundred cats had joined ranks against him.

At five steps away, they all looked up at him.

This time the ice wall of their eyes smashed into Craig like a steel door slammed in his face.

The next thing he knew he was sitting dazed on the sidewalk looking up at the cats and the man dressed in gray.

"It would take a simple apology," the man said. "Nothing more. This is your last chance."

Craig stumbled to his feet and brushed off the seat of his pants. He was getting damn mad. All he wanted to do was go into his apartment and put some disinfectant on a cut. Now some crazy man and a bunch of trained cats were playing games with him. No one did that to Craig Lieberman and got away with it.

If this guy wanted to play, Craig would play. Only Craig had the law on his side and it was about time he had this Mouth guy arrested. Then Craig would see just who would apologize.

Without a word, Craig turned and headed up the street toward the Thirty-first Precinct.

And again, the cats paced him on all sides.

Craig could feel his stomach tightening as he kept telling himself he was just being foolish. A bunch of cats couldn't hurt him. They certainly couldn't act together.

It was just a trick.

Nothing more.

Fifty to sixty of the cats beat him to the police station.

They sat on the front steps of the busy station, moving only to watch something unseen in the distance or get out of the way of the people going in and out. None of the police seemed to notice anything odd, and a few people stopped to pet the large gray tom who sat up on the stone balustrade to the right of the door.

Craig strode toward the steps. There was no way they could stop him now. They wouldn't dare with all these people around. Just let one of them stray within kicking distance of his foot and they'd see just who should apologize.

Damn stupid animals.

Three paces short of the bottom step, Craig again slammed into the ice wall of their combined stare as in unison they turned to look at him.

Two

"YOU ALL RIGHT, mister?" The cop asked as he held Craig's arm and helped him sit up.

"I think so," Craig said and nodded, then quickly reached for the bump on the back of his head as sharp stabbing pains shot through his skull.

"Banged your head on the concrete pretty damn hard," the cop said, keeping his grip tight on Craig's left arm. "You sure you're all right?"

Craig let the cop help him back to his feet and hold on to him as Craig dusted off his pants.

"I'm fine," Craig said. "But don't you think you should do something about getting rid of all those cats?" Craig pointed at the steps.

The cop looked up at where Craig indicated. "You mean that old gray fellow? Hell, why would we want to do that?"

Even through the pain from the back of his head, Craig understood that he had to be careful. Real careful, or seeing all these cats was going to get him thrown into the nut house. Then he'd really hear the cats laughing.

"It must be the whack on the head," Craig said, holding the lump on his head. "But I'm seeing about fifty cats there on the precinct steps. How many are you seeing?"

The cop laughed, but still didn't let go of Craig's arm. "Only one, mister. You better get to a Doc and get yourself checked out. You went straight over backwards. Damn lucky you didn't kill yourself. You want me to get you a ride down to the emergency room?"

Craig nodded, then winced at the pain the movement caused. "Sure. I could use a lift." That would at least get him away from the cats and give him time to think. How could cats be invisible? It wasn't possible. Maybe he was sicker than he thought he was. Maybe he should have the doctor give him a good checkup. Never hurt to be careful.

"This way," the cop said and pointed at a patrol car sitting in front of the station. Two dozen cats blocked the passenger side of the car and others were moving slowly in that direction. They weren't going to let him in the car. And right now his head hurt too much to fight it.

"On second thought, I think I'll just walk home. I live close by. Thanks." Craig pulled away from the policeman and started back up the street.

This time even more cats paced along on all sides of him. Four different times Craig tried ducking suddenly into restaurants or shops, but cats filled the doors as if they knew what he was planning. Maybe they did know what he was thinking.

That just didn't seem possible.

He tried hailing a cab, but cats moved between him and the curb and he didn't dare go near the street.

A hundred cats covered the steps of his apartment building. He tried standing back and throwing rocks into the middle of the mass of fur, but after the first rock, which fell short, every time he'd raise his hand to throw, a cat jumped out of nowhere and clawed painfully at the back of his leg.

Finally, after both his pant legs were torn and one ankle was bleeding, he gave up, crossed the street, and sat on the bus stop bench facing his apartment.

He watched as his neighbors moved up and down through the cats without seeming to notice them. Why were the cats doing this to him? He'd only thrown a little rock. A cat had scratched him first. Why didn't they just leave him alone? Or find someone else?

During the next hour he made a dozen more attempts at getting inside buildings, restaurants, or cabs. All were blocked.

Craig even tried telling a cop, but like the first, the policeman just laughed.

Finally, Craig decided the quickest way out was to apologize. He'd get even later, but right now all he wanted to do was go inside. He was getting hungry.

As he slowly approached the steps, the man appeared in place of the gray tom.

Craig fought down the urge to run. "I'm ready to apologize now," he said, keeping his gaze turned away from the gray man.

"It's much too late for that," the man said. "You were given your chance. Three of them to be exact."

"Wait just a minute," Craig said and took a step forward. "I didn't do anything that bad to you or your friends. I'm sorry I threw that rock, so let's just forget it? All right?"

"I'm afraid not," the man said. "We are hunters. We do not make it a practice to let prey go just because they whimper."

"Whimper!" Craig took another step closer. "Come down here and I'll show you whimper."

"We shall see," the man in gray said, and then smiled, "just who will show who."

Craig looked quickly around. There must be a good two hundred cats sitting on the steps and along both sides of the street. He wouldn't stand a chance if he pushed it now.

He turned back to the man dressed in gray, took a deep breath, and tried to calm down. "Answer me one question. Why me? Why pick on me and let all of these other people alone?"

"Because you let us catch you," the man said. "We gave you every chance to get away. As with any prey, only the stupid or the slow get caught. I think in human terms it is called survival of the fittest."

"I'm as fit as anyone," Craig yelled at the man in gray, then whirled around and headed back across the street to the bench to plan his next move.

On the top step of the apartment building, the gray tom dozed in the warm afternoon sun.

Three

CRAIG SPENT THE night on the bench across the street from his apartment. Hunger cut ribbons from the insides of his stomach and he felt dizzy most of the morning.

The mass of cats never left the apartment steps or the surrounding doorways.

At seven a.m. he tried to sneak around to the back door of the building, but dozens of cats blocked the alley.

By two in the afternoon, he had again tried getting into nearby buildings, restaurants, and a dozen passing cabs.

Three times he had ended up on the sidewalk with another bump on the back of his head and a headache that made him cry.

Each time, the passersby just walked around him as if he wasn't there. No one stopped to help him, or even give him a second glance.

Not even the cops spoke to him any more.

Somehow, the cats had made him invisible.

He tried walking at his apartment steps with his eyes closed, thinking that if he couldn't see the cats, they wouldn't be able to drop their wall in front of him.

It didn't work.

Their ice wall felt as solid as a brick building. He didn't know how long he was out cold after that attempt.

By six p.m., the hunger was more than he could stand.

He went back across the street to try pleading with the man in gray. The man wouldn't appear.

The old gray tom just lay on the top step and stared off down the street as if it couldn't even hear Craig yelling.

That night, Craig again slept on the bench across the street from his apartment.

Four

HUNGER, THIRST, AND HEAT pounded at Craig like hammers against a block of ice.

Parts of his sanity shattered and melted with every passing hour.

At ten in the morning, he tried to throw himself into the middle of the street in front of a passing wave of traffic.

Two dozen cats stopped him at the curb.

At noon, he tried to pick up a garbage can and hit a policewoman with it. He was unconscious for over two hours.

At seven, in front of his own apartment building, he got down on his knees on the hot pavement and begged the assembled masses of cats to give him something to drink.

Not one cat even so much as looked at him.

He spent that night stretched out against the curb in front of his apartment steps.

Five

THREE DOZEN CATS slowly herded Craig Leiberman into a dead-end alley two blocks from his apartment building. It took them most of the day, as they continually had to wait for Craig to regain consciousness.

The back doors of the kitchens of three restaurants fed out onto the alley, filling the dark space between the buildings with a thick smorgasbord of smells.

Craig sat against a brick wall and drank in the odors as ten cats guarded each door.

Craig twice attempted to get at the garbage from the three restaurants. While a dozen cats stood guard, a yellow tabby and a white and gray female cat sat on top of the dumpster and clawed at Craig's hands every time he reached forward.

After the second attempt, his hands were bleeding so much, he sucked at his own blood to get moisture for his cracked mouth and lips.

Six

ON THE SIXTH day, except for one attempt to crawl down the alley, Craig Lieberman lay unconscious in the dirt of the alley.

Six cats took turns guarding him.

On the morning of the seventh day, a gray tom cat walked slowly, lazily up the alley to the body of Craig Lieberman and sniffed at his torn shirt sleeve.

Then, without hesitation, the cat raised its paw and sharply hit the man on the cheek, leaving four evenly spaced claw marks.

The man didn't move.

The old cat studied the man for a moment, then turned and strolled back up the empty alley.

Three blocks away, a construction worker named Burt Hopkins went to pet a large yellow cat that had strayed onto their work sight. The cat scratched the worker's hand and then quickly dodged Burt's kick.

And the sport began again.

A PATHETIC FALLACY

USA Today *bestselling writer, Dean Wesley Smith, takes a look at a very strange job that Connie works. She loves the sex, but she loves the killing more.*

The job certainly keeps her life exciting in more ways than she can imagine.

A story that walks a very thin line between an adult fantasy and The Twilight Zone.

Harold: The first trick.

CONNIE ROLLED SIDEWAYS on the bed. The hot, sticky air of the small New York City hotel room made the sheets seem damp from more than just the sweat of their bodies. Outside she could faintly hear the sounds of the city, the honking of the cars, the rumble of the subways, the constant hum of millions of busy people. The sounds made her feel safe, sure of herself. They always had, even as a kid.

She propped herself up on her elbow and let herself enjoy the smell of new sex mixed with Harold's cologne and his slightly sour body odor. He had his face buried in the pillow and his breathing was heavy and hard.

"You going to be all right?" she asked, rubbing his back and shoulders lightly, letting the sweat roll under her fingers, his smooth skin slick and hot. He had a great body even though he was almost fifty. He must exercise a lot.

He nodded, but didn't say a word.

She stretched, sat up cross-legged on the bed.

"That sure was nice," she said. They had made love for over an hour and she had lost count of her orgasms.

Again all he did was nod.

She smiled. She loved it when a man was totally satisfied, exhausted, and drained of energy.

Harold, she knew, worked for a brokerage firm. He had a wife and two kids. Both kids were in high school and he was worried about paying for their college. He owned a small summer place out on Long Island, but while in the city he had a flat near Central Park.

She patted his naked, white rump and leaned toward the night-stand. With a quick snap of the wrist she opened the drawer and pulled out a small revolver. Earlier, while Harold was in the bathroom, she had loaded it and made sure the safety was off.

Smiling, she placed the gun right against the back of Harold's neck, the barrel pointing up into his brain. With her other hand she slowly stroked his back.

He sighed.

"Feels good, doesn't it?"

She moved the gun just far enough away from his head so that when he nodded, his face still buried in the pillow, he wouldn't feel the gun.

Slowly, with her free hand, she pulled another pillow up and draped it over the gun to muffle the sound of the shot and keep the blood from spattering too much. She was planning on taking a shower anyhow, but it was easier if there was less blood.

"It was nice, Harold," she said and pulled the trigger.

The shot was no louder than she had expected. She doubted that someone passing by in the hall could have even heard it.

Harold flinched once, lay still.

She pulled the pillow off and looked at the mess she had made. Blood was soaking into the white of the pillow under his head and there was a small round hole bleeding just above the line of his hair. She had no desire to see what the bullet leaving his head had done to his face. He had had a handsome face and she wanted to remember him that way.

The smell in the room had changed from sex and sweat to a copper smell of fresh blood. God how she loved that smell, almost more than anything else.

Even the sex.

She scooted away from Harold and off the bed.

Carefully, she laid the gun on the end table beside the bed and stretched, her back to the bed.

The window was open, with only the light, white drapes pulled for privacy. She moved to the window and was almost tempted to walk out nude onto the small balcony. But doing that in the middle of the day might draw just a little too much attention and that she didn't need at the moment.

So instead, she took comfort in just pulling back the drapes, sliding open the glass door slightly and breathing in the fresh, hot air and the smells of the city.

She stood there for a time, enjoying the feel of another job well done, and some good sex.

"Well, better get showered and dressed," she finally said and turned back from the window.

Harold was gone.

"What—?"

The bed was made, no blood anywhere.

"What the hell?"

She scrambled to the obviously freshly made bed and pulled the covers aside.

Nothing.

No body, no blood.

Nothing.

She looked under the bed and then quickly checked the closet and the bathroom.

Nothing.

Absolutely nothing except a fresh hotel room. And the main door to the room was still locked and bolted from the inside.

She dropped down into the armchair facing the dark television and stared at the room, not believing what she was seeing.

Not possible, just not possible.

"Get a grip on yourself, old girl," she said aloud. Her voice sounded hollow and almost ready to crack, even to her ears. "There has to be an explanation for this. Somehow?"

She forced herself to think about what had happened. She had been hired in her usual manner to kill Harold Lindsey. She had got him up here, made love to him, and then done exactly that.

She had killed him.

One shot. Nice and clean the way she liked.

Just as she had done to men before him.

He was nothing special.

She went back over the events following his shooting. She had placed the gun on the end table.

She got up and went over to the end table and checked the drawer. There was nothing there but a bible and some information about restaurants.

She had gone to the window next, so she repeated her steps and looked out the white drapes like she had the last time.

Everything out there seemed to be the same, including the sounds of the city.

She turned around, afraid for what she might find.

Harold's body was still gone.

The bed was still made.

She was still nude.

But this time the bathroom door was closed and she was sure she had left it open.

Her heart racing, she eased closer to the door and could hear movement in there.

She was about to grab her clothes and duck for the hall when the bathroom door opened and out stepped Harold, also totally nude.

And very much alive.

She took a step back, not really wanting to believe what she was seeing.

He also stopped and the look of shock on his face matched what she was feeling.

Finally, after what seemed like an eternity he said, "Connie. What —? I mean, how? I mean—"

He stopped and just stared at her.

She glanced at the door to the hall and tried to figure if she could make it with a quick dash. He was much closer and much bigger and stronger. Even with her training it would be a close match if it came down to a fight.

After another long moment of staring at each other, Harold seemed to recover a little. He made a quick step sideways, yanked open the top drawer of the cabinet under the television and pulled out a revolver.

"Look," he said. "I don't know what's going on here. You must be Connie's twin sister or something. And I don't know how you got in here, but I don't like it."

At the sight of the gun, she cursed herself silently for being so careless. Maybe she had been dreaming about killing Harold.

Or something. Maybe a daydream, planning how she would do it.

There had to be an explanation, and she bet anything he had it.

"My name is Connie, I don't have a twin, and you think I like being here any better than you do?"

She was bluffing, but she didn't know what else to do. She stood her ground, not even bothering to cover herself.

He laughed. "I don't believe you're Connie for a moment, although you do look like her a great deal. But I happen to know for a fact that Connie is dead."

This time it was her turn to laugh. "Actually, you're the one who is dead. That gun, one shot through the back of the head."

He smiled. "Oh, really?" He pointed the gun at her. "I don't think so. You see, your husband hired me to kill you."

She heard the crack of the gun and the impact of the bullet spun her around and she dropped back onto the made bed.

The last thing she remembered was the friendly sounds of the city going about its business.

Harold: The Sixteenth Trick

SHE HAD WATCHED him for days. He worked in a moderate-sized office building off Wall Street. He had four different suits he liked to wear, two gray, one brown, and one deep blue. His ties were always bright, but not too much.

At one every afternoon he went out to lunch, usually to a small deli two blocks up. He had a regular spot at the deli and normally ate alone, reading the paper or a magazine. He was never anywhere to be seen on weekends, leaving the city on the train for Long Island and returning before work on Monday morning.

He seemed to have no regular friends or a steady girlfriend or boyfriend. This was going to be one of her easier kills.

On Tuesday, she managed to be sitting at the table next to his at the deli when he came in. The deli was a traditional New York deli, long and fairly narrow, with a big white glass counter full of meats and breads along one side and shelves lining the other walls.

The place usually smelled of sausage and garlic, with a faint odor of fresh-baked bread. There were maybe fifteen tables scattered the length of the place, with four bunched up in the back.

She made sure she was facing the front, glanced up as he approached and caught his eye. Then she smiled and he nodded hello and sat down. It was a little forward for most New Yorkers, but not so much as he would notice, considering they were sitting so close in such a small place. She left before he did, happy at the start she had made.

He went somewhere else for lunch the next day, but on Thursday he was back and again she smiled at him. And this time she said hello before pretending to go back to reading her magazine.

He returned her smile and hello and she noticed that a few times during lunch he glanced over at her.

Again she left before he did, acting as if she was slightly late, and making sure she didn't glance in his direction. But she knew the bait was in the water and the hook was in his mouth. Now it was just a matter of time.

The next day she brought along one of the current best selling novels and when she smiled and said hello as he approached he asked if the book was good. She said so far she thought it was and as soon as she finished it she would let him know. He smiled at that and they spoke briefly twice more during lunch and then she made a point of saying good-bye before she left.

By Wednesday, he had joined her for lunch and on Friday afternoon they ended up at the Crown Hotel on the seventieth floor. For her the sex was good, but as soon as they finished he rolled off the bed and went into the bathroom before she had a chance to even get her gun out of the nightstand. So she laid sprawled out on the bed, pretending to sleep, waiting for him to return.

After a minute, the toilet flushed and he came out carrying a pistol.

Her gun.

And he had it pointed at her.

"Sorry, Connie."

"What are you doing?" she demanded as she sat up on the bed and faced him.

"Just doing what your husband hired me to do."

"My husband?"

Harold laughed. "How stupid did you think I was? Did you really think that pick-up at lunch would work? On the second day I followed you home. After the third lunch I found out your name and your husband's name." Harold laughed again. "Did you know he's a very jealous man?"

She knew her mouth was open as she listened to what he was saying. She wasn't married. She lived off 45th Street and worked free-lance, doing any odd job she was hired to do that paid a great deal of money. Usually it was luring some horny man into a room and killing him. This guy was totally crazy and she was about to tell him so when he shrugged.

"It was nice," he said. "The sex, I mean." He indicated the messed sheets she was sitting on. "But now it's time to get on with it."

"No! Wait!" She held up her hand to get him to stop.

But the gun was already aimed at her.

The explosion was loud, much louder than she had expected.

The force of the impact spun her around and off the edge of the bed. The last faint thought she had was of surprise.

This just couldn't be happening.

Harold: The Twenty-second Trick.

SHE WAS RIDING him like a cowboy rides a bucking bronco, astride his hips as they thrust hard into the air. She had one hand on the wall above the bed and the other behind her on his thigh.

"Whoa there, big guy," she said, leaning forward and kissing his sweating forehead. "Let's go slow for a moment."

He smiled and kissed her back, then she sat up straight again, the pace almost relaxed.

She had been planning on killing him after they finished, just as she had done with over twenty others. But maybe she should try a little something different this time. Maybe she should do him while they're having sex. Kinky, but it might be interesting.

She rubbed his chest and then kissed him again. "Harold, you want to do me a favor?"

He smiled and kissed her back. "Anything?"

"Just close your eyes and let me ride you for a minute."

"Without moving?"

"Without moving," she said.

"I'm all yours," he said, relaxing into the bed and shutting his eyes.

Amazing how he trusted her completely, especially the first time like this.

She moved her hips slowly in a circular motion and leaned back and pulled open the drawer of the small end table next to the bed. Inside was her gun, loaded and ready.

She moved a little bit more and he moaned, opening his mouth a little.

She moved a little faster and he moaned even more, tilting his head back at just the right angle that she could point the gun between his teeth and at the roof of his mouth.

With one more good thrust she pulled the trigger.

Blood splattered over her and over a large part of the room as the pistol blew the top of his head off.

He jerked upwards and than lay quiet, amazingly still hard inside her.

"She patted his blood-splattered chest for a minute and then pulled off of him. In a smooth motion and without a look back she rolled off the bed and headed for the bathroom. What she needed now was a shower.

For the first minute the water going down the drain was pink from the blood, but she had done this before. Harold was not the first and he wouldn't be the last. This was her job and she did it. If she enjoyed it at the same time, so much the better.

She finished the shower and then took her time drying her hair before she came back out of the bathroom.

When she opened the door, Harold was sitting dressed on the made bed, her gun pointed at her.

"What—"

"Sorry I'm not going to get to partake in our little love-making session, but you see, I think that would be just a little too weird."

"Weird?" she asked.

She glanced quickly around the room. No sign of all the blood. And the room smelled fresh.

This couldn't be happening.

She had just killed him.

"Why," he said, "to make love to you and then kill you. Guess I'm just not that weird, so I've decided to just kill you." He looked up and down her naked body. "But I see that might have been a mistake. Oh, well."

He raised the gun.

She put up her hand to stop him, but the explosion sent her spinning back onto the white tiles of the bathroom floor. Her last thoughts were of watching her own blood smear across the smooth, cold surface.

Harold: The Thirty-first Trick.

SHE STOOD WITH her arm linked through his at the desk of the Crown Hotel as they registered. It had been a great two weeks tracking him until she finally got him talking in the deli. He was going to be one of her best kills. She'd have to do it in a special way for him, especially if he was good in bed.

Harold was filling out the check-in form when the clerk asked, "Did you folks have a good summer? We missed you around here."

Harold did what he could. He leaned forward and whispered "Hush, man. She doesn't know I'm married."

The clerk looked shocked for a moment, then remembered and looked embarrassed. He glanced at her and she winked at him, but the mood was spoiled. It just wasn't going to work this time.

And after such a good start, too.

But Harold gave it his best, even though he knew the clerk had messed it up.

After they made uninspired love, boring love like they used to do before the murders, he raised up on his elbow and looked at her. "You think we should go to a new hotel next time?"

She shook her head no. "They've treated us well for years. It was just a slip." She didn't say that she couldn't go back to those boring nights with him. No matter how much she loved him, they had to do something to spice things up to keep the marriage alive.

He nodded, looking thoughtful.

She rolled off the bed and went to the window.

Outside the sounds of the city covered the quiet of the room. For some reason the massiveness of those sounds soothed her, brought her back to reality, to what she was hired to do.

She must kill Harold.

She silently thanked the city for the help and turned back to face him.

But the room was empty, the bed made, and her clothes stacked neatly on the armchair.

On top of the pile was her gun, waiting.

She walked over and picked up the gun, the cold heaviness of it in her hand reassuring.

She checked it over, making sure it was fully loaded.

Then she smiled.

Harold always did know what would make her happy.

NEWSLETTER SIGN-UP

Be the first to know!

Just sign up for the Dean Wesley Smith newsletter, and keep up with the latest news, releases and so much more—even the occasional giveaway.

So, what are you waiting for? To sign up, go to deanwesleysmith.com.

But wait! There's more. Sign up for the WMG Publishing newsletter, too, and get the latest news and releases from all of the WMG authors and lines, including Kristine Kathryn Rusch, Kristine Grayson, Kris Nelscott, *Fiction River: An Original Anthology Magazine, Smith's Monthly, Pulphouse Fiction Magazine,* and so much more.

To sign up go to wmgpublishing.com.

ALSO BY DEAN WESLEY SMITH

Dead Money

POKER BOY NOVELS:

DOC HILL STORIES:

The Road Back

Eyes on My Cards

POKER BOY NOVELS:

The Slots of Saturn

They're Back

POKER BOY STORIES:

The Old Girlfriend of Doom

Dead Even

Gods Aren't Funny

Gambling Hell

Luck Be A Lady

Sighed the Snake

The Smoke That Doesn't Bark

The War of Poker

Daddy is an Undertaker

Nonexistent No More

Fighting the Fuzzy-Wuzzy

Pink Shoes and Hot Chocolate

Dried Up

The Empty Mummy Murders

Living Time

Not Saleable For Sale

Just Shoot Me Now!

For the Balance of a Heart

A Night with the Forgotten God

The Atlantis Fifty

The 13th Floor Problem

A Desert Shot

You Forgive the Night's Scream

That Lost Riddle

The Match

A Storm from the Relic

The Secrets of Yesterday

The Rules of the Game

The Library of Atlantis

The Gods Have History

Leaking Away a Life

The Rude Impossible Presumptive

In the Play of Frigid Women

The Portal of Wrong Love

Scared Money

A Beautiful History

Earth Protection League Novels:

Life of a Dream

CAPTAIN BRIAN SABER STORIES:

A Time to Dream

The Gift of a Dream

Hand and Space

Start With a Coffin

JUKEBOX STORIES:

Through the Jukebox: Five Jukebox Science Fiction Short Stories

Jukebox Gifts

Our Slaying Song Tonight

Black Betsy

The Ghost of the Garden Lounge

A Golden Dream

Mary Jo Assassin Novels:

Death Takes a Partner

Death Takes a Diamond

MARY JO ASSASSIN STORIES:

Death in the Morning

The Remodeling of a Life

Make Myself Just One More

MARBLE GRANT STORIES:

A Lady in Heat: A Marble Grant Story

A Look at His Heart: A Marble Grant Story

OTHER SHORT STORIES:

The Big Tick of Time

Long Shadow

The Matchbox Agenda

Out of Coffee Experience

Sleeping with the Goddess

If Sex is All a Dream, Then Who Cleans Up the Mess

Love with the Proper Napkin

Neighborhood

Remember

A Bubble for a Minute

Waiting for the Coin to Drop

A Pinch of How Rosie Lived

In Case of Emergency

The Mouth that Walked

A Pathetic Fallacy

As the Robot Rubs

Music in Time

The Tragic Tale of a Man in a Duster

Skiing the Graveyard of Souls

Marriage in Six Floors

Well, Maybe Not

Butchered Whale on a Red Bedspread

Two Roads, No Choices

Who's Holding Donna Now

Ambassador to the Promised Land

Santa's Snack

Sprinkle on a Memory

I'm Her Dead Husband

Variations of a Scream

Gus

The Last Burp of a Very Good Woman

A Vanilla Three-Way With a Cherry

Nostalgia 101

A Life in Whoopees

Between Showers

Squatter's Rights on the Street of Broken Men

After the Dance

Mated from the Morgue

Me and Beans and Great Big Melons

Don't Rust on Me Now

Shopping Cart Lover

Iron Eyebrows: A Romance with Too Much Hair

Mom's Paradox

The Keeper of the Morals

My Socks Rolled Down

The Romance Novel Challenge

In the Shade of the Slowboat Man

It's a Story About a Guy Who...

Standing in Line at the Intersection

Husband Dummies

On Top of the Dead

The Yellow of the Flickering Past

Cheerleader Revelation

Dead Post Bumper

Clicking Sticks

Peter the Hermit

In Search of the Perfect Orgasm

The Life and Death of Fortune Cookie Tyrant

Tumbling Down the Nighttime

Growing Pains of the Dead

The Call of the Track Ahead

Dinner on a Flying Saucer

The Great Alien Vibration

Cold Comfort

For the Delusion that Waited

The Face in the Fullness of Time

Playing in the Street

Best Eaten on a Slow Tuesday

Here to Stay on the Edge

The Stone Slept Here

To Remember a Single Minute

Something Wasted On

A Parker House Roll

The Thickness of a Warp

Unlocked Gate

Last Man Out

Shadow in the City

Another Damn Deal

Habit

Smile

The Last Short Putt of a Fearful Man

Keep Hoping for a New Tomorrow

The Wait

ABOUT THE AUTHOR

Considered one of the most prolific writers working in modern fiction, *USA Today* bestselling writer Dean Wesley Smith published almost two hundred novels in forty years, and hundreds and hundreds of short stories across many genres.

At the moment he produces novels in several major series, including the time travel Thunder Mountain novels set in the Old West, the galaxy-spanning Seeders Universe series, the urban fantasy Ghost of a Chance series, a superhero series starring Poker Boy, and a mystery series featuring the retired detectives of the Cold Poker Gang.

His monthly magazine, *Smith's Monthly*, which consists of only his own fiction, premiered in October 2013 and offers readers more than 70,000 words per issue, including a new and original novel every month.

During his career, Dean also wrote a couple dozen *Star Trek* novels, the only two original *Men in Black* novels, Spider-Man and X-Men novels, plus novels set in gaming and television worlds. Writing with his wife Kristine Kathryn Rusch under the name Kathryn Wesley, he wrote the novel for the NBC miniseries The Tenth Kingdom and other books for *Hallmark Hall of Fame* movies.

He wrote novels under dozens of pen names in the worlds of comic books and movies, including novelizations of almost a dozen films, from *The Final Fantasy* to *Steel* to *Rundown*.

Dean also worked as a fiction editor off and on, starting at Pulphouse Publishing, then at *VB Tech Journal*, then Pocket Books, and now at WMG Publishing, where he and Kristine Kathryn Rusch serve as series editors for the acclaimed *Fiction River* anthology series, which launched in 2013. In 2018, WMG Publishing Inc. launched the first issue of the reincarnated *Pulphouse Fiction Magazine*, with Dean reprising his role as editor.

For more information about Dean's books and ongoing projects, please visit his website at www.deanwesleysmith.com and sign up for his newsletter.